The story of
JOSEPHINE COX
*is as extraordinary as anything
in her novels*

BORN IN A cotton-mill house in Blackburn, she was one of ten children. Her parents, she says, brought out the worst in each other, and life was hard but not without love and laughter. At the age of sixteen, Josephine met and married 'a caring and wonderful man', and had two sons. When the boys started school, she decided to go to college and eventually gained a place at Cambridge University, though was unable to take this up as it would have meant living away from home. However, she did go into teaching, while at the same time helping to renovate the derelict council house that was their home, coping with the problems caused by her mother's unhappy home life – and writing her first full-length novel. Not surprisingly, she then won the 'Superwoman of Great Britain' Award, for which her family had secretly entered her, and this coincided with the acceptance of her novel for publication.

Josephine Cox gave up teaching in order to write full time. She says: '*I love writing, both recreating scenes and characters from my past, together with new storylines which mingle naturally with the old. I could never imagine a single day without writing, and it's been that way since as far back as I can remember.*' Her previous novels of North Country life are all available from Headline and are immensely popular.

Praise for
JOSEPHINE COX

———————

'A superlative North Country saga which will
delight Cox's many fans'
Books magazine

'Driven and passionate, she stirs a pot spiced
with incest, wife-beating . . . and murder'
The Sunday Times

'A born storyteller'
Bedfordshire Times

JOSEPHINE COX

Cradle of Thorns

HEADLINE

Copyright © 1997 Josephine Cox

The right of Josephine Cox to be identified as the Author of
the Work has been asserted by her in accordance with
the Copyright, Designs and Patents Act 1988.

First published in 1997 by
HEADLINE BOOK PUBLISHING

First published in paperback in 1997 by
HEADLINE BOOK PUBLISHING

10 9 8 7 6 5 4 3

ISBN 0 7472 4957 1

Typeset by Avon Dataset Ltd, Bidford-on-Avon, Warks

Printed and bound in Great Britain by
Caledonian International Book Manufacturing Ltd, Glasgow

HEADLINE BOOK PUBLISHING
A division of Hodder Headline PLC
338 Euston Road
London NW1 3BH

Forty years ago, my cousin Maureen gave me my first pair of high-heeled shoes – grey suede they were, and I cherished them for ages.

I met her again only a few weeks ago, and it was like rolling back the curtain of time.

We fell into each other's arms and we were kids again.

Isn't life funny?

CONTENTS

PART ONE

Summer 1890
BLACKBURN

Chapter One

'HIDE! QUICK! IF she finds you, she'll flay you alive!'
He was afraid. Not for himself, but for this lovely,
gentle creature who was his only child. Through these
many long years of guilt and loneliness, when at times
he hadn't cared whether he lived or died, Nell had been
his saviour. With her strong, beautiful spirit and smiling
blue eyes, she had brought something very special into
his life. No one, not even Nell herself, would ever know
the awful guilt he carried inside him. A terrible guilt that
haunted him day and night, and would go on doing so
until the day he died.

He knew he was a coward. For many years he
believed that through his weakness he had caused the
pain and death of someone he loved. That had always
been at the forefront of his mind. Now, though, at long
last, he realised that Nell was the real victim of his
wrongdoing. And she had no one to turn to but him.

Nell stood her ground, her rich blue eyes sparkling
with defiance as she told him softly, 'Let her do her
worst. I'm not afraid.'

'Oh, child! Child! You can't know what she's like.
You can't know how she can twist and turn a situation to
her own advantage so cleverly that you don't even know

she's doing it, until it's too late.' His voice broke. It was too late for him, but Nell still had a chance. She was young, and lovely, and had her whole life ahead of her. He couldn't, *wouldn't* let Lilian take that away from her.

Nell had always believed her father nurtured a secret. She believed it now, and because of what had happened she dared to ask, 'What is it, Dad? Why are you so afraid of her? She's hurt you, hasn't she? Oh, I don't mean the way she orders you about or the awful way she likes to humiliate you. It's something else, isn't it? Something you've never told me.' Something to do with me, she thought. Though she couldn't be certain.

He sighed, a long weary sigh that bowed his head and stooped his shoulders. He looked into those searching blue eyes. 'Yes, I can't deny it, she does order me around, and I've lost count of the times when she's humiliated me in public and private alike. But I don't mind. Not really.' How could he mind when he had brought it all on himself? He had no pride now. No ambition. No future and no love to warm his heart. 'I'm not hiding anything from you,' he lied. 'You already know the story, for I've told it to you a good many times, by way of a warning. I hoped it would make you ache to get away from here to make a life elsewhere, a good life carved out by yourself and not made by others to ensnare you. After your mam died, your Aunt Lilian asked me to stay on. Being the eldest, your grandpappy left this house and all the land and holdings to her. I was no older than you are now when all that happened. Your aunt asked me to stay and work on the land and that's what I did.' He paused, finishing sadly, 'I wasn't to know it was a lifetime sentence.'

Nell felt his despair and it became hers. 'You're asking me to go away,' she reminded him. 'How can I do that and leave you here?'

'Because you have to!' Taking her by the shoulders, he gently shook her. 'It's too late for me. I'm past my prime. I've no money and no prospects. Even when the old sod dies, I don't suppose this place will come to either of us. So you see, I'm no different to a pauper, except I've a place to stay and food to keep the body alive.' He smiled wrily. 'And good, hard labour to keep my soul from shrivelling.'

Nell was not convinced. 'But you'll never be content, will you, Dad?'

'Contentment has to be earned. I don't deserve it.' Dear God! In this poignant, agonising moment, when he looked into Nell's pretty blue eyes, he could see it all as though it was only yesterday. It all came back, his first and only love, the child that was Nell. The dreams and hopes, all gone. All long gone. 'You have to go,' he said in a hard voice. 'You have to get away from here, from *her*. If you don't she'll make your life a living hell.' He shook her again. 'You know that, don't you, child? You know she'll punish you day and night until she's broken your spirit, just like she's broken mine.'

'I won't let her.'

'You won't be able to stop her. Like I said, she'll do it without you even knowing.'

Awed by the tone of her father's voice and the seriousness of her own situation, Nell became silent. She knew he was right. This was not a happy house, and the relationship between her aunt and father had always been strained. As a child she had come to accept it, but when she grew into a woman, the questions began forming in her mind. Why did her father put up with his sister's evil ways? Why did he never respond to any woman's advances? There had been plenty.

Not yet forty, Don Reece was a good-looking man, God-fearing and not afraid of hard work. He was honest and kind, and well-respected by all who knew him. Yet he had no friends. He worked from dawn to dusk on his sister's land; he made his rounds at auction, buying and selling young horses from which he bred and trained some of the finest hunters in the country. He was a shrewd businessman, and over the years he had made his sister a handsome pile of money. Yet, in spite of having nothing to call his own, he would never cheat her. He kept her accounts meticulously and not one penny ever went missing. Lilian could now lay claim to a growing fortune but it was Don who had created it, out of the sweat off his back and the dirt on his hands.

The situation had intrigued and concerned Nell. But all her questions were met with the same answer. 'You don't have to worry your pretty little head,' he would say, 'because one day I'll stride out and forge a rich future for you and me.'

Deep in her heart, Nell knew he would never 'stride out' to forge them a future. Being rich didn't bother her. What did bother her was that her father worked his fingers to the bone for a woman who treated him with less respect than she gave her daily cleaner.

'Ssh! Listen, child.'

Nell listened, and her heart froze as Lilian's shrill voice cut the air. 'Where are you, you little slut? It's no good you hiding because I'll find you, and when I do, you'll answer for bringing shame on this house.'

In a harsh whisper Nell's father urged, 'Listen to me, child. I'm in no position to help you. Whether I like it or not, she has the upper hand.' He hated himself for being the inadequate man he was, he loathed the way he had let it happen over the years, but there was nothing he could do. Not yet. Not now. Too much time had passed. Too many memories held him at her mercy. Determined that Nell would not pay the price for his wickedness, he told her fiercely, 'You're to leave this place. Don't waste another minute. I've prepared it all. The wagon and horse are ready and waiting in the barn. You'll find food and a little money tucked under the seat. There are warm clothes and blankets to keep out the cold, and a deal of supplies – lantern, tools, everything to get you started. It's all secured on the wagon, and I've covered it with the best tarpaulin I could find. It can rain buckets and you'll be snug as a bug in a rug. Maybe you can find work until the bairn comes.'

Nell smiled into his sincere brown eyes. 'The baby isn't due for a long time yet,' she said softly. 'Widow Pryce said I was three months gone, so I should have a good five months' work in me before I'm forced to give up.'

His face wreathed in a sorry smile. 'A bairn.' He shook his head in disbelief. 'My grandchild. Oh, lass, I can't believe you'll soon be a mother. It only seems like yesterday when you were a bairn yourself.' Thinking of it now was almost too much to bear. 'I've not been much of a father,' he admitted, his eyes swimming with tears, 'but I swear to God there'll come a day when I make it up to you.'

'Just love me, like you've always loved me,' she murmured, nestling into his arms. 'Don't hate me. That's all I ask.'

Gripping her by the shoulders, he held her at arm's length. 'Hate you?' In the evening light, his face hardened like stone. 'You could never do anything that would make me hate you,' he assured her. 'But . . .' he hesitated, his voice stiffening. 'You're only a child. Tell me who the father is.'

Smiling wisely, she gave her answer. 'You've already asked me, and I've already given you my answer. I won't give you his name. There's no need for you to know. There is no need for *anyone* to know.'

'All right,' he conceded. 'But if you need him, I pray he'll be there for you.'

'I'll be fine,' she promised. 'Don't worry.'

'Ssh!' Blowing out the lantern, he hid with her behind the door. 'She's coming down the stairs. Don't make a sound.'

Hardly daring to breathe, Nell pressed herself against the wall, listening intently as the slow, deliberate footsteps descended the cellar steps. After a moment they stopped; the light from the lantern flickered over the walls as it searched for them. 'Don? Nell? Are you in there?'

Nell closed her eyes. She wanted to run out and face

the old biddy. She wanted her father to confront his sister and tell her it was none of her business, that what he and his daughter had to decide had nothing to do with her. But she knew he wouldn't do that. So against all her instincts, she remained perfectly still and silent until her aunt had gone away.

'I couldn't be certain but I didn't think she'd come down here,' Don chuckled. 'She's always been afraid of the dark. In all the years I've known her, I've never seen her go all the way down into a darkened cellar. I reckon she'd rather face a dozen stampeding elephants.' Still softly chuckling, he lit the lantern and started away.

Nell followed. Come to think of it, she had never seen her aunt go all the way into a cellar either. It was a comforting thought, to know that the old battleaxe was afraid of *something*.

With her father lighting the way, they went to the far end of the cellar then up the outer steps and across the moonlit yard to the barn. He showed her where the horse was already harnessed to the cart.

'I knew you'd see it was the only way,' he told her. 'Now be off, and God go with you.'

They clung to each other for a moment. Then in a tearful voice she told him, 'I love you, Dad. I promise I'll come back one day and she won't be able to hurt either of us any more.'

He gave no answer to that. His daughter could have no idea what was between him and her aunt, and with the help of the good Lord she never would. 'Look after yourself,' he said. Then he fell silent, busying himself opening the big barn doors and telling her, 'Go out quietly. With a bit of luck she won't even know you're gone until morning.'

As she leaned down from the cart to give him a last kiss, Nell looked up and there she was, a shadowy figure standing by the open doors, her face smiling oddly in the moonlight as she called out, 'Making a run for it, are you? So! Cowardice runs in the blood after all, eh?'

Don stepped forward. 'Leave it be,' he warned. 'She's getting away from here. She's going where you can't touch her, where you can't make her suffer a lifetime for one mistake.'

Ignoring him, Lilian began walking forward, directly in front of the horse. 'Get down from there, you slut!' she yelled. Seeing how Nell glared at her, and thinking that here was a girl with a braver heart than her father, she cunningly changed her tone. 'I'll help you to get rid of the brat. I know how to do it, and I promise I won't hurt you.' Her tone hardened. 'Afterwards, we'll just have to make sure you never get a chance to bring shame on us again.'

She was so close Nell could see the madness in her eyes. 'I'm leaving, and as soon as I can I'm coming back for my dad.' Defiant as ever, Nell made to climb down from the seat. 'I'm not afraid of you.'

Suddenly she felt herself being thrust upwards, back into the seat. 'Keep going, Nell!' her father shouted. 'She'll have to get out of the way!' Raising his arm he slapped the horse hard on the rump and sent it careering out of the barn. As he suspected, his sister jumped aside, startled but unhurt.

'Take care of yourself,' he called after his daughter. 'Don't ever come back!'

Out of the corner of his eye he saw Lilian scramble up from the ground. He didn't turn. Instead, he kept on calling out to Nell, telling her he loved her, that he would be fine; that she must never return. He went on calling, even though she was now only a distant speck in the moonlight.

When he heard the rush of air behind him, he half turned. Too late! The whip cut through the air, slicing into his back, the tip of the leather flicking across his face and making him cry out.

'You're a wicked, wicked man!' she shrieked. 'The slut may be gone, but you're not.' Her laughter was awful to hear. 'If I have my way, you'll remain here until my bones are drying in the ground.'

He thought of Nell. He thought of how she was free of this woman; Lilian could never hurt her now. And, through his pain, there shone a wonderful sense of joy.

Chapter Two

Nell sat in the lane for what seemed an age. It was cold and dark, and her mind was in turmoil. Why had she run? Why didn't she stay and fight the old battleaxe? And what about her dad? Why was he so afraid?

She didn't even want to think it, let alone say it, but it tumbled from her lips, seeming to shock the night air: 'Aunt Lilian has made a coward of my dad.' But why? What had happened between her and her brother to give her such power over him?

Nell loved her father. He may be a coward where his own welfare was concerned, but he had gone out of his way to help her, even after she'd told him she was with child. He hadn't condemned her or lectured her. When any other father might have beaten her black and blue until she revealed the name of her lover, he had consoled and advised her.

Nell would be ever grateful to him for giving her the benefit of the doubt, and for trusting her. She would never forget that, and come what may, she would keep her word and come back to this unhappy place to repay the debt she owed him and, hopefully, to root out the reason why Lilian Reece had such a hold on her younger brother.

Nell gave an involuntary shiver. Just thinking of her aunt was unnerving. Lilian Reece was a powerful, cunning woman who would stop at nothing to get her own way. She had used her younger brother to build her own fortune, eating away at his pride, sucking at his life's blood until now he had nothing left to give.

'The old cow would have done the same to you given half a chance,' Nell reminded herself. The idea was horrifying.

She was distraught at leaving her father behind. 'He could have come with me,' she muttered, 'instead of sending me away. We could have made a life together, the two of us.' Her heart sank. Two little tears escaped from her eyes as she realised just how alone she was. 'Oh, Dad, I wish you were here with me now.'

The loneliness was overwhelming. There in the deep night, on the edge of the spinney, she suddenly felt very frightened; not of the dark, or of what might be hiding in the spinney. Having been brought up in the countryside and knowing all its mysteries, Nell wasn't frightened by them. What really frightened her was the ordeal that lay ahead – having a child all alone, not knowing whether she would find work, and then not knowing when she would have to stop. What if she became penniless, at the mercy of strangers? What if the horse should fall ill? What if the cart lost a wheel? And how would she manage if she couldn't find work? After the baby was born, how would they live? *Where* would they live? So many questions and no answers.

'Come on, Nell, stop fretting,' she reprimanded herself. 'It'll be all right, you'll see. You're strong and able, and the baby isn't due for another six months. It's the middle of summer, and there's work in every field if you look for it. You'll just have to work hard and save what you can for the time when you can't go out and earn. Afterwards, you'll have to search for work where they won't mind you taking a bairn along.'

Climbing down from the cart, she walked round to where the grey cob was nuzzling at the hedge. 'Well, Clarence, old feller,' she said, gently stroking his head, 'looks like all we've got is each other, eh? But I reckon we'll be all right. As long as you don't go lame, fall ill, or decide to run out on me.'

Two big brown eyes turned on her in the moonlight, as if to say, 'Shame on you, Nell Reece! Would I ever do a thing like that?'

Winding her arms round his strong, thick neck, she hugged him close and smiled. 'I'm glad you're with me,' she confessed. 'If Dad had harnessed the old chestnut mare to the cart, I might only have got as far as the end of the lane. But it looks like he thought it through. He knew I'd have need of you, didn't he, eh? You're strong as an elephant, and gentle with it. The cart is in good fettle too. Yes, I reckon we'll be fine, old feller.'

Her mind was clearer now. She had plans to make, roads to travel, and things to do. 'At first light we'll make our way into Blackburn town and pay a call on Molly Davidson,' she decided, clambering back to her lofty seat. 'But first we'd better find somewhere safe to get a good night's sleep. Somewhere we won't be easily seen. Just in case that old bugger Lilian decides to follow us.'

She drove the horse along by the spinney and up to

where Farmer Williams' land joined the big orchard. Here she teased the wary horse along a narrow bridleway until they came to a wide, open flatland bounded on three sides by a tall hawthorn hedge. 'This is far enough away from prying eyes,' she declared, jumping down from the seat. She gave a small cry as she landed awkwardly on a mound of gorse; the sharp, thorny gorse pierced her ankle-length skirt and tore at her flesh.

Stooping to examine the damage, she felt warm sticky blood against her fingertips. 'You clumsy bugger, Nell,' she groaned. 'You'd better hope it doesn't turn nasty.' But there seemed to be no real harm done. Later she would stand in the brook and let the cool water wash over it.

'Best see to you first,' Nell told the horse, easing off his harness and tethering him loosely to the trunk of a tree. 'I expect you're as tired as I am.' She laughed out loud when the horse raised his head and gave her a sloppy kiss.

Having grown up here as a child and trudged these fields with her dad, Nell knew this area like the inside of her own mind.

'See that?' She brought the horse's attention to a series of molehills close by. In the half-light they made a dotted pattern, snaking across the field and out of sight among the overhanging branches of a great willow. 'I'd like a guinea for every time I've followed that trail on my way to the Morgans' place; every day for the past three years, up with the larks and half asleep, crossing these fields, sometimes running, sometimes walking, winter and summer, in sunshine, rain and snow.' She smiled, shaking her head. 'And all for a few shillings a week, and a spare ham leg now and then when Cook was feeling generous.'

She looked about her, imagining the fields in sunlight, a quiet smile on her face as she recalled the many hours of pleasure she had enjoyed here. 'Many's the time I've lingered in these fields when I should already have been up at the house, making the tea or setting the tray for Mrs Morgan's breakfast. One time I was so late I got a beating from the housekeeper.' She wouldn't forget that in a hurry. 'Oh, but this is such a beautiful place,' she sighed, her gaze encompassing the landscape. 'A special, secret place where you can forget all the bad things and see the wonder of nature.' If you sat very, very still, hedgehogs, badgers, fat red squirrels, and even the tiny fieldmice would emerge and look at you with bright, beady little eyes. And there was the old oak tree silhouetted on the far side of the field, where she used to sit. Sometimes she would leave home early so she could stay longer, just to watch the creatures.

Pleasure was tinged with sadness. Now she was leaving and might never come back, never again sit under that oak tree or watch the fieldmouse wash its whiskers. She might have to find work in a town or city, and even if she did find a position in the country, she would be lucky if she ever had time to linger. She had a baby to think of now; a responsibility that would tax her to the limit in every way. 'I'll never forget my quiet times here,' she murmured gratefully. 'Nor the peace they brought me.'

In the moonlight, though, the landscape took on a

different, more sinister appearance. 'If I'm right, the brook lies in that direction,' she mused, turning this way then that. 'It should run down this way to my left.' Narrowing her eyes, she stared through the darkness, ears strained as she listened for the familiar sound. Yes, there it was. The unmistakable sound of water tumbling over stone, beyond the trees, she realised with relief. Just a few steps away, in fact.

Taking the horse with her, she limped down the bank to the brook. Leaving the horse to wander, she stripped off her boots and stood, ankle deep, in the water, sighing with relief as the pain subsided. 'You'd think you'd know better than to jump into a pile of gorse,' she mumbled. She soaked her ankle for a moment longer, dried it on her skirt and, leaving the horse contentedly drinking, returned to the cart to see what her father had stowed for her in his old wicker fishing basket.

There were two thick, woolly blankets, and a bag of straw for a pillow. 'Probably couldn't steal a pillow without her knowing it,' she murmured. Holding the blankets out in the air, she grimaced at the strong smell of fish. Phew! She'd stink from here to next week if she lay under them. But she had to laugh. 'A good tracker dog would find me in minutes,' she chuckled. 'Still, Dad's heart was in the right place.'

Nell recognised the blankets; one was off her dad's bed, the other off hers. 'I expect he's left the top ones on, so the old biddy won't notice the difference if she decides to look into the rooms,' she reasoned. 'Though I can't see her demeaning herself to do that,' she muttered bitterly. 'She never has yet.' Nell and her father kept their own rooms clean and tidy. So far, there had been no cause for Lilian Reece to venture into them. But she was an unpredictable creature and not to be trusted.

A further search of the basket revealed a bundle of Nell's clothes, including her best Sunday boots, and a blue, crocheted shawl given her by Molly Davidson two years back.

There was also a lantern, a can of paraffin, some matches, two stubby candles, a length of rope, a muslin cloth containing a hunk of cheese. There was bread and a jug of cider and, tucked right down at the bottom of the basket, a small, red handkerchief containing a number of coins. 'Thanks, Dad,' she whispered gratefully. 'Seems you've thought of everything.'

Returning the goods to the basket, she was both delighted and dismayed to find her father's pocket watch hooked in the lid of the basket. The silver timepiece was the only legacy left him by his father. It was his pride and joy and, as far as Nell knew, he had never been parted from it.

Gazing at the precious old timepiece, Nell was sorely tempted to make her way back. 'How can I take this from him?' she wondered aloud. 'It's the only thing he has to treasure.'

Common sense prevailed. Her father wanted her to have it or he wouldn't have put it in the basket. What's more, if she went back now she'd be undoing everything he'd done. Her father had gone to a lot of trouble so she could escape her aunt's clutches. He had set her free. She must show him that his child had grown into a capable woman. That was what he wanted. That was what she had to prove. She owed it to her dad, and she owed it to the child inside her.

A new determination took hold of her. 'You owe it to yourself too, Nell Reece!' she muttered. 'Now, get some sleep. There are things to do tomorrow.'

Fetching the horse, she tethered it, on a long rein, to the trunk of an oak tree. 'You can lie down if you've a mind,' she told him. 'There's a soft grassy verge right here. Now, we'd both better get some sleep or we'll be fit for nothing tomorrow.'

SLEEP DIDN'T COME easily.
First she lay at the head of the cart, curled up like a dormouse, with her arms crossed over her head and her feet bent beneath her body. When she became too uncomfortable and the night air made her shiver, she got under the seat at the front and blocked the gap with the wicker basket.

After a full hour of twitching and turning and trembling from head to toe, she clambered down from the cart and made a nest in the hedge. The heat from the ground warmed her and soon she was sound asleep.

Clarence stood over her all night long, and when she woke, it was to the song of a bird balancing on a branch above her. 'Good morning to you an' all,' she replied brightly, then moaned aloud as she stood up; she felt as if she'd been run over by a carriage and four. 'I wasn't cut out to sleep under hedges,' she told

Clarence, shouting and spluttering when he shook his head and covered her in slobber.

Leading Clarence to the water's edge where he wandered at will to stretch his legs, Nell washed her hands and face in the brook. Afterwards, she returned to the cart where she emptied the basket, holding her nose as the 'fishy' contents spilled to the ground.

Carefully placing the lantern and other precious articles to one side, she took the blankets, clothes and pillow slips to the water's edge where, while Clarence took great gulps of the cool, fresh water, she dipped the fishy articles time and again into the brook, washing and pounding, until she was satisfied the smell of fish was gone.

The basket, however, wouldn't give up its odour too easily. Even after several dunkings in the brook, it still reeked of stale fish. 'I'll have to get rid of it,' she decided, strapping it to the underbelly of the cart. 'Happen Molly Davidson will swap it for something more useful.' She chuckled. 'For a softer pillow, I hope.' She hung the blankets and other garments across the tail end of the cart, 'to dry as we travel', she told the curious horse.

But there was time enough before they needed to make tracks. The day had hardly begun, and most folk would still be abed, she thought.

Leaving Clarence grazing the bank, she ate a hunk of bread and a nibble of cheese, washed down with a drop of cider that made her dizzy. 'I know you love your cider, Dad,' she chuckled, 'but I don't reckon I've got the same constitution as you.' With that she emptied away the remainder of the cider and refilled the jug with water from the brook. She would travel straighter with this inside her, she thought, raising the jug to her lips and drinking a good measure of the clear, fresh water.

A short time later, Nell was on her way.

Shackled to his harness and drawing the cart behind him as though it was part of himself, the horse lazily clopped along. The hot July sun shone down, and after the trauma of last night, the world seemed a kinder, safer place. 'First stop Blackburn town,' Nell called out to the horse. 'I'll say goodbye to Molly Davidson. Then it's on to the open road and go wherever our fancy takes us.'

In a strange way it was almost an adventure. In another, it was a frightening journey into the unknown. For a girl of seventeen, alone, three months with child, and having just lost the only home she had ever known and a father she loved, the way ahead was a daunting prospect. For Nell, though, there was no choice. There could be no going back, the only way was forward. Forward with a brave heart, on a road that might lead anywhere. To a fate she could not even begin to imagine.

MOLLY DAVIDSON WAS horrified. 'Yer never setting out on yer own!' she declared. 'Yer only a lass, an' there are all kinds o' thugs and rascals just waiting to pounce on the likes of you.' She shook her head so hard her wispy brown hair stood on end. 'I'll not have it, my girl,' she said. 'You'll stay here with me and mine. I ain't got much but yer welcome to share, yer know that.'

'I can't do that, Molly, but thanks all the same.' Nell gazed at the kindly old soul, her heart warmed by the affection she felt for this special woman.

Molly was not what you'd call a pretty thing, with her short, flyaway brown hair, floppy jowls, and a half-asleep, cherry-red face, got from drinking too much gin. But she was the salt of the earth, with a big warm heart and a door that was always open to those in need.

Molly was the proud keeper of four big sons and a small Irish husband by the name of Joe. Molly and her beloved Joe had lived on Haslingden Street all their married lives, and as the four big, boisterous children came along, the tiny house seemed to grow with them until it almost burst at the seams. Though there was never much money, the house rang with laughter, exuding a special kind of warmth which, Joe always claimed, was because there was a special woman at the helm, 'My big, beautiful Molly gal,' as he called her.

Their sons grew into fine young men. Sam, twenty-four years of age, thickset, with a shock of brown hair and strong green eyes that shone out of his pale features, was a miner in nearby Darwen.

Jack, at eighteen years old, was the moody one. An undertaker's apprentice, he was small-built, quiet and handsome, with dark hair and striking brown eyes. Molly called him her 'little mystery' because, unlike the others, he kept her guessing until she was four months pregnant, when the midwife finally confirmed Molly's belief that it wasn't colic she had but a baby in her belly. Jack was a very quiet baby, a morose youth and, later, a silent man, seeming always to be in a world of his own.

Tommy, the youngest at fifteen, was tall and slim, with a quick smile and a merry whistle on his lips from morning to night. He worked with a local merchant, helping to collect milk from the farms and delivering it throughout the local neighbourhood.

Bill, the firstborn and now twenty-six years old, was secretly Molly's favourite. Tall and handsome, with wayward dark hair and laughing dark eyes, he was lean and lithe, and hungry looking. Strong as an ox, he was unafraid and wise. Blessed with Molly's own sincere, God-fearing nature, he was loved and respected by all who knew him, and adored by Nell from the very first.

Molly loved her little house, proudly declaring to one and all, 'I shall live here until they carry me out feet first to meet me maker.'

Haslingden Street was like a second home to Nell. Long and staggered, with cobbled ground, it was packed on either side with pretty terraced houses. There was a grocery shop, a big piece of waste ground where the children played, and a lively, popular pub called the Robin Hood where, on Friday and Saturday nights, the working men would congregate and put the world to rights, Molly's Joe being the first to arrive and the last to leave.

Through the week, Joe Davidson pushed a rag-and-bone barrow round the streets, and on a Saturday he kept a stall in Blackburn market where he sold everything from old boots to copper boilers. A beloved and familiar sight, he wore a broad, cheeky grin, a flat check cap, and a pair of oversize boots that might look better on a scarecrow. In front of his stall he'd shout and holler and entice the customers by promising them the bargain of a lifetime. Usually he kept his promise but now and then he would have to deal with an irate customer who might have bought one of his woolly jumpers only to find it riddled with moth holes, or a copper boiler that started to leak. 'Well now, that's disgraceful,' Joe would declare, scratching his hairy head and wearing a puzzled frown. 'Sure, I'll have a thing or two to say when I meet up with the thieving rascal who sold it me!' But there was a twinkle in his eye and a song on his lips as he readily changed the article for another. And when the placated customer was gone, he'd chuckle and tell himself, 'One o' these days, Joe m'laddo, sure you'll find yerself in a heap o' trouble!'

On the whole, though, Joe was an honest soul; and in all his working life he had never raised his fists to a fellow man or made a single enemy. However, he did have one ear missing, on account of losing a fierce argument with a stray dog. He was never ashamed of his damaged ear. In fact he was proud of his 'war wound' and would discuss it in great detail over a pint. 'The mangy dog caught me off guard, sure he did, otherwise I'd have shown him what I were made of.' In truth, he had been frightened out of his wits when the animal leaped on him from behind.

Molly continued to argue her point with Nell. 'Me and our Joe would love to have yer here with us,' she declared. 'So, why can't yer come and stay?'

'I can't.' Nell hated to hurt her feelings.

'You'll not be intruding, if that's what worries yer. Me and Joe look on you as a daughter, and we neither of us want yer wandering the roads when yer could be at home here in a warm, comfortable bed.' She raised her

25

head and peered at Nell through narrowed eyes, her fat lips pursed into a round, crinkled hole. 'Besides, whatever will our Bill say when he finds out?' There was a certain knowing look in her eye. 'Or does he already know what yer up to?'

'No, I haven't seen him.' For a moment Nell fell quiet, wondering how she could tell Bill the truth. It would be hard, especially when he had no idea how she felt about him. 'Bill isn't here, is he?' she asked. 'It might be best if I don't see him right now.' She felt the hot blush spread over her face and neck and, sensing Molly's curious eyes on her, dared not look up.

Molly's voice gentled into her thoughts. 'He's off to his work in the fields,' she said softly. 'As always, he was out of the house before any of his brothers. He went off afore six o'clock this morning and I dare say he'll not be back till early evening.' There was a pause while she reached out to lay her hand over Nell's. 'But I'm still here, lass, and I want to help, if only you'll let me.'

Encouraged, Nell looked up. 'I know you'd help if you could,' she acknowledged gratefully, 'but you *can't* help, Molly. No one can. I have to deal with this one all by myself.' Neither her dad nor anyone else could help her out of this mess. She gave a small, bitter laugh. 'You always said, so you make your bed you'll have to lie on it. And you were right.'

Molly's suspicions were confirmed but it brought her no pleasure. 'You're with child, aren't you, lass?' she asked gently.

Nell nodded, her young heart burning with shame.

'Will yer tell me who the father is?'

'I can't.'

'Yer mean you *won't*.'

'All right then, I won't.' Enough damage had been done without dragging innocent folk into it.

'Will he take care of you?'

Nell replied in a defiant voice, 'I don't need him to take care of me.' The voice softened. 'I can take care of myself.'

Molly's smile was bitter-sweet. 'I understand.'

'Do you?' Taken by surprise, she wondered if Molly had guessed who the father was. She hoped not.

Molly sensed Nell's anxiety and it only made her more determined to get to the bottom of it all. 'I could be wrong,' she went on, 'but I wouldn't be surprised if the man is in a delicate situation. I mean, he can't lay claim to you or the child because he already has a family. Am I right, lass?'

It was a moment before Nell answered. Uncertain as to whether she ought to confide in Molly, she confessed, 'I know it sounds brazen, but I don't want him to "lay claim to me and the child". You see, Molly, I don't really love him. It was one of those things that just seemed to happen. My aunt had been really vicious that morning. She caused a terrible argument between Dad and me, and I went to work feeling upset. I was crying in the barn, and . . . he found me crying. He took me aside. One thing led to another, and . . .' She shrugged her shoulders, blushing fiery red at the memory. 'The truth is, I haven't told him I'm with child.'

'Oh, but you *must* tell him!' Molly was adamant.

Equally adamant, Nell replied firmly, 'No. It wouldn't do any good.'

Molly thought a while, all kinds of questions pushing through her mind. She had seen how Nell looked at her son. He had always viewed Nell as no more than a beloved sister, but maybe their relationship had changed and she hadn't noticed. Her imagination ran riot. 'Tell me the truth, lass,' she said cautiously. 'Is Bill the father? Has my son got you with child?'

Nell was shocked. 'No, Molly! *No!*' Her heart turned somersaults. What an idea. Bill, the father of her child? Oh, but it would be so wonderful. She had loved Molly's son since the first time she'd laid eyes on him. She had loved him when she was only high enough to hold his hand, and she had loved him ever since. 'Oh, Molly,' her lovely blue eyes lit from within, 'do you think I'd be going away if Bill was the father?' Before Molly could speak, Nell answered her own question. 'You know he would never let me leave. Bill isn't that kind of man.' She shook her head sadly. 'No, Molly, I might wish it but your son didn't get me with child.' Clutching Molly's fat, dimpled hand, she chuckled. 'I'm sorry not to be carrying your first grandchild.'

'So am I,' Molly laughed. 'So am I. Oh, lass, why won't yer tell Bill how yer feel?'

'Because he doesn't feel the same way, and because it's too late. I'm carrying another man's child.' Her sad, soft smile was incredibly beautiful. 'If I thought Bill could ever love me as a woman, do you really think I would have let any other man near me?' She shook her head. 'Oh, Molly, you can't know how much I love Bill, have

28

always loved him. When I was little, I looked up to him like the hero he is, laughing when he carried me on his shoulders or when he ducked us both in the stream on a hot summer's day, missing him when he was out of sight. Dreaming of him. Loving him like a brother. Later, when I grew older, I loved him all the more, but in a different way. It was hard, Molly, trying to pretend I still saw him as a brother, when all the time it was more than that. If we hadn't both been working at the same place it might have been easier, but seeing him every day was like a kind of torture. I'd be going about my work at the big house and he'd be there at every turn. One minute I'd be upstairs, shaking the sheets out of the window, and there he'd be, leading the horse down from the field or chopping wood outside the big barn.' She closed her eyes and saw him clearly in her mind. 'With the sun shining down on him, and the wind rustling his long, dark hair, he looked like a god.'

'He's a good-looking young feller, I'll not deny that,' said Molly, her voice soft with a mother's love. 'He could have been arrogant or hard-natured, but he's not, and never has been. Bill is a good, honest man, whose heart is as kind as it's strong.' Watching Nell's sorry little face, she told her, 'I wouldn't blame any lass for loving him but I'm glad it's you, and I know deep down here,' she tapped her chest, 'there'll come a day when he realises yer ain't a little lass no more, and yer ain't his sister neither. God willing, he'll see how you've grown and blossomed, and he'll know yer all the woman he'll ever want.'

Nell could hope for nothing better but it had to be

Bill's own eyes that saw her as a woman. 'Promise you won't say anything to him,' she urged now. 'You won't tell him how I feel, will you, Molly?'

'God bless yer, course I won't,' Molly assured her, 'if that's what yer truly want.'

'It is.' Saddened, Nell turned away, her gaze shifting to the window. Outside, the cherry tree was in full bloom, the same tree where six years before when she was only eleven years old Bill had strung a swing from bough to bough for her. The swing was still there but the child had long gone.

'Bill may never feel the same way about me, but I do love him so.' She raised her eyes to Molly's quiet face. 'I've never told that to anyone else, Molly, and neither must you. Bill especially mustn't know. If there comes a day, like you said, when he realises he could love me as a woman, then that will be the best day of my life, but right now he still loves me like a sister, and that's the way he may always love me. I have to face that fact. More than anything, I don't want to make him feel guilty about my feelings for him.'

'I understand, lass.' Molly's old heart was breaking for this lovely slip of a girl. 'You have my word. It'll stay our secret.'

'Thank you, Molly.' Nell had let her tongue run away with her, and it was reassuring to know her secret would go no further. She and Bill still enjoyed a unique and wonderful friendship, and nothing must be allowed to spoil that.

The older woman gazed in silence at the small face before her, at those strong, bright blue eyes and that thick cloud of wavy golden hair. She looked at Nell's slight figure, and the way she seemed to be pressed into the chair, like a small child, alone yet stubbornly independent. Her heart went out to this young creature who was without a mother to confide in or a home where she might feel comfortable. Cursed with a spiteful aunt for a guardian and a weak, foolish father who had shown her little companionship over the years, Nell was now being thrown out into the world, with no roots and no prospect for the future. It was a sorry state of affairs.

Molly's anger spilled over into her homely features. She blamed Don Reece and his sister Lilian for Nell's lonely existence. She blamed Don Reece because he was too steeped in the past to see how his own lovely daughter needed him. She blamed Lilian Reece for wrapping a conspiracy round the long-ago past, which had brought about a dangerous and unfortunate situation, the root cause of Nell's unhappiness even though she had taken no part in it.

There was never any proof that Lilian Reece had done what she was rumoured to have done. It was one of those things no one spoke about out loud. One of those 'family' issues that other folk kept their noses out of.

Nell seemed to have taken the brunt of it. The child, then the girl, and now the blossoming woman had never known the love of a mother, nor of a father. She had grown wild and free, like the creatures in the fields. All too often she had been left to her own devices, her young carefree nature curbed by the selfish, demanding woman who was her aunt.

Molly had always longed for a daughter, and when Nell had come into their lives she seemed to fill the gap in her heart. That was twelve years ago now, when Nell was five and Bill a strapping young man of fourteen. It was two days before Christmas. Bill was out gathering holly from a nearby field when he found Nell lying hurt after falling from a tree. Taking her in his arms, he ran all the way home to Molly who lovingly tended the child and afterwards took her home to her own family.

Molly got no thanks for her troubles. Instead, Lilian Reece had declared haughtily, 'The girl is a source of worry to her father and me. She has a stubborn, rebellious nature and I'm afraid she will have to learn the hard way.' She then ushered Nell inside and slammed the door in Molly's face. Later, Molly learned how Nell had been slippered by her aunt; her legs and buttocks had been so raw and sore, she could hardly sit down for days.

Molly's love for Nell had strengthened over the years. It didn't matter that the girl had let this unknown man take her innocence, or that she was determined to protect his identity. Nor did it matter that she had refused to stay here. Nell had a mind of her own, she was a strong, independent soul who would prefer to owe no debt to any man. Life had made her like that. Life had been hard and unjust but it had taught her how to survive, and that was good.

'I won't press you for the man's name,' Molly promised, 'but I need to be sure you'll be all right.'

'Don't worry. I'll be fine.'

'Where will you go?'

'I'm not sure, but I won't stay round here. There's work all over, and I'm strong enough yet to turn my hand to anything.' She went on to describe how her father had provided her with plenty of supplies. 'There's enough to keep me going for a while. Besides, it shouldn't be too long before I find work.'

'What about money?' Molly wasn't altogether satisfied.

'I told you, I'm all right.'

'I expect that aunt of yours has taken your wages for this week, eh?'

Nell shook her head. 'I don't think so. But she'll have them quick enough when she finds out they're still waiting to be collected.'

Wide-eyed and indignant, Molly sat up. 'What? Yer mean yer ain't got yer wages yet?'

Nell shook her head. She couldn't explain why she dared not go back to the Morgan house. 'Don't need them,' she muttered.

Molly wouldn't have it. 'Stuff and nonsense!' she declared angrily. 'Yer worked for 'em, didn't yer? Worked bloody hard an' all!'

'I don't need my wages,' Nell lied. 'Aunt Lilian can have them.'

Molly shook her fist. 'That woman don't deserve *nothing* from you. All these years she's run you and yer dad into the ground. Yer fetch and carry for her. Yer cook and clean, and work like a dog to keep the peace in that house. Don't think I don't know. Don't think the whole bloody neighbourhood don't know what a dance she's led yer. I know how yer come home from a hard day's grind at the Morgan estate only to start all over again with that wicked old bat standing over yer.' Red in the face and growing angrier with every word, she wound her fists together. 'I could strangle her with me own two hands for what she's done to you over the years.'

'That's all in the past now.' Nell's mind was filled with thoughts of her dad, and the knowledge that while she'd got away, he was still there. 'Oh, Molly, I wish my dad had come with me.'

Molly was momentarily lost for words. It was on the tip of her tongue to say how her dad was tied by things that happened before Nell was born, but she wasn't certain and never could be, so it was wiser to keep her own counsel. 'Did yer ask him to come with yer?'

'I begged him to but he wouldn't.' She looked into Molly's eyes and searched for an answer. 'Why wouldn't he come with me, Molly? Why does he stay there when he's so unhappy?'

Molly took a moment to answer, always wary of saying things that might not be true and afraid to stir up muddy waters. 'Yer daddy's a grown man,' she replied. 'He made his choice and yer must respect that.'

Try as she might, Nell could not respect her father's decision to stay. 'I've promised him I'll come back some day,' she murmured. It was a promise she meant to keep. 'When I've had the baby and made a new life, I'll come back for him.'

'I know you will,' Molly said. 'You were always a woman of your word.' She wouldn't let the other matter go. 'But now I'd like yer to make *me* a promise too.'

'If I can.'

'When yer leave here, I want yer to go and collect yer wages. You've earned that money, lass, and it riles my blood to think the old bat might get her greedy mitts on it.'

When Nell hesitated, Molly saw there was something troubling her. 'What's wrong, lass? Is there a partic'lar reason why yer can't go back to the Morgan estate?'

'No.' Another lie.

Molly continued to stare at her, a terrible thought entering her head. 'My God, lass!' She clapped her hand over her mouth and took a deep breath. 'It's somebody there, ain't it? Some bad, cowardly feller that's got you with child?'

This time Nell could answer truthfully, because Vincent Morgan was not a bad, cowardly feller. 'No, Molly. It's just that I'd rather not see Bill, in case he tries to talk me out of going.' Also, she was afraid that if he looked at her in a certain way she might blurt out her love for him. Then she would have to tell him about the child and he might demand to know who the father was and go after him. Nell inwardly shivered. It was all too dangerous and she couldn't risk it. 'There is another reason,' she admitted.

'Oh aye, and what might that be?'

'Just that I've started my journey. I've come away from there and now I don't want to turn the wagon round. It would be like turning tail.'

'Then yer can sit yer "tail" here while *I* go and collect yer wages,' Molly decided. 'The only good thing yer aunt ever did was to teach yer how to read an' write. And you took the time to teach my son, God love yer.' She scrambled out of her chair and was soon rummaging round in the drawer. 'I want yer to scribble a note. Tell them up at the estate that yer ill and want me to fetch yer wages.' She threw a pile of papers and other paraphernalia out of the drawer on to the dresser top. 'Damn and bugger it! I could have sworn our Bill had writing paper in here.'

Nell felt she was making a nuisance of herself. 'All right, you win,' she conceded, helping Molly return the stuff to the drawer. 'If it'll make you happy, I'll go and collect my wages.'

Molly gave her a suspicious look. 'Yer wouldn't say one thing and do another, would yer?'

'You know I wouldn't.' Nell closed the drawer. 'I'll go right now.'

'Oh no yer won't, my gal!' Molly retorted. 'You'll not leave Molly's house on an empty stomach. Bill came home last night with a box o' new-laid eggs. Sit yer arse down an' I'll have a couple fried up in no time.'

'Honestly, Molly, I'm not hungry.'

Molly wouldn't take no for an answer. 'Soft-yolked, the way yer like 'em?'

'I've already had a meal.' It wasn't much, but it would do.

'I'll turn 'em over so they're gently cooked on both sides.' Molly grinned impishly. 'I've got newly baked bread straight out of the oven this very morning.'

All this talk of new-laid eggs and bread straight out of the oven was making Nell hungry. As a rule she didn't have much of an appetite; she assumed the rising hunger must be because she was pregnant. 'Crusty, is it, the bread?' she asked.

'Aye, lass. Soft on the inside, an' all brown and crackly on the crust.' She licked her lips. 'There's a big fat tub of newly churned butter in the larder an' all,' she chuckled. 'Bill fetched it home when he brought the eggs.'

That did it. Nell was ravenous. 'I'll set the table and make us a fresh brew of tea,' she said, limping into the kitchen.

Molly noticed at once. 'What have yer done, lass? Yer weren't limping when yer came in.'

Nell had deliberately tried not to limp when she first came in because she knew what an old fusspot Molly was. 'It's nothing,' she said. 'I expect I've got cramp from sitting in the chair too long.'

Molly drew her to a halt, at the same time bending her head to examine Nell's ankle. There was a trickle of blood over the bone. 'Looks like you've cut yer ankle, lass.'

Ignoring Nell's protests, Molly pushed her into the chair and went to fetch hot water and flannel. In no time at all she had Nell's shoe off and her leg stretched up on the stool. 'My! Look at this,' she exclaimed, her brown eyes wide as she stared at the birthmark on the sole of Nell's foot. 'I ain't never seen this birthmark afore.'

'That's because you've never seen the sole of my foot before.'

'By, but it's lovely.' Holding the small foot between her hands, Molly gazed at the mark. 'It's like a painting,' she said. 'Like a half-moon over a forest.'

Nell laughed. 'What an imagination you've got, Molly. It's just a brown splodge with a spot over. The sole of my foot is the best place for it, I reckon.' The odd thing was, the man who had bedded her had seen the same image in the mark as Molly had. Vincent too, had likened it to a painting.

Subdued by thoughts of him and the consequences of their impulsive act, Nell tugged her foot from Molly's hands. 'I'd best be on my way,' she said, eager to put as much distance between herself and Vincent Morgan as possible.

Molly would have none of it. 'You'll go when I'm done,' she retorted, grabbing the foot once more and wedging it in her lap. 'The cuts are deep and festering, and I'll not be content till I've tended 'em. So yer might as well sit still and stop complaining. And then you're going to eat.'

Knowing Molly would have her own way, Nell did as she was told. It was only minutes before the ankle was bathed and bandaged. Molly gave Nell a piece of her mind. 'Yer little sod! Why didn't yer tell me you'd hurt yerself, eh? And how did yer do it? Climbing trees, were yer? You've allus been a devil for climbing trees.'

'I jumped off the cart on to some gorse.'

'Well, yer shouldn't be jumping, not with a bairn inside yer. From now on, you'll have to be more careful, my girl.'

'Oh, I will.' In the face of Molly's chastising, Nell felt like a naughty child. Her face melted into a warm, grateful smile. 'Thanks for doing my ankle. Now, will you stop fussing? I'll make the tea and you cook the eggs. Then I'll wash the dishes and be on my way.'

Soon the little house was filled with the sounds and aroma of eggs sizzling in the pan and, after a minute, the delicious smell of bacon frying. Turning a couple of rashers in the pan, Molly chirped, 'That'll put hairs on yer chest, my girl.'

The kettle shrieked and bubbled on the stove, and Molly came over all nostalgic when Nell began softly singing an old tune favoured by her dad. 'My Joe used to sing that to me when we were courting,' Molly mused, her brown eyes all misty and faraway. 'He were a daft old bugger even then.'

They sat at the table and ate their wonderful breakfast. They chatted and laughed and Molly kept asking for reassurances from Nell that she would be all right.

Afterwards, Nell washed the dishes and Molly wiped, and soon it was time for Nell to leave. 'I don't want yer going hungry, lass,' Molly told her, wrapping a chunk of cooked ham and crispy bread into a muslin cloth. 'This is all fresh and it'll keep for days, but don't swing it under the wagon or the dogs'll gather from miles round and take the lot when yer not looking.'

At the door they hugged and cried, and finally Molly wiped her eyes on the corner of her apron.

'I do love you, Molly,' Nell whispered, and that started Molly crying all over again.

Outside, Nell climbed into the driving seat and collected the reins. One sharp click of the tongue and the old horse, bowing his long, beautiful head, started off down the street. Nell turned to wave. 'I'll write,' she promised Molly.

'You'd better, my gal!' Molly yelled.

'Look after yourself, Molly,' Nell suggested and Molly beamed from ear to ear.

'I will! I will! Take care of yerself, lass,' she called out. She watched with moist eyes as horse and wagon turned the corner. 'God bless and love yer, Nell,' she sniffled, and blew so hard into her hankie her ears popped and she couldn't hear a thing until she'd gone back into the kitchen and had a tipple of gin. 'Any excuse,' she said, rolling her eyes with pleasure. 'Besides, the good Lord knows it keeps out the cold.'

Then she looked out of the window and sighed, and wondered if she'd ever see Nell again.

MAKING HER WAY back along the same road over which she had fled her aunt's house was a nerve-racking experience. Nell's emotions were mixed. One minute she was prepared to face the old tyrant and let her know what she thought of her, and the next minute she was desperately afraid the two of them might come face to face. 'As long as she doesn't take her spite out on my dad, that's all I care,' she muttered, slowing the old horse to a crawl. 'Oh, I wish I was older. I wish I had money enough so my dad could start his own business and not have to rely on that old bugger for a roof over his head.'

And yet Don Reece had a strong back and two strong arms. He was capable and intelligent, and if he put his mind to it, there was nothing he couldn't do. Nell knew that, and it made his dogged determination to stay with his sister all the more puzzling. 'She'd better not make his life more of a misery or there'll come a day when she'll answer to me!' For one, dark moment she felt capable of committing murder.

Deep inside, though, she felt her father could take care of himself. In a way he had already proved that by helping her to make good her escape, and even facing up to his sister. 'If I didn't think he'd be all right,' she told herself, 'I would never have left him.' All the same, had she done right? 'Yes,' she answered, but it might be different when the child was born, because then her aunt could never separate her from it.

Many times since discovering that she was with child, Nell had hated herself. She hated herself now. She hated the fact that she was unworldly and penniless. But she loved the child inside her with an intense passion, vowing that this child would know the love of a mother. She herself had longed for a mother but that poor soul had died long ago, when she was born. Her father had not kept the truth from her. 'Your lovely mam gave her life so you could live,' he told her. He described her as 'a lovely little woman, small and strong like yerself, with the same pretty big blue eyes and mass of wild curly hair'.

In spite of her persistent questions, he had never told her anything else, and the one and only time her aunt spoke of her was when she found Nell searching the local churchyard for her mother's grave. She had dragged her away from the place, warning her in a hard voice, 'You'll not find her here, my girl. Her folk took her away, to be buried with her own.'

That night, Nell was sent to bed early. There was a lot of whispering from downstairs, and the next morning her father informed her that she was to put her mother out of her mind and never again ask after her. 'She's gone and we can none of us bring her back,' he said sadly. 'I've told you what she was like, and how much I loved her. Your mam was the best thing that ever happened to me and now I'll never see her again. I've had to accept that and you have to do the same or drive your poor father out of his mind.' He had cried then, sobbing like a baby. 'Oh, lass, let there be no more questions. No more searching the churchyard for that dear soul or turning your mind over with thoughts of what might have been.' He had taken her in his arms and held her for a precious moment, and when he released her, his face was stiff with grief and his voice trembling. 'Your mother was my whole world. I never loved anyone before and I'll never love anyone again.' Then he pushed her away, and from that moment on there was a blanket of silence over the entire subject, and Nell never again asked any questions. But she dreamed, and wished, and imagined the woman who had been her mother, and her heart was sore. Her mother remained a mystery, alive in her imagination but never speaking to her, never holding her, never being there when she was needed. Nell had never known her mother, and never would. That was the greatest regret of her life.

It made her determined. Every minute of every day and night, she would be there for her own child, to hold and to love it, and to answer its searching questions, however hard that might be. But, by the very nature of its birth, the child would know regrets, just like she did. Her own bairn would grow without the love of a father. And what could she say when it began to ask the very same questions she herself had asked as a child? There would have to be answers. It was obvious she didn't get with child all by herself.

Thank God, it would be years before that particular dilemma presented itself. For now, she had other, more pressing matters on her mind.

SHE DIDN'T GO straight up the main drive to the big house. Instead, she drew the horse to a standstill by the tall hedge where she prayed she might not be seen.

Climbing down from the wagon, she tethered the horse to a five-bar gate and peered cautiously through the hedge, making certain there was no one about, particularly the man of the house, the young and kindly Vincent Morgan. Of all the people who might see her, he was the one she must avoid at all costs.

There was no one in sight. Relieved, she climbed over the five-bar gate, hurrying towards the rear of the house and muttering to herself all the way, 'I'll tell the housekeeper I was too ill to work this morning and I'm not much better now but that my aunt got me out of my sickbed because she wants my wages. And it's more than my life's worth to go home without them.'

Making the sign of the cross on her forehead, she asked the good Lord to forgive her. 'You must know, if I'm to keep body and soul together, I need my wages

43

more than she does,' she explained defiantly. Nell had got into the habit of confiding in the Lord a long time ago, when she realised there were precious few folk down here to share her worries with.

Picking up the hem of her skirt, she went quickly across the field and up the rise that led to the stable yard. Once on top of the rise, she took a moment to pause, surveying all around her – the green and beautiful landscape, meandering brooks, old, broad trees and clusters of forest, the many farmhouses nestling between the valleys, and a fine blue sky above it all. 'It's so beautiful,' Nell breathed. 'How I'll miss it.' Though she comforted herself with the knowledge that she was free now to wander at will and maybe find a place equally beautiful.

Shifting her gaze, she let it linger on the house where Vincent Morgan lived and where she had worked ever since her back was broad and strong enough to carry out the duties of general maid and skivvy.

The house was a splendid sight. Big and sprawling, it had sheltered many generations of Morgans, the last being Vincent Morgan, direct and only descendant of Joshua Morgan who went to his maker two years ago; but not before seeing his only son married to a lovely, gentle soul by the name of Rosalyn. The old man went to his grave believing the family line to be secured, and with Rosalyn Morgan now carrying his son's child, it seemed his last wishes might be realised.

Standing proud and magnificent in all its glory, the old house made a fine sight in the morning sun. Built some two hundred years ago, it was bent and ancient, like the late, old man who had loved it with a passion that lived on in his son. The front of the house was liberally studded with great thick timbers, criss-crossed in places, like the feathers of a bird's tail. There were numerous chimneys and a myriad of windows with small, square panes and arched, red-brick canopies over.

The gardens were a picture to delight the senses. At this time of year, the blossoms were spectacular, in their blues and reds, with a backdrop of variegated greenery, and rows upon rows of tiny yellow and pink flowers grew round the many shrubs like garlands round a woman's neck. A vast area of lawn surrounded the gardens at the front, while a broad, sweeping drive curved up to the front porch.

Over to the left, and feeding from the main drive, a winding crazy-paved path led round to the back of the house, and it was along this path that Nell went now, going carefully over the nicks and cracks and softly chanting an old nursery rhyme that Bill had taught her.

She almost leaped out of her skin when a voice boomed out behind her, 'Nell Reece! What the devil d'you think you're doing?'

White-faced and anxious, Nell swung round, her stricken blue eyes looking straight into the hard face of a tall, thin, and very stiff young woman by the name of Miss Merry; the most ill-fitting name anyone could have bestowed on her. The housekeeper at the Morgan place was far from merry. In fact, it was common knowledge that Agatha Merry was the sourest, most miserable soul ever born; though as far as Nell was concerned, she came a close second to her own Aunt Lilian.

'I've been sent for my wages,' Nell answered, her cool, bold expression belying the turmoil inside her.

Miss Merry regarded her through narrowed eyes. 'Have you now?' she demanded, a nasty little smile shaping her bony features. 'And may I ask why you weren't here this morning when everyone else stood in line to take their wages?'

'I was poorly this morning, and I'm poorly now. I have to get back to my sickbed.' Doing her best to look feverish, Nell discreetly sucked in her breath and held it until her face turned a frightening shade of crimson.

The hag was not impressed. 'You don't look poorly to me. In fact, I'd go so far as say you have a healthy, ruddy colour.' Snorting like a pig she went on, 'Rather disgusting, I think.'

Releasing her breath in a rush, Nell feigned weakness. 'Please, Miss Merry, I'm close to fainting dead at yer feet,' she pleaded. 'Let me have my wages, and I'll be on my way.' Panicking now, she was beginning to wish she'd never let Molly persuade her to come back here.

The woman smiled sweetly. 'Don't mistake me, my dear,' she cooed. 'I never said you *couldn't* have your wages.'

Astonished, Nell gave a small curtsy. 'Oh, thank you, miss.'

Miss Merry smiled cruelly. 'You may have your wages when you've done a day's work and not before.' Taking Nell by the scruff of her neck, she yanked her forward, her voice shaking with anger. 'And if I ever catch you skiving off work again, you'll be shown the

46

door, never mind wages! Out on your scruffy ear, without a minute's notice. Do I make myself clear?' She gave Nell a sound shaking for good measure.

Incensed, Nell struggled. 'Let me go, you old bat! I've earned them wages and I'm not leaving without 'em. And I don't give tuppence for your bleedin' work, 'cause once I get what's owed me I'll be off and you'll never clap eyes on me again.'

'Why, you little monster!' Miss Merry had never been challenged before, and was beside herself with rage. 'I'll have the skin off your hide for that.' Grasping a handful of Nell's hair, she propelled her forward, with Nell twisting and writhing, and silently praying that *he* would not suddenly appear round the corner.

Her worst fears materialised when, at that precise moment, Vincent Morgan emerged from the arch that led directly to the stables. He was riding a big, black stallion, a magnificent creature with a temper that only he and Bill Davidson could master.

Astonished at the scene before him, he pulled the animal up, demanding of the irate Miss Merry, 'Whatever's going on here? Let the girl go this instant!'

Realising that Nell was getting the better of her anyway, the frustrated woman shoved her aside with a feeling of relief. 'This isn't the first time Nell Reece has caused trouble,' she lied. 'I'm always having to go behind her. She's stubborn and arrogant, and a bad influence on the other servants.'

Nell wasn't having that. 'You're a liar!'

'Did you hear that?' Miss Merry's long scrawny finger was trembling as she pointed at Nell. 'Did you hear the way she dares speak to her betters? What's more, she didn't turn up for her wages this morning and now she's arrived late for work, demanding her wages, and threatening that once she's got them she'll be away and won't be back.' She gave a gruff little laugh. 'As if I care about that. Good riddance, that's what I say.'

'Bring her wages.' He climbed down from his horse.

'What?' Miss Merry thought she'd misheard.

'I said, bring the girl's wages.' He smiled, but there was an authority about him that defied challenge.

Miss Merry glared at Nell, then she glared at Vincent Morgan then, realising he meant what he'd said, spluttered an apology. 'Sorry, sir. Of course. I'll get them now.' With that, she went off at a smart pace, cursing a world that had brought her to this. 'I could have been someone,' she complained. 'I could serve in the best houses in the land, with gentry who know riffraff when they see it. I've a good mind to give in my notice and seek a new position.'

No sooner had the remark spilled from her lips than the force of her own words brought her to a halt. Her hand flew to her mouth and her small, surprisingly attractive brown eyes rolled with horror. Lowering the hand, she also lowered her head. 'Agatha Merry, how could you even think such a thing?' A thin, pleasurable smile flitted over her features, and her voice became a loving, regretful whisper. 'You know you could never leave this house. Not while Vincent Morgan is here.' She adored the man, and hated his weak, soppy wife.

Agatha Merry was an embittered, lonely creature. If she thought for one minute it would get her the love of

Vincent Morgan, she would even be prepared to kill for him.

Nell wanted the ground to open and swallow her up. 'I'm sorry, sir, only I'm going away,' she explained. 'I wouldn't have come back, but I need my wages.'

Vincent Morgan was an intelligent and fair young man. Not immediately attractive to the eye, he was of medium height, with thick, homely features and fine sandy-coloured hair, but he had a pair of innocent, pale green eyes and an honest charm that seemed to please the ladies. At only twenty-six years of age, he had shouldered the responsibilities of his father's estate with pride and ability but he was not a happy man. Having married for the purpose of producing an heir, he found himself trapped in a loveless relationship and though his wife now carried his child, she was not the companion he had hoped for. Timid and weak, Rosalyn spurned his advances and so he took his pleasure wherever he could find it.

'Don't go, Nell,' he said softly. He had been approaching her but stopped when she began backing away. 'I'm sure we can find you other work. Better paid. More responsibility. After all, you're a very capable young woman.'

'It isn't that.' Nell could hardly look him in the eye. 'You see, I'm going away. I'm leaving the area.'

'It's my fault, isn't it?' he said. 'The reason why you're going? It's because I took advantage of you, isn't it?' When she didn't answer, he went on, 'I don't want you to leave, Nell. Oh, I know I shouldn't have taken advantage of you, especially when you were crying and

49

upset, but I thought you wanted me too.' He paused. 'I was wrong, wasn't I? And now you hate me.'

Nell shook her head. 'No, I don't hate you.' She wanted him to know that. 'I did . . .' The hot flush of shame spread over her face. 'I did . . .' Dear God, how could she ever bring herself to say it?

'Go on, please.'

'I was sad and lonely, and yes, you're right, I did want you too.' Just that one time. Never before, and never, *never* again.

'I'm glad.' He looked relieved. 'I wouldn't want to think I'd taken you against your will, or that my selfish actions had forced you to leave.' A coward at heart, he needed reassuring.

She almost told him. It was on the tip of her tongue but she held back. 'It isn't all your fault, what happened between us. I'm leaving because I want to, and I won't trouble you or yours ever again.'

'I'll miss you. I'll miss you as you go about your work, and the way you greet everyone with that bright sunny smile. The mistress is bound to ask where you've gone. She's grown very fond of you, Nell. What shall I tell her?'

Rosalyn's image came into her mind; a slim, frail creature with long, brown, flowing hair and sad, pale eyes. For one fleeting moment Nell felt sorry that she was leaving, but then she reminded herself that she hardly spoke two words a day to the mistress except when she took her breakfast and later collected her tray. On those occasions Rosalyn Morgan would chat to her, asking her to stay a moment longer, but it was not a friendship, more one woman subconsciously reaching out to another. Of the two, Nell the servant was the stronger, but Rosalyn was the mistress. That was the way of things.

Shrugging off his complimentary remarks, Nell smiled. 'The mistress won't miss me, sir, and neither will you. After a while you'll be glad I've gone, you'll see.'

'Where will you go?' He was glad already. He had a soft spot for Nell but after his foolhardy action and in spite of her reassurances, he feared she could be trouble.

'I don't know yet.'

'Will you be all right?'

'I'll be fine, thank you, sir.' It seemed odd, calling him 'sir' when she had lain in his arms and conceived a child by him. She felt bold, and somehow equal to him. 'I have my horse and wagon, and supplies enough to keep me going until I find work.'

'I wish you well.' Now that she was going, he wanted it to be quickly. Glancing at the approaching figure, he told Nell, 'Here comes the unhappy Miss Merry with your wages. Take them and go, with my blessing.'

'Thank you, sir.'

'Goodbye, my dear.'

'Goodbye, sir.'

Nell watched him climb back on to his horse. He didn't immediately ride away. Instead he waited for the housekeeper to hand over the wages to Nell, after which he merely nodded his head, then spurred the impatient horse into a gallop. In a matter of minutes he was out of sight and to the watching Nell it was as though he had never existed. But he would go on existing in the new, warm life's blood she carried inside her.

'Won't do you no good staring after *him*,' Miss Merry sneered. 'You're not fit to wipe his boots.' For a long time she had known how the mistress turned him away with every excuse, and oh, how she longed for him to tap on her bedroom door. He hadn't so far, but she lived in hope.

'I wasn't staring after him.' Nell's heart turned over with the idea that Miss Merry might have seen them in the barn that day.

'Liar! Your sort are two a penny. Entice the master and force money out of him afterwards. I've seen it all before.' Jealousy burned in her eyes like a beacon. 'I know all about you, Nell Reece.'

'I don't know what you mean.' Though she could feel the colour drain from her face, Nell proudly squared up to her.

For what seemed an age Miss Merry stared at Nell. She saw how her threats had shaken the girl, and it made her wonder. Suspicions crept into her mind and formed on her lips. 'I was meaning how you take advantage of the mistress,' she said. 'Lingering with her while she chats to you, like you were an old friend instead of a lowly scullery maid. That's what I meant when I said I knew all about you.' She narrowed her eyes to dark, accusing slits. 'What did you think I meant?'

Relieved, Nell defended herself. 'I didn't think anything in particular, and anyway, I can't help it if the mistress wants to talk.'

'Maybe not.' Miss Merry continued to stare at Nell

who began checking the contents of her wage packet. She didn't trust this woman. If there was one coin short, there would be hell to pay.

'It's all here,' she said finally. 'I'll be on my way.'

As she turned, Miss Merry's long bony hand grabbed her by the hair and swung her round. 'Not so fast, you little baggage.' Her eyes stuck out like hatpins as she pressed her face close to Nell's. 'Happen I've missed something, eh?' she whispered. 'Happen there's more to you than I've given you credit for. Happen you were staring after the master just now because you're more pally with him than you are with his wife.' An awful gleam came into her eyes. 'Is that it, eh? Have you and him been up to something you shouldn't?'

Desperately afraid, Nell kept her head. 'You're mad!'

'Not so mad I didn't see how the two of you were head bent in conversation just now.'

Kicking out, Nell shouted, 'Let go, you crazy bitch!'

The woman's answer was to tighten the fist clasped round Nell's hair. When Nell cried out in pain, she raised her arm and digging thumb and finger either side of Nell's mouth, viciously squeezed. 'What have you two been up to, eh? You'd better tell me or I'll draw your hair out by the roots.' To emphasise her threat, she gave a tug on Nell's hair that almost bent her double. 'I don't think you heard me. I asked, what have you been up to with the master?'

'Nothing!'

'You're a liar.'

'I'm not, and if he knew what you were saying, you'd be kicked out like the troublemaker you are.'

'I've an idea he's bedded you.' Her jealousy became a kind of madness. 'Tell me, damn your eyes! Has he bedded you?'

Defiant and determined, Nell called her bluff. 'Ask *him*,' she hissed. 'Ask the master what you've just asked me. Tell him about your filthy suspicions, and like as not you'll either be horse-whipped or sent packing with your tail between your legs.' Desperate to make good her escape, Nell deliberately glanced towards the direction he'd gone. 'Here's the master now. Go on then, ask him!'

Startled, the housekeeper loosened her grip and swung round. Thankful her ploy had worked, Nell quickly pulled free. 'You've got a bad tongue in your head,' she told the furious woman. 'Thank your lucky stars I'm not vindictive or I might tell the master what you've been saying.' Fleeing across the field, she called out, 'Nobody bedded me, d'you hear? Nobody!' Going like the wind, she surreptitiously made the sign of the cross on her forehead. 'God forgive me for the liar I am,' she said. Nell had not told as many lies in the whole of her life as she'd told today.

Behind her, Miss Merry remained still for a moment, shoulders bowed, cursing her lot in life while the jealousy inside her ran its course. 'I wonder,' she murmured as she made her way back to the house. 'Was she telling the truth? Am I going mad after all? Do I want him so much that I'm beginning to imagine things?' She couldn't be sure, but one thing was certain. 'I daren't put my suspicions to the master, nor anyone else, come to that. Not if I want to keep my place in this house.' A sad, slow smile lit her face. 'Not if I want to be where *he* is.' To be close to Vincent Morgan, to watch his every move and secretly love him. That was what she craved. With every beat of her bitter heart.

Some short way from the house, she turned to stare where only a few moments before she and Nell had confronted each other. 'I can tell you this, Nell Reece,' she muttered. 'Whether he's bedded you or whether he hasn't, I'll see to it that you don't set foot inside this house ever again.' A long sigh escaped from her narrow chest. 'I envy you, all the same. You're ten years younger than me and twice as bold. You're also the prettiest thing I've ever seen. Though I might kill the pair of you, I wouldn't blame the master if he *had* bedded you.'

Lowering her head, she wiped the palms of her hands over her face and groaned. 'I'm twenty-seven years old and no man has ever cast his eyes over me. I'm thin and ugly, and growing into a crusty old maid.' She closed her eyes and faced the skies. 'Vincent Morgan looks at me but he doesn't even know I'm there. No woman on this earth could please him the way I would, and afterwards he'd never want another.'

Suddenly she was laughing, a hard, bitter sound that melted away as she entered the house. She made her way to the kitchen where she rounded on Cook who was up to her neck in pastry and preserves and had forgotten to put the kettle on for the housekeeper's elevenses.

WITH HER WAGES secured and in a lighter frame of mind, Nell went in search of Molly's son, Bill Davidson. Now that she was here, she didn't want to leave without saying goodbye to him, and anyway, if she went away without a word, it was in his nature to come looking for her and that would never do, at least not while he still treated her as his little sister. Since working at the big house, she had come to know his routine as well as she knew her own. At this time he'd be checking the sheep in the far meadow. After she'd seen him, her intention was to travel as far south as she could before midday. Then a brief rest for her and the horse. Afterwards she would begin to search for work at the farms along the way. 'Can't work where I'm known,' she told the old horse. 'Don't want Aunt Lilian finding out where I am or she'll put the poison in, then I'll not find work anywhere.'

Just as she thought, Bill was busy at work in the far meadow. Feeling as though she had all the time in the world, Nell didn't go straight to him. Instead she turned the horse and cart into the field and sat watching him for a long time, enjoying the knowledge that while she could see him, he could not see her. 'You're a handsome feller, Bill Davidson,' she murmured, and her heart leaped, like it always did when she set eyes on him.

He was certainly an extraordinarily good-looking man. Tall and lean yet broad of shoulder, with an upright stride and that thick mop of longish dark hair, he made a striking sight. He seemed at one with nature. Out there in that long, quiet meadow, beneath the vast and magnificent sky, all alone except for the creatures grazing below and the birds winging above, he seemed a million miles from civilisation.

Suddenly, his voice lifted in song. The song was

'Paddy Boy'. Nell had heard him sing this before and it had touched her heart then. On this glorious morning, his melodic voice came to her on the crest of a warm breeze, touching all the emotions she felt for him and bathing her sorry heart with bitter-sweet pleasure.

She began softly crying, the big generous tears flowing down her face and salting her mouth. She loved this man more than she had ever thought it was possible to love anyone. But he was not hers to love. That was why she cried. That and the sound of his beautiful, plaintive song.

She stayed until the last note had died away. For a long time she sat there, her lovely blue eyes focused on him as he went to the aid of a sheep caught on its back and unable to right itself. She saw him raise and comfort the frightened creature before it ran off to test the strength of its tired legs. She heard him laugh at its antics, and saw how he called the dog and fussed him for his skill in ushering the sheep back to the fold.

Torn between going to him and leaving right then, her mind was made up when he strode away in the opposite direction with the dog at his heels. 'Happen it's just as well,' she mused. 'If I faced him now, he might see the truth in my eyes.' He might see how she would rather stay here with him; or that the love she felt for him was not the love of a sister. 'I can't face him,' she whispered. 'I'd have to lie and I don't want to.'

When at last he was gone from sight, Nell left the meadow by the same way she'd entered. Once on the lane, she swung to the right, heading south by way of the river bridge. Next stop would be Accrington and the many farms thereabouts.

It was as she came over the bridge that the accident happened.

The way was treacherously narrow with a wooden fence on either side and a drop of some twenty feet to the river below. Though Nell had negotiated this route many times and knew its every tiny rut, she had always been on foot. To take a horse and cart across was a new experience for her.

The wooden fencing was old and rickety, and the ground edges had begun to crumble. Two of the rotted posts were hanging loose and where the ground was disturbed the fencing snaked up and down, like the ocean waves.

Engrossed in stretching her neck to look over the meadow for signs of Bill, she didn't see the bird flutter and rise from the wooden fencing post. But the horse saw it and was startled.

The first Nell knew of the danger was when the frightened horse went up on its hind legs, causing the cart to lurch to one side. The rear wheels caught the old fencing and in a matter of seconds there was nothing between the cart and the river but a breath of air. 'Dear God!' Nell cried. It took all her might to calm the horse. By that time, she realised with horror, one false move would send her, the cart and the terrified horse over the edge. 'Easy, boy,' she murmured. 'Take it easy now.' Turning her head, she saw how the front left wheel was embedded in the crumbling ground at the edge of the parapet, while the rear one was hanging in mid-air. With every second that passed, and with agonising slowness, the cart began to shift. The front wheel dug deeper and deeper into the soft, pliable surface, sending a hail of debris tumbling into the river below, then suddenly both wheels were spinning in mid-air, the cart was resting on its axle to one side, and all the while the edge was disintegrating, sucking the cart towards the yawning chasm below.

Frantic, Nell forced herself to stay calm as she urged the horse on with soothing words. 'Pull hard, old feller,' she urged. 'Come on, you can do it.' He had the heart and the strength but was frozen with fear. 'Come on, old feller,' she persisted, holding her breath as she gave a very slight slap of the reins. 'Easy now.'

Encouraged and trusting, the horse tried vainly to pull away. There was a grinding sound from the rear as the axle scraped along the ground. Then a sigh of relief from Nell as the cart seemed to move forward. But just when she believed they might make it, a section of ground broke from beneath them and the cart lurched again. This time it settled into a lopsided pitch that threw Nell out of her seat and left her straddling the cart, her feet anchored by the iron rim, and her fingers gripping the iron legs of the seat. She couldn't move. It was more than her life was worth to shift even an inch. One glance at the horse told her that he could panic at any minute. Big-eyed and frothing at the mouth, he was trapped by his harness and being slowly drawn towards the edge of the parapet. 'Easy now.' Though bruised and afraid, Nell knew she had to instil calm in him. 'Stand fast, old feller,' she told him. Beneath her breath she prayed, 'Please

God, don't take us all over.' Her mind was racing as she tried to think of a way out.

She daren't press forward and couldn't go backward. Already her stash of supplies was sliding to the side of the cart. Any minute now, the whole lot would go over the edge.

She tightened her grip on the iron struts, stiffened her toes on the cart's rim and prayed he was close enough to hear her. Taking a deep breath she called out his name. 'Bill! Help!'

No answer.

'*Bill!*' Beneath her breath, she added, 'For pity's sake, where are you?'

Time and again she called his name. But it was no use. 'He can't hear me,' she groaned. Hot and exhausted, she reasoned with herself. 'If I sit up, the whole lot will go, and if I try and slide forward, the horse could rear and send us all down anyway. I can't go over the side on to the ground because it's only my weight that's stopping the cart slipping any further.' What then? What to do? 'I can't lie here until we're found. It could be hours, maybe days. We can't hold out that long.' Try again. 'Bill!' Her voice sailed to the heavens. And slowly died.

Beneath the dry, merciless sun, Nell held on for all she was worth. Drifting in and out of awareness, she had no idea how long they were there. Her body was sore and aching and her fingers incredibly painful. The tips of her toes were crippled with cramp, eased only when she made herself twiddle them every so often. The sweat trickled over her back; her arms felt as though they were being drawn out of their sockets and now she was so stiff she couldn't move even if she wanted to. It seemed as though she and the old horse were the only two souls left in the whole world.

'Stay quiet, old feller,' she kept saying, hoping he was listening, still trusting. 'Someone's bound to come along.' She was trying to convince herself as much as the old horse.

HAVING HERDED THE sheep back to the fold, Bill made his way down the riverbank, cutting the reeds as he went. 'Old Jed will be glad of these for thatching the cottage,' he remarked to the dog at his side. 'By, it'll be grand when it's all done up and we can move in.' Tickling the dog under the chin he mused, 'Our own place, eh? What d'you think to that?' Jed Braithwaite had worked at the big house for many years and had been given the task of restoring the old lodge. The idea was that now old Jed was getting on in years, it might be a good idea for Bill to live on the estate. Bill was thankful to be given the chance to be independent and spent every minute God sent helping Jed do the place up. It would take some long time yet because over the years the lodge had been left to fall into shameful disrepair. It might be habitable by spring next year and though he would miss his old mam, Bill was really looking forward to moving in. 'It's not as if we'll be too far from Haslingden Street,' he said aloud, 'and if I know Molly Davidson, she'll be poking around, bringing her fresh-baked muffins and making sure her big bad son is looking after himself.' He laughed out loud. 'It's just as well I'm moving out or she'd have me there till I'm old and grey.'

As he reached out to slice off a clump of especially tall, fine reeds, he was alarmed when a shower of rubble fell to the ground only inches away. 'What the devil?' Judging that it must have come from the bridge, he immediately looked up and to his astonishment saw the two cartwheels hanging over the edge. As he stared up, numerous small and solid lumps of earth and debris were hitting the ground beside him. 'Jesus, Mary and Joseph! The bridge is falling apart!'

The bridge had been put there as a temporary measure many years ago in the wake of a bad flood, when the old bridge was swept away. Only recently anxious voices had been raised in favour of demolishing the makeshift bridge as a matter of urgency. Bill's voice had been the strongest of them all. 'Bloody councillors might listen and replace the old structure now,' he muttered.

With the dog hard on his heels, he ran towards the thick stone buttress which supported the bridge above the field. Weathered by the passage of time, the stone surface was smooth as silk, with only the worn cracks between the stone blocks offering a slim foothold. It was a difficult, slippery climb to the top but it was the quickest way up. If he went by way of the field and then round the road, Bill knew it would take him at least twice as long.

Three times he almost lost his footing but he would not be beaten. When he stumbled on to the bridge, his nails were torn and bleeding and he felt as if he'd climbed a mountain but he could see the cart and with renewed determination he went towards it.

Having worked with animals all his life, he knew how any sudden movement on his part could send the horse into a panic. Slowing his steps, he began speaking softly to the horse. 'All right, my beauty, all right. I'll soon have you out of there.' When he recognised the horse, he was shocked. 'Why, it's Don Reece's old gelding.' Not for one minute did he think it was Nell who was in trouble. He couldn't see anyone in the cart until he came closer and saw her hanging on for dear life. 'Good God! Nell!'

Not daring to move, Nell smiled up at him while silently sending up a prayer of thanks.

His dark eyes took in the situation at a glance. There was no time to make any kind of a lifeline for Nell. 'If I try and move you first, we might all go down,' he called. As he spoke, he was already tearing at the fencing posts. 'Hold on, Nell. I'll have to lead him off, away from the bridge altogether. Do you know what I'm saying, Nell?' He didn't want to frighten her by spelling it out.

Nell felt the earth shudder beneath her. My God! The awful realisation took her breath away. The whole bridge was going! From one end to the other, huge cracks were appearing. Unable to speak, she merely nodded.

Breaking off a number of railing posts, Bill quickly made a solid base over the splitting ground. Then, taking the horse by the head collar, he urged it forward, bracing it with his own weight so as to give it confidence. Slowly, agonisingly, the animal moved, inching the cart forward with him until the overhanging wheels began to butt up against the posts. This was the hardest part. This was the moment that would test both their strengths. 'That's it, old son,' he said. 'Nearly there. Keep coming forward. Come on, that's it.'

Bearing the full weight of both horse and cart, Bill imagined he heard his back breaking; but it was the sound of the bridge disintegrating beneath him. Great rivers of sweat ran down his back, and his arms were almost wrenched out, but he couldn't stop. He had to keep going. He had to keep going because Nell was in mortal danger and if anything happened to her he would not want to live himself.

Suddenly, there was a lurch as the front wheel was forced up and then over the posts. 'Hold on tight, Nell,' he warned. And she did, relieved that at last she was on more level ground and in less pain because of it. But she still couldn't move. She still dared not loosen her grip.

'Be ready for any sudden movement,' he called out, confirming her fears. 'We're not home and dry yet.'

The back wheel ground up over the posts and they were almost there.

Almost.

The horse was clear, and so was the cart now and Bill led them to where the bridge joined the grassy track. Behind them the bridge was breaking off in huge chunks but they seemed far enough away from any immediate danger. Anxious to get Nell out of the cart, Bill ran to her and opened his arms. 'Come on, sweetheart.' He had always called her 'sweetheart' and it made her smile.

'Let's have you down from there,' he said, reaching up to lift her out.

As Nell leaned forward into his arms, there came an almighty cracking sound from the far side of the cart. For a moment Nell believed the cart had broken its back after the struggle. But it wasn't that. It was the earth beneath them; bitten off by the weight of the falling bridge, it was tearing away like a man might tear away a piece of bread. As it reared up under them, the cart toppled backwards and Nell lost her balance.

It all happened in a split second; one extraordinary, terrifying second that seemed to last a lifetime. As she struggled to right herself, she stared into Bill's face and it was alive with horror. Desperately trying to keep his own balance, he grabbed at her clothing. 'Don't look down!' he shouted. 'Look at me, Nell, look at me!' When she turned, he almost had her. But the cart rocked violently, throwing them separate ways; he to the bank, Nell through the air. He saw her fall, and his heart went with her. 'No! Nell!'

Even before she hit the water and disappeared beneath the surface, he had kicked off his shoes and thrown himself off the bank, his dark, desperate eyes scanning the water where she'd plummeted. Like a slim, folded arrow he sliced into the cool depths, the water rippling over his sweating body.

In a minute he found her and, taking her by the scruff of the neck, he swam with her to the surface where he dragged her unconscious body to the bank. Breathless and gasping for air, he laid her face up, his distraught gaze ravishing her cold, bleached face. 'Dear God above, don't let her die,' he pleaded. Rolling her over, he pressed on her back to force the water up from her lungs. 'Come on, sweetheart,' he muttered. 'Come on . . . come on.' When she groaned and moved, he worked all the harder until at last she began coughing out the water from her lungs. 'That's it,' he laughed, the relief ebbing through him. 'That's my girl!'

Nell could hear his voice but she couldn't speak. She felt herself drifting in a strange place, a cold and frightening abyss where the waters lapped over her head and the darkness closed in around her like a suffocating fog. She felt herself being lifted. She felt safe, cradled, and the movement of someone walking with her. She felt his warm, affectionate lips cover her mouth, filling her lungs with his breath.

Then she felt no more.

Chapter Three

'Nell. Nell, can you hear me?' Rosalyn Morgan had stayed close to Nell ever since Bill had brought her to the house yesterday after her terrible ordeal. Like the kindly soul she was, Rosalyn had insisted that Nell be put to bed in her home. 'We can't have her moved anywhere else,' she told her worried husband. 'The girl is in a bad way and I would be failing in my duty if I didn't take her in and have her attended by the very best.'

Recognising the soft, quiet voice of her employer, Nell wondered where she was.

'Nell, can you hear me?' the voice persisted. There was a moment before it spoke again. 'All right, my dear. I'll leave you now.'

There was the familiar sound of shoes tapping against polished floorboards, then the sound of a door opening and closing, and afterwards silence.

Nell wanted to open her eyes but she was afraid. Why was Rosalyn Morgan talking to her like that? Where was she? She felt odd ... tired, and a little suspicious. Why wasn't she ambling along the roads, making her way to Accrington? Why was she with Rosalyn Morgan and where was Bill?

Suddenly, like a bad dream that lingered after waking, she saw it all – the bridge breaking up, the cart sliding into the railing, the river below and herself falling. It wasn't a nightmare. It had happened. It had really happened. And Bill. Where was he? The more aware she became, the more she feared. Inside, she was burning. Outside, she was cool. Deliciously cool.

Intrigued and still a little afraid, she opened her eyes.

At first she couldn't understand. The room was vaguely familiar. There was a sense of richness – the windows dressed in blue velvet curtains, a pretty crystal chandelier hanging from the centre of the ceiling. There was a feeling of wealth and grandeur. 'I know this room,' she murmured, her fuddled mind trying to recognise the opulent surroundings. Her gaze fell on the bedside lamp. It was tall and slender, with the figure of a lady at the base and, above, a tasselled shade of pale blue silk.

There came a light tap on the door. When it opened, a small, squat little man carrying a black bag appeared. He was alone. As he came towards her, his round face smiling, Nell pressed herself down, deeper into the bed, until only her blue eyes peered over the top of the bedclothes.

The man's smile broadened and his little eyes disappeared into the fleshy folds of his cheeks. 'Ah! I see you're awake,' he said. Placing the black bag on the dresser, he came to the bed where he tenderly laid his hand over her forehead. 'You're a very fortunate young lady,' he said, in a firm, authoritative voice. 'If Bill

Davidson hadn't been there to drag you out of the river, I dread to think what might have happened.'

It was all coming back now. Bill holding on to her – but he couldn't. He couldn't because the ground was breaking up and she was falling through the air. What then? She knew nothing after that. Until now. 'Are you saying Bill dived in and saved me from drowning?'

'That's exactly what I'm saying, young lady. He dived in and got you out, then he ran across the fields with you to this house. Mr Morgan was out shooting at the time but his good wife was home and took you in at once. She insisted that you should be given the best possible care and that money should be no object.' His round face creased into a grin. 'That's why I'm here, you see.' Presenting himself with the smallest measure of pride, he announced, 'Dr Frederick Fellows at your service. I'm pleased to say you're recovering very well. But then I'm not surprised by that. You're young and strong and you seem to have a will of iron.'

Nell had seen Dr Fellows at the house on previous occasions but she had never spoken two words to the quaint little man; nor he to her. Now, though, she took an instant liking to him.

Her first thought was for the man she had always loved. 'Is Bill all right?'

'If you mean young Mr Davidson, he's as fit as ever.' A great sigh came from his bulbous chest. 'What it must be to have a fine, strong body like that.' He went on, 'He's fine, the horse is all right, and the cart is mended – your young man has seen to that.' A thought struck him, making him wonder. He had already discovered that Nell was pregnant. That knowledge, and the knowledge that Bill Davidson had put his own life at risk without a moment's hesitation, made him put two and two together, prompting him to ask, 'Is he your young man?'

'No.' All the wishing in the world wouldn't change that. In her mind's eye she could see him, reaching out to her, and for the rest of her life she would see his dark, stricken eyes, filled with terror as she fell from his clutches.

'It's fortunate you didn't have a young flighty gelding in harness or he might have pulled you all to your deaths.'

'Oh, Clarence is a fine old horse. My dad wanted me to have him because he's sensible.'

'Your dad too, by the sound of it.'

'Is the horse fit enough to travel? I mean, he's not young any more and he was so frightened.' The old horse had been there for most of her growing life. When things overwhelmed her, she would often sit in the barn talking to him, telling him her deepest secrets.

Going to the dresser, Dr Fellows picked up his bag and brought it to the bed. 'Old horses are like old doctors, you have to shoot them, or they'll never die.'

'What about the cart? That was my aunt's, but Dad told me he'd earned it ten times over and that I was to take good care of it. He gave me enough supplies to last until I could get a good position. I suppose the supplies were lost in the river.'

The doctor opened his bag and pulled down the bedclothes. Placing his stethoscope in his ears, he listened to her chest. 'From what I understand, everything was secured.' His gaze fell on the angry red weal across her temple. 'It's you I'm concerned about, young lady. You took a nasty knock on the head when you fell.'

Feeling stronger by the minute, Nell was bold. 'Thank you for your trouble, Doctor, but I'm recovered now and I won't be needing you any more.'

Clearing his throat, he said smartly, 'You do seem to have recovered well enough to get out of bed but I first want to give you a thorough examination.'

'I have to leave this house,' she confided worriedly. 'I should never have been brought back here.'

'Considering the urgency of your situation at the time, I'm afraid young Mr Davidson had no choice but to get you to the nearest dwelling as quickly as possible. The nearest dwelling was this house, and that's where he brought you.' Staring down at her with a scowl of disapproval, he chided, 'Really, my dear, you should be immeasurably grateful.'

Nell was mortified. 'Oh, don't misunderstand me, Doctor. I'm eternally grateful to Bill, and the mistress, and you of course, but . . . well, you don't understand. I can't be discovered here. I *have* to get away.' In as few words as possible she had to make him see her desperation.

He smiled on her then like an old, wise man. 'Your need to get away,' he ventured softly, 'wouldn't be because you're with child, would it?'

She couldn't bring herself to answer. Instead she buried her face in her hands and wondered how many people he had told. Had he told the master? Did Vincent Morgan guess that she carried his child? What would the mistress think of her? How many other people knew of her shame, and how long would it be before her Aunt Lilian came here to take her away?

The doctor was speaking again. 'You're little more than a child yourself,' he observed. 'You do understand, don't you, Nell, that if you were taken against your will, the culprit can be made to answer? Who was it? You must not be afraid to point him out.'

Nell was both relieved and surprised. Relieved, because his remarks suggested that he had not yet told the master of her condition. And surprised that he should think she'd been taken against her will. What had happened between her and Vincent Morgan was a terrible mistake but it wasn't sordid, not in the way the good doctor was suggesting.

'Well, what have you to say?'

'It wasn't like that.' She could not bring herself to look him in the eye.

'Hm.' A moment's pause, then, 'So, you were not taken against your will?'

'No, sir.'

'You wouldn't be protecting the scoundrel, would you?'

'No, sir.' She looked up then, opening her heart a chink. 'I have to go away. You see, my aunt wants me to be rid of the baby.'

'And you don't agree to that?' It wasn't unheard of

for a young girl to find herself in trouble then have it all hushed up.

Nell was horrified. 'No! I won't let her do it. But I'm afraid because she's capable of anything.'

'You make her sound like a monster.'

'Oh, she is!' Nell was in full sail. 'She's a dreadful woman. She owns everything, the house, the land, every stick of furniture in the place, and every penny that my dad's earned for her. You'd never believe she was his sister. His only family, apart from me, and she treats him like dirt. I've never understood why he lets her do that. I wanted him to come away with me but he wouldn't.'

'Some people prefer the devil they know.'

'I mean to come back for him. Some day, I'll take him away from her and she won't be able to do a thing about it!' The tears were flowing now. Tears of frustration and long-held anger.

'Did your father want you to stay? I mean, wasn't he concerned that you were setting out on your own, and so young?'

Nell shook her head. 'He told me to go. He said he loved me but that she would make my life a misery the way she's made his. He said I was to stay away and not come back until I knew it was safe – when the baby's born and she can't make me be rid of it.'

'I see. And how will you know that?' Unsure whether she was telling the truth, he did sense an essence of real tragedy about her young life. So he listened like a good doctor should.

Weakened by her tirade, Nell leaned back and

let the comfort wash over her. Placing her hands over her stomach, she asked, 'My baby's safe, isn't it, Doctor?'

'Yes. As far as I can see, the ordeal has done it no harm.' He smiled, that same sweet, old-fashioned smile that had made her confide in him. 'You're a remarkably strong young lady, and I do believe you'll have a remarkably strong baby.'

Nell gave a little laugh. 'At least it should be able to swim, wouldn't you say?'

He laughed also. 'I think you might be right.' In a more serious tone, he said, 'Raising a baby won't be easy. Have you thought about that?'

'I've thought of nothing else.'

'And you won't be deterred?'

'No.'

'Stubborn, eh?'

'So my dad says.'

'When were you thinking to resume your journey?'

'Today.' Nell was eager to be gone. 'Right now would not be soon enough.'

Drawing a deep breath, he stood up, his soft face composed into a picture of contentment as he looked down on her. 'You're an astonishing young thing, I must say.' He gave a sigh. 'I suppose I'd better examine you before you leap out of the window and make good your escape, eh?'

Nell chuckled. 'I don't feel much like leaping.'

'You do surprise me.'

She lay still then while he examined her limbs and joints; he listened to her heart and looked into her eyes until he was assured that she really might be able to travel. 'I don't believe this is an injury received in the accident.' Pointing to her bruised and cut ankle, he asked, 'How was it done?'

'A thorn went into it.'

'It's badly festered.'

'That's because I haven't been able to tend it myself with herbs and natural things, like Molly taught me.'

He grinned. 'I see. And I'm just an old quack, is that it?'

'I didn't say that.'

'You didn't have to.' Thankfully, he was still amused by her honest cheek and chatty tongue. The girl is an angel, he thought, with no more fear of her betters than a cat has of a king.

Nell hadn't asked before, so she asked now, 'How long have I been lying here?'

'Overnight. You became fitful. It was necessary for me to give you a sedative.'

'Overnight!' Nell was alarmed at the implications. 'I wish you hadn't kept me here.'

'I had little choice.'

'Sir?'

'Yes?'

Taking a deep breath, Nell voiced what had been on her mind since he mentioned her being pregnant. 'Have you told anyone . . . about me being with child?' She waited anxiously for his answer.

'I'm a doctor. Your secret won't go beyond these four walls.'

'Thank you, sir.' What a blessed relief. Vincent

Morgan was a powerful man. If he wanted the child, nothing would stop him taking it from her.

She gave a cry when he squeezed her ankle. 'Crikey! That bloody hurt!'

'Language, if you don't mind!' He squeezed the ankle once more and this time she merely shivered with pain. 'It's swollen with pus,' he observed ruefully. 'I'm afraid it will have to be lanced.'

'Will that mean I can't leave today?'

'We'll see.'

'If you won't let me leave, I won't let you lance it.'

He stared at her then, his small, comical eyes bright. 'I must say, you're the boldest little thing I've ever come across.'

'If I don't take care of myself, nobody else will.' She had never been able to rely on her father. Her aunt was unapproachable, and the only real friends she'd known were Molly and her family. Nell had taken great care never to abuse that wonderful friendship, and so for the most part she had kept her own counsel and looked to herself to survive.

'Well now, that's a sorry state of affairs.' He was curious. All he knew of Nell was that she worked in this house and lived some miles away. Apart from that scant knowledge, he had never heard of her or her family.

With a wisdom older than her years, Nell answered philosophically, 'You do what you can with what the good Lord sees fit to give you.'

Her remark made him think. Not long ago he had had a wife and children – two boys and a girl. Now his wife was gone and his children had grown and moved away. They didn't write or call any more, and he was a lonely man. All he had left was his practice, and if he had given less time to that and more to his family, he might not be plagued by so many regrets.

Nell wondered why he'd gone so quiet. He sat on the edge of her bed, quite still, either deep in thought or suddenly unwell. 'Are you all right, sir?' she asked tentatively.

He looked up. 'Miles away,' he answered. Then he turned her ankle to examine it again. 'I dare say if the cut is just small enough to release the pressure, you might be able to hobble on it. I would rather you didn't but somehow I have a feeling you would leave anyway, once my back was turned.'

'I would because I have no choice. To tell the truth, I'm worried in case Aunt Lilian has been here already.' Her tired blue eyes grew big and round. 'Has she? Has she been here already?'

'You forget, I'm just a visitor,' he told her. 'It isn't me you should be asking.'

'Who then?'

At that moment the door opened and in walked the mistress, tall and frail, moving with a steady, careful step and looking older than her twenty-eight years. Her pale eyes were too large in her narrow face but her flowing brown hair shone like the bright side of a penny. With her was a weasel-faced servant by the name of Freda.

As Rosalyn Morgan approached, she first addressed Dr Fellows who gave an explanation as to Nell's concern about her aunt. 'You're not to worry, my dear.' Turning to Nell, Rosalyn's thin features ventured a smile but the smile didn't lift her face. 'The only visitor to come to this house last evening was Mrs Davidson. A dear soul, laden with new honey and advice.' She gave a small, tinkling laugh. 'She was quite adamant as to how you should be tended.'

Nell laughed also. 'That's Molly,' she said. 'My friend.'

'She also brought two freshly baked apple pies. You were in no fit condition to eat them so the dear soul insisted that I had them anyway.' She rolled her eyes. 'Cook was not pleased, I can tell you. She imagined I was about to replace her. However, once she was assured I meant no such thing, she smothered the pies in cream and served them for supper. They were a credit to your friend.'

Nell laughed with delight. 'Oh, Molly is the best cook in the world. There's nothing she doesn't know.'

'I'm sure. However, I had to send her away, together with the young man who saved you, though I've issued him with regular bulletins through the kitchen. I am sorry, my dear, but,' she glanced at the doctor, 'I was advised there should be no visitors.'

'Yes, ma'am.' Nell was disappointed.

'But I told her that I would let you know how concerned she was.'

'Thank you, ma'am.'

'So you see, my dear,' she looked first at Nell, then at the doctor, then back at Nell, 'there have been no visitors to your bedside and certainly not your good aunt.' She gave Nell a peculiar look. 'If you like, I can arrange for someone to fetch her at once.'

Nell startled them all with her sharp reply. '*No!* Please, I don't want her here!' Embarrassed by her outburst, she bowed her head. 'Sorry, ma'am, but I would rather she wasn't fetched.'

'Then she won't be.'

Freda had stayed by the door, listening intently to everything that was being said. Old and cantankerous, the miserable creature knew everything about everybody. Nell hoped she didn't know about her; if she found out that she was carrying a child, the news would be halfway across Lancashire in no time.

'I'm almost finished here,' Dr Fellows told Rosalyn. 'The patient is in surprisingly good form, but I am concerned about her ankle. I'm told it was pierced by a thorn. It won't mend until the poison is released.' He glanced at Nell. 'I've already informed this young lady it will have to be lanced in order to release the poison.'

It was too much for Rosalyn. 'Oh, my dear!' Raising her hands she spread them in front of her, as though pushing away something threatening. 'Is that necessary?'

'I'm afraid so,' Dr Fellows said. 'It will take only a minute and afterwards the ankle should mend quickly. The trouble is, this young woman insists she wants to leave as soon as possible, and I'm saying she should not put weight on the ankle for some time.' He gave Nell a friendly glower. 'I wonder if you might persuade her to stay a day longer.'

Before Rosalyn could say a word, Nell spoke up. 'I'm

thankful for all your help, honest to God, but I need to go. If you have to cut the ankle that's all right, but if you mean to keep me here against my will, then you can leave my ankle alone and I'll be on my way.'

'Is she strong enough to leave?' Rosalyn asked the doctor.

He smiled. 'She's strong enough to lay down the law, I know that much.'

Coming closer to the bed, Rosalyn tried to persuade Nell. 'I really would like you to stay a while longer, at least until you're more able.'

'I'm able now, ma'am. I really am.' The truth was, she felt as if she'd been shot from a cannon. Her bones ached as if they'd been stretched on the rack and it hurt her to breathe. But she couldn't stay. She daren't stay. Every minute she stayed was a minute closer to falling into her aunt's clutches.

'I can't keep you here against your will, child,' Rosalyn said gently, 'but I must insist you allow the good doctor to tend your ankle the best way he can. Afterwards, if you insist on leaving, that has to be your choice. However, I hope you can enjoy a hearty meal before you depart my house.'

'Thank you, ma'am.' That would be no hardship; she was so hungry her stomach was turning somersaults.

Smiling, Rosalyn turned away and her eye caught sight of Nell's swollen ankle. Morbid curiosity made her examine it more closely; where the flesh was torn, there was a dark, ugly swelling, and the skin all around was an unsightly criss-cross of red cuts. 'I see what the doctor means,' she remarked, turning a paler, sickly colour.

'Oh, and what's this?' Her curiosity was aroused by the distinctive mark on the sole of Nell's foot.

Stretching her neck, Nell saw what she meant. 'That's my birthmark,' she told her. 'I always think it looks like I've walked in dog's muck but Molly thinks it's lovely. She says it looks like a half-moon over the forest.'

Rosalyn agreed. 'Yes, she's right. That's exactly what it looks like.'

Intrigued, Freda leaned forward to have a peep too. So did the doctor. 'Hm, so it does,' he said, and reminded himself why he was here. 'Now, I'd like hot water and clean sheets, and a bar of carbolic. The sooner I lance this little mess the better.'

With a smile of encouragement at Nell, Rosalyn left the room, accompanied by Freda. Dr Fellows set about getting Nell ready and by the time he had wiped the wound and folded the sheet beneath it, Freda was back. 'The mistress says I'm to stay and help if needed,' the old biddy grumbled through her large, gappy teeth.

When the doctor beckoned, she scurried over, her piggy eyes alight with enthusiasm. She relished a bit of blood and gore. She liked to see suffering and tears, as long as she wasn't at the receiving end.

If she expected to see Nell cry, she was bitterly disappointed. Nell set herself for the pain and throughout the ten minutes or so that it took the good doctor to open up the ankle and scoop out the badness, she made not a sound, nor did she shed a single tear.

Feeling cheated, Freda gathered up the soiled articles and shuffled away. 'Bleedin' jobs I get,' she muttered on leaving. 'I've got better things to do with me time.'

Washing his hands in the bowl of water, the doctor commented, 'There goes a miserable old thing.'

Nell managed a little chuckle. 'I think she's upset because you didn't chop off my leg.'

'Heaven forbid!' Returning to the bed, Dr Fellows made sure the ankle was clean and smartly dressed, then he looked into Nell's blue eyes, saying with a tenderness that endeared him to her, 'Do as I ask, my dear. Give the ankle time to heal before you set out again.'

Nell didn't want to reward him with a lie so she merely smiled up at him, leaving him to ponder on her intentions. 'I'm really hungry,' she told him. 'I could eat a scabby donkey.'

He laughed out loud. 'At least you haven't lost your appetite. I suppose I should be grateful for small mercies.' As he made his departure, he had one last thing to say. 'If I don't see you again, take care of yourself, young lady, and be sure to keep that wound clean.'

'I will. Doctor?'

'Mmm?'

'Thank you.'

He nodded and made his way downstairs to make his report and present his bill.

VINCENT MORGAN WAS in the library, discussing Nell with his wife. 'If she insists on leaving, you have no right to persuade her otherwise.'

'But why should she leave?' Rosalyn had been

puzzled when she had received the news that Nell had severed her employ in this house. 'And why on earth would she want to leave the area, a young girl like that, on her own? Why did Mrs Molly Davidson advise me not to call Nell's family? "Nell wouldn't thank you" was what she said.' Rosalyn had been tempted to override Molly's advice. 'It was my first thought, to inform her father and aunt, but Mrs Davidson said it would cause trouble.' She recalled how certain and worried Molly had been. 'I don't know why,' she murmured, 'but I believed her. That's why I didn't send for her father. Now, with the girl threatening to leave and the doctor saying she should stay, I'm not sure what to do.'

'You do nothing, my sweet.' The last thing he wanted was for Nell's father to turn up here. He wouldn't be able to look the man in the eye. 'Apparently there is a family dispute. It has nothing to do with us, and as far as I'm concerned, that's an end to it.' He was shaking inside. Nell couldn't leave soon enough for him. If it should ever come out that he had bedded the girl, his reputation would be in tatters, and his marriage too.

So engrossed in his fear was he that when a knock came on the door he almost jumped out of his skin. Glancing at his wife, he appeared momentarily confused, then he cleared his throat. 'Come!' At least his voice sounded authoritative.

Dr Fellows poked his head round the door. 'I've finished with the girl,' he said. 'Unfortunately she is adamant she won't stay, so I don't suppose I'll be tending her again.' He gave one of his little smiles. 'What a stubborn young thing. I've no doubt she'll be gone as soon as she's dressed.'

Rosalyn gave a cry and would have left the room, no doubt to talk to Nell and at least persuade her to have something to eat. Her husband put his arm round her shoulder, effectively keeping her there.

'Thank you, Doctor,' he said brightly. 'Like me and my good wife, you've done all you can. Send your account. It will, of course, be settled promptly as usual.'

'I have it here.' Taking a slip of paper from his waistcoat pocket, the doctor laid it on the desk. 'I like to keep things in good order, as you know.'

'Of course.' Keeping a wary eye on his wife, Vincent went to his desk and perused the bill. Satisfied it was not excessive, he plucked a cheque book from the desk drawer and swiftly wrote into it. Giving the signed cheque to Dr Fellows, he smiled. 'Thank you again.' With a curt nod of the head, he bade him farewell. 'Good day to you, sir. I'm sure you're right in thinking you won't tend the girl again. Like you, I believe she's bound to be gone soon.' His relief was immense.

Ever since Nell had been brought here, Vincent Morgan had not enjoyed a minute's peace. First he was smitten with guilt at the pitiful sight of Nell, then he was smitten with fear when his own wife took it on herself to oversee the girl's recovery. If he'd refused to have Nell here, it would have raised questions, so he was forced to appear willing and equally concerned. His marriage was not very satisfactory but it was a suitable marriage nevertheless, and now that Rosalyn was carrying his child, he must conform. To suffer a loveless marriage was not too high a price to pay for a son and heir.

Rosalyn walked with the good doctor into the hallway. 'And how are you?' he asked, eyeing her up and down and noting how unusually tired she appeared. 'You've endured a hectic time recently. It's bound to have taken its toll.' There were times when he wondered whether this frail and precious woman could ever muster the strength needed to deliver a child. Yet she had endured her pregnancy well so far and had shown signs of determination he had not detected in her before.

Rosalyn showed the same determination now. 'I'm due for a check-up the day after tomorrow,' she reminded him, just a little cynically. 'I think I might survive until then.'

Already she was dreading the check-up. As always, she hated the doctor's hands on her nakedness, and afterwards, when he'd gone, she would feel dirty and used. But it wasn't his fault. It was hers. At heart she was a timid, frightened creature who trembled every time a man came near; even her husband, who was tender and gentle as any man could be.

'Very well,' the doctor agreed. 'But you do look tired. Will you allow me to recommend a tonic?' He paused, setting his black bag on the hallway table and searching inside it even as he spoke. 'Three times a day with meals,' he told her, handing out a small bottle of liquid, 'and mind you take care of yourself, Mrs Morgan. I wouldn't want you to risk losing this baby because of that young woman upstairs.'

She stared at him in astonishment. 'I don't want you to go away thinking that young lady has been any trouble to me,' she corrected. 'Nell Reece is a likeable, honest young thing, and I'm only too glad to have been here when she needed help.'

'Of course.' He shuffled uncomfortably. 'I was not implying that she might have deliberately caused you trouble. I merely state the fact that you have suffered a certain amount of anxiety which, in your condition, can only aggravate your wellbeing. Naturally, I have been very concerned.'

'Why?' She continued to accuse him with her large, pale eyes. 'Because I'm weak and frail, and because, like everyone else, you see in me a foolish, helpless woman without design or purpose?'

Greatly embarrassed, he blustered and fussed. 'Oh, but my dear, I meant no such thing! What I meant was . . . you saw how the girl was when she was brought here, and you have taken care of her yourself ever since. I know for a fact that you stayed with her through the night. I saw for myself how you cared for her, and how you made your servants care for her. I saw a strength in you that was astonishing.' Bristling, he told her in a calm, quiet voice, 'Ma'am, you do me an injustice. How could I ever see you as a weak and foolish woman? You are kind and thoughtful, and if it hadn't been for you, that girl upstairs would not have recovered so quickly.'

Rosalyn bowed her head. 'Thank you, Doctor, but I had little to do with the girl's swift recovery. Always a fighter, Nell Reece is strong and wilful, with a zest for life that leaves me breathless.' Thinking of Nell made her look up and smile.

The doctor smiled back. 'I know exactly what you

mean,' he admitted. 'She made me wonder who was the doctor, me or her. Nevertheless, I insist that, along with young Davidson, you played a crucial part in bringing her back to health and I will not have you saying otherwise.'

'If that's the case then I'm glad. Nell is a delightful young thing. From the first day she came to work here, she's filled this grim old house with sunshine.' A flush of sadness rose in her features. 'I'll be very sorry when she leaves.'

'Hmm!' He knew exactly what Rosalyn was trying to say, for he, too, had felt years younger in Nell's bright company. 'She's certainly a determined rascal. I suspect if she means to go, then she'll go.' Something Nell had said came to mind. 'What do you know about this aunt of hers? Lilian, isn't it?'

'Only that Nell doesn't want to see her and that she has good reason for taking against the woman.'

'What reason?'

Rosalyn shrugged her narrow shoulders. 'Who knows what goes on in any family?' In my own family too, she thought bitterly.

For some time now she had suspected Vincent of seeing other women but she could never prove it, and anyhow she blamed herself. If a man didn't get his rights at home, from his own wife, who could blame him if he looked elsewhere? She didn't enjoy that side of marriage and there were times when she even felt grateful he could be satisfied in some other woman's arms. Maybe when the baby was born she would feel differently. Maybe she would not shrink when Vincent's body lay on hers and his mouth covered her nipples. Maybe then

87

he would not feel the need to use other women. One thing was certain. She must not risk her marriage because of his weakness. Especially when she, too, was guilty of being weak.

'If the aunt means to tame the girl, I'd say she has her work cut out.' Dr Fellows was still thinking of Nell.

Rosalyn laughed. 'I see you've got to know her very well in a short time.'

'Enough to realise she will let no one and nothing interfere with her plans.' Puzzled, he scratched his head. 'There appears to be something very bad between the girl and her aunt though. I can't help but wonder how that came about. Certainly the girl is infuriatingly strong-minded, but I wouldn't have thought she was a troublemaker.'

Rosalyn nodded. 'Your instincts serve you well. Nell is a good, kind soul, and if there are bad feelings between her and her aunt, I would say the fault lies with the woman and not the child.' She wanted him to go now. He was a fine doctor and a decent man, with only one fault as far as she could tell, and that was his tendency to chatter. 'I'll go to her now,' she said, hoping that would speed him on his way.

'Good day then. I'll see you the day after tomorrow, as arranged.'

'Thank you. Good day.'

A maid handed the doctor his hat and jacket, and he prepared to leave.

When the maid stepped forward to open the door, all three were taken aback to see a sour-faced and ill-tempered woman standing on the step, her fist raised ready to strike the door knocker. 'I ought to inform the authorities,' she shrieked, her beady eyes looking straight at Rosalyn. 'It was your bounden duty to inform me that my niece was injured and being held at this house. I've come for her! Send her out this minute or you'll answer to the magistrates.'

Cool and calm, Rosalyn inquired, 'Who are you?'

'Who am I?' Her face seemed to crumple with rage. 'Lilian Reece, that's who I am. The girl's aunt.'

'The girl's aunt?' Rosalyn stepped forward.

'Turn her over to me and I'll be on my way.'

'I'm afraid I can't do that, Mrs Reece.'

'Miss Reece, if you please! And what do you mean, you can't do that?'

'Your niece won't see you.'

'You're lying! What the devil's going on here?'

The doctor stepped forward. 'I'm Dr Fellows,' he said sternly. 'Your niece is recovering well from her ordeal but as yet I can't allow her to have visitors. She is certainly in no fit state to travel.'

'Nonsense! I've come to collect her and collect her I will.'

Rosalyn had been studying the older woman's face and it came to her that Nell might have every reason to be afraid. 'I'd like you to leave now,' she said. 'You heard what the doctor said. Your niece is not well enough to travel and even if she was, I doubt if it would matter to you. As I've said, and as you persistently choose to ignore, your niece does not want to see you.' Sternly regarding the other woman she asked, 'How did you know your niece was here?'

Lilian smiled. 'There is very little I don't know,' she said, 'and people talk.' She waved her hand impatiently. 'No matter! The girl is not yet seventeen. She doesn't know her own mind. It's obvious to me that she needs taking in hand, and as her legal guardian that falls to me. I've never shirked my responsibilities and I never will. She must be given into my care. We have urgent matters to attend to.' Things such as ridding the girl of the brat she was carrying, then finding out who put her that way and making him pay the price. The sooner she got the girl back home the better, before Don found out she was here. Taking a deep breath that seemed to lift her from the ground, she asserted, 'Understand this. I have no intention of leaving here without my niece.'

Deciding this was no time to be tactful, Rosalyn was blunt. 'I don't want to have you forcibly removed from here, but if you persist you will leave me no choice. Please be sensible. For the time being, your niece is in my care and it's her wishes I'm concerned with. Not yours.'

'I'll call the authorities.'

'You must do as you wish.' Rosalyn was firm.

'What did she tell you?' Suddenly Lilian's anger became a deep, niggling worry.

Seeing the woman's anxiety, Rosalyn quizzed her. 'What do you mean?' She felt there was something wrong here. Something rotten and evil. 'What could she tell me?'

Defensive now, Lilian retorted, 'I'm sure I don't know. There is nothing Nell could say that would cause me trouble but being the wicked little thing she is, I've no doubt she might try and blacken my name, but I'm a good woman, and a generous benefactor. The girl owes me a great deal and it's time she realised that.' For one, fleeting moment, when Rosalyn Morgan had called her bluff about going to the authorities, she had actually believed that Nell had found out her age-old secret. But no. It was impossible. Nell did not know the truth and neither did her father. In fact, no one knew and no one ever would. For years now, she had let the girl believe her mother had died giving her life. She had let the man blame himself. It suited her to encourage his awful guilt. Merciless in her condemnation of that ill-fated affair, she had played on his sense of guilt until, now, he was a shambling shadow of his former self, believing as he did that he, and he alone, had caused the death of Nell's mother.

He loathed himself, punished himself and came to believe every terrible lie his sister fed him. Because of his blind passion, he had sent a lovely and wonderful woman to her grave. That was what Lilian constantly told him.

And yet, in truth, all he had ever done was to adore her.

'Of course we have our little arguments,' she continued guardedly. 'Nell can be unbelievably lazy and when I have occasion to punish her, she tends to hold longstanding grudges. So you can see why I feared she might turn you against me.'

'Yes, I do see.' In fact, Rosalyn was beginning to see a whole lot more than she had originally suspected. This woman was a very real danger to Nell. She knew that now.

'Her father, my brother, you understand, will expect me to bring her home.'

'Why isn't he here himself, wanting to see Nell?'

'Because he has work to do.' The lies fell thick and fast. In fact she had not told him about Nell's accident. 'My brother and I work long, hard hours,' she continued smugly. 'At this very moment he's deep in the spinney, gathering logs for the winter. Being a landowner yourself, though of course on a much grander scale than our humble little farmstead, you will understand how we have to stay ahead of the seasons. That's why he wasn't able to come and why I'm here to speak on his behalf. Don't believe for one minute that he loves his daughter any the less because he couldn't leave his work.' Jealousy raged through her. 'In fact, he worships the ground she walks on.' A dark, dangerous emotion betrayed itself in her agitated manner.

The doctor and Rosalyn glanced at each other, each thinking how this woman had shown herself to be not only hard and cunning, but also unstable. She should be persuaded to leave as soon as possible.

It was Dr Fellows who spoke. 'I'm sorry,' he said, 'it isn't advisable to worry your niece just now.'

Realising she was fighting a losing battle, Lilian decided to turn on the tears. 'You've no idea what I've been through with that girl,' she cried. 'I raised her when she had no mother to call her own. I provided for her and her father when they had no home and no prospects.' Taking a handkerchief from her pocket, she blew her nose and dabbed at her eyes. 'All these years I've looked out for that ungrateful wretch and now see how she repays me!'

Rosalyn was curious. 'And how does she repay you?'

'Oh, you may well ask!' The statement was delivered with a puff of the chest and a squint of the eye. 'Rebellious! Wayward! Always daring me. Expecting wages for work she does round the house and farm when she should be doing it in gratitude for being housed and fed all these years. She persistently takes her father's side against me, and tries her damnedest to come between us. She resents the fact that her father and I have a very good relationship and always have had. We were brother and sister long before she came on the scene and we'll be brother and sister long after she's gone away.' She eyed them with contempt. 'I expect she's told you how she was running away when she went into the river, hasn't she?'

Rosalyn shook her head. 'She's told us nothing, and we ask for nothing.'

This was Lilian's opening, and she took it. 'Ah! So she hasn't told you how she caused a fearful argument between me and my brother? She hasn't explained how she stole certain items from my barn, then made good her escape on my own horse and cart?'

'I don't think any of this is my business, Miss Reece, but I find it curious that Nell found it necessary to "make good her escape".' Rosalyn's fears were being confirmed with every word this dreadful woman uttered. 'Is she a prisoner in your house then?'

'No, of course not!' The smile trembled on Lilian's

lying mouth. 'A prisoner indeed! Dear me, whatever next? I only meant that the girl took it into her head to take off to goodness only knows where. She took provisions from my house and barn but, well, I dare say she'll have an explanation.'

'So you don't intend punishing her?'

'Good heavens, no.' Lilian felt herself getting out of her depth. 'But she doesn't belong here. She belongs with me and her father, in our own home. Besides which, there are urgent family matters to be attended to and they will not wait.' Every minute that passed the girl grew bigger with the seed inside her. The sooner it was got out, the better. 'Now, will you please let me take her away?'

UPSTAIRS, NELL LISTENED with a sinking heart. 'You won't take me,' she muttered, her face pressed to the window. 'I'd rather have died in the river than go back with you.'

Turning from the window, she made her way across to the wardrobe. The short walk from the bed to the window had seemed hard and long, with her every limb aching. Her temple throbbed, and her ankle felt like a lead weight. Now, going to the wardrobe seemed to sap her remaining strength so that she was obliged to lean on the wardrobe door a moment to regain her breath and mentally calm herself. 'She can't take you against your will,' she promised herself. But she wasn't reassured. 'She's already making you out to be a thief and a troublemaker. Who'll believe you against her, eh?'

94

It took another minute or two to locate her clothes, all washed and beautifully ironed, and placed on the inner shelves. 'Quick now, gal,' she told herself, 'or she'll have the constabulary after you. What then, eh? Locked up for a thief, that's what, and if she has anything to do with it, you'll never again see the light of day.'

God! That was a terrible prospect. So terrible that Nell seemed to find a rush of strength that got her dressed and away down the stairs while Lilian was still arguing her rights with the doctor and the mistress.

Leaving by the back door, Nell made her way across the yard to the stables. 'Let them keep her there,' she prayed. 'Just let me get away, Lord, that's all I ask.'

In the stables she found the old horse, fed and watered and looking none the worse for his adventures. The cart was in the adjoining barn, mended by Bill and as good as new. The supplies were piled high on the ground nearby, with only the perishables gone.

'Oh, Bill.' His name ushered softly on her lips. Her blue eyes turned to the fields, eagerly searching for him. But he was nowhere to be seen. 'How can I thank you?' she murmured. 'How can I say goodbye?'

There was no easy way if she was to stay out of Aunt Lilian's clutches. But thoughts of Bill softened her resolve. He would help her. Bill and his mam would stand by her. Then she thought of the baby and knew she had no choice. 'I have to go,' she decided firmly. 'I can't let Aunt Lilian hurt the baby or me! Once it's born I won't be afraid.'

As quickly as her strength would allow, Nell set about preparing to leave. First there was the heavy harness to be got from the nails on the wall. Then the horse had to be taken from the stable and led through to the barn where she harnessed him up. Next, she secured the supplies in the cart. When that was done, she collected a nosebag filled with hay from one of the empty stables and strapped it to the side of the cart. 'At least you'll have something to eat,' she told the horse.

Content and pleased to see her, he kept nuzzling his big nose into her shoulder, until now it was wet with dribble. 'Gerroff!' she protested good-naturedly. Then she embraced his big face and her heart was lighter for it.

Her own stomach was rumbling with hunger. 'Wish I'd had time for that hearty meal the mistress offered,' she sighed.

When everything was ready she paused, wishing there was some way she might leave Bill a message, though what she would say in it she wasn't sure. With mixed feelings she climbed on to the seat and took up the reins. Quietly, she coaxed the horse out the back way. 'Won't do no good for them to see me go,' she muttered. 'Soon as ever I get myself some paying work and a place to stay, I'll write the mistress and thank her properly.'

Once clear of the house, she urged the horse to take up a smarter pace and she began to relax. Molly played large in her mind. 'I'll miss Molly,' she mused. Molly had been everything to her.

Raising her face to the warm sunshine, she spotted Bill in the fields; that tall, familiar figure she had come to cherish. Bent to his work, he wasn't looking in her direction. Her heart knotted inside.

She forced herself to look away. 'I'll miss you too, Bill,' she whispered brokenly. 'More than you'll ever know.'

Chapter Four

MOLLY STOOD OVER the kitchen range, one eye on the pan of bubbling vegetables and the other eye on her eldest son. 'Any sign of your dad or the others?' she asked. She knew full well the others would not be on their way home yet but she felt obliged to speak. Anything to break the unnerving silence.

Standing by the window, Bill appeared not to have heard. Instead, he seemed intent on watching for someone. 'I can't understand it,' he muttered. 'What made her take off like that?'

'Bill!' Turning from the stove, Molly folded her arms and gave him her full attention. 'For Lord's sake, man, did you hear what I said?'

He swung round. 'What? Oh, sorry, Mam.' He gave her one of those free, easy smiles that made her proud. 'Did you say something?'

Returning his smile she groaned. 'I might as well shout at the wall for all the notice you've been taking of me.' Crossing the room, she came to his side. 'What is it, son?' she asked, looking up to his troubled dark eyes. 'What's bothering you that yer can't talk to yer old mam about, eh?' She had an idea what bothered him but it wasn't wise to go into that too much, especially since she'd promised Nell she would not betray her secret love for Bill. Sure that he was thinking of Nell, Molly hoped he was beginning to realise how he loved her, and not just as a sister.

Her hopes were dashed with his reply. 'I know it isn't really my place to worry about Nell.' He stared out of the window again, his mind away down the road somewhere, with a slip of a girl who had the heart of a lion. 'But she's like a sister to me,' he murmured, 'and I can't help feeling responsible for her.'

'I know what you're saying,' she answered. 'I feel responsible for her an' all but the lass is nearly seventeen. She's strong-minded and more capable than I ever was at her age.'

'All the same, Mam.' Nell's leaving was something he couldn't seem to get to grips with.

'All the same nothing.' Molly felt the need to be cautious. 'I told yer what Nell said to me, didn't I? I said as how she came here and explained how she wanted to make her own way in the world and that her dad went along with the idea. If her own father thinks she'll be all right then we have to trust her, don't we? Think on that, me laddo. What right have we to say that Nell ain't able to leave these parts and make a new life for herself?'

He shrugged his broad shoulders. 'You're right, Mam. Nell's a sensible girl. I'm sure she wouldn't do anything without thinking it through first.' Still, he couldn't help but wish she'd talked it through with him.

'There y'are then. The lass promised to write, and have yer ever known her break a promise?'

'No. I never have.' Nell was always as good as her

word. Always honest and loyal, and laughing, and always there. But now she was gone. It left a cold, empty feeling inside him.

'I can say, hand on heart, that I've never known that lovely lass break a promise in all the years I've watched her grow,' Molly declared. 'So we can believe she will write, just like she said, and she'll put all our minds at rest, and one day I expect she'll walk through that door with her bright blue eyes sparkling. She'll have any number of tales to tell us.' Her homely face crinkled into a grin. 'I've no doubt they'll fetch tears to yer eyes one minute and have yer laughing out loud the next.'

Bill smiled. 'Remember when she told us about her Aunt Lilian, the day she went to catch a chicken for dinner and the chicken had other ideas? When Lilian went after it with the chopper, it flew up, caught hold of her nose and wouldn't let go.' He chuckled at the memory. 'Nell said they must have heard her aunt screaming from one end of Lancashire to the next.'

Molly grinned. 'Aye, and when Nell's dad heard her screaming, he ran out, slipped in the mud, and fell on top of Lilian, chicken an' all. Lilian panicked and threw the chopper across the yard, whereupon it sliced past Nell's ear by a whisker and killed the poor old cockerel stone dead. By, I'll not forget that lively little tale in a hurry. And the way Nell told it had me in stitches.'

Though Bill's smile lingered on his mouth, there was a deal of regret in his voice as he asked quietly, 'Do you really think she'll come back?'

'Aye. I do.'

'I've half a mind to go after her.'

'Why would you want to do that?' Molly held her breath.

'I've already said. Nell's like a sister to me.'

Crestfallen, Molly advised against it. 'She wouldn't thank you for it.' That was the last thing Nell would want. If Bill found her and discovered she was with child, there was no telling what he might do. Besides, if he wasn't ready to declare his love as a man and not a brother, it would be better if he didn't find her at all.

Bill turned her reply over in his mind. 'I'm not ruling it out,' he said firmly. 'If we don't hear from Nell inside a week, I'm taking leave to go after her.'

'Then we'll just have to hope she gets in touch, eh?'

Molly had no idea what the week would bring. She had learned from experience that it was never wise to speculate. Just when you thought you'd got the better of life, fate had a funny way of turning all your plans upside-down.

'Look,' she pointed out of the window. 'Here's yer dad, and I'll lay a pound to a penny yer brothers ain't far behind.' Moving back to the stove, she lifted the pan of vegetables. 'If yer want to freshen up, you'd best jump to it 'cause once they crowd into that washroom, there'll be no room to bend yer bleedin' elbows.'

As Bill made his way out, she flung open the window. 'Gerra move on, you lot!' she called out. 'I'll have the dinner on the table afore yer can say Jack Robinson!'

In fact it was a good half hour later when Molly had her five beloved men round the big pine table. Her husband, Joe, headed the table at one end, while Bill was at the other end. Jack and Sam sat side by side down one length of the table, with Tommy and Molly opposite, Molly nearest to the top of the table where she could chat easily to the incorrigible Joe.

'I hope you're all hungry,' she said pleasantly, looking proudly at her fine family, 'because there's a big pork joint, enough vegetables to sink a pirate ship, and apple pie with cream for afters.'

Joe smacked his lips. 'What would any man do without a woman like yerself, Molly Davidson?' he asked with a twinkle in his blue Irish eyes. 'You're a little angel, so you are.'

Molly flustered with pleasure and young Tommy winked at his dad. 'Mam ain't so little, Dad,' he said. 'And if she keeps feeding us up like this we'll all be round as barrels.'

'Why, yer cheeky young rascal!' Molly laughed. 'Are yer implying yer poor mam's round as a barrel then?'

'Shame on yer, Mam. Would I do that?' He would, and did, but with a gleam in his eye that told her he didn't mean a word of it.

'I've a good mind to put yer over me knee and smack yer arse.'

Joe laughed at that. 'Them days is long gone, me little darling,' he chuckled. 'Your wee lads are past all that now.' He gave her a sly grin. 'But I'll not complain if yer put me over yer knee. Sure I wouldn't mind me arse being smacked.'

That sent laughter round the table.

Tickled pink, Molly found an excuse to get up. 'If yer buggers know what's good for yer, you'll treat yer mam with a bit of respect, especially if yer after a slice of her best apple pie!' She tried to sound serious, but the smile on her face betrayed her love for each and every one, and especially for Bill who was unusually quiet, steeped in thoughts of Nell.

He remained quiet throughout dinner, even prompting one or two probing remarks from his brothers. 'Lost a pound and found a farthing, is it?' Tommy teased.

Sam, too, had noticed how quiet Bill was. 'Naw, I don't reckon it's money trouble,' he told Tommy. 'Bill ain't like you. He don't count every coin in his pocket twice over. He's more than likely got the sack for working too bloody hard. Six of a morning till nightfall, seven days a week, if he gets the chance.'

Being the misery in the family, Jack made the most cutting comment. 'I expect he's gone sweet on some woman and been turned down. Is that it, Bill? Mind you, it's about time. You allus seem to get whatever you set your cap at. I mean, look how you drew the landlady's daughter down at the Rose and Crown. Any one of us would have fancied our chances but she only had eyes for you.' He tutted loudly. 'What riles me is, you don't even know she's alive!' Winking at his brothers, he taunted, 'I don't reckon he thinks she's good enough for him, lads. I reckon he's looking for the perfect woman and he ain't found her yet.'

'Nor is he likely to,' Sam sighed, ' 'cause there's no such thing as the perfect woman.' He knew, because he'd searched high and low and was still disappointed.

Bill was in no mood to rise to their jibes. Instead he told them, 'Eat your dinners, you lot, and try minding your own business.'

'Touchy, aren't you?' Tommy said, and got a ticking off from Molly for talking with his mouth full.

Bill merely smiled and ate his meal, and let himself dwell on thoughts of Nell. Where was she now? Was she safe? Would she really get in touch, like his mam said? No matter. Mam was right. It wasn't his place to tell Nell what she should or shouldn't do. After all, he might feel like a brother to her but in actual fact he was no relation at all and, like Mam said, Nell would not thank him for treating her with less credit than she deserved.

There followed a few minutes of silence while everyone enjoyed the meal and reflected on the conversation.

In the midst of the quiet, Joe gave Molly a look that said, 'What's wrong with Bill?'

Molly's pursed lips and gentle shake of the head warned him to leave it until the two of them could talk.

THE TIME FOR Molly and Joe to talk came two hours later, after the table was cleared, the crockery washed and put away, and the three younger men each doing what they loved best: Tommy was down at the canal where he would fish till dark; Sam had gone to meet his sweetheart at the end of the street; Jack was up in his room reading. Bill was restless. First he went for a walk. Then he went to the room he shared with Jack. Then he came down and sat in the kitchen. 'I'm making a brew for me and yer dad,' Molly said. 'D'yer want one?'

Bill said yes and thanked her, but when she turned

round again, he was gone. Hearing the back door slam shut, she went to the window and there he was, at the bottom of the yard, with his shirt stripped off and chopping wood as if his life depended on it. 'It ain't for me to tell yer what's wrong, son,' she murmured. 'Swinging the axe to the wood won't get rid of your frustration.' Molly realised he was confused about his feelings for Nell. She also knew he must come to terms with it in his own good time.

Joe looked up and smiled as she went into the parlour. 'Thought I were getting a cup of tea,' he said. 'Been to milk a cow, have ye?'

'Less of yer cheek,' she laughed. She handed him a mug of tea, settled herself into the chair opposite and said, as she always did, 'Now then, yer old bugger, what have yer been up to today? What have yer got to tell me, eh?' Like Nell, Joe always had a tale to tell.

He regarded her with some surprise. 'Sure, I thought you'd have summat to tell me.'

'Why's that?' Molly was hoping he'd forgotten that intimate little glance she'd given him at the dinner table. She'd made a promise to keep Nell's secret. Bill was all part of that and she didn't want to betray either of them, not even to Joe.

Joe watched her, patiently waiting for an explanation. There was a time many years back when he had suffered a degree of resentment against Bill because Molly seemed to feel more for her firstborn than she did for those that followed. She tried hard not to show it and to her credit she always treated the four boys alike, outwardly loving them equally. Thankfully, they never caught sight of that small, private corner of her heart that was reserved for Bill alone. Joe knew though. Loving Molly the way he did, how could he not know? There was jealousy, a feeling of being left out of her affections. But it was all in his mind and, anyway, that was then and this was now. Now, he loved Bill with the same deep, abiding pride as Molly did. Bill was special. A leader. A man whom others would always look up to. Certainly his brothers went to him in times of trouble. Bill, though, would turn to no one, except maybe Molly who knew him as well as she knew herself.

'What's ailing Bill?' Joe wanted to know. 'Is he in some kind of trouble?'

Molly shook her head and sipped her tea. After a while she answered, 'He's worried about Nell.'

'I expect he is. We're all worried about Nell. That damned bridge should have been shored up long ago. It's a wonder the pair of them weren't killed!' He drank from his mug and peered at her over the top. 'Thank God our lad were at hand when the bridge started to fall or she'd not have lived to tell the tale. How is the lass?'

'She's taken off.'

'Taken off?' He looked confused. 'How can she have taken off? I thought the doctor said she were too ill, even for visitors?'

'Well, he were wrong, weren't he, 'cause the lass were here and now she's gone, lock, stock and barrel.'

'Why in the name o' God would she do that?' He could never understand women.

'Because she doesn't get on with her aunt and

because she thinks she'll make a better life for herself away from these parts.' Molly hated herself for deceiving her man but she would hate herself even more if she betrayed Nell's confidence. She toyed with the idea of telling Joe how Nell felt about their son, and how she was afraid to tell him in case it spoiled their very special friendship. And, as a woman, Molly could see how that might happen. Also, she wondered what Joe would say if he knew Nell was with child but that the lass would not tell who the father was. It was a pretty messy business whichever way she looked at it, and only time would tell how it would end. She decided against telling Joe. In Molly's opinion, no man could be trusted with a secret, and that included Joe, bless his simple heart.

'What does Nell's father say about her taking off?'

'He says she's capable.'

'Oh aye! Well, capable or not, I'd never let a young lass o' mine go wandering the highways, I can tell you that! There's folk out there who'd cut your throat for a shilling.' He stared at Molly with disgust. 'What's got into her father, eh? Mind you, he were never forceful enough. I mean, what man would let his sister run his life the way Lilian Reece does? The old tyrant never lets him forget it's *her* house, *her* farm, and *her* money that keeps them out of the workhouse. She works that man from dawn to dusk and pays him less than you'd pay a skivvy off the streets. By, I'd not stand for that. Sure, my pride wouldn't let me.'

'Pride comes before a fall.' Molly was a fount of wisdom.

'No wonder Nell wanted out.' Like any decent sort,

Joe had long wondered about the brother and sister at Reece Farm. 'I don't understand it,' he said. 'Why does he let his sister treat him like that? Be Jaysus, it drives me mad just thinking about it.'

'Don't think about it then.'

Joe was persistent. 'Don't ye think it's odd, though? A grown man the like of Don Reece buckling under to his sister when he's got the strength and know-how to run his own farm. There are any number of gentry hereabouts who would rent him a farm, so why should he cling to her, eh? What is it that makes him obliged to spend his life making money for her and never having his own roof over his head?'

His words sent Molly back over the years. When her dear old mammy was nearing her end, she had rambled on about something that had happened years before, at Reece Farm. With her senses going and her spirit already on its way to meet the maker, the old dear was incoherent and confused. Saddened by losing her mammy, Molly took little notice of her ramblings about the Reece family. But since then, her words had come back to haunt her. If she remembered right, it was something about a girl, and an indiscretion. There was a suggestion of bad doings and Lilian Reece was right in the middle of it all. Unclear, muttered words from a dying old woman.

Intrigued though she was, Molly would never repeat those words. Not to anyone. There was a danger in repeating such things. Oh, there were rumours. There had always been rumours, whispered and furtive though they may be. But Molly had decided long ago that she would not be drawn into a whispering campaign that could destroy Nell's family.

WEARY AND ACHING, Don Reece loaded the logs on to the wagon and started on his way back.

Deep in the woods, he knew nothing of what was going on in the outside world. He know nothing of Nell's predicament and believed she was long gone, and he was glad of that. At least now she had a chance to make her own way. Even with a child in tow, Nell would manage, he was sure. He felt proud. He also felt sad, hoping she would keep her word and come back one day to see him.

He thought about that, and it brought a smile to his face. 'I'll be a grandad,' he murmured. 'Think on that, Don Reece. You'll be a grandad.' He prayed he would make a better grandad than he had a father.

He thought how Nell was so like her mother. 'Oh, Nell.' He sighed long and noisily. 'You and your mam are like peas in a pod. The same build and colouring. The same warm, strong nature and bright smile.' He sighed again, eyes closed and heart aching. So many regrets. Such a terrible, shocking waste. If it hadn't been for Nell, he might have brought his life to an end a long time ago. Nell had kept him sane. She alone had given him a reason for living. Even then, he couldn't repay her by being the father she deserved.

In this mood he tended to think about things that were best forgotten. He thought about what had happened when he was a young and happy man. He had not been happy since, and doubted if he would ever be happy again.

The smile slid from his face. 'Dear God, let things be different this time,' he prayed. 'Unlike her mother, let Nell hold the bairn in her arms.' The tears glistened in his tired eyes. 'Let her live to see it grow, that's all I ask.'

As he travelled the country lanes, the darkness closed in. The birds stopped singing, and he knew he must be nearing home. 'Funny how the birds don't sing so loud the nearer to Lilian they get.' He gave a sour laugh. 'I know just how they feel.'

Arms folded and stern-faced, Lilian was waiting for him at the gate. 'That daughter of yours is a bad 'un!' she said. 'It's a pity she didn't fall to her death when that bridge collapsed. That way we'd be rid of her *and* the bastard she carries!'

White-faced and angry, he swung off the wagon. 'What the devil are you talking about, woman?' He came at her in two strides. 'What bridge? What d'you mean, fall to her death?'

Realising she had said too much, Lilian backed off. 'I mean what I say,' she said lamely.

'Answer me, woman!' He shook her by the shoulders. 'What's happened to Nell?'

Hard-eyed and stiff, she stared at him. 'Take your hands off me, you maniac.' Cunningly, she turned his rage to weakness. 'Or would you really like to hurt me? Would you turn on someone who's taken care of you and your little bastard all these years?'

It was as though she'd slapped him hard in the face.

Abruptly, he let her go. 'Is she hurt?' He was like a child again, pliable in her hands.

'What if she is?'

'Don't hate her, Lil. None of it was her fault.'

'Nor mine.'

'I know that.'

'The girl wouldn't be here if it wasn't for me.'

'I know that too.'

'You have a great deal to answer for.'

He bowed his head. 'I don't need reminding.'

Lilian watched him grovel for a minute or two before telling him, 'The girl's all right, so stop whining and get the logs unloaded.'

'What happened?'

'The bridge collapsed and she went over. Young Bill Davidson was at hand and went in after her.' She sniffed and coughed, and kept him waiting. 'The pair of them came out of it all right. They say the devil looks after his own.'

'Why didn't you send for me?'

'Because she wasn't badly injured and because you can't spare the time to run about after a stupid girl who can't take care of herself. Anyway, you've got enough to occupy your mind here. There's work to be done without gallivanting all over the place. The birds aren't touching the berries this year and that's always a sign of a hard winter. We need a good store of logs put by or we'll rue the day, and well you know it.'

Knowing her fears to be true, he made no comment. Instead, he began striding to the house. 'Is Nell inside?'

'No, she's not.' Lilian ran to keep up with him. 'She

knows better than to come back here. She knows I'd flay her alive after what she's done.' Though she wanted her back here, so she could be rid of the little bastard before it could be born.

Ignoring her, he searched every room. A few minutes later he ran down the stairs and stood holding the banister, his face contorted with worry. 'Where is she?'

She enjoyed seeing him squirm. 'Young Davidson took her to the Morgan place. Rosalyn Morgan sent for the doctor and your precious Nell has been living the life of a lady for the best part of twenty-four hours, eating the finest food and being treated by the Morgans' very own practitioner. I can just imagine the little hussy lying in bed like she belonged there.' She gave a spiteful laugh. 'Coarse muslin against silken sheets, that's all she is, and it's all she'll ever be.'

'I wouldn't count on it. Nell has it in her to do well.'

'She'll *never* do well!'

'I don't want you going anywhere near her.'

'You're too late, I've already been there.' Once he was hurting, it was like an obsession with her. She had to keep on hurting him, torturing his already wounded mind.

The wide, cunning grin sent him half crazy. 'What have you done?' he said through gritted teeth. 'I swear to God, if you've hurt her . . .'

Softly laughing, she swung away. 'I've done nothing. The girl will be her own ruin.' She rounded on him then, her face a study in loathing. 'She's gone, and good riddance. While I was on the front step arguing with the

113

lady of the house and the good doctor, the little thief ran off, taking my horse and cart with her.' Tossing her head defiantly, she added, 'I hope she never comes back because if she ever shows her face again, I'll lay an axe to her.'

Without a word, Don turned and strode out of the house. He didn't know what to believe. Was she telling him the truth or was she taunting him, like she always did where Nell was concerned?

Later, when the old biddy was in bed, he would make his way over to the Morgan place and find out exactly what was going on.

THE EVENING SEEMED never-ending. Lilian sat by the window in her rocking chair; back and forth she went, eyes closed and softly humming a tune. Occasionally she would peep out of one eye to regard her brother with some satisfaction. He was unusually restless, pacing the floor one minute and throwing himself into a chair the next.

Don was a troubled man, and that pleased her. If the day ever came when he was content with his lot, that would be the day she lost her hold over him. If it was up to her, that day would never come, and she was prepared to do anything to make sure of it.

She felt very pleased with herself. So much so that she could afford to be kind. 'You look worn out,' she cooed. 'D'you fancy a drop of elderberry wine?'

He looked at her as though she'd gone mad. 'By, you must be feeling generous! I've never been offered any of your precious wine before.' She bought the wine by the jugful and always hid it where he would not find it.

'Well, I'm offering you some now. Do you want it or not?'

'No, thank you all the same.'

'Very well. It won't stop me from having a sip or two.'

'I've no doubt.' He wished she would drink enough to send her off to bed – or send her to her maker while she slept.

She left the room and returned a few minutes later with a brown jug in one hand and a glass in the other. As she sat down, she seemed to read his mind. 'It's no good you waiting for me to retire to my bed because I'm not the least bit tired.'

'Why would I be waiting for you to go to bed?' It was uncanny the way she seemed to know what he was thinking. Or maybe he was just pathetically transparent.

Pouring the red liquid into the glass, she took a long, leisurely sip. 'My, but that's good.' Noisily smacking her lips, she raised her gaze and fixed it on his face. 'I wouldn't go to the Morgans' place if I was you.'

'What makes you think I'll go to the Morgans' place?' He could never outwit her.

'They won't thank you for it. I should think they've had enough trouble from this family, what with having that ungrateful girl palmed on them and then me telling them a truth or two.' She snorted with disgust. 'If you turn up there, they'll likely set the dogs on you. I wouldn't blame them either.'

'I'll do as I think fit.'

'My, my. Back-chatting me now, eh? You'd better think hard before you start on that route, my man.' Squaring her shoulders, she took another drink, softly hiccupped, and eyeing him with contempt said, 'If your darling daughter knew what you'd done, she'd hate you for the rest of your miserable life.'

'If I thought you'd tell, I swear to God, Lil,' his face darkened, 'I'd have to kill you first.'

He had a rage in him but most times he kept it well under control. Now, though, he could gladly have put his two hands round his sister's throat and squeezed until her eyes popped out.

The clock struck eight, then nine thirty. Then it was quarter to ten, and after a long, back-breaking day, he was feeling bone weary and ready for his own bed. His sister was still sipping away at her elderberry wine, now and then smiling at him, content in the knowledge that she still had the upper hand.

As the mantelpiece clock chimed ten, she stood up. 'I'm off to my bed.' Going across the room on unsteady legs, she instructed, 'Don't be long down here, and mind you lock all the doors when you come up.' She turned to see if he was listening and almost fell over. 'Did you hear what I said?'

'I heard.'

'Goodnight then.'

'Goodnight.' With any luck she'd quickly fall asleep so he could get about his business. 'Don't worry. I'll see the doors are locked.' He couldn't look her in the eye. She could read him too well.

'You're a secretive sod, Don Reece.'

He bowed his head lower, his voice a mere whisper. 'And you're a miserable bugger.'

'What's that you said?'

'I said nothing. The booze is playing tricks on you.'

'Hmm. Mind what I said, and don't be down here burning paraffin till all hours. It costs money.'

'It's *me* that earns the money!'

She was already out of the door and shuffling her way up the stairs, muttering with every step.

Ten minutes later he crept up the stairs to see if she was asleep. There was no sound so he inched the door open and there she was, stretched out on the floor, fully clothed and snoring like an old sow. 'You're a black-hearted old biddy,' he murmured, looking down on her. 'I should leave you lying there until your bones ache as much as mine.' But it wasn't in his nature.

Lifting her up, he carried her to the bed and wrapped her in a blanket. 'That's as much as I'd do for any poor soul.' Hurrying to the door, he muttered under his breath, 'And now, whether you like it or whether you don't, I'm off to find out about Nell.'

It took him a few minutes to saddle the horse and another ten before he was standing on the doorstep of the Morgan house.

'Who's there?' The maid sounded nervous.

For an answer he knocked again, and this time she opened it, a small, big-eyed creature with flyaway yellow hair and her white, frilly cap on crooked. Peering at him through bleary eyes and momentarily disorientated by the half-light, she stifled a yawn. 'Yes?' She was twenty-nine years old but come ten o'clock of an evening she felt a hundred and one.

'I'm Don Reece.' He gave her a friendly smile. 'I've come to see about my daughter, Nell.'

'Oh.' Stepping back, she invited him in. 'I'll get the master.'

Vincent Morgan was in the study, counting his lucky stars that Nell was gone and he was not betrayed. When the maid announced the visitor's name, his fears returned with a vengeance. 'Take him into the drawing room,' he ordered. 'I'll be along in a moment.'

As she was about to leave the room, he called her back. 'Where's the mistress?'

'In her room, sir.'

'Good. Don't disturb her. She needs her rest.'

'Yes, sir.'

After she'd gone, he paced the floor. 'What the hell does he want?' he asked himself. 'Surely to God Nell didn't tell him I'd bedded her.' He thought on that, and then his face broke into a shaky smile. 'No, she wouldn't.' Slipping on his jacket, he made ready to face Nell's father. 'You've nothing to fear,' he told himself in the mirror. 'Calm and confident, that's all you need to be.'

One more heartening measure of whisky, and he was prepared for anything.

As instructed, the maid showed Don into the drawing room, a large, grand place with oak chandeliers and wood panelling. There was a thick-pile rug on the floor and silver in the cabinet, and he felt totally out of place amidst such finery. 'Thank you, miss,' he said to the maid. 'I'm sorry to have bothered you so late of an evening.'

The skinny little face grinned from ear to ear. 'To tell the truth I was having a kip in the kitchen. It's better you woke me than the master, or I might have got a scolding.'

He took a liking to her straight away. 'All the same, I am sorry.'

Regarding him for a moment, she thought how good-looking he could be if only he didn't seem so sad. With his straight brown hair and quiet eyes, he made a pleasing sight. 'The master will be along shortly,' she said gently. 'Make yourself comfortable.'

'Excuse me, miss.'

'Yes, sir?' He seemed more of a gentleman than many of the toffs who frequented this house.

'Do you know about my daughter?'

'Oh, yes, sir! Terrible accident that.'

'I'm told she was brought here.'

'Yes, sir. The mistress made certain she was well cared for.'

'But she's not here any more?' He was hoping Lilian had lied.

'No, sir.'

'I need to know if she was all right when she left.'

'I'm sorry, sir.' She shook her head sympathetically. 'The master would know more about that than I do. You'll have to ask him.'

Vincent Morgan's soft voice startled her. 'Thank you, Meg. A pot of tea for two, if you please.'

'Yes, sir.' With that she scurried away, leaving Don thinking how nice she was and how suited to the pretty name of Meg.

Don was standing, cap in hand. 'I'm sorry to have

called so late,' he apologised, 'only I weren't aware she'd had an accident. You see, I've been camping out in the forest, gathering logs and such, ready for the winter.'

'I understand.' Gesturing for him to be seated, Vincent dropped into the chair opposite. 'Your sister did explain.' Waves of relief swept over him. Obviously this man didn't know he'd bedded Nell or he'd be in a far different mood. But then he shouldn't be too surprised. Nell had promised she wouldn't tell, and he should have believed her.

'I hope my sister didn't upset anyone.' The look on Vincent's face confirmed his fears.

'I'm afraid she did get on the wrong side of me. I had to ask her to leave.'

'My sister is not the most discreet person in the world. I just want you to know she was not talking for me.'

'Of course.'

'My sister said Nell ran off.' Don wasn't sure how much he could confide in this man but God only knew how much he needed someone to talk to.

'She did.' Vincent smiled easily. 'Took her horse and cart and went away at a gallop, so I'm told.'

Don visibly relaxed. 'So she was recovered from the accident.'

'Apparently so.' In spite of his own guilt, Vincent felt comfortable in this man's presence. 'When your daughter was brought here, she was shocked and bruised. She suffered a nasty knock on the head during her fall but according to the doctor she wasn't seriously injured. In fact he made the comment that she was as strong as a lion.'

'Nell was always strong, even as a bairn.' Don

couldn't help but look proud. 'When she was three years old, I came out of the house to see her trying to lift a new-born lamb into her arms. Covered in blood and muck she was, but by, you should have seen the look of joy on her face. The lass might be small-built and she might have a dainty look about her, but don't you believe it. Nell were always strong for her size.'

The tea arrived. 'Thank you, Meg.' Vincent Morgan waited until she had poured the tea and departed before speaking again. 'Your daughter received the very best medical care while she was here.'

'Did she say where she was headed?'

'Not that I know of.' That was the last thing he would want to know. 'Maybe she's gone to a relative.'

'Her aunt and myself are the only relatives Nell has.'

'I see.'

'Did she say . . . anything else?' Nervous, he broached the forbidden subject.

Regarding him with the smallest rising of anxiety, Vincent dared to ask, 'About what?'

Putting down his cup of tea, Don cleared his throat, then he coughed a little and in a sombre whisper confided, 'Nell had a boy friend. Her aunt and I knew nothing about him.'

Swallowing the hard knot in his throat, Vincent also put his cup on the table. 'Most young girls have boy friends,' he said, trying to grin but not quite managing it. 'It's to be expected. I mean, your daughter is a lovely young thing.' He pulled himself up short, wishing he hadn't said that. 'She's well liked by everyone here,' he finished lamely.

'I'd like to find out who the young man was.' If he could only lay hands on him, he might have more than a word or two to say.

'Well now, she was very friendly with young Bill Davidson.' Desperately trying to distract suspicion from himself, Vincent went on hurriedly, 'I've seen the two of them together on many an occasion. Sometimes they would walk across the fields together on their way home. Other times they might wander through the orchard at the end of a working day.' That was true but it had all seemed innocent. However, he wasn't about to tell that to Don Reece. 'Do you know the young man?'

Don smiled. 'Yes, I know him, well enough to be certain they're not lovers. Bill and Nell grew up together, and now he feels responsible for her, protects her, if you know what I mean. Like a brother might protect a sister.' He stood up. 'Nell won't be that far away, I'm sure, and if she needs me, she'll know where I am. Please, tell your good lady I much appreciate her looking after Nell.'

Vincent was curious. 'You don't seem too concerned about her whereabouts.' And here he'd been worried that Nell's father might beat the sweat and blood out of him.

Looking him in the eye, Don said in a quiet manner, 'Nell means everything to me, and if I don't appear too concerned about where she is, it's only because I know she's better off than if she stayed at home. I'm ashamed to say I haven't been the father I ought to have been. And her aunt has given the girl nothing but tears and trials since the day she was born.'

'I'm sorry.' In those brief, revealing moments,

Vincent Morgan saw the strength of Nell's father, and felt the lesser man because of it. 'I had no idea.'

Don bowed his head. 'There are things folk have no way of knowing.' He sighed, saying in a burst, 'And Nell being with child is one of them.'

Rocked to the roots of his soul, Vincent stared at him. For a moment it seemed he couldn't speak, then he opened his mouth to ask hoarsely, '*What* did you say?'

Don, too, was shocked by what he'd confided in this man who was almost a stranger to him. 'I shouldn't have told you,' he croaked, 'but, being the gentleman you are, I'm sure you'll be discreet with the knowledge. There's no danger of her aunt spreading the word because she's too ashamed. Unfortunately my sister has a hard, unforgiving heart. She wanted the girl to be rid of the child. Nell rebelled and there was holy hell to pay. That's why Nell ran away.' His features seemed suddenly to droop with age, 'I think the culprit should be made to pay for what he's done but Nell wouldn't tell me his name. She's like that, always defending somebody or other.' He smiled at the image of Nell's urchin face in his mind. 'Anyhow, I know it's not Bill Davidson. I'll be off now. Goodbye, Mr Morgan, and thank you. I'll not fetch my troubles to your door again, I can promise you that.'

LONG AFTER DON Reece had ridden away, Vincent sat, head in hands, recalling Don's words, 'She's with child.' The news had come like a bolt out of the blue. 'You fool, Morgan!' He thumped his fists together. 'You bloody fool!'

The news had brought on a raging thirst. Going to the dresser, he poured a stiff drink and threw it down his throat. 'What else did you expect?' he demanded of himself. 'You should have realised. What made you think you could make your own wife pregnant, yet not that slip of a girl? Sod and bugger it! You've put the cat among the pigeons now.'

He took to pacing the floor, head down one minute, raised in anguish the next. Then he was at the dresser again, pouring another drink and smiling to himself. 'You'll just have to deny it. If she goes against her word and says you're the father, you'll have to look after your own, whatever the consequences to the girl. She'll be all right. She's strong and independent, her own father said so.' He swilled the drink down. 'Nell is an honest sort. She promised not to tell I'd bedded her and I don't expect she'll tell I fathered her child.' He sat down.

'Wait a minute,' he cautioned himself. 'She never told me she was with child, and that was a particular deceit, so why should I trust her at all? What if she comes back for money? What if she can't make her own way and looks to me as a source of income? Let her try it,' he muttered, 'and it'll be the worst day's work she's ever done!'

He sat in the chair a while longer, his hands running feverishly through his hair, his mind in turmoil. After a time, he walked to the window and stared into the night. 'Don't betray me, Nell,' he whispered. 'I don't want to hurt you. Please, whatever happens, don't betray me.'

He almost had a heart attack when the door opened

to admit his wife. 'I can't sleep,' she said, coming to him. 'The baby won't let me rest.'

Taking her in his arms, he held her tenderly, his free hand roving over her stomach. 'I do love you,' he murmured. 'I know you must often wonder but I really do.' He had had his share of women but that was only a basic need. It didn't involve the heart.

Like a lamb to the slaughter, she looked up at him. 'I know you do,' she whispered, 'and I'm sorry I can't be a proper wife to you.'

He bent his head and kissed her on the mouth. It was a kiss of shame, a kiss of regret. When it was over, he asked softly, 'Will you be a proper wife to me now . . . tonight?'

'I can't.' She drew away. 'It's the baby, you see. I have no strength. Maybe after the baby is born things will be different.' She began to cry.

'It's all right, Rosalyn. It doesn't matter.' But it did matter. It mattered like hell! That was why, the minute she'd gone to sleep, he'd be out of the house looking for comfort.

Chapter Five

'COME ON, DEARIE.' The woman was huge but extraordinarily gentle as she coaxed her patient to take the medicine from the spoon. 'Please, Mary, don't be difficult.' The big woman had been given the task of curbing Mary's rebellious nature. Instead she had grown to love and respect her. 'I don't want to report you, but I'll have no choice if you keep being difficult.'

Small-built, with a cap of wavy golden hair and deep blue eyes, Mary sat up in bed. 'I don't want to get you in trouble, Amy, but I hate the medicine. It makes me sleep and I don't want to sleep. I want to get out of this room and get on with my work. It's the only thing that keeps me sane.' She squeezed Amy's hand. 'Oh, and you, Amy. You help keep me sane too. What would I do without you?'

'Take the medicine, Mary. It's good for you.'

Mary was quiet.

'Will you? For me?'

Still quiet.

Amy pushed the spoon to Mary's mouth. 'Come on. Just one sip. At least I won't be lying when I tell them you took it.'

'Tell them the truth,' Mary suggested defiantly. 'Tell them I refused.'

The big woman blew out a long, heavy sigh. 'Honest to God, Mary, you'll be the death of me yet.'

'You mean they'll be the death of *me*.'

'Oh, now look!' Amy sank so hard on to the bed it groaned beneath her weight, tipping so low to one side that Mary almost rolled out. 'They don't mean you no harm. I know they can be a pain in the arse at times but you know they mean well enough.'

Mary was quiet once more, her mind spinning back over that part of her life she knew. When she had first opened her eyes, in this very bed, in this very room, she knew nothing before that moment. That was seventeen long years ago. Since then she had come to realise that she was destined to spend the rest of her days in the Convent of St Mary Magdalen.

She looked up at Amy, at the scruffy mop of greying hair and the large, round face with its pea-like green eyes, and she was sorry for giving her so much trouble. 'I'm sorry,' she murmured. 'I know you're only trying to help, and I suppose the nuns do mean well but they never really talk to me. They smile and pass the time of day, and they give me my work schedule, but they never help me understand who I am or why I'm here. Whenever I ask, they say, "As long as God knows who you are, you'll never be lost." '

'But that's true,' Amy said. 'We're the sheep and he's the shepherd. He knows every one of his flock and he'll *never* let you get lost.' Amy had come straight from an orphanage forty years before. Unlike Mary, she had never questioned her origins, but was content to live within the hallowed walls of this peaceful sanctuary.

Set in rolling countryside, the village of Woburn was one of the most picturesque villages in the south of England; so breathtakingly beautiful that a body could live out its whole life here and never want to venture away. Once, she had gone out to Leighton Market with Sister Annette but the noise and bustle had frightened her so much she had nightmares for a whole month.

'We're very lucky, you and me,' Amy scolded Mary now. 'Not everyone gets to live in a lovely place like this.'

'But why am I here, Amy? Who brought me to this place? Sometimes, when I'm lying here in my bed, I think about it and it drives me crazy.'

'You know why you're here. You got left at the door one night in a snowstorm. When Sister Bridget found you the next morning, you were nearly frozen to the bone. They took you in and made you well, and now this is your home. It isn't so bad, is it? Here, with me?' She rolled her eyes to blink away the tears. In a small, sad voice she asked, 'You would never leave me, would you, Mary?'

'No. I would never leave you, Amy.'

'Why can't you be happy?'

'Because I'm a cripple.' Now it was Mary's turn to choke back the tears. 'Because my mind is bright and busy and my body won't let me do the things I want to do.'

'I made you a runabout though, didn't I?' The pea-green eyes sparkled with pride.

'Yes, you did, Amy, and it's wonderful but it's not the same as having two strong legs to walk on.'

'I had to beg the sisters to let me have that hospital trolley. They didn't want to. You know that, don't you?'

'Yes, Amy. I know that.'

'Then it took me all day just to saw the sides off.'

'You're a good friend, and I'm very grateful.'

'If you take your medicine, you can ride in it tomorrow, and if you feel strong enough you'll be able to get on with your work.'

Mary smiled. 'That's just it, Amy. I always feel strong enough inside.' Making a hard fist, she thumped it against her chest. 'I'm not *ill.* It was the heat of the oven that made me keel over yesterday. I was black-leading the fire grate and Cook had a pig roasting in the big oven. The smell and the heat overpowered me, that's all.' She gripped her hands together, rocking back and forth, like a bird trapped in a cage and yearning to get out. 'There was no need for them to make such a fuss.'

'But you looked really poorly.'

'Well, I'm not! I'm as healthy as you or them!' Closing her eyes she laid her head against the pillow. 'It's my *legs* that are useless. I might as well have them chopped off, for all the good they are.' Her eyes moistened. 'According to the nuns, I'm thirty years old, maybe thirty-one, thirty-two, they're not sure. That's not too old, is it, Amy? But I might as well be ninety. In my mind I can walk, and run, and dance. Through my dreams, I skip and jump and climb the hills outside this convent. I stand on the top of the hills and look right across the valleys but in reality I can't do any of those things.' As she talked, she grew excited. 'Oh, Amy! I want all the things any woman wants, to find a good man and have his children. I dream of playing with children, Amy, *my* children, *my* family. And that's what hurts. I'm not ill. I don't want medicine to put me to sleep. I want the use of my legs. I want to get out of here and live a normal life.' The tears fell but she brushed them away. 'I would gladly give half my life if only I could hold my own child in my arms.'

She paused, letting Amy digest the words so she could try and understand. 'Don't you see, Amy? I can't do that, and I never will.' The truth was harsh, unbearable. And yet she had to bear it. What else could she do? Except for Amy, she had no friends. The only way she could move from one place to the next was thanks to the 'runabout' Amy had made for her. Like it or not, she was trapped here, part of the furniture. Like the timber struts that held up the walls, she was securely woven into the fabric of this institution. Her day was like clockwork. Days and nights. Weeks, months, and years. Always the same.

Always the same!

She would rise with the others at five o'clock in the morning when the day would begin with prayers in the hall. Then breakfast, and away to work. First the kitchen chores; then clean the grates and polish those parts of the furniture within her reach; then shake the mats and shine the silver from yesterday's evening meal. The day was filled with purpose and went quickly.

In the evening, after service in the chapel, she would sit on a special chair at the servants' table in the dining hall. Here she would eat her meal and afterwards she would go to the conservatory at the back of the house and quietly dream, but without hope. There was no hope for the likes of her. No hope, no future, and no prospect of ever touching God's beautiful world outside these four walls.

Amy's voice gentled into her mind. 'You could be happy here, Mary, if only you'd stop wanting the impossible.'

'Oh, Amy, if only I could believe that. If only I could find the same contentment you've found, things might be different. But I haven't and they aren't. So I'll go on dreaming and praying and cursing the people who brought me here, robbed of my memory, and with my spine so damaged it would have been kinder if they'd drowned me in the nearest river.'

Amy put her hands to her face, her eyes widening with shock. 'That's a terrible thing to say, Mary!'

Mary bowed her head. 'Maybe it is,' she admitted. 'All the same, there are days when I wish I hadn't been born.'

The older woman grinned. 'I hope you've worked up a good appetite.'

'Why?'

'It's Cook's special today – plum-duff. If you're after ending it all, ask for a second helping. That'll turn yer toes up and end your troubles.'

T HE SOUND OF laughter echoed down the halls. 'What ever's that?' Sister Bridget asked her colleague.

'Laughter,' she answered. 'And doesn't it make your heart feel good?'

When the two nuns parted company, Sister Bridget made her way to the office where she searched in the big wall cabinet for a certain file. A brown, ageing file, tied with string and inscribed with the name 'Mary'.

When at last she laid her hands on the file, she sat at the desk, opened it, took out the two sheets of yellowing paper and carefully perused them, her old eyes straining to read the thin, scrawled handwriting.

Afterwards, she sat a moment, dwelling on the night these papers were slipped beneath the convent door. They told nothing of the girl's background then and the passage of years had done nothing to reveal their grim secret.

Sister Bridget had always liked Mary. In spite of her terrible handicap, Mary was a fighter. Spirited and likeable, she had brought sunshine to this place. Oh, there were times when she could be infuriating but that was all part of her nature. Unlike some of the wretched creatures who had walked these hallowed floors, Mary was honest and good.

The sharp knock on the door made her jump. 'Who is it?'

'Sister Anne.'

'Come.' She made no attempt to hide the papers.

Compared to her ailing colleague, Sister Anne was still blessed with good health. Some years younger, she had a brisker step and a quicker mind. It was this that Sister Bridget turned to now. 'I want you to see something,' she said, gesturing to her to sit. 'Take a look at these and tell me what you make of them.' Pushing the papers towards her, she watched Sister Anne pick them up and begin to read.

After a moment or two, Sister Anne commented, 'I don't understand. This is merely a list of instructions.' Holding one sheet up, she went on, 'It asks that you take care of the child, bring her close to God and make her see the error of her ways. It insists that you have a duty to this sinner and that, for her punishment, she must never again be allowed outside these walls.' She paused, saying in a quieter voice, 'It also states a considerable amount of money is enclosed for the child's keep and lodging, for as long as it may live.'

'What do you make of the other note?'

Sister Anne looked again. 'It is full of despair.' Her voice trembled with compassion. 'Well-written. In a different hand.'

'Go on, Sister.'

Holding the paper up, she went on. 'This appears to be some sort of a confession.' She read out loud, ' "May God forgive me, for I have sinned. I have brought a terrible shame on my family. From this day on, I am banished, without hope." '

The two nuns were silent for a moment. Then in a sombre voice, Sister Bridget asked, 'Would you say that was a *willing* confession?'

'I don't know. They could be the words of a sinner repented, but there is something about the wording that suggests it might have been dictated. Especially where it says the sinner is "banished without hope".' She plucked at her lip with her teeth, as she always did when puzzled. 'It suggests the writer is banished by some other person.'

'My sentiments exactly!' A belief strengthened by

the fact that someone had deliberately stripped the girl of all family identity on that night.

Reaching out, Sister Bridget took hold of the papers. 'Listen to me,' she said earnestly. 'Listen carefully to all I have to say.' She felt tired, ancient, ready to meet her maker. It was only right that someone else should now help to carry this burden, and Sister Anne was a compassionate, kindly soul.

In a quiet, intimate voice, she continued, 'Only two people knew about these papers, myself and the Mother Superior. Seventeen years ago we found them in that envelope,' she pointed to a long brown envelope lying beside the file. 'As you see, the envelope was addressed to Mary Magdalen Convent. It was pushed underneath the main door, sometime during the night. On the very same morning we discovered a sorry creature huddled on the outer step. She was very young, fourteen, fifteen. It was hard to be sure, especially as the girl was slightly built and desperately undernourished. In the end, we took it upon ourselves to place her age at fourteen years.' After a moment's pause she explained, 'You know the girl as Mary.'

'Good Heavens!' Sister Anne sat up with interest. 'Of course I knew Mary had been left at the convent but I wasn't aware of these papers or the circumstances.'

'We could never be sure that these papers were left by the same person who abandoned Mary but it all seemed to point that way. We tried everything we could to locate the person who had left the papers and to find out who might have left Mary here, but nothing ever came of our inquiries. In the end it was decided to simply follow the instructions and assume the papers did, in fact, relate to Mary.'

'Has no one ever come forward? Not to this day?'

'No one. The papers were put away and the money placed in trust on Mary's behalf. It was agreed that Mary should never know the full truth. While she's here in God's house, she will always be taken care of. She knows nothing of the money and unless someone comes forward to claim her as family, it will remain locked in trust for her until, and if, she ever needs it.' She shook her head despairingly. 'In my opinion it can only make her dream of things she can never achieve.'

'I understand.' Sister Anne was quick to agree. 'I also understand how there still remains a nagging doubt.' She was deeply intrigued by the tale. 'The note of instruction refers to a "child". Yet, at the age of fourteen or fifteen, Mary was more than a child; she was nearly a woman.'

'Of course, but whoever wrote the instructions could not see that, or *chose* not to see it.'

'And no one else was left here that night?'

'Apart from Mary, the only foundling left with us on that particular night was a newborn who was later collected by the distraught father and reunited with its mother. They both denied leaving any notes. Indeed, they couldn't even write their own names, as is often the case.'

'It does seem then that the notes must have been left by the same person who left Mary.'

'Unless whoever pushed the notes under the door had a change of heart and took the child away again, before the night was over. They would not have been able to retrieve the notes from inside. If that was the case, then the notes need not relate to Mary at all.'

'But what about the confession?'

'Indeed. As you can see, the handwriting is thin and crooked, as though written by someone who is either ill or old. Either way, it was penned by an educated person.'

'Or *dictated* by an educated person. The same person who wrote the instructions perhaps.' Sister Anne pointed to the second paper. 'See? This one is written in a different, stronger style of writing. It carries a sense of outrage. Written by a harsher, unforgiving soul.'

'Yes, my thoughts exactly.' Sister Bridget grew excited. After all this time, being able to discuss it with another being was immensely satisfying. 'There was nothing by which we might have identified the girl,' she revealed now. 'Whoever put her there made certain they could not be traced.' In her mind's eye she saw Mary as she had been on that night. 'The girl's head was cruelly shaved. She had been stripped of all clothing, and by the time we discovered her, she was close to freezing.' Controlling the rage that threatened to overwhelm her, she added calmly, 'They didn't even have enough forgiveness in their sad hearts to sound the bell so that we could find her earlier than the morning.'

Appalled, Sister Anne commented, 'If you ask me, it wasn't the girl who needed punishment but the monsters who left her here.' She pointed to a dark stain at the top of the confession. 'Because of its age and condition, it's hard to tell, but I believe this could be a bloodstain.'

'It *is* blood.' Sinking deeper into the chair, Sister Bridget sighed, as though suddenly a great weight had been lifted from her. Casting her mind back to that morning, she recalled it as clearly as though it was yesterday. 'I was the first person to tend Mary. I cleaned and washed her, made her comfortable and, God forgive me, I kept a certain discovery to myself because I believed the girl had been punished and hurt enough. I felt in my heart that God would understand my reason for keeping silent.'

'What discovery?' Sister Anne inquired. 'And why did you keep silent about it?'

'That poor young girl had been badly beaten.' She pointed to the bloodstain. 'Her back was pitted with the stamp of whip leather, long, deep rivers from shoulder to waist, still bloody, though the blood had congealed during the night. There was a small pool of blood on the step. To this day it cannot be scrubbed away.'

'Such cruelty! But there was something else, wasn't there? Something you wanted no one to know?'

'From what I could tell, the girl had not long borne a child.'

'A child? Can you be sure?' To think that such a young girl could have borne a child and then been abandoned was beyond understanding.

'Many years ago we took in young women who had fallen by the wayside. Sometimes they were with child and it fell to me to see these unfortunates through the worst times before they could be found a home for themselves and the infants. I saw how it was. I watched them give birth and cared for them afterwards. I helped

138

to bring their milk forth and sat with them while they learned how to care for the newborn. Over the years I got to know all there is to know.' She studied Sister Anne's face. 'So yes,' she said with conviction. 'I can be sure she had given birth.'

Shocked, the other nun merely shook her head and sat, quietly mulling over the facts.

'The girl had not been cared for after the birth. She was raw and unclean and even without a child to suck her breasts, the milk came forth and had to be dried up before infection set in.'

'When she was better, didn't she ask questions? Didn't she want to know what had happened to her newborn?'

'She had no memory then, and as you know she has no memory now. But at night when the world slept, she would cry out and I would come running. Always it was the same nightmare, with her calling out for her baby. Other times, she would call out someone's name. It was hard to decipher, all her cries were mingled one with the other. As I have said, all my discreet inquiries in the area came to nothing. I have a feeling she was brought here from some miles away, to where she was not known.'

'The man who got her with child. Do you think it was he who brought her here?'

'Any man, or woman come to that, is certainly capable of beating another until the blood flows and the life begins to ebb.' She thumped the table. 'But what man would get a woman with child and then treat her so badly? What man would abandon her and burden

himself with the newborn?' Her features softened. 'I saw
her face when she called out the name. I felt the love she
had for him. No, Sister, I don't think it was the man who
brought her here. I believe it was someone else. Maybe
the man was also beaten. Maybe the newborn was given
away. Who can tell?'

'You say she called out in her sleep. Did she
remember anything in her *waking* hours?'

'Nothing. She never has and I have never pressed
her. I did not tell her she had given birth to a child,
because I had no child to put into her arms.' Sister
Bridget had been greatly saddened by that. 'For a long
time she despaired, never smiling, not wanting to speak.
Always afraid because she was crippled and helpless, in
a strange place, with strangers, and no identity of her
own.' She shivered. 'Can you imagine how it must have
been?'

'I *daren't* imagine.'

'With so much of a burden to carry, and so young in
life, I could not torture her any more and so I chose to
remain silent. I pray you understand.'

'Was it the beatings that crippled her?'

'That, and an unusually difficult birth. She was badly
torn, and crudely stitched inside. In these particular
circumstances shock, too, can have a devastating effect
on a young girl.' Her face darkened with passion.
'Whoever attended the birth of Mary's child was little
more than a butcher.'

'Have you never discussed this with anyone else?'

'Never.'

'Did you use *any* of the money towards Mary's keep?'

'That isn't our way, and you know it. Our vow is to care for all the poor and helpless when they find their way to God's house. The wealthier people of Woburn have always been generous to that purpose.'

'It's a great deal of money?'

'Yes, it is, and it grows more in value as the years pass.'

'But the person who left instructions gave you permission to use it on Mary's behalf.'

'The money has not been needed, and besides, we were never sure whether it belonged to Mary.' She bent her head, as though in silent prayer. 'I feel sure the money rightfully belongs to Mary. As Mother Superior, I am now guardian of both the money and the girl. It is an awesome duty.'

'Could some of the money not be spent to buy her a Bath chair? It would be more dignified than that runabout Amy made for her.'

'For some time now I've toyed with the idea,' Sister Bridget admitted. 'I only hesitate because I'm afraid it might make her too bold. It might give her impossible ideas and make her think she can be independent. But she will never be independent, poor soul. Her dreams always aspire beyond her capabilities. In a Bath chair she might sneak off at any time and be at the mercy of any rogue outside these walls.'

'I understand. And I suppose, with the care and attention Amy put into that runabout, it can't be all that different from a Bath chair. The runabout is padded with cushions; it has a tall, sloping back for her to rest against, and a platform where her legs can be bent in a comfortable sitting position. It also has wheels.' She chuckled. 'In fact, I'm surprised Mary hasn't already sneaked off in that.'

'Oh, but she has.' Sister Bridget smiled at the memory. 'About five years ago, Sister Margaret was woken by a noise in the gardens. On going out with a lantern, she found Mary lying upside-down on the ground with the runabout on top of her.' The smile became a frown. 'She had got almost as far as the gates, obviously with the intention of going out, on to the open road, though of course she would not admit it. The only reason she hadn't got further than the convent grounds was because the wheels on the runabout were too small. The wheels on a Bath chair are big and capable and the whole thing would be far more manageable. So you see my dilemma.' Going to the window, where she stood quiet for a moment, Sister Bridget suddenly turned to say with conviction, 'The money is best untouched. It has already been made over to Mary in trust, if ever she should need it.'

'Do you think she ever will?'

'Who knows, Sister? Mary is quite unique. She's a cripple and will probably always be a cripple but she's warm and generous, a restless spirit with a desperate yearning to see the world before she dies. Yet she has always refused offers of being taken on trips outside. She is impossibly stubborn! She has to do it herself or not at all. That's the way she sees it and she has set herself an impossible target.' She paused, thinking of Mary and wishing it might have been different. 'Someone with the kind of affliction she has been cursed with hardly ever lives long. Even if she was offered the money now, she probably wouldn't want it. You know how fiercely independent she can be.'

Sister Anne smiled. 'We *all* know how independent she can be!'

'Apart from which, if she was told about the money, she would not rest until she knew it all – the shocking manner in which we found her, the papers, the callous instructions there. She would have to know about the unbelievable cruelty of the people who abandoned her. And, God forbid, she would also have to be told that she had recently given birth to a child and that the child was not left here with her.' Her voice broke. 'Can you imagine what that knowledge would do to her?'

'It could break her spirit for ever.'

'I refuse to risk it. Never a day goes by when she doesn't ask questions, and somehow we have managed to avoid the whole truth. I pray we can continue to keep it from her. As for the money, there might come a day when it will help her to realise some of her ambitions. Until that day, it will be kept safe.'

Sister Anne nodded. 'I think the decision is a wise one.'

'One more thing.'

'Yes, Sister?'

'Have you ever seen Mary's handwriting?'

'Never.'

'Nor me. But have you seen the way she cringes from pen and paper? As though it represents something fearful?'

'Why yes! Only the other day, Amy tried to coax

143

her to write her name, and she was very distressed.'

Sister Bridget's suspicions were confirmed. 'It seems to me that the act of writing has particular bad memories for Mary. Now then, why would that be, do you think?'

The younger nun stared up with astonished eyes. 'Of course! Her fear would be understandable if she had been forced to write a confession!'

Sister Bridget looked steadily at her. There was no need for words. The truth was there, in both their faces.

A short time later, Sister Bridget was alone again. Collecting the papers from the desk, she carefully returned them to where they had lain these many years. As she turned the key in the lock, she wondered if it would be as many years again before they saw daylight.

For now though, Mary was in their care and, God willing, she would never again be alone or unwanted.

S OME TWO HUNDRED miles away in the north of England, Lilian Reece crept out of bed to listen at the door. For the second time in a minute, she raised her voice and called out, 'Who's there? Don? Is that you?'

He replied in a gruff, tired voice, 'It's all right. Go back to sleep.' He had been enjoying a quiet jug of ale until she woke and began shouting from the upper regions. Now, to his annoyance, he could hear her coming down the stairs, the slippered feet dropping her weight on each step, with a muted *thump, thump*. 'Is there no peace?' he groaned. 'Day and night she's pecking at me like a bird at a crumb.'

The shuffling footsteps carried her across the

hallway to the kitchen. 'What the devil are you doing up at this hour?' she demanded from the doorway.

She made no attempt to enter. When dressed in her severe day clothes and hard buckled shoes, with her mind active and wary of saying the wrong thing, she was capable of anything. But now, in the early hours of the morning, wearing only her nightgown, with her feet bare and her hair hanging loose and the sleep dulling her senses, she felt strangely vulnerable. More than that, she felt afraid. Afraid of the terrible wrong she had done this man, her own brother. Afraid of the memories which, even after all these years, came into her dreams to haunt her. What if he should look into her eyes and see the awful truth behind them? What if he could tell what she was thinking? What then? Her brother was a peaceful man, a quiet and tolerant being. But if he knew what she had done!

Riveted with fear, the strength ebbed from her legs as he suddenly looked up, his voice filled with contempt as he demanded, 'Seen a ghost, have you?'

'What do you mean?' Startled, she took an involuntary step backwards.

He stared at her a moment longer before taking another sip from the jug. 'Get back to bed,' he muttered, replacing the jug on the table. 'Leave a man to his thoughts.'

'I can't sleep. Not with you lumbering about down here.'

'Got a bad conscience, have you?'

'There's nothing wrong with *my* conscience!'

'Then you should sleep through an earthquake.' He

turned his head, his dark accusing eyes staring at her through the half-light. 'I hope you're proud of yourself.'

'I've done nothing wrong.'

'You've done nothing *right* either!' The alcohol had filled him with false courage. 'If it hadn't been for you, she might not have gone. You drove her away. D'you hear me? You and your black heart drove my girl away!'

'Nell has a mind of her own. If she'd agreed to be rid of the child, she could have stayed here. But she was defiant and now I don't want her under my roof.'

'*Your* roof. You never tire of reminding me, do you?'

'You *need* to be reminded.' She spoke in a softer, more menacing voice. 'I mean, it wouldn't do to let you forget, would it?'

'I made a terrible mistake. I fell in love. Do you mean to haunt me to my grave because of it?'

'It's not *me* that haunts you. It's what you did, all those years ago.' Her confidence returning, she told him cruelly, 'Your conscience will never let you forget.'

He raised his face to her, his dark eyes filled with anguish. 'I don't *want* to forget.' Bowing his head, he began to cry.

His heartfelt sobs momentarily shamed her. For one trembling moment she was tempted to console him. But then she reminded herself. Let him suffer, she thought callously. As long as he suffers, I know I won't lose him.

'I'm going to my bed,' she told him. 'Don't stay down too long, will you?'

When she'd gone, he was quite still, the heartache washing through him. Warmed with booze and filled with memories of the girl he had loved and lost seventeen years before, he wouldn't have minded dying there and then. Life was too painful. He was ready to face his maker. Whatever punishment awaited him could not be worse than the weight of his terrible sin. If he had not made Mary with child, she might still be here today.

Lurching across the room, he flung open the drawer and took out a kitchen knife. Pressing the blade to his wrist, he cut through the outer skin. The crimson blood spurted over his hand. He closed his eyes, preparing to end it all.

But then he thought of Nell and his heartache was tenfold. Letting the knife drop to the floor, he groaned, 'I'm sorry, Nell. I shouldn't be thinking of suicide. God forgive me, but I robbed you of a mother. I won't wrong you again, child. If ever you return, I'll be here for you.'

After washing the wound and wrapping a makeshift bandage round it, he made his way towards the stairs.

Upstairs, Lilian Reece was muttering over the contents of a small wooden box. 'I thought this would be an end to it but now I see the sins of the mother are visited on the daughter.' Her voice broke, as if she was softly crying. Filled with a terrible guilt, she fell to her knees and began praying.

As he passed her room, Don heard her quiet mutterings. 'Talking to yourself now, is it?' He smiled. 'You ought to ask the Lord's forgiveness, you heartless bitch!'

Inside the room, Lilian thought she heard something. Scrambling from her knees, she grabbed the box and began cramming the contents in – the golden, blood-stained hair, a small silver ring, and a piece of paper, written in the spidery scrawl of an 'educated' woman:

> Mary Rush,
> delivered of an infant on this night
> of January 1st, 1873.
> The infant is kept.
> The mother given into the care of
> the Convent of Mary Magdalen
> in the town of Woburn,
> in the county of Bedfordshire.

Replacing the box in the back of the cupboard, Lilian quickly climbed into her bed. But she couldn't sleep. Somehow, she feared that the years were unravelling the secret she had fought so hard to keep hidden.

BILL DAVIDSON WENT quietly out of the house, softly closing the door behind him and hoping he had not woken his mam from her well-earned slumbers.

He waited a moment, satisfied she was still in the land of dreams. 'See you in the morning, Mam.' He looked up at the window, his smile half-hearted. 'At least one of us is able to sleep.'

He hurried down the street, nearly leaping out of his skin when a cat launched itself from a wall and landed on his shoulder. 'Jesus!' He ducked instinctively and, in the blink of an eye, the cat was gone, apparently more startled than Bill himself.

Imagining she heard the front door close and now the sudden wail of a cat in the street below, Molly crept out of bed and peeped through the curtains. Bill was hurrying away, his broad shoulders and strong stride instantly recognisable. She glanced at the bedside clock. 'Bugger me, it's two o'clock of a morning. Where the devil is he off to?' All evening he had been restless. He was the last one left downstairs when she finally decided she couldn't keep her eyes open a minute longer, and now he was off down the street, striding out as if he had a purpose in mind.

When he was out of sight, she got back into bed and cuddled up to the warm body of her husband. 'By, yer bloody freezing, woman!' Joe complained. Then he wound his arms round her ample waist. 'I'll soon have yer warm, sure I will,' he chuckled.

If was half an hour later when the two of them disentangled themselves and fell asleep, exhausted from the physical effort of making love. 'I ain't so young as I used to be,' he muttered before he closed his eyes.

'You're just as randy though, yer bugger!' Molly smiled. There was a fleeting thought for Bill, and where he might be heading, before she, too, closed her tired eyes.

The moon was already dipping in the skies as Bill strode through the streets towards the inn. The early morning air was cool and refreshing and, in the eerie quietness, he felt as though he was the only man alive in the world. It was a lonely feeling.

When he got to the inn, he stood in the street, staring up at her room. 'What the hell am I doing here?' he asked himself. But he knew what he was doing there. He was lonely for company. He needed someone to talk to;

someone of his own age. He needed a woman, in the same way any man might need a woman.

He almost turned away, but his need was strong, and Kate Jordan was always willing.

She was willing now.

When he threw a stone to wake her, she opened the window and gestured for him to go to the back door.

'Come in,' she said, grabbing him by the coat sleeve. 'Quick! Before my dad hears us.'

She led the way up to her room, occasionally glancing back with a warm smile. She had had an idea he might be here tonight. If she had her way, he'd be here every night and never leave.

Kate Jordan was in love with Bill, and always had been. Tall and slim, with vivacious dark hair and handsome features, she was every man's dream. Bill liked her but he didn't love her. He had never pretended otherwise and she respected him for that.

Closing the bedroom door behind them, she put the lamp on the mantelpiece and regarded him with interest. The halo of light fell on his face. His dark eyes glistened like wet coal, and his strong manly figure seemed to fill that small, shadowy room. As always when she saw him, her passion was roused. 'Couldn't you sleep?' she asked softly.

He shook his head. 'There's no sleep in me.'

'Need a drink?' She went to the chest of drawers and drew out a small bottle of gin. 'Just as well I saved it.'

'No.' He held out his arms. 'It's not drink I need. It's you.'

Thrilled, she snuggled close. 'Want to make love?'

'Not yet.'

Pulling away, she looked at him with renewed interest. 'What's wrong?'

He shrugged his shoulders. 'I had to get out of the house.' He curled his fingers through her long, dark hair. 'I felt lonely. Thought you might be feeling the same.' He had never felt that kind of loneliness before. It was unsettling.

He led her to the couch where he pulled her down beside him. Wrapping his arm round her, he asked, 'What do you want out of life, Kate?'

'You.' She looked up with adoring eyes.

He laughed softly. 'What else do you want?'

'Oh. Security. Money. An inn of my own.'

'Children?'

'Not if I can help it.'

It wasn't the reply he'd expected. 'I thought all women wanted children.'

'Not me.' She gave a gruff little laugh. 'I'm too bloody selfish.'

'Marriage?'

'Is that a proposal?'

'No.'

She grinned, but there was a seriousness in her manner when she spoke. 'What if I won't take no for an answer?'

''Fraid you'll have to.'

'Is the idea of marrying me so awful?'

'I'm not ready for that sort of commitment.'

'I can wait.' She stroked her manicured fingers over his face. 'I'll wait for ever if I have to.'

'You might have to wait a long time.' He didn't want her getting the wrong idea. 'I've no plans to marry. You've known that all along.' Why couldn't he get Nell out of his mind?

'A man like you should be married. It's not safe to have you running loose.' She got up then, a little disappointed. 'It would serve you right if I told you to piss off.' Turning away, she poured herself a measure of gin.

He came and stood behind her, bending his head to kiss her neck. 'Do you want me to piss off?'

'You know I don't.' The touch of his mouth against her skin drove her crazy.

Sliding his hands beneath her nightgown, he caressed her, his strong, tender fingers finding the curve of her thighs, his stomach pressing against her back, and his open mouth kissing the soft, warm nape of her neck.

Unable to bear it any longer, she put her arms above her head and tore off her nightgown. Writhing in his arms, she turned to face him, her eyes alight with excitement. 'No other man can get round me like you do.'

His dark eyes appraised her nakedness. 'You're a beautiful woman,' he whispered. 'Any man would be proud to have you.'

'To have me, yes. But not to keep me.' There was bitterness in her.

He had no words to comfort her. Nell was too alive in his mind.

Both naked, they fell on to the bed, he on top, her beneath. 'Be rough,' she pleaded, opening herself to him.

He wasn't rough. He was demanding but tender. He

was thoughtful yet greedy, fired with a need so deep he had to force himself to wait for her to be satisfied. Then, when he fell away, exhausted, he wished he could make promises. But he couldn't.

Not while Nell lingered so heavily on his mind.

PART TWO

Autumn 1890
ON THE ROAD

Chapter Six

NELL WAS AT her wits' end.

For weeks now she had felt unusually tired. She had put it down to the hot summer, but now that was behind her and with the coming of October the days had grown cooler, which was a blessed relief. The nights, however, were bitter, and try as she might she could not keep warm. Moreover, the farmers hereabouts wouldn't take her on because now that she was six months gone her condition was bold enough for everyone to see.

Up to this past month, she had managed to disguise it by tying her shawl tight round her stomach, loosening the waist on her skirt, and wearing a smock over the top. By doing that, she looked more chubby than pregnant. In the kitchen of a farmer's house, where she'd managed to find work, no one was any the wiser. Lately though, she'd suddenly burst out of shape, and every eye was drawn immediately to the bulging mound about her midriff. One glance at her and every cook, every housekeeper and landowner had sent her packing.

After a rough night in Bedford town, she had travelled about four miles along the main road before cutting off to narrower lanes which would take her into the farming community. At every stop along the way she had tried for work and been turned away. It was a heart-destroying experience.

Mid-morning now, ambling along the lanes and singing softly to herself, Nell did not give up hope. Instead, she kept her eyes open and stayed alert. There must be any number of farms in these isolated places where folk might find it hard to get help. 'There must be work hereabouts,' she muttered, her blue eyes scanning the fields. 'And I'm not ready for the knacker's yard yet.'

It was late morning when she saw him in the field, a small, round fellow with a face like the rising sun. Wearing a shabby jacket and a flat tweed cap, he might have been a scarecrow. 'I'm looking for work,' she called from the cart. 'I can turn my hand to most things.'

'Bugger off!' He eyed her swollen belly with contempt. 'It's all I can do to keep my own body and soul together without taking on a scruffy little floozy who's got herself in trouble. Go on! Bugger off afore I take a pitchfork to you.'

Grunting and swearing, he commenced offloading wooden boxes from his handcart. Judging by his foul temper and the rivers of sweat on his face, he'd been working hard for some time.

Nell was furious. 'You mind your manners, you bad-tempered old sod!' It had been a hard day for her too, and she was in no mood for niceties. 'I'm no floozy. What's more, I wouldn't work for you if you paid me double the rate.' When he stared up in amazement, she cocked her head, snorted her disapproval and, taking up the reins, drove the horse on. 'Floozy indeed!' In truth she was close to tears but she would die before letting him see that.

'Hey!' His voice sailed after her.

Nell ignored him. If he insulted her again, she might have to spit in his eye.

'Hey, you proud bugger, come back here.'

'Woa, old feller.' Bringing the horse to a halt, she looked round. 'What do you want?'

'You're a feisty little thing, I'll give you that.' He took his cap off and scratched his balding head. 'You might be able to help me an' all.'

'Doing what?' Beggars can't be choosers, she thought.

'Come back here an' I'll tell yer. I ain't got patience nor energy to yell from one end o' Bedfordshire to the other.'

Clambering down from the cart, Nell made her way back. 'What work are you offering?' Since fending for herself she'd learned to come straight to the point.

'Helping me shift stuff from the big barn over by the cottage there to this field shelter.'

Nell glanced down at the wooden boxes. They were filled with ripening apples and vegetables. 'I can't lift them boxes, if that's what you're after,' she warned.

His gaze fell to her midriff. 'I can see that,' he laughed. 'Yer belly's riper than these 'ere apples.'

'Have you brought me back to insult me?' Her eyes flashed with anger.

'No, no.' He could see Nell was not the usual, common type who had one bairn after another, and all by different men. 'We ain't got off on the right foot, have

we, eh?' he chuckled. 'Let's start again.' He looked at
the boxes and he looked at her, and he knew he would
have to do all the hard work. 'I'm not asking you to lift
these 'ere boxes. I'm asking for the use of your horse
and cart, and mebbe you'll mek us a bite to eat while I
work. How does that sound?'

It sounded all right to Nell. It would be the first work
she'd had in ages, but she didn't show her excitement.
'What wages are you offering?'

'Threepence for every time I fetch the horse and cart
across the field. Does that suit you?'

'How many times do you expect to cross the field?'

'Nine, mebbe ten times.'

'Sixpence a time then.'

'You're a bleedin' robber!'

'Take it or leave it.' She couldn't help but notice how
exhausted he was and how bow-legged every time he
lifted one of those heavy boxes. 'By the looks of you, I'd
say you need me more than I need you.'

'Fourpence.'

'Sixpence. Or I'm on my way.'

Blowing out his cheeks, he looked at the sturdy old
horse and the sizeable cart. 'All right then, sixpence. And
I hope you can make a good stew 'cause I've had nowt
to eat since yesterday.'

He told her to take the horse and cart along the lane
and into the field through a break in the hedge.

'You'll find root vegetables and meat in the larder,'
he told her. 'I ain't had time to light a fire but there's
kindling wood and matches aside the fire range.' Leading
the horse and cart towards the big barn, he called out,

'You'll have to search about for whatever else you need.'

When Nell stepped inside the cottage, she had the shock of her life. 'By, it's like a pigsty in here!' The windows were bare. The floor was strewn with broken pottery. Wisps of straw were blown about everywhere, and there was an inch of dust on every surface. The shelves were empty and the only furniture in the sitting room was a three-legged stool, a chair and a small pine table. 'Looks like the robbers have been in,' she muttered. There was a sense of desolation about the place, which made her uneasy.

Glancing out of the window she saw him loading the cart with crates. 'Wonder what you're up to, you old devil?' she said aloud.

She found the meat and root vegetables. The meat was a miserable scrag end of lamb that had seen better days, and the vegetables had been there so long they were growing whiskers. The black cauldron in the fire grate was big enough to take a fine stew but first the fire had to be lit.

Collecting the kindling wood from the hearth, she laid some of the smaller pieces inside the grate, then used larger sticks to build up a pyramid. That done, she put a match to it and in no time at all the fire was crackling and spitting. After enduring the cold autumn nights, the sight of a cheery fire and the warmth it emanated was a pure delight to her.

Fetching a pail of water from the pump outside, Nell poured some into the cauldron which she had first placed on the flames; the remainder she poured into a large earthenware bowl she found in one of the cupboards. Next, she set about preparing the meal. She scraped and washed the vegetables, then chopped the meat into sizeable chunks. Afterwards she dunked the whole lot into the cauldron and stirred in a pinch of pepper and a cube of salt. When it was gently simmering, she kept the fire going by pushing fragments of wood into the flames. The aroma soon filled the room, making her stomach sing and her heart bounce. 'By, Nell, couldn't you make a pretty place out of this cottage, eh?' she remarked, looking round with smiling blue eyes.

While the meal was bubbling away, she scouted around. The entire cottage was built on one floor only. There were two tiny bedrooms, both in need of a good scrub. The sitting room was larger, dressed with scatter rugs that had seen better days, and a large beamed fireplace that was perfect for huddling round on a cold winter's night. The only room with curtains at the window was the larger of the two bedrooms, though the curtains hung from a crooked pole and even when closed, as Nell discovered, you could see daylight through the many moth holes. The flagged floors struck cold, and the stone walls were stained and dusty. In one corner of the sitting room, the ceiling was open to the skies, and though now somewhat disguised by the aroma of cooking food, a pungent smell of dampness pervaded every nook and cranny.

Yet for all that there was a wonderful sense of peace and tranquillity about the place. Nell felt oddly at home here. 'I've been travelling too long,' she murmured. The road was a poor companion for a lonely soul, she thought, and every day took her further away from those she knew and loved.

Thoughts of home and her father invaded her mind. Other, warmer thoughts of Molly and Bill touched her heart and, for one nostalgic minute, she felt like turning round and making her way back. But how could she? Nothing had changed.

The sound of water boiling over sent her running to the kitchen and, sure enough, the cauldron was spurting its contents over the rim and on to the flames beneath. Quickly she lifted the lid and cocked it to one side, letting the steam escape. The smell was delicious. Dipping the ladle in, she tasted the thick, fatty juice. 'Another half hour and it'll be done to a treat,' she observed.

Weariness settling on her, she returned to the sitting room and gazed out of the window. The horse and cart were being led across the field, back and forth, taking piles of stuff to the shelter. 'Why would he do that?' she asked herself. 'It looks like he's already emptied this cottage, and now he's emptying the barn and stacking it half a mile away.' She was puzzled. 'It seems an odd thing to be doing.'

She leaned into the windowsill, spreading her arms and letting the stone sill take her weight while her soft gaze roved round the room. 'I could make a real home out of this place,' she mused. 'Big copper pans hanging in the fireplace, with a log basket and brassware in the hearth.' She could see it all clearly in her mind's eye. 'Peg rugs on the floor, and pretty curtains at the windows.'

Growing excited, she wandered about, imagining all

the things she would do. 'I'd have a dresser in that corner,' she decided, pointing to the corner by the kitchen door, 'with wide shelves dressed with pretty ware, and big, deep drawers beneath to hold all my precious things.'

A shy smile crept into her lovely face as she glanced at the alcove beside the fireplace. 'Over there I'd have the baby's cradle.' She knew exactly the way it would be. 'A beautiful wooden cradle with wide, safe rockers and covered with the prettiest, softest eiderdown. Oh, and there'd be a bonnet of wicker covering the top where she lays her head, to keep the chill away.'

She giggled. 'What makes you think it will be a girl?' she asked herself. 'Because I want a girl.' That did seem selfish, she thought, when all that mattered was for the child to be born healthy and safe. 'But I won't be disappointed if it's a boy,' she added.

Though Nell had conceived in circumstances she wished had never happened, there was no turning back. Already she was dreaming of the day when she would hold the child in her arms.

Returning to the kitchen, she warmed herself by the fire, feeling for the first time a sense of envy. 'I hope I find a little cottage like this,' she mused, 'where I can raise my baby and keep out the world.' But not Bill, she thought fondly. She would never want to keep out Bill.

She went round the cottage again, each time seeing something new, like the damp patch in the bedroom sill, and the intricate spider's web in the sitting room. The tiny black spider was at home, hunched in a ball and looking as forlorn as she felt. 'Waiting for your dinner, eh?' she murmured. 'Hoping some poor unsuspecting fly will find its way into your parlour?' She raised her arm, ready to brush the web away. 'I don't suppose I could tempt you to a plate of stew?' she asked. The spider didn't move. Instead it tightened its body and stiffened, seeming to brace itself against losing its home.

'All right.' Nell lowered her arm. 'I know how you feel.' She turned away and almost at once her gaze went to the mantelpiece. Something caught her eye, something she hadn't noticed before, maybe because she had been too close, and the mantelpiece too high. Now, though, from the far end of the room, she could see the corner of what looked like a photograph.

It was a photograph. On tiptoe she brought it down and looked into the face there; the kind and lovely face of a woman probably in her late fifties. She was dark-haired and dark-eyed, and her long, fine hands, which rested on her lap in a formal manner, were pale and smooth, like those of a young girl.

While Nell gazed at the photograph, so did the man who was looking over her shoulder. Not realising he was there, Nell was surprised when he spoke softly. 'She'll be the last memory I take from this place,' he said, his voice hoarse with emotion.

'She's beautiful.' Nell could hardly take her eyes off the woman's face. 'Who is she?' Handing him the photograph, she could see he was close to tears.

Thrusting the photograph in his pocket, he looked away. 'Is the food ready?'

Realising he did not want to discuss it, Nell didn't

press the point. 'I'll go and see,' she said. 'The stew should be nicely done by now.'

It was done to perfection. 'Wash your hands,' she said, seeing how his hands were torn and bleeding and his nails like the inside of a coal mine. 'Then, when you've fetched the cauldron to the table, I'll dish up.'

'You're a bossy young miss.' He did as he was told all the same. 'By, that smells grand!' he exclaimed when she began dishing up the food. 'I hope it tastes as good.'

'It will.' Nell had already laid the table with what meagre items she could find. 'There are no knives in the drawer,' she explained. 'All I could find were these forks and spoons.'

'Forks for stabbing the meat and veg,' he smiled, 'and a spoon for scooping up the gravy. What else do you want?'

'Nothing.' She could see the logic of what he was saying. Looking out of the window, she saw the horse tucking into a bag of hay. 'I'm glad you've fed him,' she said. 'He's worked hard.'

'He ain't the only one.' He stared at his full plate. 'I like plenty of gravy,' he said, licking his lips. 'Thick as sludge and running over the edges or it ain't worth having.' His stomach rumbled. 'Come on! Get a move on, woman!'

Nell didn't dare put another spoonful on. 'Happen you'd like to eat it straight from the pan,' she suggested with a wicked smile. 'Or what about the horse trough outside? That might be even better.'

His face hardened with anger but then he saw the determination in her eyes and gave a bark of laughter.

'You're a gutsy little bugger. Happen I should ask you to stay around after all.' His respect for Nell grew by the minute. 'I see you've set two places at the table,' he observed with a smile.

'That's right. Two people, two places at the table.'

'You never asked.'

'Didn't think I needed to,' she said, putting a full plate in front of herself. 'I've been working hard too, or hadn't you noticed?'

He picked up his fork and stabbed a large chunk of meat. Popping it into his mouth, he sighed with pleasure. 'You're a good cook,' he said. 'I reckon you've earned the right to sit at my table.'

'I'm glad you think so. If I thought you meant to send me away hungry, I'd have tipped the food away first.'

He eyed her from behind his spoon. 'I reckon you would an' all.' Pointing at the three-legged stool, he told her, 'Sit down, have your meal, then if you've any sense you'll be on your way as fast as you can.' He cast an anxious glance towards the doorway. Seeing nothing, he got out of his chair and looked through the window. 'The buggers will be here soon, damn their eyes!' he muttered. Returning to the table, he gobbled down his food as though it was his last.

'Is there something wrong?'

Slurping the last spoonful of gravy, he wiped his mouth with the back of his hand. 'What makes you say that?'

'You're acting strangely, that's all. First you wouldn't give me work, then you used the horse and cart to take stuff out of one barn into another. The house is half empty, you're choking your food down, and now you're watching for someone who, I suspect, is out to cause you trouble.'

'You think too much.' Taking out the photograph, he stood it in front of him. 'She was like that,' he said quietly. 'She was a thinker. The wisest, gentlest woman I've ever known.'

Nell sensed the loneliness in him. She knew about loneliness. 'Who was she?' she asked again, hoping this time to get an answer.

With a sad smile, he turned the photograph so she could see the woman's face. 'Her name was Anne Louise,' he revealed. 'We were married for thirty-four years and there was never a day in all that time when we didn't find pleasure in each other's company.' With the tips of his fingers he tenderly stroked the photograph. 'She's been dead these past three months.' Going to the window he looked out again, before saying, 'You wouldn't think so to look at it now, but this garden was filled with flowers she planted with her own hands.' He shook his head, lost in memories of her. 'Funny thing, but when the flowers faded before their time, she went with them.' He paused, gulping back the tears. 'After she'd gone, it was like my whole world had come to an end.'

Nell came to his side, her gaze reaching out to the parched and untidy ground outside. 'I can imagine why she loved it here,' she murmured. 'It takes hold of you, doesn't it?' Intrigued as to why the cottage had been half emptied, and why he should be shifting all his goods down to the field shelter, she said, 'I can't understand why anyone would want to leave this lovely place.'

Suddenly he was angry again. 'What makes you think I want to leave here?' he snapped. 'You know nothing about it.' Grabbing her by the arm, he spun her round. 'You'd best take your belongings and go. Now!'

Shocked, Nell tried desperately to make amends. 'I'm sorry,' she apologised. 'You just seem so worried, and I'd like to help if I can.'

He hung his head. 'No one can help.'

'I'm not afraid.' He had been good to her, and she owed him.

Grabbing her by the arm, he propelled her to the door. 'You should be afraid! Now, get away from here before you're caught up in things that don't concern you.' He took her outside, to where the horse was drinking at the trough. 'I'm grateful to you,' he said, 'but I don't want you here when they come.'

Struggling to get out of his vice-like grip, Nell wanted to know, 'When *who* comes? Who are these people? Do they mean to hurt you?'

'You ask too many questions.' Digging into his pocket he drew out a handful of shillings. 'Here's your wages,' he told her. 'I've put a few crates of fruit and veg on the back of the cart. Now be off with you!' Without further ado, he bundled her on to the cart. The minute she had the reins in her hands, he slapped the horse on the rump and sent it careering across the field, with the cart and Nell bumping up and down as they went. 'Good luck, young 'un!' the man called after her.

Nell managed to take the horse in hand and bring

him to a steady gait. 'I've never stayed where I'm not wanted,' she muttered defiantly, 'and I'm not about to start now.'

Yet, as she drove away, she was deeply troubled. So troubled that she drew the horse to a halt and climbed down. The lane was narrow and the ditches on either side were steep. Inch by inch, she turned the horse about. 'The old man's in trouble,' she argued with herself. 'I have to go back.'

As she got to the break in the hedge, she saw a plume of smoke rising high in the air. 'Good God! The cottage is alight!' There was no time to negotiate the horse and cart through the hedge so she jumped down and set off as fast as her feet would let her. Heavy with child and weighed down by a good helping of stew, she seemed to take for ever to cross the field. Then she saw the old man come running from the cottage. 'Jesus Christ!' He was shocked to see her there. 'What the hell are you doing here?'

'I had to come back.' Gasping for breath, she looked up to where the rising smoke turned the sky black. 'The cottage, it's on fire.'

Coming at her like a bull at a gate, he propelled her into the field shelter. 'You shouldn't have come back!' he yelled. 'These buggers are capable of murder!'

The acrid smell of burning clung to him. There was smut on his face and a great sense of agitation about him. 'I fired the cottage,' he told her in short spurts of breath. 'The buggers can have it now.'

Nell was shocked to her roots. 'You've done *what*?'

The sound of men's voices sailed through the air.

'Ssh!' Putting his fingers to her lips, he bade her be silent. For what seemed a lifetime, he held her there, pressed against the timber wall, his eyes like those of a madman.

Presently the voices dimmed and he smiled. 'They've gone looking the other way,' he breathed. 'They'll not find us here. This shelter isn't on the land map. As far as they're concerned, it doesn't exist.'

'What have you done? Why did you set fire to the cottage?' The idea of that delightful little home being put to the torch was deeply saddening.

'I had to.' Going carefully to the door, he looked out. Satisfied there was no one watching, he explained, 'I was a market gardener, like my father before me. I've always made a good living and paid my dues along the way. In all my life I've never owed any man or woman. Things were all right when Anne Louise was alive. Afterwards, well, I just lost heart. Most of the harvest went rotten. There didn't seem no point in going to market, and I soon fell behind with the rent. A few days ago the squire got court permission to call in the bailiffs and throw me out. I went to see him, tried to reason with him. "I'll sell everything I own to put it right," I told him, but he didn't want to know. He's had his sights set on that cottage for his fancy piece, somewhere to go where he'll not be seen. And there's a fair bit of land attached to it, all good fertile soil. I've put sweat and blood into that place over the years.'

The sweat was running down his brow as he spoke. 'When I knew he meant to have it away from me, I could hear Anne Louise saying what a bloody fool I'd been. That's when I decided they would never set foot inside.

171

That cottage has been mine and my wife's all these years, and I couldn't bear the thought of him in there with his floozy. So I've set fire to it and I hope to God it burns to the ground.'

Nell didn't agree. 'You shouldn't have done it.' She thought of the happy years he must have spent there, he and his wife, and it struck her as cruel for him to have repaid it by laying a torch to its foundations. But she didn't want to add to his burden so she simply asked, 'What will you do now?'

He made a circle with his arms, embracing the many boxes and crates stacked high. 'Most of the harvest went to rot but there's enough here to get me started. Once I've got money in my pocket, I'll work my way to the other side of the world. It shouldn't be too difficult. There are ships leaving for foreign parts all the time.' Reaching into his pocket he drew out the photograph of his love. 'As long as I've got her with me, I'll not want for anything else.'

Nell was serious. 'How will you sell the fruit and veg?'

'Don't you worry. There's plenty round the market who'll pay a pretty penny for this little lot.'

'You can have the use of my horse and cart if you like.'

He looked into those bright blue eyes and was sorry he didn't have time to get to know her better. 'Bless you, that won't be necessary. Market traders have their own means of transport. They'll soon shift these crates.' He grinned. 'But not before they've laid the money in my hand.'

Nell's mind was working feverishly. 'Suppose the bailiff's men find it here? If they seize it all, you'll have nothing.'

He had no time to think on her remark before they heard yelling. 'God Almighty, they're searching the area,' he groaned, peering through a chink in the window. 'You're right. If they look long and hard enough, they're bound to find it, and us.' He couldn't risk it. 'If they find me, there'll be no need for crates or such. After what I've done, the squire will be out for blood.' He shook her by the shoulders. 'I told you not to come back but I'm glad you did. We'll load as much as we can on to the cart and get it to a market staller I know. There's always a chance the squire's men won't discover the shelter, in which case I can come back under cover of darkness for the rest.'

The next few minutes were frantic. The old man worked until his bones ached, and Nell did what she could to help, though all she could carry were the smaller boxes and odd items of furniture.

It was when she had taken a chair to the cart and come back for another that she saw the cradle. Made of wood and covered in cobwebs, it could have been the very one she had imagined back at the cottage. 'It's yours if you want it,' the old man said. 'We never had any children, and you've got one in the making.' He glanced at her belly and chuckled. 'If you do much more lifting, it'll be on its way and causing us more trouble than we can handle.'

To Nell it was the most beautiful thing she had ever seen, though it needed some repair. 'Thank you,' she whispered, and was too choked to say more. She never dreamed she would own such a lovely thing as that cradle.

Lifting it on to the back of the cart, he covered it with a tarpaulin. 'Wood needs to be kept dry,' he told her, 'and that sheet is big enough for you to make a tent out of should there come a storm.'

'How did you know I was travelling the road?' Certain she hadn't mentioned it to him, she wondered how he could have guessed.

He pointed to the supplies her father had given her, and the bucket and tools slung beneath the belly of the cart. 'It doesn't take a magician to see you carry all your belongings with you,' he observed. 'I expect you've had a rough time of it, eh?'

'What do you mean?' Shame put Nell on the defensive.

'You being with child and only a slip of a girl yourself. I bet the family didn't take too kindly to that. Threw you out, did they?'

'Sort of.' Not her father, she thought proudly. He would never have thrown her out if it hadn't been for that sister of his.

He pursed his lips and sighed through his nose. 'Families can be a blessing,' he commented thoughtfully, 'or they can be the very devil.'

Over his shoulder she could see men approaching. 'They're coming this way!' she hissed. 'Three of them. And they're carrying shotguns.'

There was no time for him to look round because suddenly they caught sight of him. 'He's here!' one of the men yelled. 'I've got the bugger cornered.'

The old man lifted Nell bodily and put her on the cart. 'Keep going and don't turn back,' he warned. 'Whatever happens, *don't turn back.*'

'Get on the cart,' Nell urged. 'We'll outrun them.'

'There's no time! Make for a hamlet called Ridgmont, find a man by the name of Albert Slater. He'll take the goods from you and you can be on your way. Tell him John Butler sent you and I'll make my way there when I've got rid of these blighters. Now go on! For once in your life, do as you're told.'

The men were close now. Too close for her to waste any more time. 'I'll find him,' she promised as he ran out of sight. 'For God's sake, be careful.' Even as she spoke, shots rang out. 'Get on, you lazy old bugger!' she called, slapping the reins against the horse's rump. 'Move your arse or we'll all be meat for the crows.'

THE JOURNEY TO Ridgmont was painstakingly slow. There were few signs along the narrow, meandering lanes, and Nell had to stop and ask the way several times.

At last, just as the sun was beginning to lose its glory, she came into Ridgmont hamlet by way of the Ampthill Road. 'My! This is a lovely place,' she remarked, looking from one side of the street to the other. The old square church with its pretty tower stood to the left of her, and to the right was an ancient inn with black-timbered gables and flower-filled gardens. Both sides of the street were lined with quaint cottages. Children played outside. There were bairns in prams and mothers chatting, and a lazy, easy feeling to the place that immediately put Nell at ease.

Stopping the cart outside the inn, Nell got down and went inside. 'I'm looking for a man by the name of Albert Slater,' she told the astonished proprietor. 'Can you point me in the right direction?'

A big man with mutton-chop whiskers and a belly like the side of a ship, he was a formidable sight. 'We don't usually have women in here,' he snarled, his beady eyes falling on her swollen stomach.

'I don't mean to stay,' she explained. 'I need directions, that's all.'

'I don't know any Albert Slater,' he lied, 'so you'd best ask elsewhere.' His face was hard, unyielding. As he spoke, he lifted the hatch and pushed open the door. 'I've never had to physically throw out a woman in your condition,' he threatened, 'but there's always a first time.'

Nell didn't like him, and said so. 'You're a bad-tempered devil to be keeping an inn,' she told him. 'I wonder you have any custom at all.'

He jerked his head at the door. 'Out!'

Defiant as ever, Nell drew herself up to her full height. 'I reckon you know where Albert Slater lives.' She'd seen the flicker of interest in the man's face when she'd mentioned that name. 'But don't you worry, I'll find him, with or without your help.'

As she flounced out, he smiled to himself. 'And the best of luck, you little baggage.' Drawing a pint of ale, he drank it down in one go. 'I'd give a month's takings to see Slater's face when he claps eyes on you.'

Nell found a young woman standing by the cart. 'He's a pig!' she said. 'He knows Albert Slater all right.'

Astonished, Nell took stock of the girl. Thin and wiry, she couldn't have been much older than she was herself, but she looked worn by the years and her eyes carried the scars of trouble. She wore a frilly white cap and a waist pinafore. 'I don't suppose the old bugger pays you much either, does he?' From the young woman's appearance, Nell guessed she worked for the landlord.

'He doesn't pay me *anything*,' she answered with a wistful smile. 'But then why should he? He married me, and now he gets the best of both worlds. He acts like a dog in bed and works me like a dog during the day. I get board and lodging and manage to steal a few shillings now and then. I get to drink the slops in the cellar, and I'm allowed one day off a week to ride the bus into Bedford.' Shrugging her thin shoulders she quipped, 'What more could any woman want?'

'I'm sorry.'

'Don't be sorry. You look like you've got your own troubles.' Her gaze travelled over Nell's shabby appearance. The boots she'd left home in were dusty from the road and her clothes were the worse for wear. She'd torn her skirt on a bramble bush and patched it with a square from her petticoat, and now, after helping to shift the crates and then the long journey afterwards, she was incredibly weary.

'Don't let looks fool you,' Nell said defensively. 'It's been a long day, that's all. I'll be right as rain after a dip in the brook and a good night's sleep.'

'You'll have to travel a mile or two before you find a brook round here.'

'My time's my own.' Nell treasured that. 'The sooner

I find Albert Slater, the sooner I can be on my way.'

The young woman spat in the dirt. '*He* could have told you. Him and Albert Slater are sworn enemies. Albert's a decent sort, keeps himself to himself. Sometimes you might not see him for days on end.' Her smile brightened. 'You've not met him before, then?'

Nell shook her head. 'No, but I'm obliged to do business with him.'

'You'll like him. Albert deals fair and square. He can be a good friend and a bad enemy, and he's not afraid to speak out when he sees wrong being done.'

Nell liked him already. 'Where can I find him?'

Taking Nell to the edge of the walkway, the young woman pointed to a house some way down the street. 'See that big place with the long windows and gated archway through to the yard?'

Nell's gaze followed the line of houses down the street. The house in question was painted black and white, with a huge archway to the side, and a market barrow parked at the road edge outside. 'I see the one,' Nell confirmed. 'Will he be home, d'you think?'

The young woman laughed. 'He's always home. Haven't I said, sometimes you don't see him for days on end, except for market days and that's not for another week.'

Nell thanked her and got back on the cart. The young woman followed her. 'When's it due?' she asked, eyeing Nell's bulge with envy.

'I'm not certain to the day,' Nell admitted, 'but I reckon it should be another twelve weeks.'

'First one, is it?'

178

Shame suffusing her face, Nell merely nodded.

'Oh, I see.' The young woman assessed the situation. 'Some man had his way and dumped you, is that it?'

Now it was pride that flooded Nell. 'No. I dumped *him*!'

That made her smile. 'Good for you!' The smile became a frown. 'I wish I had that kind of courage.'

'Would it take that much courage for you to leave him?' Nell had taken to her. In an odd sort of way she could see something of herself in this young woman. They had both been caught in a bad situation.

'One day I *will* leave,' she answered, 'but I'm not ready yet.' Returning to the question of Nell's condition, she asked, 'Have you seen somebody yet, about the birthing, I mean?'

'There's time enough.' Nell had avoided thinking about the day. 'When I need help, I dare say it won't be hard to find.'

'Watch out for the backstreet crows. They'll tear you wide open and take your money into the bargain.'

A shard of fear shot through Nell but she sounded confident as she told the young woman, 'Thanks for the warning, but I expect there are two good women for every old crow. I'll just have to be sure and find one.'

'Good luck then.'

'And good luck to you.'

TWICE NELL PULLED the bell-cord and twice she had the feeling that someone was watching from the window. She waited. No one came. She stepped back, glancing at the bay window. The curtain fluttered. 'Is anyone home?' Stony silence. This time she knocked hard on the door. 'There's someone in there,' she cursed, 'and I'm not going away until they answer.'

'All right, we ain't deaf!' The gruff voice came from an upstairs window. 'What's your business?'

'I'm sorry,' she apologised, looking up, 'only I couldn't get anyone to hear me.' The man didn't look at all like she might have expected. He had a big ruddy face, dishevelled whiskers and a permanent frown creasing his swarthy forehead. 'Are you Albert Slater?'

He seemed taken aback. 'And if I am, what's it to you?'

'Your friend, John Butler, is in trouble. You have to help him.' Exasperated, she added, 'And that's all I'm saying on the doorstep!'

'Whose is the cart?'

'Mine.'

'What's in the crates?'

'Let me in and I'll tell you.' She was puzzled. The description the girl had given her of Albert Slater bore no relation whatsoever to this man.

The window slammed shut, followed by a series of noises from inside the house. She could hear him coughing, then a rattling sound as he unbolted the front door. In a minute the door was inched open and his face appeared. It was even more unpleasant up close. 'You'd better come in.'

The house stank to high heaven. The windows were tightly closed and the curtains half shut. There was half-eaten food on the table, and brown ale spilled down the chair.

Trying hard not to wrinkle her nose, Nell told him what had happened. 'He got most of the stuff out before the bailiffs came, then he set fire to the place. When I left, the bailiffs were out for his blood.' This man didn't seem the compassionate kind, but she appealed to him all the same. 'I mean to go back for him. Will you come?'

'Well, now, that's a silly plan. If he says he'll make his way here, then you can be certain he will. No doubt he'll come over the fields, so it's no good going back by road because we'll be bound to miss each other. No. The sensible thing is to stay and wait for him to turn up here.'

'All the same, I have to try.' She didn't like this man and couldn't understand how he'd earned such a likeable reputation.

'Sit down.' Throwing himself into an armchair, he gestured for her to be seated in the one opposite. He stroked his stubbly chin while he studied the facts. 'We'll do as he says and wait. That's the best thing by my reckoning.' In truth, the best thing by his reckoning was to keep the girl for a bit of entertainment, though it was a shame she'd already been violated. The virgins were always the best, and he should know because he had had enough of them in his time. As for this John Butler who had sent her, he didn't know him and didn't care to. But he'd done him a favour all the same. The girl was tasty, and the horse and cart was bound to come in useful when the time came to make a getaway. Meanwhile he would have to get it out of sight before it raised suspicion, and he would need to make certain the girl stayed here until he was good and ready to let her go.

But what about John Butler? If he should show up

here, it could complicate matters. 'Butler told you to get the produce to me and that he'd turn up here later, isn't that what you said?'

Nell had declined the offer to sit down, fearing she might take the stink with her when she left. 'That's right,' she confirmed. 'That's what he told me.' She was still wondering if she'd come to the right house. 'Are you sure you know who I'm talking about? Maybe I've come to the wrong house. Maybe there's another Albert Slater hereabouts?'

He creased with laughter. 'There's no other Albert Slater that I know of,' he assured her in a softer manner. 'And o' course I'm acquainted with this 'ere feller. We've done plenty of business in the past, and I dare say we'll do plenty in the future.' Leaning forward, he offered, 'Will you have a drink? You look as if a drop of the good stuff wouldn't do you no harm.'

'Thank you kindly but no.' Nell had no intention of staying a minute longer than was necessary, though she was weakened by the day's adventures. Her back felt as though she'd spent the day carrying a sack of coal, and her stomach had grown so heavy it seemed to pull her down.

He saw this and took advantage of it. 'Me and the lad will fetch the cart round the back,' he coaxed. 'Once we've offloaded it, we'll see what we can do about going back for John Butler.' He gestured to the chair again. 'Meanwhile, take the weight off your feet and make yourself comfortable.'

Nell stood her ground though she was sorely tempted.

'Kit!' the man yelled to the ceiling. 'Get down here,

you lazy bastard!' Smiling at Nell, he said in a syrupy voice, 'These lazy lads have to be chivvied along, don't you think?'

The indignant urchin came tumbling down the stairs. 'What's all the shoutin' about?' Small and wiry, with a broad Cockney accent, he had a shock of dark hair and pear-shaped green eyes, so big they seemed too large for his face. Catching sight of Nell he grinned from ear to ear. 'Hello, who's this then, hey?'

'Never you mind.' Before the boy could take his fascinated gaze off Nell, the man had crossed the room and slapped him hard across the head. 'Ain't I told you before about asking questions?' He thrust the boy from him. 'In the kitchen and make the lady a cup of tea or summat. Can't you see she's burdened? And travelled a long way into the bargain.'

The boy's gaze went from Nell's face to her midriff. 'I ain't blind!' he protested. 'And I ain't deaf neither, so you don't need to shout.'

'When you've seen her comfortable, I want you out the back. I'm fetching a horse and cart round and there's work to be done.' In case he wasn't listening, he gave the boy's ear a vicious tweak. It was spiteful enough to make the boy twist away and flee to the kitchen, hand clapped over his ear and his lips moving in silent abuse. 'He'll be back before you know it,' the man told Nell. 'When he's seen you all right, send him out the back, there's a good girl.'

'You're not to touch the wooden cradle at the back of the cart,' Nell instructed. 'It was a gift and I don't want it damaged.'

'Hang me if I even go near it,' he joked. When he saw she wasn't smiling, he left the room and went out of the front door. Nell thought the place seemed a deal cleaner with him gone.

The boy was soon back. 'Why don't you sit yourself down?' he suggested. 'If you don't mind me saying, you look well and truly knackered.'

Nell felt a bubble of laughter rising in her. Such big words from a small parcel, she thought. 'You're right,' she confessed. 'Knackered is exactly the way I would put it.' She glanced at the seat of the chair out of the corner of her eye. It was stained and filthy. 'But I'm all right perched here on the arm.'

He gave a cheeky grin, cocking his head to look at her. 'That seat ain't fit for a lady like you.' Placing the cup in the hearth, he took off his jacket and slung it over the seat of the chair. 'There! Now you can sit yourself down without fear of soiling your skirt.' His laugh was infectious. 'Mind you, I ain't promising you won't catch a flea or two off me jacket. I took it off a scarecrow some weeks back, and I swear to God it's alive.'

He was so cheeky and brash and full of himself that Nell couldn't disappoint him. Besides, she was out on her feet. 'If I do catch a flea,' she said, dropping into the chair, 'you'll know about it, my lad!'

'What's this 'ere business all about?' he queried, handing her the cup. 'I don't like the sound of "work to be done". And whose horse and cart is he talking about anyway?'

'The horse and cart belong to me. It's loaded with crates of fruit and veg. When it's offloaded, your dad's coming back with me to find the man who sent me. He might be hurt, you see.'

Sniggering, the boy jerked a thumb towards the back window. 'He ain't me dad.'

'If he's not your dad, who is he then?'

For a long minute the boy seemed reluctant to say more. 'How do I know I can trust you?' he asked suspiciously. 'I don't know you from the chimney sweep.'

'I don't know you either,' Nell reminded him, 'or that man outside. For all I know you could be a pair of imposters.'

Looking at her with his big green eyes, he seemed such a pathetic little thing, but when he spoke, he was a wise old man. 'Naw, we ain't no imposters,' he assured her with a tut. 'The geezer outside is old man Slater. He found me rummaging for food in the midden and brought me inside. He give me as much food as I could eat, an' then he give me me own room to sleep in.' He rolled his eyes. 'I ain't never 'ad me own room before. Cor! It's a bleedin' treat, I can tell yer.'

'Where's your family?'

'Ain't never 'ad none.'

Nell felt drawn to the lad. 'Everybody has a family of sorts.'

'Not me. Soon as ever I could walk, I knew I were on me own. I were brought up in an orphanage, an' soon as I got the chance, I ran off. That's when I came to this house an' old man Slater took me in.'

'Is Kit your real name?'

Shrugging his shoulders, he said casually, 'Who knows? Don't matter though, does it?' In spite of his bravado, there was a quiver in his voice.

Nell knew exactly what he meant. 'No, I don't suppose it does matter.'

'Well, that's my story,' he said chirpily. 'I reckon you'd best tell me yours.' He sat cross-legged on the floor, his huge green eyes swivelled up to her. 'I have to keep one step ahead of this 'ere gent. At first I reckoned he'd taken me in out of the goodness of his 'eart, but I soon found out he'd got himself a cheap workhorse.' His thin, dirty features broke into a grin. 'He's a cunning old ratbag but his bark's worse than his bite. I could do worse, I reckon.'

Nell felt less anxious at his words. There must be some good in a man who would take this boy in and give him a home. And even if he was expected to work in exchange, there was nothing wrong with that. She had been made to work like a dog all her life, and that in itself had never hurt her. In fact, there were times when work had been her saviour. Still, why was Slater so different from what she'd been told to expect? 'Do you know anything about him?' she asked.

'Only that he's got a brother who he's not seen for years. He's expecting him any day, that's what he says, but you're the first to knock on that door in a week – that's how long I've been here.'

'So, before you came along, he lived here alone?'

''S right.'

The old man back at the cottage played on her mind. 'Won't he be wanting you to help offload?' She had to get back.

'Aw, let him wait.'

He was visibly startled when Slater's voice carried in from the yard. 'Kit! Where the hell are you?'

He chuckled. 'Looks like the old sod's missing me.' Like a spring uncoiling, he rose from the floor. 'I'd best be off before he throws a fit.' Still chuckling, he ran out to the yard, straight into a mouthful of abuse.

Nell drank her tea and let her gaze wander round the room. It had the distinct markings of a man: big heavy furniture, dark carpets and moth-eaten curtains. There was an air of neglect that most women wouldn't tolerate, and the pungent smell of pipe tobacco lingered in the air like a thick, choking cloud. 'This place needs a woman's touch,' she muttered, sipping at the hot, welcoming tea. 'But not mine. I'd sleep in a ditch before I'd stay here.'

Assured by the fact that she had found the right man, even though he did seem short-tempered and gruff, and comforted by the heat emanating from the small fire in the grate, Nell relaxed for a while. 'It'll take them some time to offload that cart,' she reasoned, 'so I might as well rest while I've got the chance.'

Her ankle was still giving her trouble. 'Damn the thing!' she cursed, rubbing the palm of her hand over the tender bone. 'You'd think it would be better by now.' Every day she'd found a way to bathe and dress it, and still it gave her grief. As if that wasn't enough to contend with, the child in her belly was never still; kicking and struggling, it sapped her strength and made the days seem never-ending. The child had been extra active today. 'Be still,' she murmured, placing her hand over the bulge. 'Give me room to breathe.'

Leaning back in the chair, she sipped at the tea and closed her eyes, letting the gentle heat flow over her and enjoying the rest. Her eyelids grew heavy. 'Mustn't go to sleep,' she warned herself. 'I've got to be ready when they've finished . . . must get back to the old man.' Like a tidal wave the weariness flowed through her. 'Must get . . . back to the . . . old man . . .' Her senses began to dim.

Out in the yard, Slater was heaving a crate off the cart when he realised Kit had stopped working and was moving towards the cellar.

'Hey!' Grabbing the boy by the scruff of the neck, Slater yanked him back from the cellar steps. 'You bugger, what did I tell you?'

Surly at being treated like a two-year-old, Kit glared at him. 'Can't remember.' He remembered well enough but his curiosity was getting the better of him. Why was Slater so secretive about the contents of his cellar?

'Liar!' Slater shook him so hard his eyes rolled like thrown dice. 'You remember all right. I told you to keep out of the cellar, and here you are, trying to sneak in the minute my back's turned.'

'Sorry, guv.' Kit looked suitably sheepish but he wasn't a bit sorry.

'You will be if I catch you at it again.' Thrusting the boy away, he gestured to the half-emptied cart. 'Get the rest of them crates off and pile 'em up here.' Pointing to a cleared area at the top of the cellar steps, he grumbled, 'I'll take them down into the cellar, not you, and you'd best remember that or you can piss off, back to the orphanage where you came from.'

That was enough to shut Kit up. He toiled for the next half-hour, unloading the crates and piling them up on the spot where he'd been shown, all the while looking daggers at the older man. 'Send me back to the orphanage, would you?' he muttered as he worked. 'That's for me to say, not you.'

Once, when Slater was in the cellar, he dared to walk halfway down the steps and peer in, but suddenly Slater was on his way back and he had to run for it. 'What's the crafty bugger got in there?' he mused. 'Must be worth a bob or two or he wouldn't be so bleedin' jumpy.' An idea came to him then. 'It might pay me to bide me time till he's snoring in his bed tonight. Then I might just take a little gander in that there cellar.' He'd picked many a lock in his time so it shouldn't be too difficult.

Half an hour later the work was done. Slater carefully locked the cellar door. Delighted with his little hoard, he told the boy, 'That lot should fetch a pretty penny. The furniture is good, solid stuff, and that cradle is a work of art. We'll have to shift the fruit and veg a bit quick though, before it goes rotten.'

Kit recalled what Nell had said, and he was on her side. 'That cradle's not yours to sell,' he reminded him. 'She'll be up in arms when she knows you took it off the cart.' His reward was a slap round the ear.

'Keep your trap shut then,' Slater told him. 'If she doesn't look under the sheet she won't even know it's gone.'

He led the way inside, with Kit following at a safe distance. 'That's where you're wrong, you old bastard,' he muttered under his breath. 'She'll know because I'll tell her!'

Slater entered the room first, and what he saw brought a smile to his face. 'Well now, isn't that a pretty sight?'

Nell was fast asleep, the cup still in her hand and her head lolling to one side. Her legs were stretched out towards the fire, a snippet of frilly petticoat peeping from beneath her skirt, and her fair hair shining like gold in the firelight.

Kit would have gone to her but the man stopped him. 'Don't wake her,' he whispered. 'Let a hungry man get his fill first.'

'She wants to get back to the old feller.' Kit didn't like the glitter in Slater's eyes. 'She'll not thank us for letting her sleep.'

Slater spun round. 'Get back out and unharness the animal,' he hissed. 'Turn it loose in the back field and hide the cart in the barn.'

'What's the point o' that?' Kit nodded in Nell's direction. 'You heard what she said, she'll be looking to leave the minute she's awake.'

Slater's grin was evil. 'We'd be sorry creatures if we didn't persuade her to stay the night,' he murmured. 'A woman in her condition needs her rest, and look at her.' He turned and smiled at the sleeping figure. 'The poor little sod's out on her feet.'

'If I turn the horse loose he might not come back.'

'Don't be so bloody daft!' Slater snarled. 'The thing has to eat, doesn't it? It can't live on fresh air. We've no food here so it can get a belly full of grass from the field.

It'll be back. Horses always find their way back.'

'Maybe, but–'

'But nothing. I've given you a job to do, so get out and do it.' He pressed his face close to the boy's. 'Unless you want to be turned out an' all.'

The boy's sorry gaze went to Nell's quiet face. 'You ain't gonna touch her, are you?'

Slater looked shocked, then he smiled, asking softly, 'What kind of a man d'you think I am? You surely can't think I'd take advantage of a helpless woman? Besides, haven't I just said how she needs her rest?'

Unsure, Kit hesitated. 'All right then, but you'd better be telling the truth.'

Scowling, Slater tried hard not to let his feelings show. Instead he said sweetly, 'I'm going into the kitchen to make meself a nightcap, then I'm off to me bed for a good night's sleep. Does that satisfy you?'

It didn't. But he had to trust him, and anyway, the sooner he got the work done, the sooner he could get back and keep an eye on things.

Outside, he paused to peer in through the window, and sure enough he saw Slater go off in the direction of the kitchen. 'Right!' He glanced at the horse which seemed content enough for the moment. 'I'll see to you later,' he said. Then he hurried towards the cellar and cautiously went down the steps. His heart was fluttering like a bird's wings, and his tongue was so dry it stuck to the roof of his mouth. 'Hurry up, Kit!' he gabbled. 'For Gawd's sake, hurry up!'

The lock was more difficult than he'd imagined. 'If only I had more time I'd do it,' he told himself, 'but there ain't no time, so it'll have to be brute force. He won't know any better than what someone else came and broke in during the night.' He put his hands together in a gesture of prayer. 'Unless you want him to break me poor neck, don't let him catch me at it.'

Prising a piece of wood from the door frame, he wedged it tight behind the lock and forced it upwards. There was a sound of creaking, and then a sharp, surprising snap as the lock sprang open. 'I ain't lost the old touch yet,' he congratulated himself. Sneaking down the stairs, he recalled how Slater had replaced a box of matches on the ledge just inside the doorway. 'Quick now, let's see what he's hiding that's so bleedin' precious.'

The matches were easily found. After he'd struck one he crept forward. 'Phew! What a stink!' It was so overwhelming, he held his nose, tempted to turn tail and run. 'No. You wanted to find out what was down here, so you'd best get on with it.'

The crates were piled to the right and the furniture to the left, leaving a narrow way between. As he felt his way forward, the match went out and burned his fingers. 'Ouch! Bleedin' thing.' He lit another and pressed on.

'There ain't nothing down here that I can see,' he muttered. 'But why was he so eager to keep me out?' Apart from the furniture and crates, the only other money spinner he could see was a handsome pile of coal beneath the manhole in the far corner. 'Batty old sod,' he muttered. 'Bet he thought it was a joke, making me think there was valuables down 'ere.' He squealed as the second match burned down to his fingers.

As he struck another, his attention was caught by a bulky sack lying in a niche, so cleverly hidden it was a wonder he'd seen it at all. 'Maybe this is what he's been hiding, eh?' A huge smile crossed his face as he dragged the sack into the doorway. 'It's bleedin' heavy, I know that.' His face went red from the effort. 'Better be worth me while.' When he dropped the sack, it seemed to sigh and roll before coming to rest at his feet. 'Silver, I shouldn't wonder. Outta one of the big houses hereabouts.'

Being nearer the door now, and with the light shining down from the sitting room, he blew out the match. 'Don't need to draw attention to meself. I've been out here too long as it is.'

Half expecting to see the crown jewels, he gingerly opened the mouth of the bag. Straight away he was knocked back by the stink. 'Jesus! Smells like rotten eggs and dead dogs rolled into one.' All the same, his curiosity got the better of him. He'd come this far and now he had to know.

Slowly, he opened the bag wider, and when he saw what was staring back at him, he fell against the wall, his eyes sticking out like beacons and his mouth open in a silent scream. Horrible though it was, he couldn't look away.

The man's face was upturned, his eyes bulging open and the fine cord still knotted round his neck. There was a thin line where the blood had oozed out and run down his shirt. On his face was a sinister grimace, almost as though he'd been caught in the middle of a smile which was held for all time.

'Christ Almighty!' Kit was visibly trembling. 'What's he done? Gawd, what's he done?' Even now he couldn't believe that Slater was capable of committing murder.

Too much time had passed. He took a moment to gather his wits. 'If he finds out I've been here, he'll do for me too.' Quickly, and with his face turned away, he took the sack by the legs and dragged it back where he'd found it. Now he knew why it was so heavy.

Grabbing the wooden cradle, he fled that place as if the devil himself was after him.

Once outside, he took great gulps of air into his lungs. Then he set about making good the door. 'Maybe 'e didn't do it,' he muttered as he worked. 'Maybe 'e doesn't even know it's in 'ere.' He wanted to believe that, but his deeper instincts told him otherwise.

Another, different instinct told him not to unharness the horse. 'I don't know what 'e's up to,' he told the dozing creature, 'but I'm leaving you ready for a quick getaway.' The cradle was more cumbersome than he thought, but he managed to sling it on to the cart and hide it beneath the tarpaulin. 'It ain't his to keep,' he said, 'and neither is *she*.'

NELL WOKE WITH a cry. He was all over her. 'Take your mucky hands off me!' she told him, striking out and scoring his face. 'Get off! Leave me be!' His hand was up her skirt, frantically tugging at her knickers; his face was against hers and she could feel the sweat on his skin. She opened her mouth to scream but he pressed his hand over her face. 'It won't matter to me whether you suffocate or not,' he warned her grimly. 'You've got me riled and now I can't be calmed.'

He was greatly excited and sweating profusely as his groping hands laid bare her thighs. Filled with a terrible anger and desperately afraid for her baby, Nell pleaded with her eyes but he merely smiled into them. 'You're a handsome little thing, and it ain't as if I'm the first, is it? You've had a man before, so you know what to expect.' Unbuttoning his trouser front, he lurched forward, ready to thrust himself into her. His weight was crippling. Frantic, Nell tried to push him off but her efforts were fruitless against his brute strength. 'Don't struggle,' he hissed at her. 'I've killed once. Twice won't matter.'

Just when she feared it was too late, there was a scream from the doorway. 'Filthy bastard!' Kit launched himself through the air, landing on Slater's back with a thump. 'Murderer!' he cried. Swinging on the big fellow and pummelling him with his puny fists, he shouted, 'I know what you hid in the cellar.' Incensed, the big man roared out, locking his great arms round the boy. The two of them rolled to the floor, with Kit fighting like a tiger, but he was no match for the heavier man. Pinning him to the ground, Slater put his two hands round Kit's throat and began squeezing. For one awful minute, Nell thought the boy would pay with his life.

Scrambling out of the chair, she rushed to the fireplace and picked up the poker. Raising her arm, she was about to bring it down on the back of Slater's head when he spun round and grabbed her by the ankle. With a cry of pain she fell to the ground. The poker rolled within the boy's grasp and without a second thought he grabbed it and clubbed Slater.

Any other man might have been knocked unconscious by the blow, but not Slater. Moaning in agony, he crumpled into a ball, his hands over his face and the blood trickling through his fingers.

'Out the back, quick!' Kit propelled Nell out of the house and into the yard where the horse was standing, head down and deep in slumber. When he heard Nell's voice, he was suddenly alert. 'There's no time to open the gates,' Kit shouted. As he spoke, Slater appeared at the back door. Slowly, he advanced on them.

Grabbing the reins, Nell told Kit to hold on. At first, when she swung the horse and cart towards the gates, Slater watched in amazement, then when it was clear what she was about to do, he cowered against the wall and covered his face with his arms.

'Jesus!' The boy was having the time of his life. 'You're mad as a bleedin' hatter!' he yelled.

Grim-faced and praying the horse would not be hurt, she urged him on, across the yard and straight into the centre of the gates where she knew they would give way more easily. 'Go on, feller!' she yelled, and he did. Like a battering ram he went, head down, chest braced, and the gates were flung asunder, with splinters flying in all directions.

'Bleedin' Nora!' Kit ducked, laughing and screeching as they came into the street and safety. 'Keep going,' he yelled. 'Keep going, you bugger!'

They sped through the village and didn't stop until they reached a quiet lane. Nell climbed down, took up the lantern and gave it to the boy. The two of them went to inspect the horse who was snorting and excited. 'All right, are you, old feller?' she asked lovingly. 'I'm sorry we had to do that, but we didn't have much choice.'

Apart from a small cut over his brow, the horse had suffered no apparent damage. 'He seems all right,' she told Kit. 'I'll be able to check him better in the daylight.' Relieved that the water bucket was still slung beneath the cart, she brought it to the horse. 'We lost a fair measure in the run, but there's enough for us all.' She gave Kit first swig, then herself, and finally the horse. He stuck his head down and it seemed as though he'd drink every last drop, but when Nell checked, there was still enough to bathe his wound.

Tearing a strip of muslin from her skirt, she dipped it into the water and applied it to the cut above his brow. 'It doesn't seem too deep,' she observed in the half-light. 'I dare say he's had worse in his time.' While she prodded and dabbed, the horse stood perfectly still, seeming grateful to be out of that yard and on the open road again.

A moment later they were on their way. 'Where to now?' Kit was nervous. Everything had happened so fast and there was no telling what Slater might do. He could follow them, and he'd already proved he was capable of murder.

'I have to find the old man,' Nell answered, heading the horse and cart in the direction she remembered. 'I need to know he's all right. He was in real trouble. I should never have left him.'

'I heard you tell Slater the old man was on the run from the bailiffs. Is that the truth?'

'Course it was the truth!'

'Then you did right to leave. What's the use of you both being caught?'

'You may be right,' Nell had to admit, 'but I still feel bad about it, and now there's even more to be reckoned with.'

'How's that?'

'All that stuff on the cart was his. His lovely furniture. The fruit and veg which he risked his life to save. He meant to sell it so he could get a new start, and now it's all gone. How am I going to tell him?'

'You just tell him. There ain't no easy way that I can see.' Kit sighed, leaning back into the hard wooden seat. 'One thing's for sure, *I* ain't going back there for it. Neither will you, if you value your life.'

'That man Slater was meant to be his friend.' How right her instincts had been about that sorry creature. 'Is he really a murderer?'

Pretending not to have heard her, the boy sniffled. 'It's all the excitement,' he lied. 'I always get the sniffles when I'm shook up.' Hugging himself in the cool night air, he grumbled on, 'For a girl, you've got some spunk. You went through them gates like a bat out of hell.' He coughed and sniffled again. 'I reckon I'm catching a bleedin' cold, thanks to you.'

'Kit!'

'What?'

'Is he a murderer?' There were all manner of questions in her mind.

He suspected she wouldn't give up, so he answered honestly. 'Too bleedin' true.'

'How d'you know?'

'I just know, that's all.'

She looked at him. 'You said he had something hidden in the cellar.'

'I don't think you want to know about that, lady.'

'The name's Nell.'

'Pretty name.' In the light of the rising moon, he gave her a long stare. 'Pretty face too.'

'So what was it?' Nell persisted.

'What?'

'The thing he had hidden in the cellar. What was it?'

'I ain't saying.'

Stopping the cart, Nell told him, 'We'd better part company here.'

His face opened with horror. 'What? You mean you're throwing me off? In the middle o' nowhere?'

'I don't want to but I will.'

'What the bleedin' hell for? I saved you from him, didn't I?'

'Yes, and I'm very grateful.'

'You'd be daft to get rid o' me. Who knows, I might even come in useful again.'

'Maybe.' Nell really liked him; sensing a kindred spirit in this brash little waif, she admitted, 'I dare say you'll make a fine travelling companion too, but we have to be honest with each other or it's no good.'

He took a moment to consider her comment before saying firmly, 'I were only thinking o' you, Nell. What I found in that cellar made me 'air stand on end. It ain't summat you should know about, not when you're in *that* condition.' He glanced at her big, round belly. 'I might frighten you into 'aving it 'ere and now.' He looked genuinely scared. 'Honest to Gawd, Nell, I wouldn't know what to do.'

Nell's laughter put him at ease. 'I'm not about to have the baby here and now,' she told him. 'I'm not squeamish either. You can tell me what you found and I promise not to pass out.' His anxiety endeared him to her all the more. It showed that, for all his cheek and swagger, he was just a little lad in the dark.

'I found a dead man,' he whispered, 'trussed up in a sack, with a cord round his neck.' He ran his finger across his throat, shivering. 'He were staring at me, grinning like. It were awful!'

Nell sat rigid on her seat. She had never seen death close up, and here, in this place, it was hard to imagine. The moonlight filtered through the overhanging branches and the gentle breeze rustled the treetops. Now and then the moon floated behind sinister shadows, throwing the world into a strange, shifting darkness. The night grew chilly, and the sounds of creatures were all around. This was the world Nell knew and loved. This was the world she had come to hide in when things became too much to bear.

It had become a lonely existence; long days and quiet, fleeting nights. During these times she would think of Bill and long to be near him. But that was just a dream, and dreams rarely came true for someone like her. And so she spent her waking hours wisely, and gathered her strength during the sleeping hours. The night was her friend, and she had come to know there was nothing in the dark to hurt her.

Kit, however, was more used to daylight and people all around – markets, race meetings, busy places where he could mingle unobtrusively. He'd wait his chance and pick pockets and, like any small boy, hated the idea of what might be lurking in the depths of a night like this. 'You don't reckon the bugger's followed us, do yer?' His huge green eyes darted nervously in one direction then another. An owl cried out and he nearly had a fit. 'Gawd help us, I thought that were him!'

'Well, it wasn't, so stop worrying. Anyway, if he turns up, we'll just run him over.' Nell chuckled. It helped to clear her mind of the awful things he'd described.

'It ain't funny.'

'That man in the cellar.' Nell had a shocking thought. 'Do you think he was the real Albert Slater?'

'I dunno.' Kit was puzzled. 'What makes you think that?'

Nell recalled the descriptions she'd been given about the Albert Slater she had been sent to find. 'The old man said he was a good bloke, and the girl at the inn described him as fair and square, someone who wasn't afraid to speak out against wrongdoing. You wouldn't think it was the same man, would you?' The more she thought about it, the more she was convinced he was an imposter. 'The old man trusted Albert Slater. How could anybody trust that man back there?'

'So?'

'You said he'd got a brother, didn't you?'

'That's right.' He caught his breath. 'Hey, you don't

reckon that were his brother in the cellar, d'you?' He sat bolt upright in his seat. 'P'raps Slater killed him and took possession o' the 'ouse! Maybe that's why he yelled blue murder if I so much as showed me face at the winder. Every time we went out it were at night, an' that were only to steal food from any place we could break in.' Only now did he fully realise the kind of man he'd been living with. 'Gawd Almighty! I might have been killed in me bed!' Staring at Nell, he asked in a hushed voice, 'D'you really think he killed his own brother?'

'Whether it's his own brother or not, we both heard him admit to killing,' Nell recalled. 'First chance we get, we'll have to let the authorities know. If there's any justice, he'll hang for it.'

'By the time we get near to any constabulary, he'll be long gone, taking your goods and the body too, I shouldn't wonder.'

'How will he shift them? There was no cart or wagon that I could see.'

'That won't stop him. He'll steal one.'

'When we've found the old man, we'll go straight to the authorities and tell them what we know. Don't you worry, they'll find him. He'll pay for what he's done.'

'I ain't got nobody now.' The boy's voice was suspiciously croaky.

'That's where you're wrong,' Nell told him softly. 'You've got me.' Reaching out to take hold of his hand, she was astonished at how cold it was. 'By! You're freezing. Hold on, I'll get you a blanket.'

'I'm all right,' he told her sharply. 'I ain't no bleedin'

sissy, an' I ain't cold neither.' He cocked his head towards the back of the cart. 'Slater had your cradle an' I grabbed it back, so I expect he's 'ad your blankets away an' all.'

'He took the cradle?' In the chaos Nell had forgotten. 'And you got it back?'

'I nearly left it, I don't mind admitting.' He shivered again at the thought of that dead man's eyes.

'Thank you, Kit.' If the cradle had been lost, she would have had to go back for it. 'The old man gave me that cradle and it means a lot to me.' She looked over her shoulder to where the sheet was secured at the back end of the cart. 'Shall I see if there's a blanket for you?'

He glared at her. 'I already told you, I don't want no sissy blanket.'

'Have it your own way.' She clicked her tongue and the horse moved off, his big round hooves making a soft, muffled sound as they plodded along the lane.

They continued in silence for a long time; out of the lane and on to the highway, going at a trot, closer and closer to the burned-out cottage and that brave old man. And all the time the boy clattered his teeth and shivered, and felt ashamed that he'd betrayed his fears of the night to this slip of a girl. He wanted her to be proud of him, to know she could rely on him any time, anywhere. Now he felt he'd shown himself to be less of a man than he thought he was. The dark had always frightened him, and he hated the cold. There was no fat on his bones to keep it out, and right now he felt as though he was dying.

Nell had grown used to the cold. She'd lived in it

and slept in it and was now hardened to it. All the same, it was growing chillier by the minute. Winter was never far away, and October nights could be spiteful, as this one was.

Kit broke the silence. 'Just now,' he said through chattering teeth, 'when I wouldn't tell you about that dead man?'

'Yes?' Nell was relieved he was talking again.

'Would you really have thrown me off?'

Nell's blue eyes glittered with mischief. 'I might have.'

'*Would* you though?'

'You know I wouldn't. Like you said, you did save me back there.' The thought of that man touching her bare flesh made her cringe. As soon as they'd made sure John Butler was all right, she meant to take a dip in the nearest brook.

Kit grinned, his small, straight teeth surprisingly white in the moonlight. 'I knew you were joshing,' he lied. He fell silent again, thankful to be seated on the cart and leaving that house behind. But he was so tired. In a disgruntled voice he inquired, 'How far is it to where we're going?'

'Not too far now.'

'How do you know that?'

'Instinct.' Living in harmony with the elements had honed her sense of direction.

'What if he's dead?' Death was real to him now. He sensed it everywhere.

Nell was shocked. 'I don't want to think about that.' Yet she *had* thought about it. Every minute since he'd sent her away, she had feared for the old man.

The idea of death shocked them both into silence. No words were spoken for a long time. The quiet night was pierced only by the occasional cry of a night thing, and the soft clip-clop of the horse's hooves.

They must have been travelling for twenty minutes when she glanced at the boy. He was slumped to one side, his arms folded and his face white as chalk. 'Kit? Are you all right?' He was so still, she was afraid.

She stopped the cart and leaned over. He was fast asleep. 'Been a busy day, has it?' she murmured, a soft smile gathering on her lovely features. 'Ah, you should be in your own bed, with a dad and mammy downstairs, and a little friend of your own age to meet of a morning.'

Placing the palm of her hand on his cheek, she felt his flesh shiver. 'You might be a man in a hurry,' she said, 'but right now you're only a lad and whether you like it or not, you're getting a blanket.'

Thankfully, the two blankets were still there; big, brown and woolly, they were serviceable and warm. 'It wasn't out of the goodness of your heart that you left them for me, Slater you bugger!' she muttered. 'Though if it hadn't been for the boy there, you might have taken something much more precious, an' that's a fact.'

Drawing one of the blankets from beneath the tarpaulin, she made her way back to Kit who was still fast asleep and cold as a dead fish. 'I owe you a lot,' she murmured as she covered him in the blanket. 'I'll not forget that in a hurry.' She made him comfortable and, resuming her own seat, she took up the reins and softly urged the horse onward. 'Let's find the old one,' she said, 'and pray to God the devils didn't get him.'

Before the horse could put a foot forward, there came a scream that made her blood curdle.

It was the boy.

Realising he was still fast asleep, she dropped the reins and gathered him in her arms. 'Ssh! It's all right,' she murmured. 'Nell's got you now. She won't let nobody hurt you.'

The boy trembled uncontrollably. 'Ssh!' Sliding beneath the blanket with him, she rocked him back and forth in her weary arms, like a mother might rock a baby. 'Ssh, Kit, it's all right.'

'It weren't me!' he called out. 'I didn't know, I swear to Gawd I didn't know. Don't hurt me! Please don't hurt me!' His arms flailed the air and his feet kicked out, catching Nell hard on the ankle that was already giving her grief. 'Get him away! He's looking at me, get him away!' His cries broke into deep racking sobs, shaking his body.

'Ssh!' Nell held on to him, gently easing his fears and softly murmuring against his face. Gradually the cries lessened; the trembling continued for a minute or two, and then he was still, though whimpering now, and very cold to the touch.

She stayed with him, quiet and still, willing the warmth from her body into his. In the moonlight she looked down into his face, such a small face, so grubby and proud. 'Who do you belong to?' she asked softly. 'What brought you to this, eh?' She rocked him, back and forth, back and forth, until her arms felt like lead and her back was throbbing, but she would not leave him until he was safe. 'No man should see what you've seen,' she whispered. 'No man would have been braver.' Her smile was that of a proud woman. 'You're a precious little feller, and I'll never turn you away.' Suddenly tears were rolling down her face. 'I know someone who would make a fine father for you,' she said, her heart aching. 'And that's Bill.'

Bill was always on her mind. Through the minutes and hours, and even when she was crashing through that gate back there, Bill was with her. He would always be with her in spirit. 'He's a good man,' she went on. 'A warm and wonderful man, who I may never see again.' The thought was crippling.

Thinking of him was soothing to her troubled mind. Closing her eyes, she invited him into her heart, and it was a wonderful thing. Sometimes she would consciously keep him out because it caused her pain, but tonight, with the boy sleeping against her breast, the moonlight flickering above and the child inside her, warm and safe, she was filled with a wonderful sense of peace.

By the time the moon dipped low, Nell was deeply asleep.

For the first time in a long time, she was close to another human being; a lonely little soul who had looked to her for comfort and reassurance. In comforting him, she had comforted herself. Over the past months, without her realising it, Nell had missed that vital closeness with another being. Everyone needed someone, and at this vulnerable time in her young life, Nell more than most.

The night closed in, and still they slept, he with his head on her shoulder, she with her arms about him. In those few precious hours while they slept, the bond that had already formed between them grew and strengthened.

When the sun rose on the first birdsong, Nell woke with a start.

'Kit!' Digging him in the ribs, she tried to gather her wits. 'It's morning,' she said, running her hands through her tousled hair. 'We've slept right through the night.' Her first thought was for the old man. 'There's no time for breakfast,' she told Kit before he'd hardly opened his eyes. 'We've got to push on. We can't be that far away now.'

He looked at the blanket and he looked at her. ''Ere!' He rolled out of the blanket. 'What's been goin' on?'

'You had a nightmare,' she explained, 'and you wouldn't stop shivering, so I got in the blanket with you. I wasn't supposed to fall asleep.'

He glared at her, his face one big, disapproving frown. 'You mean you an' me, together?'

'That's what I said.' Nell was amused. Beneath the grime, he was actually blushing.

'You 'ad no bleedin' right!'

'It's my cart.' It was all she could do not to laugh.

'That don't give you no right neither.'

Digging into her skirt pocket, Nell drew out a small comb. Running it through her hair, she told him, 'I'm sorry, it won't happen again. Now we'd best get on our way. We've wasted enough time already.' Settling into her seat, she explained, 'I know you must be hungry, and so am I.' She glanced at the horse who was wide awake and taking his fill of the lush grass beneath the tree. 'There's a brook about four miles away,' she said. 'I wouldn't mind betting it's teeming with fish. We'll have fresh water, and who knows? There might be a miller close by who'll give us some bread for an hour's work. I'll show you how to make a camp fire, and to tell you the truth both of us could do with a dip in the brook.' She wrinkled her nose. 'We've brought the stink from that house with us, I reckon.'

'I ain't dippin' in no brook with you, lady!'

'Nell!'

'Don't make no difference, I still ain't going in that brook with you watching.'

His face was so funny, Nell laughed out loud. 'I'm nearly old enough to be your mother.'

'No, you ain't. I don't know how old I am, an' you can't be above what – sixteen?'

Nell was indignant. 'Never you mind! What are you? Nine?'

'I'm twelve if I'm a day!'

'Nine!' She straightened her skirt and set to leave. 'Ten!'

'All right then, ten.' She smiled at him. 'Happen I'm not old enough to be your mother but there's nothing to say we can't be friends, is there?'

'Don't suppose so.'

'Stop arguing then and pull that blanket up. It's touching the cart wheel. I don't want it snarled up.'

'Bossy bugger, ain't you?'

'So they tell me.'

'I ain't ready to go anywhere yet.'

'Why's that?'

'I want a piss.'

'I beg your pardon?' The look she gave him spoke volumes.

'Sorry, Nell.' And he looked it. 'But I have to go or I'll wet me pants. Honest to Gawd.'

'Behind the tree. Hurry up, Kit. Please!'

The huge, sad eyes bored into hers. 'You won't leave me, will you?'

'Never,' she said, and her warm, generous smile was all the reassurance he needed.

When at last they got started, Nell was frantic. Suppose the old man was gone? Where would she find him then? 'What if he's already making his way to that house?' she suggested. 'We'll have to go back. He won't know what he's walking into. He probably doesn't know that man from Adam, and like Slater said, he's killed once, twice won't matter.'

'I ain't going back there.' That was the little boy speaking.

'I'll have to go on my own then.' Nell was determined.

'If you go, I go an' all.' That was the little man speaking.

'Let's hope we find him first.' Nell half hoped to meet the old man along the road. 'He might well be travelling the same road as us,' she said. 'Keep your eyes peeled for him. He's small, with a weathered, round face and a sour expression.'

'Bad-tempered old sod, is he?'

Nell smiled, recalling how he'd snapped at her. 'You could say that,' she confirmed, 'but his heart's in the right place.'

Nell recalled the way he had fought to defend what was his. She knew little of him but, during the short time she'd spent in his company, she had learned to respect him. A man like that, old and alone, deserved a friend, and though she could not help him in practical terms, she hoped she could at least be his friend.

'I know Slater were bad,' Kit said, 'but he were the only friend I ever had.' He looked up at her, his mind ticking over, asking questions that wouldn't stay in. 'Have *you* got a friend, Nell?'

'I've got you, haven't I?'

'Naw. I mean yes, but what about where you come from? Did you have a friend there?'

'A very good friend, by the name of Molly.' Nell's heart never ached more than it ached at that moment. 'I miss her.'

'Ain't you seen her in a long time?'

'No, but I've managed to get word to her now and then. Course she can't get word to me because I never know where I am from one day to the next.'

'Is she pretty?'

Nell laughed out loud. 'Not what you'd call pretty,' she admitted, 'but she's much more than that. She's good and kind, and has a heart of gold.' She paused, composing herself enough to tell him, 'I love her very much.'

'What about a boy friend?'

Nell shook her head. 'I don't have a boy friend.' Turning, she saw how he was looking at her in puzzlement. 'I know what you're thinking,' she said, 'but I'm not lying. It wasn't a boy friend who did this. It was more . . .' She couldn't think of the right way to explain. He was just a boy, and she was out of her depth. 'It was the man I worked for,' she said regretfully. 'A bad mistake.'

'Does that mean you'll give the bairn away when it comes?'

Shaken by the very idea, Nell said stonily, 'If anybody tries to take this bairn from me, they'll rue the day.'

'Why ain't you got a boy friend? You're a good-looker.'

'Maybe I don't want one.'

'All girls want a boy friend.'

'I'm not a girl. I'm a grown woman.'

'Same thing.' He gave her a sly glance. 'You love him, and he don't love you, I'll bet that's the truth.'

Nell had to smile. 'You're too old for your years,' she told him. 'All right, there is someone, and no, he doesn't love me. At least, not in the same way I love him.' As she talked, memories of Bill warmed her heart. 'He's like a brother to me. Over the years I came to love him in a different way, but he never knew, and now he never will.' That was the sadness of it, that Bill would never know how she really felt about him.

'Why didn't you tell him?'

'Because there would have been no point. We had something very special between us, and I didn't

212

want to lose that by making him feel guilty.'

He made a grim face. 'Women!' Rolling his eyes, he snuggled down. 'I'll never understand 'em.'

Nell chuckled. Then she set her sights on the road ahead, determined to get to John Butler as fast as she could.

B Y THE TIME they rounded the lane that would take them to the field where she'd left the old man, it was pouring with rain. 'I'm bleedin' drenched!' Kit complained, poking his finger through a tear in the tarpaulin. 'This thing's full of holes.'

When the rain started, Nell had taken the tarpaulin off the cradle and put it over the two of them but it hadn't kept out the rain; now they were both soaked to the skin. 'We'll see if the old man's got a decent sheet we can have,' she promised. 'Stop moaning and keep your eyes open.'

With the rain coming down in torrents and the sky blocked by clouds, the day had taken on a darker face. It was difficult to see anything, but Nell stayed vigilant. 'Here!' Bringing the cart to a halt, she pointed to the break in the hedge. 'This is where I took the cart in,' she explained, 'and there's the shelter where he hid all his stuff.' Somewhere in the back of her mind, Nell had half expected the shelter to be razed to the ground. 'And it's still standing.'

'Thank Gawd for that,' Kit cried. 'Run the bleedin' cart in the field then so we can get out the rain.'

'We'll have to walk from here,' she told him. 'The

rain's muddied the field ankle-deep. If I take the cart in there, I might not get it out again in a hurry.' Jumping down, she attended to the horse. Undoing the harness, she dropped the shafts and led him by his halter into the field. 'Come on, old feller. Let's get you in the dry,' she said, and the sound of her voice was soothing to his ears.

'Hey! Wait for me.' Kit wouldn't be left behind. By the time Nell reached the shelter, he was there beside her. 'Why ain't the doors pulled to?' he wondered aloud. 'You'd think the silly old sod would want to keep out the rain.'

'When I left, he'd set fire to the cottage and was being fired at by the bailiffs. What time would he have to shut the doors?'

It was dry in the shelter, and surprisingly warm. Nell commented on that.

'These old wood buildings hold the heat,' Kit explained with the wisdom of an old owl. 'There ain't no sign o' your old man though, is there?'

Nell looked round the barn. It was small but cosy. The back wall was stacked with all manner of items – pieces of furniture; wheelbarrows and other tools of the land. There was a delightful old rocking chair which Nell assumed must have belonged to his wife, and a few boxes showing crockery and jars of various shapes and sizes. The remaining crates of fruit and produce were stacked to one side. 'I can't understand it,' she said. 'All his possessions are still here. Why didn't the bailiffs take them?'

'Maybe they didn't find 'em.' Poking about in a crate, Kit drew out a big rosy apple. Sinking his teeth in it, he spoke while he chewed, the juice running down his chin. 'It's all right 'ere, ain't it? Are we staying?'

Nell wasn't listening. 'The bailiffs were up at the cottage. They saw him down here and started towards us. The old man seemed certain he could dodge them. He told me he'd make his way to Albert Slater's and that I was to get there as fast as I could.'

'You did your part, Nell. It weren't your fault if poor Albert went an' got himself done in.' He finished off the apple and found another, while Nell decided to take another look around.

HOURS PASSED AND still there was no sign of the old man.

'The bugger's run off an' 'e ain't coming back.' Kit was tired. Nell left the horse to his own devices and came to sit beside him. 'Think about it, Kit,' she urged. 'If the bailiffs had found the goods, they'd have taken them, wouldn't they?'

'The buggers'll take your eyeteeth if you so much as open your mouth.'

Nell agreed. 'Right. So they didn't come this far, and they didn't find the goods. And if that's the case, why didn't the old man close the doors after they'd gone?'

'Search me.' By this time he was grappling with the horse for the rosiest apple in the crate.

'I'll tell you why.' Nell leaped to her feet. 'They didn't find this little lot because the old man led them away from here.'

'You mean they've got him?' Fearing the worst, his

215

eyes swivelled in his head. 'That'll be the last you'll see of him then.'

Nell was pacing the floor. 'Either they took him off or he managed to get away. If he got away, why didn't he turn up at Slater's? And why didn't we see him along the road?'

'He probably kept to the fields.'

'Maybe, but I don't think so. I think he would have waited till they'd gone and then come back to secure this barn. He would never have left the doors wide open for any passing Gypsy to help himself.' She gestured with her two hands, encompassing the things hidden there. 'All this stuff is so precious to him, the produce and the money it can bring him. And his wife's things especially.'

'You're getting all worked up for nothing.' Pausing to slap the horse round the ear when it nicked the apple from his fist, he sorted another from the crate. 'Look, Nell. If I were that old man and the bailiffs were after me, I'd be away like the wind. I wouldn't stop to find out if they'd found this place or not.'

'I don't know what to think.'

'I'm tellin' you! I've had to run a time or two from people like that, an' if it were me, I'd stay hidden till they stopped looking for me, then I'd keep to the ditches and make my way to where I was going. That's what he's done, and that's how we missed him.' He nodded towards the doors. 'I expect he's at Slater's house now.'

'Well, if he is, I hope Slater's long gone.'

'If he ain't long gone, he'll be lying to save his life. Knowing him, he'll probably tell the old man you stole his crates an' that the pair of 'em should be out looking for us.'

Nell bolted the door. 'That settles it,' she declared. 'As soon as the rain stops, we're heading back.'

'What? You must be mad.'

'I made a promise, and leave them apples alone. You'll get colic.'

'Tell that to the 'orse.' He glanced at Clarence who was already on his third apple. 'What's good for 'im is good for me.'

Nell tethered the horse away from the crates, then she found a bucket and filled it with rainwater. Placing it where the animal could reach, she told Kit, 'I'm sure the old man won't mind us helping ourselves to a few apples. Get some sleep now. I'll wake you when the rain stops and we'll be on our way.'

CURLED UP IN the corner amidst the paraphernalia, Kit slept soundly, his belly filled with apples and his clothes dried stiff on his back.

The horse slept standing up, his head bowed and one leg crooked comfortably at the joint; he even snored a little, the flap of skin round his lips shivering in the rush of air. He was warm and dry, and thankfully he, too, had taken his fill of apples without suffering too much.

Nell couldn't sleep; a few minutes' snoozing and a few minutes' listening, always alert, even when her eyes were closed.

The rain fell ceaselessly, though inside the shelter

she felt cosy enough. 'So this is my family now,' she thought, glancing at the sleeping boy and smiling at the horse as he snored. 'God help me then.' She chuckled softly, tried to get comfortable enough to sleep, but remained wide awake and anxious.

She pushed back one of the doors and peered out. 'Looks like the heavens are full of a storm,' she murmured, her eyes scanning the dark, shifting skies.

Lowering her gaze, she looked to the horizon, searching for the old man. 'Where are you?' she whispered. 'Did they take you away, or have you found a worse fate at Slater's house?' She looked again at the sky. 'If it doesn't clear soon, I'll start back anyway.' The idea of returning to that house and its gruesome secret was a dreadful prospect, but what choice had she? And anyway, she had nowhere else in particular to go. 'We'll call at the constabulary first,' she decided. 'Better safe than sorry.' She was restless, aching to be gone.

She closed the door, curled up beside the boy and slept for an hour. When she woke he was still fast asleep, but the light of day was already creeping through the chink in the shutters. She cocked an ear and listened. It was blissfully quiet. No more pitter-patter of rain or the howling wind driving against the side of the barn. 'Thank God!' She sprang up and cried out in pain; her ankle was worse, and she didn't need to take off her boot to know it was badly infected again.

Nell's cry of pain woke the boy. 'What the 'ell's up?' His eyes stuck out like hard green marbles, softening when he saw there was nothing to be afraid of. Rubbing his eyes awake, he asked sleepily, 'What's going on?'

'It's all right.' Nell was quick to reassure him. She made no mention of her ankle. 'It's morning,' she told him with a smile. 'The rain's stopped, so we can get on our way.' Gritting her teeth, she stood up. 'Can you harness the horse?'

'Course I can.' He was indignant. 'Anybody can strap a horse to a cart.'

Nell wasn't convinced. 'You're sure now? I want to go up to the cottage.'

'I thought you said he burned it down.'

'He did.'

'So why do you want to go up there?'

'I need . . .' She blushed to the roots of her hair. 'I need to wash, and as I recall there's a water pump up there.'

He stared at her with astonishment. 'I reckon you won't want washing after being out in all that rain.' He saw how embarrassed she was and gave a cheeky grin. 'Oh, I see. You don't have to go to the cottage though. You can squat behind a bush. I ain't gonna watch.'

She gave him a playful push. 'No, you ain't,' she mimicked. 'You can squat behind a bush if you like but I'm not used to that.' So far she had managed to keep a semblance of dignity and she wasn't going to lower her standards now. But she was growing bigger with every passing day and it was getting more and more difficult to hold herself for as long as she used to. 'I won't be long,' she promised. 'Make sure you secure the doors.'

'Are we taking this stuff with us?' He gestured to the crates and furniture.

'I've thought about that and I don't believe we

should. It's not ours, and until we know what the old man wants, it's best to leave it where it is.' Without waiting for his comments, she opened the doors to a field of mud. 'It's a good job we didn't bring the cart in,' she observed, 'or we'd have sunk axle deep. As it is, we might still have a job getting out of the lane.'

The field sloped to the lane and the rain had washed soil and mud to the bottom, depositing it around the gap in the hedge. The higher up the field she got, the easier it was to walk without slipping and sliding, though her ankle was causing her considerable pain.

The cottage was a pitiful sight. Rafters, beams, doors and windows were all blackened ash. 'Oh, and it was such a pretty place.'

The pump was broken but the trough was overfilled, with rainwater swilling over the sides and making little rivers all around. The water inside was clear enough for Nell to see the bottom, and it tasted sweet as dew. Splashing her face and neck, she ran her dampened fingers through her hair, feeling refreshed and all the better for it. Then she made her way into the cottage.

Oddly enough, the place seemed strong and alive as ever, in spite of the fire damage. The wind whistled through the open rafters, like some merry flautist from a distance. Entranced, she lingered in the burnt remains of what had been the kitchen. In her mind's eye she could see it as she had seen it when she was here before. The fire range was now open to the elements and the stove where she'd prepared the stew was curled and deformed, almost beyond recognition.

The bedrooms, too, were pitiful. The rain had put

the fire out but not before it had done immense damage. The stone walls were blackened, soot and dirt in each and every crevice, and the cupboards gaped, their doors burnt to cinders. 'It's a crying shame.' Nell fondly touched her hand against the cottage walls. 'The old man would never have done this if he hadn't been desperate,' she murmured, as though talking to the cottage itself. 'This was his home, where he was happy with his woman.'

While she wandered through the place, someone else was there, curled up in the fireplace in the sitting room. Shot through the chest, he was losing his life's blood. Yet he could hear her voice, and it gave him hope.

Nell came as far as the sitting-room entrance. She looked in and was horrified by the extent of the damage. 'This is where he must have started the fire,' she mused, 'at the very heart of the cottage.'

She couldn't go any further. Turning from the carnage, she began her way back, unaware that the old man was dying only a few steps from where she had stood.

He heard her go, and all of his courage went with her. His blood trailed from his hiding place, staining the floor where he and his wife had sat, side by side in the winter evenings, with the fire roaring in the hearth and their hearts content in each other's company.

He thought of his wife, and of the terrible thing he had done to this place where they had known such happiness. Tears meandered down his face but in his despair he found a new strength.

Nell was halfway down the field when she felt the

urge to turn round. At first she imagined it might have been the wind calling. She turned and was shocked to see the old man staggering towards her. The next moment he crumpled to the ground, lying so still she feared he must be dead. 'Dear God.' She ran to him, calling out for Kit as she went.

The old man wasn't dead but he wasn't far from it. 'You came back.' That was all he said, but for Nell it was enough.

'I had to,' she whispered, and was comforted that he knew.

Kit fell to his knees beside her. 'Is he dead?'

Nell shook her head. 'We have to get him to a doctor.'

'You can't help carry him,' Kit reminded her, blunt as ever. 'Not like that, you can't.' He stared at her round belly. 'He's too 'eavy for me. We'll need to get help.'

'There is no help and there's no time to fetch anybody. And anyway, how do we know who's his friend and who's his enemy?' She had to think quickly. The wind was getting up again. 'Go back to the shelter,' she told Kit. 'Find something we can lay him on. If we can't carry him, we'll push him to the cart. After that, we'll do the best we can.'

'What am I supposed to be looking for?'

'Just go, Kit,' she yelled. 'Use your common sense.'

As she spoke, the wind dropped eerily and suddenly the skies emptied. The rain fell with a vengeance, soaking them in minutes. It was all the encouragement the boy needed. Turning tail, he ran like the wind. 'Hurry, Kit,' Nell called after him. She wasn't only thinking of the old man. Already chilled to the bone and trembling uncontrollably, she was deeply concerned that her baby might be in danger.

It seemed an age before Kit returned, dragging an old door. 'This is all I could find,' he apologised. The rain was dripping off his nose and his clothes were stuck to his back. 'I'm sorry, Nell.'

'Don't be sorry.' Taking hold of the door, she laid it beside the old man. 'You've done well, Kit. This is perfect.'

Taking great care, the two of them rolled the old man on to the door. Peeling off her shawl, Nell used it to secure him. 'You take the front and I'll take the back. Go slowly,' she warned.

Thankfully, the gentle slope of the field made the journey that much easier, but it was a slow, miserable task. The rain pelted them mercilessly, and the wind cut through to their bones, but eventually they got to the lane. 'We ain't gonna get him on that cart.' Cold and drained, Kit had lost patience.

'We're not leaving him now,' Nell said defiantly. But Kit was right. How in God's name would they get the old man on to the cart?

She had an idea. 'Loose the horse,' she said, 'then turn the cart round, with the arms of the shaft resting on this boulder.' Indicating the smooth stone on the edge of the field, she explained, 'If we can raise the end of the door so it rests on the shaft, we should be able to push the door up, along the shaft, and on to the cart.'

Kit did as he was told, and after Nell had made certain the old man was still tightly secured to the door, she and the boy set to. They propped one end of the door against the boulder, raising it inch by inch along the shaft, until they had it safely on board. 'If 'e ain't dead by now, he bleedin' well should be!' Kit almost wished he was back with Slater.

After covering the old man with the tarpaulin, Nell and Kit drew the door right to the front of the cart behind the seat, where it would be most sheltered from the elements. 'Where to now?' the boy asked.

'We have to find a doctor, and quick.'

'When I ran away from the orphanage, I came across a place where they might help this geezer.' He jerked a thumb in the direction of the old man. 'It's called the Convent of Saint Mary Magdalen. One of the nuns told me. They're kind, and they give you food.' He longed to be warm and dry, with hot broth in his belly. 'If they ain't got a doctor there, they'll soon get one,' he suggested hopefully.

'Where is this convent?' Nell was willing to try anything.

'I don't know the name o' the place 'cause I can't read signs, but I can find me way from Slater's house.' He winked. 'I've been there a time or two when the old bugger wouldn't feed me.'

Nell didn't relish the idea of going by way of Slater's house but there was no reason why he should see them, assuming he hadn't made off by now. 'Right. The Convent of Saint Mary Magdalen. That's where we're headed.'

As they edged out of the lane, the wheels sank deeper and deeper in the mud until Nell despaired of them ever getting out. But the horse was strong and big-hearted enough to pull them free eventually. Once on the open road, they made better headway. Gradually the wind ceased and the rain became a light shower. But they were a sorry pair, and there was hardly a word uttered throughout the journey.

As they came back through the hamlet of Ridgmont, Nell deliberately picked up pace as she drove by Slater's house. It was quiet there, the big gates still smashed open and not a soul in sight. 'The bugger's done a runner,' Kit said, and Nell thought he must be right.

'We'll tell the nuns what happened there,' she decided. 'They'll know what to do.'

Following the boy's directions, they continued on their way. 'This is Woburn,' she read from the sign as they entered the village. 'How far now to the convent?'

In fact it was only a matter of minutes before they entered the grounds of Mary Magdalen and Nell was pulling on the bell-rope. The nun who answered the door ushered Nell inside and soon all three were receiving attention. The old man was swiftly ushered to the sickbay where he was skilfully tended by Sister Teresa who had studied medicine and knew what was needed.

While the old man was being cared for, Nell and Kit were ushered to the great kitchen. 'Cor!' Kit was famished. 'It's warm in 'ere, ain't it, Nell?'

Nell was entranced. The kitchen was huge, with a run of tall, arched windows across one wall and a dresser that stretched the entire length of another. Reaching right up to the ceiling, festooned with copper pans and all manner of cooking implements, it made a wonderful sight. There was nothing grand or sumptuous about the kitchen. Like the convent itself, it was simply a big, quiet place where peace and beauty pervaded every nook and cranny.

Right in the centre of the room was a long pine table with numerous chairs all round and earthenware jars of immense proportion in the process of being filled with homemade jam. 'We make most of our own food here,' the nun explained. Wiping her hands on her pinafore, she came forward to greet them. 'It's all right, my dear,' she told the young novice who had brought them. 'I'll take care of them now.'

Nell and Kit sat at the table and food was quickly brought – hot, homemade broth, just as Kit remembered it, and round chunks of bread with soft insides and a brown crusty top.

'Will the old man be all right?' Nell asked tentatively. 'He was shot by the bailiffs and I don't know how long he lay there in the cold.'

'We'll do the best we can,' the nun promised. 'Now, eat your food while I find you both some dry clothes.' With that she disappeared and was gone for some long time.

'I told you they were kind, didn't I, hey?' Kit was looking for some sort of praise and got it when Nell told him he'd done the right thing in bringing them here.

'I want to see the old man,' she said, glancing towards the door. 'I want him to know we haven't forsaken him.'

Slurping a spoonful of broth, Kit looked at her inquiringly. 'Is he a relative o' yours?'

Nell, too, was enjoying the broth. Swallowing a piece of vegetable, she told him, 'No. In fact I don't know him all that well.'

'Then why the bleedin' hell are you so worried about him?'

Pointing to the crucifix hanging on the wall, Nell suggested, 'I should watch my tongue if I were you.'

'What? You reckon I'll be struck dead?' He grinned.

'You never know.'

'This is God's house, ain't it?'

'Yes.'

'An' he made me, didn't he?'

She smiled.

'Well then, he should know I don't mean nuffin' bad.' He sounded brash but he watched his tongue from then on anyway.

They were both startled when a voice from the doorway said, 'D'you want some more food?'

'I've had enough, thank you,' Nell answered, 'but maybe Kit would like some more.' She regarded the newcomer with interest. The woman was huge, with a kindly face and a cumbersome bearing. 'You've all been very kind,' Nell told her. 'I don't know how to thank you.'

The big woman filled the kettle from the copper tap and wedged it on the fire. 'It isn't me you should be thanking,' she advised with a homely smile. 'You see, the nuns took me in when nobody else wanted me. I've lived here a long time.' For one quiet moment, she paused to dream, before saying wistfully, 'I expect I'll end my days here too.'

Making the tea, she brought them each a mug filled to the brim. 'I have to be sparing with the tea,' she said. 'Sister Anne says I mustn't be too generous because the nuns have to buy it in and it costs a lot of money.'

She went on to explain how the nuns grew their own vegetables and stored the summer harvest for the winter months. 'Sister Margaret looks after the greenhouse and the tomatoes and that kind of thing. The other nuns all take turns in looking after the vegetable garden, and me and Mary help wherever we're allowed.' Reaching out, she shook hands with them both. 'I'm Amy,' she said proudly. 'What are your names?'

Nell gave her their names and explained what they were doing here. 'We brought in an old man,' she said. 'He's badly hurt and we were just wondering if we could see him.'

'Not me, thank you very much!' Kit piped up. 'I reckon he's already a goner, an' they ain't tellin' us.'

Amy looked at him more closely. 'You've been here before, haven't you?' she said. 'I remember you ate three bowls of broth and spilled the last one all down yourself.'

'I never!' Looking embarrassed, he quickly changed the subject. 'We've to be on our way quick,' he gabbled. 'Find out about the old man and we'll be off.'

Before she left, Amy looked long and hard at Nell. 'You've got blue eyes and golden hair,' she said thoughtfully. 'And you're real pretty, just like my friend Mary.'

The minute she was gone, Kit asked worriedly, 'You don't reckon they'll keep us here an' all, d'you, Nell?'

'Course not. Why would they do that?'

'You heard 'er. She's been 'ere a long time. They make her work an' all. Sounds worse than the bleedin' workhouse!' Glancing up at the crucifix, he clapped his hand over his mouth. 'Can't we go now, Nell?' he asked sheepishly, turning his back to the wall.

'Soon,' she promised, 'when I know about the old man. And don't forget, the nun's gone to get us dry clothes.'

No sooner had she said that than the same nun returned. 'These should fit,' she said, laying the clothes out on the table. There was a shirt and trousers for Kit and a dress with a shawl for Nell. 'The local people are generous with their cast-offs,' she said, smiling at them in turn, 'but we don't get much in the way of boy's clothes.' Looking Kit up and down, she seemed satisfied the clothes would fit. 'There are underclothes in the wash-house,' she explained. 'As soon as you've had enough to eat and drink, I'll take you there.'

As they made their way to the wash-house, the nun saw that Nell was limping badly. 'Are you hurt?' she asked, noting the red, raw skin above the rim of Nell's boot.

'It's nothing,' Nell assured her. 'The prick of a thorn, that's all.'

'Perhaps we should take a look at it.'

Nell declined. She knew the nun meant well but, like Kit, she didn't want to stay here longer than was necessary. Besides, once she was on her way again, she could tend the ankle herself. 'I'm more concerned about the old man we brought in,' she said. 'Can I see him?'

'I'm sure that will be all right.' The nun showed them

into the wash-house. 'Sister Bridget would like to speak to you first. I'll wait outside,' she said, 'then I'll take you to her.'

Inside the old stone building there was a bowl filled with cold water, and beside it a chair containing a towel and a bar of carbolic. Kit poked his elbow into the bowl. 'Bleedin' Nora!' he squealed. 'It's *cold*.'

Nell laughed. 'I suppose the nuns are used to it,' she said. 'Come on. Hurry up. The sooner you get washed and put the clothes on, the sooner we can see the old man.'

'I ain't washing.'

'You are.' Nell handed him the soap.

'All right then.' He could see she was determined. 'Just a cat lick,' and she watched over him just to make sure.

Afterwards she had a wash while he stood behind her out of her sight and put on the clean underwear.

Nell was next. Kit turned his back while she stripped to her petticoat and quickly changed into the clean dress. 'That feels good,' she said. Thankfully the dress was roomy enough to slide over her protruding stomach. It felt soft and feminine, and for a minute she wished she was slim and pretty again. The dress had a pattern of red and cream squares, with a flouncy hem and a lace neckline. 'What does it look like, Kit?' she asked, momentarily ashamed that she should worry about how she looked at a time like this. But she was still a woman, though big and clumsy, and her spirits needed a little boost.

Kit was astonished at the transformation. 'That Amy

were right,' he admitted. 'You really are pretty.' And he meant it. Nell's face shone, her cheeks were rosy, and her golden hair wild and natural. Now, when she smiled, she was positively beautiful.

'Come on then,' she declared, grabbing him by the arm. 'We're fed and washed and Sister Bridget is waiting.'

S ister Bridget had been told of the visitors, and now Amy was contributing her opinion. 'They're real nice,' she said. 'And the girl has golden hair, just like Mary.'

'Thank you, Amy.' Sister Bridget uncrossed her arms and got out of her seat. 'You go and see if you're needed in the sickbay, there's a dear.'

'Can I take Mary for a walk in the garden?'

'Not today. It's far too cold.' Gently, she ushered Amy out. 'We'll see what the weather's like tomorrow,' she promised. 'Now off you go.' She watched the big woman lumber down the corridor, then she went back to her desk and awaited the arrival of her two visitors. She was curious to know how the old man had come to be shot.

The knock came on the door and she called them in. When they stepped inside, Sister Bridget was shocked to her roots. Looking at Nell was like looking at Mary when she was first brought here. For the briefest moment before she composed herself, she could only stare, unable to speak. Then she said, 'Please, sit down and tell me who you are.' Her mind was playing tricks. Could this girl be the child born to Mary some seventeen years ago?

The nun who had brought them could not understand what had so shocked Sister Bridget but she noticed how she could not take her eyes off the young woman, and it made her curious.

'I'm Nell, and this is Kit.' Nell was thankful to be seated, her ankle was agony and she needed to take the weight off it. 'We're very grateful to you for everything,' she went on, 'but I'd like to see the old man, John Butler, now.' Remembering her manners, she added, 'If that's all right.'

Sister Bridget was still shaken. She needed a moment to assess the situation. There were questions to be asked and, if this young woman really was Mary's daughter, there were important decisions to be made. It would be a real shock to Mary if she knew she had a daughter. It would also be a shock for the girl to learn that her mother was crippled and in a wheelchair. Still, she mustn't jump to conclusions. Just because this visitor bore an uncanny resemblance to Mary didn't mean she was necessarily her daughter.

'Please, let me see him.' Nell's voice gentled into the nun's fragmented thoughts.

'Forgive me.' Sister Bridget stood up. 'When you get to my age your mind begins to wander,' she apologised. Addressing the other nun, she said, 'Take her along, would you?' To Nell she added, 'Afterwards, I'd like to talk to you.'

Nell merely nodded. Everyone had been so kind, and she was very grateful, but she was impatient to leave the place. She had noticed the way the nun had looked at her, as if she was shocked, or as if she had been expecting someone else. It was unsettling and Nell only wanted to be back on the open road now.

Sister Bridget's eyes followed Nell to the door. 'You've hurt your ankle,' she remarked, seeing the limp. Without waiting for Nell's answer, she instructed the other nun, 'Tend to it while she's in the sickbay.' The nun nodded, closed the door, and Sister Bridget leaned back in her chair. 'It's uncanny,' she murmured. 'But it has been a long time and my memory isn't what it was.' Yet when Nell walked through that door, the years had rolled away and it had seemed like only yesterday; the same small build, those vivid blue eyes, and that thick, curly cap of golden hair. Even the quick, pretty way she smiled. The girl was Mary seventeen years ago.

⁂

THE OLD MAN was awake. 'They tell me . . . I'll live,' he whispered, and even uttering those few words seemed to drain him.

'Ssh.' Nell sat beside him, her hand in his. Kit had gone to check on the horse. 'Rest now. Everything's going to be fine.' She was thrilled to see him awake. For a short time earlier, she had been ready to believe Kit when he claimed the old man had died and the nuns didn't want to tell them.

He closed his eyes, clutching her hand as if he wouldn't let it go. 'I thought . . .' He sighed and couldn't go on.

Nell squeezed his hand. 'I know what you thought,'

she said. 'You thought I wouldn't come back. But I did and now you're going to be well, so please, rest. The nuns are kind. They'll take good care of you.'

Opening his eyes, he gazed at her, the tears trickling down his face. 'The . . . cottage . . .' A sob caught in his throat and he was lost for words.

'Oh now, don't you worry about the cottage,' she told him firmly. 'It's a sturdy place. All it needs is a new roof and a few doors, a good clean-up and it'll be right as ever.' She made herself sound cheerful. 'It'll take more than one setback to finish it off. Just like yourself,' she laughed. 'The pair of you will see many a summer yet.'

His eyes smiled through the tears. 'Thank you,' he murmured. He gazed at her a moment longer, taking in her image: the strong square chin and those wonderful blue eyes; the wild sunny hair and that unforgettable smile. And, as his senses closed on him, he knew he would never forget her.

Leading her from the bed, the nun informed Nell, 'We'll take a look at your ankle now.'

Still uneasy because of the way Sister Bridget had stared at her, Nell wanted to leave as soon as possible. 'No need,' she answered brightly. 'It's all right now.'

'Are you sure? It won't take a minute.'

When Nell insisted she was sure, the nun didn't press her.

Kit returned to the sickbay, but remained at the door, unwilling to enter where death might be.

'Poor old sod, I expect 'e's a goner now,' he whispered as the nun and Nell stepped into the corridor.

'No, he isn't.' Seeing how the nun threw Kit a

disapproving glance, Nell gently shook him. 'And I think you've forgotten where you are.'

Sheepishly he stared up at the nun. 'Sorry, lady . . . er, miss.' Biting his tongue, he dropped his gaze momentarily to the floor then, looking up with big, rolling eyes, muttered soulfully, 'Sorry.'

As they followed the nun down the corridor, Nell felt sick with pain. Kit noticed. 'Why don't you let 'em take a look at it?'

As it turned out, Nell had little choice because as they came to the top of the stairs, she couldn't even put her foot to the ground.

Glancing down, the nun observed how the ankle was so swollen, the rim of Nell's boot was digging into the flesh. 'Don't worry,' she said, 'I'll bring Amy. She's marvellous with this sort of thing. We're nearer to the kitchen than the sickbay now. Can you walk a short distance?'

Grey with pain, Nell assured her she could.

The nun settled her in the kitchen, with Kit watching over her, and set a pan of water to heat on the stove. 'I'll be back with Amy in no time at all,' she promised, and with that she hurried away.

SISTER BRIDGET WAS deep in thought when there was a knock on her door. 'Yes?'

It was Sister Anne. 'You sent for me?'

'I did. Please sit down. There's something I need to discuss with you.'

As clearly and precisely as possible, she conveyed

her thoughts to her colleague; about Mary, and the young woman who had come to their door this very day, and their striking similarity to one another. 'I feel I should be doing something about it, but I'm not sure what,' she concluded.

'Where is the young woman now?'

'I'm told she's in the kitchen where Amy is tending to her ankle.'

'Would you like me to ask a few discreet questions?'

'I was hoping you might. The girl might think me too authoritative.'

Sister Anne smiled.

NELL'S ANKLE WAS a mess. 'You should be thankful it isn't any worse.' Amy was tender but firm as she finished bathing the wound and began applying a bandage. Looking up, she scolded Nell severely. 'If gangrene had set in, you could well have lost the leg. Why didn't you get it seen to before?'

Nell was deeply humbled by Amy's kind, simple manner. 'There always seemed to be something more important.' In her own defence she added, 'I've tried to keep it clean though, and I've used the herbs that grow along the roadside.' Having lived in the countryside all her life, Nell knew a little about the medicinal properties of natural plants.

Amy regretted being hard on her. The girl reminded her strongly of Mary, and it wasn't just the features. It was something in the manner of her smile, and the way she looked at you with those honest eyes that twinkled with goodness. She liked her, and because she was so like Mary, and Mary was the dearest thing on this earth to her, Amy spoke in a softer voice. 'You must have been in a lot of pain.'

Nell couldn't deny it. 'It feels more comfortable now than it has in a long time,' she admitted gratefully.

Sister Anne entered the kitchen while these two were chatting. She bustled about making a brew of strong tea. 'Travelled a long way, have you?' she inquired of Nell casually.

'Miles and miles!' Kit broke in. 'And we have summat to tell you an' all, ain't we, Nell?' He was bursting to tell them about Slater and the dead man in the cellar. Moreover, he wanted them to know how Slater had stolen the old man's belongings and nearly took Nell against her will. 'Nell says you'll know what to do.'

Sister Anne came and sat alongside Nell. 'Have you been on the road a long time then?' she queried.

'Long enough.' Nell was on her guard and she didn't know why. It was as if she was being quietly observed.

'Which part of the country do you hail from?'

'North.'

Sister Anne tried to remember everything she had been told about this girl and her young companion. 'You're travelling the road with a horse and cart, but if you don't mind me saying so, you don't look like Gypsies.' The boy might, she thought, but not Nell. 'You're not brother and sister, are you?'

'No, we ain't,' Kit informed her, 'but I wouldn't mind if we were, 'cause Nell's a good sort. She saved the old man and she didn't throw me out, even though I deserved it.' He wasn't sure whether to trust the nuns but then he decided they hadn't done them any harm so why not. 'I ain't got no family, y'see,' he muttered, 'but Nell says I've got 'er, an' that'll do for me.'

Sister Anne regarded Nell, thinking how lovely she was, and if the boy's tale was anything to go by, she had a kind heart too. 'Have you no family of your own either?' she asked Nell gently. 'No mother or father?' If the girl had a mother then Sister Bridget's theory didn't hold water.

Nell answered the direct question honestly. 'I have a father,' she said, 'and an aunt who I don't get on with, but I never knew my mother. She died when I was born.'

Thinking she might be on to something but sensing Nell's reluctance to talk, Sister Anne didn't pursue the subject for the moment. 'Tea!' she said, springing out of her chair. 'I'm sure we could all do with a good, strong cup of tea.'

It was too much of a temptation for Kit. 'I don't suppose you've got a cake as well, 'ave you?'

Nell glared at him. 'Kit!'

Sister Anne put up her hand. 'It's all right,' she assured her. 'We don't have much in the way of cakes but I'm sure we could find a pot of jam and some fresh bread.' And, in a surprisingly short time, that was exactly what she did.

While Kit tucked in and Amy put the finishing touches to Nell's bandage, Sister Anne proceeded with her questioning. 'So your mother died when you were born? That's a sad thing.'

Nell sipped her tea. Over the years she had been

conditioned never to crave for the impossible. 'My aunt says you can't miss what you've never had,' she replied philosophically.

Sensing the regret in Nell's voice, Sister Anne was cautious. 'But you do, don't you, Nell?'

'I suppose so.'

'This aunt of yours, the one you don't get on with. Why is that? I would have thought an aunt might take the place of your mother – try to make it up to you somehow.'

'She's cruel.' Nell recalled all the awful beatings she'd taken from Lilian over the years, and her deep dislike of that creature trembled in her voice.

'I see.' Sister Anne was thinking of what she'd been told with regard to the manner in which Mary was found. She had been delivered of a child, and someone, some wicked, unforgiving person had taken the child and turned Mary out of their lives for ever. 'Did your aunt turn you out, child?'

Nell didn't want to say anything more.

'Was it because of the child you're carrying?'

This time Nell's answer was marbled with anger. 'She wanted to kill my baby. I couldn't let her do that.'

Sister Anne was horrified. 'Of course not! What about the baby's father? Why didn't he take care of you?' She glanced at Kit who was as surprised by Nell's outburst as anyone. 'I take it there is just you and the boy?'

Subdued now, Nell looked at Kit and nodded. 'Just me and the boy,' she confirmed.

'What about your father?' Now that she had Nell's

confidence, the good sister was not about to leave it at that.

Nell was beginning to feel homesick for her father; for Molly, and Bill. What were they doing right now? No doubt Molly was chasing about in the kitchen, getting the meal ready for her big, strapping lads. Probably her father would be chopping wood with Lilian standing over him. Bill might be out in the fields with his dog. She could see him so clearly, tall and strong, and just now she would have given almost anything to be in his arms. Holding fast the image, she murmured, 'My father's a good man. But he's a coward. My aunt rules him with a rod of iron.' God forgive her! She shouldn't have called him a coward. But he was, she reminded herself. All those times when she was being beaten, where was he? Why did he never stand up to Lilian?

It was hard to love someone when half the time they didn't seem to know you existed. So many times she had longed for him to sit her on his knee and talk and laugh with her. When she was small, her dad had seemed so distant. Now it was different. Physically he was further away than ever but he was real to her. He had stood up to Lilian. He had fought on his daughter's side, and that made Nell proud.

Convinced there was something of great interest here, Sister Anne wanted to convey all she had learned to her anxious colleague. 'Finish your tea,' she told Nell. 'Amy will bring you to Sister Bridget's office when you're ready.'

While Nell finished her tea, Amy made certain the bandage was secure, then she helped herself to a cup of tea and gave Kit a slice of cake. 'I don't want you to tell lies,' she imparted intimately to the boy, 'but if anybody mentions cake, just don't say anything.' She gave Nell a merry wink. 'That way they won't know, and I won't get in trouble.'

A sound at the door made them all turn.

To Amy the strange sight was familiar and dear, but to Nell and Kit the appearance of a small, attractive woman in a flat, four-wheeled conveyance was a bit of a shock. The woman was pretty but her legs were thin and limp, stretched out before her. She didn't speak immediately. Instead she looked from one to the other, her blue eyes resting longer on Nell's face.

Beneath Mary's inquisitive gaze, Nell felt oddly drawn to her. 'Hello,' she said. 'I'm Nell, and this is Kit.' She gestured to the boy but neither of them moved, in case they frightened her away.

Mary remained by the door, unsure and nervous. There was something about Nell that made her sad. Something about the face, the soft eyes, and especially the fact that she was obviously with child. 'I was looking for Amy,' she replied in a small voice, her gaze never leaving Nell's face.

'I'm here.' Amy was seated to the side of the door, where Mary couldn't see her right away. Now she stood up and came forward. 'I've to wait until these two are ready to be taken to Sister Bridget,' she explained, winking again at Nell. 'But you can come in and join us if you want, then we'll go and sit in the conservatory.'

'I don't want to come in,' Mary replied. Still, she didn't take her gaze from Nell. 'I'll wait in the

241

conservatory.' With practised skill she spun the runabout round and went away at astonishing speed.

Nell was entranced. 'She's lovely.'

Amy laughed. 'She's a bugger, if there ever was one.'

'What's her name?'

'Mary.' As briefly as she could, Amy explained how Mary was found 'nearly dead' outside the convent many years since. 'Bad people left her there, and nobody knows who they were.' Her face clouded over as she told Nell, 'They made her a cripple.' There was just the slightest tremble in her voice, but she choked it back and with a smile told Nell proudly, 'I made her that runabout and now she can go where she wants, but not to the town. She can go to the conservatory, and sometimes we go for walks in the garden. She likes that best of all.'

'D'yer think 'er folks will ever come for 'er?' Kit asked.

'Don't know.'

'She's like me,' he declared. 'I ain't got no folks either.'

'Mary doesn't need anybody else.' Amy always worried that Mary had a family somewhere and that one day they might come and claim her. 'I'm her family,' she said, 'and this convent is her home.' She became silent, pacing the floor and occasionally staring out of the door to see if Sister Anne was coming back to see where they'd got to.

Kit had been thinking, ever since Mary had appeared at the door. Now he had to remark, 'That woman and you look the same, Nell, except the woman's older. She's thinner than you an' all, but that's because you're fat with a bairn.'

Nell wondered about Kit's remark; Amy herself had made the same observation earlier. 'Can't they do anything about her legs?' she asked.

'Her legs won't work any more and that's that.' Amy went silent again. She knew what Kit had said was right, and it unsettled her. Also, she'd noticed the birthmark on Nell's foot. Mary had one exactly the same. 'It's time you two went, isn't it?' she asked. Recalling the way Mary had looked at Nell made her nervous.

'We're going now, Amy.' Nell sensed they were no longer welcome, and anyway she didn't particularly want to speak to Sister Bridget. It would only be a series of questions, and she'd had enough of them for one day. 'Will you do something for me, Amy?' she asked.

'What?'

Placing her cup and saucer in the sink, Nell went into great detail about the old man's belongings. She even drew a small map on a piece of paper supplied by Amy. 'We've made everything secure,' she said, 'but it's best the nuns should know where it is.'

Amy perused the drawing. 'I'll tell them,' she promised.

'Ain't you gonna tell her about Slater?' Kit wouldn't rest until that man was put away behind bars.

Nell had not forgotten but she didn't want to over-awe Amy, so she wrote it all down – the street and the house, and every little detail she could recall. 'He may already have gone but the nuns will inform the authorities and then it's up to them,' she said to Kit.

T HE HORSE WAS waiting patiently. 'We're on our way, old feller,' Nell said, nuzzling up to him, 'and we won't be coming back.'

Kit was surprised. 'What about the old man? Ain't you coming back to see 'im?'

'No.' Manoeuvring the cart out of the narrow yard, Nell glanced back at the convent. 'He'll get well now. He'll collect his belongings and travel the world like he said.' Her smile was wistful. 'We've done the best we could for him, and now he doesn't need us any more.'

Kit was relieved. 'Thank Gawd for that!' Having run away from one big institution, he didn't relish the possibility of being incarcerated in another, like Amy and that poor crippled woman who looked like Nell.

As they left the grounds of the convent, Nell and Kit were closely observed.

The two nuns watched from the office window. 'Maybe it's just as well they've gone,' Sister Bridget mused. 'There was something about the girl that made me uneasy.'

'You're right though,' Sister Anne commented. 'She and Mary do bear a striking resemblance, and it's possible that there is a link somewhere in their backgrounds.'

'Maybe,' Sister Bridget answered, 'but sometimes it's better not to know than to know and be sorry.'

M ARY LOVED THE conservatory. She sat by the window with Amy at her side, her nose pressed to the windowpane. She, too, was watching Nell's departing figure. 'I liked that girl,' she murmured. 'Why was she here?'

'They brought the old man.' Amy had mixed feelings about Nell's departure. On the one hand she felt afraid, and on the other, like Mary, she had taken a strong liking to Nell. 'Sister Anne said they saved his life.'

'Is he family?'

'I don't think so.'

'The girl – Nell, isn't it?'

'What about her?'

'She's with child.'

'About to drop it any day, I should think.' In the silence that followed, Amy thought her friend was crying. 'Are you crying, Mary?' she asked, bending her neck to see.

Without turning round, Mary reached behind her to take hold of Amy's big, warm hand. 'I wish I had a child,' she murmured. 'I wouldn't be able to run and chase it in play, but I'd make a good mother all the same. Wouldn't I, Amy?'

Crying too, Amy hugged her close. 'Oh, Mary, haven't I told you before, you shouldn't dream about what you can't have.'

'I know, but sometimes there's a big empty ache inside me. I try so hard, Amy, but it won't go away.'

They held each other, their eyes drawn to Nell as she paused at the gates to look back. One glance, and then she was gone.

THEY WERE SOME way down the lane before Kit thought it wise to speak. 'Cat got your tongue?' he asked warily.

'Don't be cheeky.' She playfully pulled his hair and he laughed like a boy should.

'You ain't said a bleedin' word since we left that place,' he complained. 'Thinking about the old man, are you?'

'Yes,' her smile was warm and reassuring, 'and about where we should be heading. We'll need to look for work, and a roof over our heads.' Making a face at him she said, 'Now that I'm lumbered with you, I've got more than enough to think about, wouldn't you say?'

But it wasn't just Kit she was thinking of, nor was it the baby, or the loved ones she'd left behind.

She was thinking of the one called Mary. And wondering if their paths would ever cross again.

PART THREE

Christmas Eve
1890
A NEW LIFE

Chapter Seven

IT WAS CHRISTMAS Eve and the snow fell from the skies with a vengeance. Undeterred by the biting cold, and picking their way along the slippery pavements underfoot, the shoppers spilled into Blackburn town.

Not everyone had money enough for fancy presents and bags filled with food. Some poor folk had to be content with scraps from the butcher's counter, or bread left over from the day before; and others, more unfortunate, resorted to begging on the streets.

Laden down with all kinds of Christmas fare, Bill and Molly pushed their way through the market. 'It's like the last-minute rush for a packed tram,' Bill groaned, pressing himself to a wall while two women and a small, irate man squeezed past; one of the women was tall, elegant and wrinkled beneath her make-up, and it was only when he looked close that Bill realised it was actually a man dressed as a woman. He had to look away and smile when the person gave him a cheeky wink. 'By! You're old enough to be his mother!' Molly yelled. 'Get off home to yer old man, and your grandkids!'

When Bill burst out laughing, she glared at him. 'What are you laughing at?'

Leaning towards her, he whispered, 'Ssh, Mam. That woman was a feller.'

Molly was shocked. 'Never!' Wide-eyed, she stared after the threesome and when the same person turned round and smiled straight at her, she blushed crimson and hurried on. 'Come away, our Bill,' she muttered. 'By, I've never known the like.' Then she chuckled, shook her head and said in a small, wondering voice, 'It's a funny old world an' that's a fact.'

'Hold on a minute.' Bringing Molly to a halt, Bill shuffled his own burden and took some of her load. 'God only knows why you've bought all this,' he said. Molly had purchased a small tree, a large turkey, two chickens and a mountain of vegetables; there were presents for each of the family, and all the usual attributes to making a festive meal.

'I've bought nothing I don't need,' she retorted. 'I've a big family to feed. With everyone in work and paying their old mam their dues, thank the good Lord I can afford to treat 'em right.'

'You could invite half the neighbourhood to Christmas dinner with this little lot.' Bill glanced at the pile of shopping distributed between the two of them. 'You don't need to make a big show for me, Mam. You know that.'

Pausing to rest, Molly regarded this son of hers, and her heart swelled with pride. Bill had drawn every woman's eye from one end of the market to the other; even that one who wasn't a woman had thought him deserving of a naughty wink. Bill was an eyeful for anyone. With his dark strength and twinkling black eyes, he had something very rare – good looks combined with a sense of humour and a deep, ingrained honesty that a body could see at a glance. 'Come on, son,' she said, 'it's time we had a drop o' summat to keep the cold out.'

They were only a short walk away from the Sun public house, and the minute Molly set off towards the end of Ainsworth Street, Bill knew exactly where she was headed. 'You'll get thrown out,' he warned with a grin. 'You know what happened the last time you set foot in there.'

Defiant as ever, Molly marched along the street, bent almost double beneath the weight of her shopping and with a look of grim determination on her face. 'You're not to say a word,' she told him. 'Any arguments and I'll be the one to deal with it.'

Smiling but keeping the laughter from his voice, Bill answered sternly, 'I wouldn't dream of it, Mam.'

A busy old inn, set on the corner of King Street, the Sun was frequented by men of all ages and means; there had been more punch-ups and differences of opinion in that place than anywhere else in the whole of Blackburn. But it was a long-time, favourite meeting place. On Saturday it was a haven for all those men who sought refuge from the many trials of a working life. They might be seeking relief from a long, demanding week in the pits some distance from their homes, or the mills on their doorsteps, or their wives and families, or they'd be sneaking a quiet drink away from their clinging sweethearts. Whatever the reason, they flocked there by the dozen, propping up the bar and staggering home when the last shout was called.

'Remember what I said,' Molly muttered as the two of them went in through the door. 'Any arguments and it'll be me that deals with it. All right?'

'Just as you say, Mam.' It was more than his life was worth to let her see he was smiling.

Molly went through the door in full sail, head high and a face like a thunderbolt. 'Two pints o' the best, landlord,' she said, dropping her shopping at the nearest table and instructing Bill to do the same, which he did before returning to her side, ready to defend her should she get herself in any trouble.

All eyes turned her way. There were a few gasps of disbelief, and a sense of anticipation as to how the landlord might deal with this particular situation. In one corner a man in a flat cap started laying odds on her being thrown out. When he laid his cap on the counter, coins were dropped into it at an astonishing rate. Bill saw this and winked mischievously, awaiting the outcome as eagerly as the rest of them.

The landlord was a stocky fellow with a droopy moustache and a ruddy face. 'What did you say?' He leaned over the counter towards her, his pink, bulbous eyes sticking out and his mouth set in a thin, angry line.

Like a bulldog bristling for a fight, Molly drew herself up to her full height. 'Deaf, are ye?' she taunted, puffing out her chest. 'I want two pints o' yer best, and be quick about it.' Returning his stare, she silently dared him to challenge her. 'I'm that parched me tongue's stuck to the roof o' me mouth.'

'Get out of here, Molly Davidson, or I'll have you chucked out.' He glanced up when Bill stepped forward.

'I'll serve you, Bill,' he promised warily, 'but not your mam.'

Molly gave Bill a glance that said, '*My* business, remember?' He nodded, and she was satisfied. All the same, Bill stood ready. If anyone made a move towards his mam, they'd answer to him.

'You might as well leave, Molly.' The landlord was adamant. 'I'll not serve you.'

Stiff and unyielding, Molly stood her ground. 'Oh? And why's that?'

He stared at her in disbelief. 'You know why,' he snarled.

'You'll have to remind me,' she replied sweetly, 'because I've forgotten.' Molly was lying, and the men loved her for it. They sensed a fight brewing, and grew excited.

'Women aren't welcome in this place.' In fact, women didn't even step through the door, except for one daring officer of the Salvation Army and a few street women who were soon shovelled out on the end of his toe.

'Ain't my money good enough for ye then?'

'It's not that, and well you know it.'

'Think this place is sacred, do yer?' Molly was stony-faced. 'Think a woman ain't got no rights?'

'Not here, they haven't, and especially not you.'

'You might as well serve me, Edward Black, 'cause I'm not leaving till I've had me thirst quenched.'

Tension heightened and the man's cap was filled to brimming.

Molly saw the landlord anxiously glance towards his

living quarters. 'Oh, I see,' she smiled. 'Want to fetch the dog out to chase me off, is that it? Not man enough to do it yourself, eh?'

'I'm warning you.' Feeling the weight of opinion against him, he quickly altered his tone. 'You'd best leave, Molly. I don't want no trouble.'

'And you'll get none.' The smallest grin was beginning to lift the corners of her mouth. 'Two pints o' the best, please.'

'Then you'll be gone, will you?'

'Aye.' Realising she was getting the better of him, Molly teased, 'If one don't quench me thirst, I might want another, so you'd best make sure yer fill the jar to the top. An' not with froth neither.' Having said her piece, she led Bill to the table where she set her shopping all around and told him to relax. 'See, I told yer there weren't gonna be no trouble.'

He smiled at her with affection. 'Are you sure, Mam?' he asked, his dark eyes twinkling. 'Don't forget, I heard what happened here before.' The smile became a grin. 'In fact the whole of Blackburn must have heard about you causing an uproar.'

'That's water under the bridge,' she said grandly. 'I ain't got time for all that.' Nodding to the irate landlord, she commented, 'Anyway, it's his fault. If he hadn't bragged to all and sundry that he'd never let me set foot in his place again, I wouldn't have felt the need to put him right, now would I?'

'Well, you've got him worried now.'

The landlord brought the pints and set them on the table. 'There's no froth on these,' he said nervously.

Molly had to agree. 'Happen they'll do the trick then,' she answered smugly. 'Then I'll be on me way before you know it.'

As he went away, the landlord glanced at Bill; he seemed to be silently pleading with him to take his mother out as quickly as he could.

Bill merely smiled and nodded. 'You serve a good pint,' he remarked disarmingly. With that he chinked his glass against Molly's and the two of them settled back on the bench. 'You're a bugger, our Mam,' he laughed. 'Remind me not to get on the wrong side of you.'

They relaxed for a time, during which Molly raised the matter of Christmas Day. 'I want it to be the best yet,' she told him. 'I don't suppose it'll be too long afore me an' your dad are on our own and you boys have carved out a life for yourselves.'

'I've got no plans for leaving just yet.' There *was* something he had to tell her but he didn't think this was the time, especially as she was so excited about Christmas.

Molly knew him too well. 'Come on. Out with it, son. What's on your mind?' She put her pint on the table and waited for an answer.

He hesitated, not wanting to spoil her pleasure.

'You might as well tell me 'cause I'll not rest now.'

'It's not important.' It might have been if Nell was here, but as she wasn't, it didn't matter too much either way.

'So, tell me.'

'Vincent Morgan's offered me the cottage.' He took a long gulp from his jug. 'It's the one Jed and I were rebuilding before he died, in the meadow.' Momentarily closing his eyes, he thought of Nell. When he first started the work there, she used to sit on the bridge and watch him. But she was a child. Just a child.

Molly sighed. 'By! That's in a lovely spot, meadow all around, spinney behind, and the brook right on your doorstep.' Like Bill, she recalled how Nell used to sit on the bridge and wait for him to finish work so he could walk her home. 'Nell was enchanted with that cottage.'

'Aye, she was.' His handsome features lifted in a smile. 'She used to say how she'd have a cottage like that one day.'

'Will you take it?' In her heart Molly had Bill and Nell tied together, and nothing could make her untie that knot. If he took the cottage, who was to say that one day he and Nell wouldn't make a fine family there?

'I haven't thought too much about it but I suppose I'll need to branch out on my own soon enough.'

'Want to leave me, eh?'

'Mebbe.' He had to be honest. 'If I do take the cottage though, I'll not be so far away I can't keep an eye on you.'

Molly laughed. 'So you think I need watching, eh?'

Looking at her now, with her wild hair and her round, brown eyes, he thought she'd been the best mother any son could have. Molly was a law unto herself. She was kind and gentle, and generous with her affections. She could be loud and raucous, and wouldn't listen to a word of advice from any man, but there was no one quite like her. 'Yes,' he admitted with a grin. 'I'd say you needed watching.'

'So, when does he want word on the cottage?'

'What with this weather, and all the other jobs that need doing round the farm, I haven't been able to get on with it as fast as I'd like, but I plan to have it finished by early spring. I expect that's when he'll want word.'

'Take it, son.' It took a lot of courage for Molly to say that. Bill was her strength when everyone else let her down. Her little home would not be the same without him.

'Want to be rid of me, do you?'

'I have my reasons.' Nell was her reason. Nell and her son, walking down the aisle together.

'I'll think on it.'

They sat quietly for a time, much to the relief of the landlord.

Presently, Molly's thoughts found form in a question. 'How's that wife of his?'

'Who?' Bill had been lost in his own thoughts. 'Morgan's wife, d'you mean?'

'Aye. Morgan's wife. Last I heard she were a poorly thing. Folks say she ain't carrying that child none too well neither.'

'I wouldn't know about that. I get on with my work and mind my own business.'

'Not like me, eh?' Molly chuckled. 'But that's 'cause you're a feller an' I'm a nosy old bag.'

'I dare say folks are right though,' Bill admitted. 'The doctor's been out to the house a lot lately. I've seen him from the meadow, driving his carriage along the lane. I know for a fact he's journeyed out at least three times in a week.'

Molly did some quick calculations. 'If I remember

rightly, the Morgan bairn should be due early in the New Year, same as . . .' She bit her tongue, mortified that she had almost given away Nell's secret.

Bill hadn't missed her slip of the tongue. He gave her a cheeky smile. 'Don't tell me *you're* adding to the family, Mam?'

Molly blushed pink. 'Give over, you silly arse!'

'Who then? You said the Morgan bairn was due the same as . . . who?'

'I were rambling, that's all.' She tried to make light of it. 'When you get old, your mind wanders.'

'Not yours, Mam. You're sharp as a tack.'

'Aye, well, what's wrong with the woman? What does she keep wanting a doctor for?'

'You just said yourself, she's due a bairn in the New Year.'

'Mebbe, but a woman don't need pampering every two minutes just 'cause she's having a bairn. When I were having you lads, I never asked nobody for anything, and when I started the birthing, the only other person in the room were old Martha Langden from number ten – the poor old sod's been gone this past year, Lord rest 'er soul.' She made a swift sign of the cross. 'Still, that Rosalyn Morgan is a puny little thing, ain't she? Let's hope she can get through the birthing without any difficulties, 'cause if gossip's right, Vincent Morgan might throw her out lock, stock and barrel if she doesn't produce him an heir.'

Bill was shocked. 'Whoever told you that must be looking for trouble. As far as I can see, they seem all right together.'

'Ah, well. Men don't see the things us women see. Our butcher's lass is the scullery maid up at the house, and she says that marriage is coming apart at the seams.'

'Honest to God, you women!' Drawing in a deep breath, Bill held it a moment while he pondered his mother's comments, then in a rush of air he said, 'Drink up, Mam. It's time we were off.' He was out of his depth. The Morgans had their troubles like any other couples, and there were things he could have told his mam that would make her eyes pop out. But it was none of his business, and nobody else's either.

Molly was in no hurry. 'I had another letter from her today,' she said, her old brown eyes sparkling with pleasure.

He didn't have to ask who the letter was from. 'Is she all right? On her way home for Christmas, is she?'

Molly shook her head. 'I don't reckon so.'

'Can I read it?'

'I ain't got it with me,' she lied. In fact the letter was in her bag which was standing right beside her on the floor.

'I thought you asked her to come home for Christmas.' Suddenly his mood had changed. The smile was gone from his mouth and the twinkle from his dark eyes. 'What's her excuse this time?'

'I told you she'd moved on, didn't I?'

'You said she never stays in one place long enough to lay down roots, if that's what you mean.'

'Since she last wrote, she's found honest work in a baker's shop and they're so run off their feet over Christmas and New Year, they've asked her to stay on –

given her a pay rise into the bargain, she says.' Molly was thrilled to have heard from Nell. 'The lass seems to be doing well enough. Going from strength to strength.' She cocked her head and pursed her lips. 'Oh aye, she's doing well, is our lass.'

'So we'll not see her for a while yet then?' His heart had sunk to his boots with every word Molly uttered.

'You never know with Nell,' she said. 'Like a will-o'-the-wisp, she is, here one day, gone the next. It wouldn't surprise me if she didn't turn up on the doorstep Christmas morning like she'd never been away.' She could cut out her tongue for lying, but she'd made Nell a promise, and promises were sacred.

'She never should have gone away in the first place.' He wanted her back. Dear God! How he wanted her back. 'For two pins I'd go and fetch her back this very night.'

Aware he might be about to ask where Nell was living, Molly quizzed him. 'Why would yer want to fetch her back, son?' Maybe this once he would let her know what he was really thinking. Maybe this once he would admit how much he loved Nell, and that he wanted her back because he yearned to make her his wife. Molly hoped he might say these things, but she didn't think he would somehow. Bill had always been one to keep his deeper thoughts to himself.

Just as she feared, he gave nothing away. 'Because she's too young to be gallivanting all over the place,' he replied after a moment's thought. 'And because I feel responsible for her. I mean, Nell's like a sister to me.'

'I see.' Molly gave a long, drawn-out sigh. 'And that's

the only reason yer want to fetch her back, is it?'

His dark eyes raked her face. 'What are you getting at?' he asked. 'What other reason could there be?' For a moment he wondered if she'd guessed that he was beginning to think of Nell in a new and different way. A way that frightened and excited him all at once.

'Just wondered how you felt, that's all, son,' she answered lightly.

'Well, now you know,' he told her. But she didn't know, he thought. How could she? His feelings were so mixed up these days, he didn't even know himself how he felt.

Molly wished she could say it straight out – do yer love Nell like a man loves a woman? If yer fetch her back, will yer make her yer wife? And will yer still want her when yer know she's carrying another man's child? If he could answer 'yes' to all these questions, then she would gladly tell him how to find Nell. But he wasn't ready yet. Maybe he never would be, and that saddened her.

'I can't help worrying about her,' he admitted now. 'Maybe I could go and see her, make her see how dangerous it is for her to be travelling the roads. Oh, I know how she needs her independence, and I respect that, but surely to God she can have it without traipsing the country from one end to the other.'

'You'd be wasting yer breath,' Molly retorted, 'because I told her the very same an' it got me nowhere. I even offered her a home here with us, but she wouldn't be persuaded.' Molly knew why. Nell was with child. The lass needed to deal with that in her own way.

'She's a stubborn bugger!'

'Always has been.' A smile chased away the frown. 'Nell's a law unto herself, an' she'll not come home till she's good and ready.' What then? she thought. What would Bill have to say when Nell turned up with a bairn in her arms?

Bill was still looking for a way. 'I could talk to Morgan. I'm sure I could get him to let Nell take on the cottage. He might even find her work at the house again. Rosalyn Morgan liked Nell. She was asking after her only the other day.' Leaning forward and groaning like a man in anguish, he ran his hands through his thick, dark hair. 'That way Nell would have her independence. There'd be no need to go off looking for it.' And she would be here where he could watch over her and stroll with her like they used to; and talk, and laugh and just maybe, with her safe, he might feel more content in himself. 'I don't like the idea of her in some strange place, with people she doesn't know and maybe can't trust.'

'I know, son.'

'She shouldn't have taken off like that. It was a foolhardy thing to do.'

'Nell is her own woman, and we have to accept that. All right, I agree with yer, son. Mebbe she shouldn't have gone, an' mebbe it were a foolhardy thing to do. But she were never happy at home. That aunt of hers made her life a misery. Her own father ain't got the guts of a rabbit, and she had precious little to look forward to.'

'I know all that, Mam, but I only wish she'd talked

it through with one of us first.'

'She *did* talk it through – with me.'

'And you couldn't change her mind, eh?' He smiled. 'She's a stubborn bugger, like I said.' And well able to take care of herself if he would only admit it.

'I'll 'ave another then we'll be on our way.' Molly winked at the landlord who trembled in his boots. 'One for the road, landlord, quick as yer like.'

Half an hour later and merry from the drink, Molly was ready for off. As she got out of her seat, her little brown eyes caught sight of a man who must have entered when she and Bill were deep in conversation. 'Ain't that Len Armitage?' she asked Bill. 'Little shit! An' look what he's got clinging to his arm, eh?' The man's companion was obviously a street woman. A tall, slim creature with yellow hair and painted face, she was all over him, laughing and giggling and holding on to him as if she might fall over if she let go.

In a minute, Molly was across the room and confronting the little man whose face turned a pale shade of grey when he saw her. 'You should be ashamed, Len Armitage!' Molly told him; by this time she was beginning to feel the effects of the two pints she'd consumed. The little man's face was shifting from one end of his head to the other, and the whole bar was dancing a jig round her. 'What would yer missus say if I told her you were out with a floozy?' Glaring at the yellow-haired woman, she was disconcerted to see how the painted eyes dropped to her mouth and back again in a trice. Blinking, Molly focused again. 'Reckon I'm drunk,' she muttered.

In front of his woman, the little man found his daring. Turning to the landlord, he said in a very loud voice, 'You want to be careful who you let in, landlord. Decent folk like me are partic'lar who they drink with.'

In a move that took him by surprise, Molly swung her bag at him. 'Yer sorry little bugger!' she screamed. 'There's yer poor wife waiting at home while you bide yer time in 'ere with a woman off the streets, laughing an' giggling an' spending the money yer should be taking home to yer family. Shame on yer, I say. Shame on yer.' Another mighty swipe with her bag sent him staggering backwards. 'Don't think I'll not tell 'er,' she warned, ''cause I'll be going straight round there when I leave 'ere. Yer can count on that.'

Stepping forward, Bill touched his mother on the arm. 'Come away, Mam. Leave folks to their own business, eh?' Like Molly, he despised what the little man was up to. It was common knowledge Len's wife and seven kids went without because of his drinking and gambling.

Mistaking Bill's words as a gesture of support, and desperate to be seen as a man of stature in the eyes of his woman friend, Len Armitage jabbed a finger at Molly. 'Listen to your son,' he snarled. 'What I do is my business an' I'll not answer to you nor any other bugger. So piss off afore I knock yer out the door.'

By this time every man was betting furiously on whether Molly would be thrown out by Len or by the landlord.

In fact, it was Bill who stepped in. A formidable sight, he stood over the little fellow, his dark eyes burning with anger. When he issued a warning, it was in a soft whisper that made the other man tremble. 'What my mother says is the truth. There's no call to talk to her like that. I think an apology might be in order, don't you?'

'Hey!' The shout came from the back of the room. Almost immediately a big man emerged from the crowd. Big and bald, he boomed, 'You and your loud-mouthed mother had best do what the man says and piss off. Now!'

Bill stared at him but didn't reply. Instead he returned his attention to Len. 'Well? I still haven't heard you apologise.'

Another voice yelled, 'Molly's right. You're a bad lot, Len Armitage. Happen a bloody good thrashing is what you deserve.'

'Shut your mouth if you know what's good for you!' Pushing him roughly aside, the big, balding man strode across the room. Squaring up to Bill, he invited, 'You and me, Davidson. How about it?'

'Go on, son!' Thoroughly enjoying herself, Molly watched from the table on the other side of the room, where she'd returned to finish her beer. 'Show the bugger what yer made of!'

When Bill turned to see where she'd got to, the big man landed a blow on the back of his neck. Taken by surprise, he was momentarily stunned.

'Now happen you'll do what's best,' the big man boasted. 'Sod off and take the old bitch with you!'

Silenced by a well-placed punch on the mouth, he reeled backwards, knocking into one man who stumbled

265

sideways and knocked into another. Tempers flew, and soon the whole place was in uproar, with fists flying and the sound of bone crunching bone. Tables and chairs were thrown about and there was Molly in the middle, laughing and shouting, 'Go on, yer buggers! You're all as bad as one another.'

Dodging the blows and landing a few of his own, Bill grabbed Len by the scruff of the neck and carried him to where Molly was leaping about with excitement. 'He's got something to say,' he explained, thrusting the arrogant little man forward and glaring at him. 'That's right, isn't it?'

There was a pause while Len wondered how he would keep his self-respect after this. If he had been more of a man he might have been tempted to have a go at Bill, but he was a renowned coward so he decided against it. 'All right.' He bit his tongue, hating every minute he was made to stand there. One dark night, when they least expected it, he might be able to get his own back on Molly and her son, but for now he would have to show willing. 'I'm . . . sorry.' He stiffened with rage. 'Damn the buggers,' he hissed under his breath.

It wasn't as heartfelt an apology as Bill would have liked but it was an apology nevertheless.

He wasn't finished with him yet though. 'If you had any sense in that head of yours,' he told him, 'you'd value your wife and kids.' Gesturing to where his floozy was helping herself to a drink from the bar, he warned in a kindly voice, 'See sense, man! That one will take you for every penny you've got, and when she's done with you she'll be off.'

His warning struck home. Len glanced at the floozy and then suddenly he was hurrying away, out through the door and on to the street.

'Don't think you've got away with it, short-arse,' Molly yelled after him. 'Don't think I'll forget to tell your missus the next time I clap eyes on 'er.' Grinning at Bill, she said, 'I'll not tell 'er, but it'll give the bugger summat to think about all the same.'

Bill could only shake his head. 'Come on,' he said, trying not to smile. 'Let's get you home. You've caused enough trouble for one day.'

As they reached the door, the big man chased after them, determined to teach Bill a lesson. Catching him by the shoulder, he spun him round, swinging an almighty punch which sent Bill crashing through the door to the pavement.

By the time the big man had lumbered after him, Bill was back on his feet and ready. When the other man's face appeared, he flattened it with a knotted fist, the force of which left the big man nursing his bloody nose and writhing in agony on the ground.

Brushing the dust from his jacket, Bill took a firm hold of Molly's arm. With a quick smile, he commented casually, 'Isn't it amazing how a quiet afternoon can suddenly turn into a riot?' His smile became a lopsided grin. 'And to think I only came out to help you with your Christmas shopping.'

Molly glanced back at the tumult she'd caused. Two bobbies ran past blowing their whistles as the pub suddenly emptied, with everyone fleeing in all directions.

Unruffled but still a bit merry from the drink, Molly

hitched up her skirt, stuck out her chin and chuckled, 'Eeh, our Bill. I ain't seen a bloody good scrap for ages. Not since last Christmas when I went in there and saw Jack Dolly making eyes at the barmaid – and him only just wed!'

'I ought to have had more sense than to let you go in there,' Bill said. 'No wonder the landlord went white at the sight of you.' He stifled a giggle, then Molly bowed her head and sniggered like a schoolgirl. They glanced at each other and there was no holding back. As they went a pace faster for home, the sound of their laughter echoed down the street.

'By! I did enjoy it though,' Molly said. 'An' did you see how they all ran when the bobbies arrived?'

Though his nose was bleeding and the cut above his eye was swelling by the minute, Bill had to laugh. 'We'll not forget this Christmas Eve in a hurry, and that's a fact.'

T HAT NIGHT ROUND the dinner table, Joe remarked on something he'd heard being discussed in the marketplace that day. 'Remember that feller who was murdered down south? Bloke by the name of Slater?' Without waiting for an answer he went on, 'It seems old Ted the greengrocer knew him.'

Molly chuckled. 'Old Ted knows everybody,' she said, 'especially if they've been in the news.'

Joe nodded. 'You're right. The daft old sod, his mind's wandering, I reckon.'

Molly recalled the murder. 'By! It's a bad thing,

though, an' no mistake. Who in God's name could kill his own brother?'

'You'd be surprised.' With a quick smile, Tommy glanced at his brother Jack. 'If my best shirt keeps going missing, *I* just might end up strangling my own brother.'

'Never touched your shirt.' Jack, morose and moody as usual, had nothing more to say all evening.

Sam was still intrigued by the report of the murder. 'What made him do it?' he asked. 'What drove this feller Slater to murder his own flesh and blood?'

Joe shrugged his shoulders. 'Don't rightly know. All I know was he'd hidden his brother's body in the cellar and it were found by some passing tramps – a young woman and a boy. They alerted the nuns at some convent or other, then they disappeared and the authorities haven't been able to find them.' Not wanting to let his dinner go cold, he shovelled a fork filled with meat into his mouth. 'It won't matter though, because it seems they finally got a confession outta the feller. He'll hang, and so he should, the wicked devil.'

The meal continued in silence for a while. Tommy was about to ask another question but Molly wagged a finger at him. 'I don't want to hear no more about this murder,' she announced firmly. 'It's Christmas Eve and we're having us dinner. We shouldn't be talking of murders and such like. Not tonight.' Then she lightened the atmosphere by recounting what had happened at the Sun earlier.

Everyone laughed. 'You'd start a fight in a mortuary,' Joe said, and her sons agreed.

Tommy thought it hilarious. 'I wish I'd been there,'

he told her, punching the air with clenched fists.

'I hope it's a few years before you set foot inside one o' them places,' Molly retorted. 'An' if I catch yer fighting, I'll tan yer arse, so think on it, my lad.'

Sam asked about the floozy with Len Armitage and was told in a stern voice, 'She was out for all she could get, so you'd best be warned about women like that.'

Jack quietly listened and had little to say except, 'Is there any more turkey, Mam?' When he'd had a second and a third helping, followed by a dish of Molly's home-made fruit pudding, he pushed away his chair and stood up. 'I'm off for a walk,' he announced, and the sound of the door banging shut behind him signalled his departure.

'I'm surprised he can walk after eating that lot.' Joe had devoured only half the amount and was flopped in the chair, as though his legs had given out beneath him.

It wasn't long before all of Molly's sons left the house, with the exception of Bill who sat by the fireside, smoking his pipe, his dark eyes intent on the dancing flames in the fire grate and his mind elsewhere.

'Much as I might wish it, these dishes won't wash theirselves.' With a long groan Molly got up and began clearing away the crockery, after which she could be heard singing merrily as she clattered about in the kitchen.

Aware that she'd had a busy day, Bill might have offered to help if it hadn't been for the fact that Joe had already offered and been told in no uncertain terms, 'This is woman's business. Get away with you and find summat else to occupy yer mind.'

When Molly's work was done, she came and sat by the fire. Joe was gently snoring, and Bill was pacing the floor. 'Well now, you two ain't much company an' that's a fact,' she snorted. 'One sleeping, an' the other prowling like a lion in a cage.'

In no time at all, with the heat from the fire on her face and her belly full of Christmas fare, Molly herself had closed her eyes and was snoozing contentedly. Bill looked at the pair of them and smiled. 'Just look at you,' he murmured, glancing from one to the other. 'Worn to a frazzle, the pair of you.'

Quietly he tiptoed out of the room. He had half a mind to go and see Kate Jordan but his heart wasn't in it.

He peered out of the door. It was snowing. 'If I had any sense at all, I'd curl up by the fire and let my dinner settle,' he sighed. 'But I've got no sense at all these days. Too much on my mind, that's the trouble.'

All the same, he put on his overcoat and went for a walk. After the heat of the house, the cold and the snow was exhilarating. The breeze cut through his skin and made him shiver but the faster he walked the more invigorated he felt. There was something very satisfying about hearing the newly fallen snow crunch beneath your feet. Besides, he was an outdoor man. Being inside made him feel trapped; as his mam had rightly observed, like a lion in a cage.

His mind was sharper out in the air, and he was able to see more clearly. His longing for Nell was growing into something more desperate as the months went by. 'You're a bloody fool, man!' he told himself. 'Nell's never looked at you in that way. I expect she'd run a mile if she thought you had ideas about marrying her.'

J OE WOKE WITH a stretch. 'Ready for bed, are you, lass?' Feeling mischievous, he jabbed Molly in the groin. 'Wake up, ye lazy divil, or ye'll not sleep a wink in your bed tonight.'

Molly opened one brown eye. 'D'you want a clip o' the ear?' she asked.

'Now why would ye want to clip me ear?' he chided. 'Amn't I the one who loves ye like nobody else?'

'Stop prodding me then.'

'Molly, have ye seen the time?' His gaze went to the clock on the mantelpiece. 'Sure, we ought to be in our beds.'

Closing her eye, Molly shifted her weight and groaned. 'Bugger yer, Joe! Leave me be while I have a little kip.'

'Sure it's gone midnight.'

That stirred her. 'Yer what?' Sitting up in the chair, she glanced at the clock, her eyes widening with horror. 'Why didn't yer wake me, you dozy article?' She scrambled out of the chair, dazed and confused. 'Fancy letting me fall asleep. Why, I've got things to do. I ain't got the presents wrapped nor nothin'.'

'Well then, ye'll just have to get out of yer bed a bit earlier, won't ye?' He stood up, looking her in the eye and loving her for the woman she was. 'Sit down.'

Molly gaped at him. 'Yer what?'

Gently he pressed her into the chair. 'I said sit down,

an' I'll make us both a nightcap.' When she made to get up, he pressed her down again. 'Stay where ye are, woman. The men are out an' we're on us own, an' I'm waiting on ye for once.'

Before Molly could object, he was gone into the kitchen where he quickly set about making two mugs of cocoa, and into each he poured a little measure from the stone jug on the shelf. He chuckled as he poured. 'Anybody who can get the better o' Len Armitage is worth a drop o' the best.'

By now, Molly was enjoying being waited on. 'What's got into yer?' she asked when he returned with a broad smile on his cheeky face.

'Get that down ye,' he said, chinking his cup against hers. Winking, he confessed, 'I've put a little extra something in it, to keep out the cold.'

Taking a swig of the brown nectar, Molly's eyes lit up. Smacking her lips, she winked back and mimicking his broad Irish accent, she laughed, 'Joe Davidson, yer a man after me own heart, sure ye are.'

They sat and talked, like most parents do, about their children and the merciless passage of time. 'They're all growed now,' Molly said sadly. 'Even young Tommy's getting the ideas of a man.'

It was another of their sons that occupied Joe's mind. 'What's ailing the eldest?' he asked. 'What's troubling him?'

Molly said cautiously, 'What makes you think summat's ailing him?'

Sipping his drink, he regarded her through shrewd eyes. 'Ye know, don't ye?' He had been wed to Molly for many years and knew her almost as well as he knew the back of a playing card. 'Sure, ye know what's wrong, an' ye're saying nothing, isn't that the truth?'

'Bill can look after himself.'

'Is it woman trouble?'

Molly shrugged her shoulders. 'Who knows?'

He smiled at her. '*You* know.' He was convinced. 'You know an' ye won't tell.'

'All right then.' Molly suspected he would not be satisfied until she'd settled it one way or another. 'It's possible there *is* a woman behind it all,' she admitted, 'but it's not for you nor me to ask questions.'

'Hm. In other words, mind me own business, eh?'

'If you like.' She took another swig of her drink and closed her eyes with a satisfied sigh. 'Yer know how to mek a soothing nightcap, I'll give yer that, our Joe.'

'He's unhappy though.' His eldest son was special to him. 'Our Bill don't seem the same any more.'

Molly grew impatient. 'What d'yer mean?'

'I mean, after we'd had our dinner, he'd always sit and chat with his old dad but tonight he were miles away. When he'd finished his day's work he'd always walk through that door with a smile and a joke, and a lengthy account of what went on at his work.' He rolled the cup in his hands, his face troubled as he asked, 'Is it bad, Molly? This woman, she isn't married, is she?'

Molly shook her head. 'Bill's got more sense than to get involved with a married woman. No, it ain't that, an' it ain't nothin' he can't sort out in his own good time, so stop yer worrying an' take yer wife to her bed.' Her brown eyes twinkled. 'Happen she wants a bit o' comforting, eh?'

That pleased him. 'Am I right in thinking you're throwing yourself at me?'

'Mebbe.'

'You're a harlot, sure ye are. You get off to your bed now while I lock up.' He kissed her soundly on the cheek. 'It isn't often we get the house to ourselves, so let's make the most of it, eh?'

Upstairs, Molly took Nell's letters from beneath the carpet where she kept them hidden. 'Can't let anyone get hold of these,' she muttered. 'Thanks to Lilian Reece being too ashamed to talk about it and her brother under instructions to keep his mouth shut, Nell's little secret is still safe.' She cast her gaze over today's letter from Nell, posted some time back. Softly she read it aloud. 'I'm fine, Molly, though I still miss you all. I've got work now and am managing to save a few shillings. I have a new job in a baker's shop, and people are being kind, in spite of me having a belly the size of a ship! I've found a new friend. His name is Kit. It won't be too long now before the baby arrives. We'll see how it goes then. Meanwhile, I'll keep in touch. Take care and God bless, and don't worry. Love from Nell. By the way, I hope Bill is all right.'

'Aw, lass, o' course he's all right,' Molly murmured. 'I only wish to God you'd make yer way home.'

Joe's voice startled her. 'Talking to yerself now, is it?' he said from the stairs.

Quickly she put away the letters and was beginning to undress when he came into the room. 'You're a fine figure of a woman,' he told her.

275

And Molly would have walked over coals for him.

When Bill returned a short time later, he could hear the soft laughter coming from his parents' room. It made him feel good. 'It's nice to know you're still a pair of lovebirds,' he murmured. Then he thoughtfully closed the sitting-room door and put the kettle on. 'They don't need me climbing the stairs just yet. Besides, there's no sleep in me. I'd only lie there thinking of Nell, and wishing she was here.'

ROSALYN MORGAN HAD never been a strong woman, and the burden of carrying a child these many long months was almost more than she could bear. She went about the house with a pale, wan face, her footsteps dragging as though she had the weight of the world on her shoulders. She cried easily and stayed awake most nights until the dawn lit the sky.

Lying beside her, enjoying the sleep of the innocent, though he was far from that, Vincent Morgan had no idea his wife was in such distress. Or he didn't care.

When she wasn't gazing out on the sky through the open curtains, Rosalyn would sit for hours watching him, listening to the gentle rhythm of his breathing and wishing she could rest so easily. Occasionally he would sense her staring at him and open his eyes. 'For goodness sake, go to sleep,' he would groan, turning away impatiently. 'And lie down. You're making a draught in the bed.'

Over the months, her love for him had turned to indifference, then to resentment, and at times like these, when he showed such callous indifference to her distress, she learned to hate him. It only added to her burden, for she was not a vindictive person. She just wanted to be cherished. Instead, the larger she got with child, the less she was noticed.

Vincent Morgan tolerated his wife but he worshipped the child she carried, to such an extent that he was becoming obsessive about its imminent arrival. When the doctor came, he would usher him upstairs with the urgency of a man whose wife was already giving birth, and when he came back down, Vincent would be waiting. 'Is the baby all right?' he would ask nervously, as he did on this bitter cold January morning.

'The baby is fine.' Dr Fellows gave him a disapproving glance. 'But your wife is not as well as she could be. I am concerned about her.' Each time he saw Rosalyn Morgan, she seemed more and more despondent. It was clear her husband neglected her, and she had no one to whom she could turn. No friends and no family. It was a pitiful situation. 'Is it not possible for you to spend a little more time with her?' he inquired now. 'She does seem to be left on her own quite a lot.'

'Has she been complaining?'

'Well, no, but then Mrs Morgan is not the kind of woman to complain.'

'Then I suggest you treat her aches and pains and leave the welfare of my wife to me.'

'As you wish.' He clicked his black bag shut with a sharp snap.

'If my wife wants anything, she only has to ask,' Vincent added.

'I have no doubt you provide very well for your wife,' Dr Fellows said stiffly, 'but you must understand she has a very weak constitution. A woman in her condition needs company. She needs to feel wanted.' He took a deep breath. 'She needs *you*, sir. For God's sake, man, the woman is carrying your child. Show *some* compassion.'

Vincent flushed with anger. 'I don't pay you to be impertinent.'

The doctor stared at him in silence.

'I should bar you from this house,' Vincent snapped. 'Other doctors know their place.'

'Of course. You do have a choice.' Dr Fellows squared his shoulders. 'So, am I to understand that my services are no longer needed?' His bold inquiry belied the concern he felt. He did not want to be dismissed. He had brought Rosalyn Morgan through most of her pregnancy and he wanted to see her come safely to term.

Realising he would be hard pressed to find so good a doctor, and at such short notice, Vincent began to regret his words. 'I fear we have both been rather hasty,' he said nervously. 'Let's have no more of it. You will continue to attend my wife but in future confine your remarks to medical matters.' He held out his hand. 'Agreed?'

The doctor hesitated. He had just left a sobbing woman, and he knew from the town gossip that Vincent Morgan continued to see other women, sometimes even bringing them home to this very house.

'I do love her, you know.' It embarrassed Vincent to say that but in a strange way it was the truth.

The doctor took his hand. 'Take care of her,' he

murmured. 'And be thankful you're a man because bearing a child is the hardest thing in the world.'

'I understand.' Vincent was genuinely sorry for the way he treated Rosalyn. They were not suited, he should never have married her, but he had and now he must make the best of it. 'I will try,' he promised.

The doctor nodded. 'Good day to you then. I'll call in again tomorrow. The birth is very close.'

Vincent accompanied him to the door. 'This . . .' he searched for a word, 'this malaise you say my wife suffers from, will it harm the child?'

'Of course not.' The doctor spoke harshly. 'It needn't affect your wife either if you can find the time to be with her, talk to her, stroll round the gardens. The cold won't hurt her as long as she's well wrapped up, but you must not take her far from the house.'

'Of course. I'll see to it.' He meant well. He always meant well, but it never came to anything.

When he went to her room, Rosalyn was still sobbing on the bed. Seating himself beside her, he pulled her into his arms. 'I know I haven't spared you much time lately, but things will change, you'll see. I'll find time for you from now on.'

With tragic eyes, she gazed up at him. 'I'm sorry, Vincent. I don't mean to be miserable but I can't help it.'

'I know.' Holding her close like this was surprisingly pleasant. Her hair smelled of perfume, and her skin was exquisitely soft. Suddenly, in the middle of the morning, he wanted her.

'The doctor says the baby's doing fine.' Delighted

because he was holding her, Rosalyn smiled into his eyes, her face glowing with the promise of motherhood.

Slowly, his hand covered her stomach, caressing the mound that held his child; a child of his own making, someone to perpetuate the name Morgan. He never thought it might be a girl. Always when he imagined the child in his mind, it was a boy, a strong, healthy boy, with his own nature and colouring. 'We'll call him Robert Joshua,' he decided, 'after my father.'

Rosalyn didn't mind that. All she wanted was to be rid of this great, uncomfortable thing that had plagued her for months. 'What makes you think it's a boy?'

'It wouldn't dare be anything else.' His hand moved from her stomach to her breast. 'Being with child suits you,' he lied. Being with child made her ugly, he thought with repugnance. Being with child had turned her into a huge, obnoxious thing. Still, he remembered what the doctor had said and he tried to be compassionate. 'Is it so bad?' he asked. 'Does the child move inside you?' He was intrigued, oddly jealous. It was *his* child yet she was the one growing closer to it.

A faint blush tinged her face. 'Yes,' she whispered shyly. 'It doesn't move quite so much lately, but the doctor says there's no cause for concern.'

'Are you looking forward to the birth?' He wanted to be the one giving birth. He wanted to experience the child being brought into the world. He wanted to suffer the pain and the joy, but it was not to be. The realisation raised a terrible anger in him.

'I know it's cowardly but I'm afraid.' The fear showed in her face. It sickened him.

'I won't be far away,' he promised. Skilfully, his fingers undid the small pearly buttons on her dress and his hand slipped inside, caressing the warm, bare breast. The feel of it in his hand, the touch of a hardened nipple in the tips of his fingers made him wild with desire. Rosalyn, however, was flinching beneath his touch.

Gently he pressed her to the bed. 'You look so beautiful,' he lied, lifting her skirt and sliding his hand to her bare thigh. 'I need you badly, right now.' His member was bursting, standing so tall and erect, he was actually in pain. With his other hand he undid the buttons on his trousers and drew it out. 'Open your legs,' he pleaded. 'Hurry!' In a moment it would be too late.

'You can't.' His weight crushed the child inside her. It weighed on her, seeming to squeeze her lungs until she could hardly breathe. He was hurting her, frightening her. 'Don't. Please.' She tried to push him off but he was too determined.

'I won't hurt you,' he whispered. 'I only want to love you.' In that moment, when his loins were fired and his soul screaming for satisfaction, he would have said or done anything to get his own way.

Rosalyn's need was of a different kind. She needed to believe every word he uttered, and so, in the heat and rush of the moment, she let herself believe.

Looking into his eyes, she imagined she could see a kind of love there. Now, when he kissed her again, softly talking and telling her how lovely she was, and how he would take care of her, how could she resist? She wanted him to love her, needed him to hold her and to stay with her. She was lonely, and he was her husband.

Lying back on the bed and easing herself into a more comfortable position, she opened her legs. 'Be careful,' she pleaded. 'The baby.' She felt his hands parting her legs wide, then he was tugging at her underwear, and suddenly, but with immense tenderness, he was pushing into her.

At first, she lay with her legs dangling over the edge of the bed so his weight would not press too heavily on the baby, but as he neared his climax he thrust so hard into her that she was pushed backwards, with his whole weight falling on her. She didn't cry out like she might have done before because, astonishingly, she was actually enjoying his lovemaking. The huge, hard member was an intrusion into her body, and she resented that part of it, but he was with her, holding and loving her, and talking to her in a way he had not done for a very long time. Discomfort was a small price to pay for such rare joy.

Afterwards, when he climbed off and looked down on her swollen body, he felt physically sick.

'You did mean it, didn't you?' she asked, tidying herself. 'Things *will* be different from now on?'

Already he'd forgotten. Promises were merely a means to an end, and easily broken. 'If that's what I promised, you can rely on it.' He even bent to kiss her, though it turned his stomach to be so close. 'I have to go. I was supposed to see Bill Davidson at the cottage an hour ago.'

In minutes he was out of the house and striding towards the stables. 'The stallion,' he demanded of the groom. 'I need something spirited underneath me.' He was thinking of her, and of the way she had just lain there, like a great fat lump of dough. Once his son was born, he would have no need to pretend. From this day on, he would never again go to her bed.

Taken by the devil, he rode like a madman. 'God forgive me, but I can't even look on my own wife any more,' he shouted to the wind. 'When I need a woman, I'll find one who knows how to please a man!'

***

BILL DAVIDSON WAS astride the roof. 'It's as I feared,' he told Vincent. 'The thatch is rat-ridden and the timbers beneath are rotten. The whole lot needs stripping and replacing.'

He took Vincent on a tour of the cottage. 'The chimney's cracked all the way up from the hearth,' he said, 'and the floors are split. I've saved most of the window frames, and I should be able to salvage some of the good timber to be used again, but there's still a lot to do, and it's bound to cost.'

'Since old Jed passed on, the work has been neglected. I wonder, is it actually worth the saving?' In his present mood, Vincent could have demolished the bloody thing with his own bare hands. 'I haven't got money to waste.'

'We wouldn't have started this work if we thought it was a waste,' Bill responded. 'Some time back you asked us if this place should be taken down or built up, and we gave you our answer. Restored and extended, it could make a pretty penny if ever you came to sell it.'

'Meanwhile, I suppose I could try and find a tenant

for it and get part of the money back that way.'

Bill frowned. 'I thought the cottage was always mine for the asking. You didn't say anything about offering it to anybody else.'

'Nothing was written in stone.'

'All the same . . .' Bill was ready to do battle.

'Look! *If* I decide to rent it out, you'll still get first refusal. As yet nothing's been decided so there's no point discussing it.'

In the back of his mind Vincent had other ideas for the cottage. It could be an ideal place to bring his women. Taking them to the house was beginning to get too risky. If Rosalyn found out, there was no telling what she might do, and with a child due, he wanted her there. She was a lady after all, with a lady's upbringing; the women he took did not have the breeding to bring up a son of his.

'Put in as much time as you can on this,' he told Bill. 'See if we can't have it finished before the spring.'

'It'll need to be done by then,' Bill pointed out, 'what with the lambing season an' all.' There was something peculiar about Morgan today, he thought. It was making him feel very uncomfortable. 'Is there something else?'

'Such as what?'

'You seem to have something on your mind.'

'If I have, it doesn't concern you,' Vincent snapped, and changed the subject. 'That new man we've taken on, is he any good? Do we keep him?'

'He seems to be pulling his weight. I'd advise keeping him.' Bill wasn't altogether satisfied with the new man but he was prepared to give him the benefit of the doubt. 'At least for a month.' Unlike some he could mention, he would never put a man out of work unless he deserved it.

'All right, Davidson. Keep an eye on him. Good men are hard to find these days. Still, if he turns out as well as the new maid at the house, I'll be satisfied.' He grinned like a wicked schoolboy, his humour returning with the mention of the new maid. 'She makes a pretty sight for the visitor and earns her keep into the bargain.' He winked at Bill who did not give him the satisfaction of returning his smile.

As Vincent rode away, Bill's dark eyes followed him. 'It were a bad day when you wed that poor woman o' yours,' he muttered. 'There can't be a woman in the whole o' Blackburn that you haven't bedded.'

Sore at heart because Morgan had hinted he might have other ideas for the cottage, Bill returned to his work. 'I'm spending every hour God sends breathing life into this cottage,' he murmured, running a hand over the ancient timbers above the fireplace. 'And I'm telling you now, Morgan, you'll have a fight on your hands if you mean to rob me of it.'

W HEN NIGHT FELL, Vincent was still irritable. He had gone into town with the intention of finding a woman. He toured the bars of Blackburn. He went in and out of sleazy clubs, and even kissed a girl or two but none of them took his fancy. After a while he made his way home, entering the house in the early hours, only to find to his dismay that Rosalyn was waiting in her room for him.

She was sitting in front of the mirror. 'Do you think I should wear my hair like this?' she asked, piling it on top of her head. She had made up her face, and it repelled him. Wiping his thumb over her mouth, he smudged the lipstick across her cheek.

'Get that muck off,' he snarled. 'You look like a harlot.'

'I thought you'd like it.' Like a wounded child, she stared up at him.

'You were wrong.' He turned to the door. 'I'm off to my bed.'

'Please, Vincent, stay with me tonight.' She didn't want his physical attention. All she wanted was to have him near and to hear his voice. 'I'm afraid,' she confessed. 'Suppose the baby starts and I'm on my own?'

'I'm not a nursemaid,' he answered coldly.

'Please, Vincent.'

She was so pathetic he felt sorry for her. He loathed the fact that he could not love her, and he loathed himself for ever letting her believe he could.

'You'll be all right,' he said, his anger falling away. 'The doctor would have said if there was any danger of the child arriving tonight.' Sitting on the chair close beside her, he took hold of her hands, his gaze drawn to them. They were so fine, and pale, and the fingers so long and slim. A lady's hands. A sense of pride rushed through him. 'You've done so well,' he admitted, suppressing his jealousy. 'I know how hard it must be for you.' She was so like a child, he thought, with her narrow white face and those delicate pale eyes. If only he could love her, things might have been so different.

'Stay with me. Please?'

How he despised her when she clung like that. 'I'll send the new maid,' he said, dropping her hands to her lap. 'She seems a sensible little thing.' And before she could argue the point, he left the room.

Rosalyn sat still for a moment, staring at her own reflection. 'He doesn't love you, Rosalyn. He never has, and he never will.'

———

I T WAS LATE. The house was quiet and the servants were sleeping. Softly, Vincent went up the stairs to the servants' quarters. Tapping his knuckles on the small panelled door, he called in a harsh whisper, 'Maria, get dressed. The mistress needs you.'

Almost immediately the door opened and a young, brazen-faced woman appeared. Clothed in a long white nightgown and with her dark hair hanging loose about her shoulders, she smiled seductively. 'I knew you'd be here tonight,' she told him coyly. 'I've been waiting for you.'

Terrified the other servants might hear, he bundled her back inside. 'You little fool!' Shaking her by the shoulders, he thought how light she felt in his hands, how light, and warm, and desirable. 'Haven't I already warned you how delicate this whole thing is? When I want you, I'll let you know, but right now it's the mistress who's in need. She's feeling unwell. Get down to her, and keep your mouth shut.'

'Sorry, sir.' Afraid she might have overstepped the mark, she backed away. Standing before the full-length mirror and aware that he was watching, she slowly stripped off her nightgown and tantalised him by bending and moving, pretending to look for a suitable dress. 'It's all right, sir,' she breathed, turning and showing her nakedness fully to him. 'I'll only be a minute.'

Making a sound like someone in agony, he carefully closed the door. 'You little witch.'

For a long, agonising moment they stared at each other, each of them knowing he was lost, and each with their own feelings; he curled up inside with shame and longing, she jubilant. He was a man with a dangerous appetite, and she knew it.

He tore off his clothes and threw her on to the bed. Their lovemaking was wild and passionate. They played with each other, rolling about on the bed, biting and kissing, knowing every inch of the other's body. Then he lay beneath her, his hands curved to her buttocks.

'Want more, do you?' she murmured, and leaning forward placed one large breast above his mouth. When he opened his lips and sucked at the nipple, she moaned with pleasure, at the same time easing herself over him. With a sigh, she opened herself to him and, watching his face, pushed down with the whole of her body, slowly swallowing the hard member beneath her.

The expression of exquisite pleasure on his face, the small agonised cry, and the way he clutched at her with all his strength gave her a feeling of power. Now, the master was at her mercy.

LYING ON HER bed, Rosalyn was taken unawares by the jabbing pain that shot through her. At first she waited, thinking it would go away, but when the second pain came, longer and more vicious, she realised there was something very wrong. 'Vincent?' she called, but there was no answer. 'Maria?' Again, no answer.

Easing her legs round, she put her feet to the floor and waited a moment. It was obvious no one had heard her. There was no pain now, not like before, but she felt strange, as though her whole body was about to break wide open.

Standing up, she closed her eyes, letting the dizziness wash through her. Then she put on her slippers and robe and made her way very carefully out of the room.

HE LAY BENEATH her, breathless and aching with emotion. 'Don't tease,' he pleaded through gritted teeth. 'You're driving me mad!' But it was what he wanted and she knew it.

Neither of them heard the door open. It was only when the cool draught flickered across the floor and touched them that they looked up. When they saw Rosalyn standing there, they were both transfixed with horror.

Her face grey with shock, Rosalyn stared down on their naked bodies, and though her lips moved, no sound came out until a spasm of agony gripped her. 'You . . . you . . .' She turned away, gasping and sobbing. Though the pain was fierce, she somehow staggered across the landing.

'Rosalyn!' Throwing the girl off, Vincent quickly dressed and went after her. She was at the top of the stairs, bent double in pain and sobbing bitterly.

'Stay away!' she cried. 'STAY AWAY FROM ME!' She turned to look at him and for as long as he lived he would not forget the expression in her eyes; it was a mirror of his own terrible hatred.

'I'm sorry,' he said, coming towards her, arms outstretched. 'I'm so sorry.'

She edged away, her body ravaged by a rhythm of pain, but the pain he had caused her was far greater. 'You only ever wanted the child,' she told him. 'You never really wanted me.'

In that same moment when he realised her intention and launched himself at her, she smiled, and before he could catch her she threw herself forward, arms outstretched as though flying. His voice screamed after her, 'NO . . . O . . . O!' His stricken eyes looked down, watching her bounce from one step to the next, the awful, muffled sound echoing in his ears as he raced after her. Behind him, the servants gathered, covering their faces in horror – all but Maria who did not dare come out of her room.

There was nothing anyone could do. Rosalyn had chosen her own way, and the child went with her.

'You won't have either of us now,' she said brokenly when he cradled her in his arms.

There was no pain now, only a sense of regret.

She touched his tear-stained face, and her smile faded. In its place was a world of sadness. 'I do . . . love you,' she whispered. And, while she was still looking up at him, death came and took her gently by the hand.

IT SNOWED HEAVEN'S hardest when they buried Rosalyn Morgan, with the child still inside her.

There were many good people there. The Morgans had very few friends and did little socialising, so the mourners were made up from the working community; farming neighbours and a smattering of townsfolk, including Molly, who had come because her son was part of that little world, and because Nell had spoken kindly of Rosalyn Morgan. She cried for the woman herself, and she cried for Nell. These two lovely souls were with child. One, now lying in that cold grave, was gone for ever. The other was too far away for Molly to hold, and oh, how she ached to see her again.

All the servants were there, except the girl, Maria, who had brought all this about. No one knew where she'd gone and no one cared, least of all Vincent Morgan.

It was given out that the mistress of the Morgan house had suffered a fatal fall. Only Vincent Morgan and the servants knew the truth behind the tragedy, that the mistress had thrown herself down the stairs after finding her husband in bed with a maidservant. There were those who would have liked to shout it from the rooftops, like the old cook who had seen the Morgans married and then parted in such a terrible manner. But, like the other servants at the house, her tongue was stilled by the fear of losing job and home if she should ever betray the master. He had warned them all, and not one of them dared to disobey.

Besides, it could be argued that it truly had been an accident, and yet they had seen her face, they had seen how she flung wide her arms as she went, and they whispered to each other, it was no accident. Rosalyn Morgan took her own miserable life.

Bill was there, heartsick at the loss of such a good woman. Like many others, he knew of Morgan's insatiable taste for other women. Unlike the others though, he laid the blame for this terrible thing squarely on that man's shoulders.

Dr Fellows was there too. Inside the splendid church of St Peter's, he sang as proud as any man; he walked behind the coffin when it was carried to its last resting place, and afterwards when the service was being read he bowed his head and quietly wept.

Don Reece did not go to the church service. Instead, he waited outside along with all the other curious folk. When the procession moved into the churchyard, he followed at a discreet distance. 'Such a pity,' said a stocky woman in a red hat. 'And her with child an' all.'

He merely nodded, not wishing to get involved in a conversation about the late Rosalyn Morgan.

Molly saw him there and smiled. Later, she spoke to him. 'I hope I'm not intruding,' she said, 'but I know if Nell was here, she would have been at the service.'

Don agreed. 'That lady was kind to my girl when she needed help. Like you, I thought I should come for Nell's sake, to say thank you.' They walked on, these two people who had always been close to Nell. They talked of her, wishing she was here, and wondering how she was doing.

The mourners were dispersing. Only Vincent Morgan stood beside the open grave, his face white as chalk and his heart filled with bitterness. His eyes raked the brass plaque which bore her name, and when he spoke, low and trembling, it was with murder in his heart. 'You took my son,' he murmured. 'I won't forgive you for that.' Stooping to the ground, he clutched a handful of earth and threw it with considerable force on to the coffin. 'Damn you to hell!' he muttered. 'Damn you to hell!' Then he swung away and strode towards his waiting carriage.

'Have you heard from Nell lately?' Molly asked Don.

'Not since a month back. Mind you, it wouldn't surprise me if her aunt hasn't got the letters hidden somewhere. She's a wicked old bugger – if you'll excuse me.' He was embarrassed. Molly might be rough and ready but he had no right to use such language in her company.

'Away with yer!' Molly was not bashful. 'I've used stronger language than that in my time.'

'I'm worried about Nell. Mebbe I shouldn't have sent her away.' It had plagued his conscience ever since.

'I don't suppose you had much choice,' Molly suggested. 'Nell told me how her aunt was insisting that she have the baby scraped away. I knew she was with child, you know.'

'Oh aye. Lilian even had one of them backstreet women lined up to do it. Nell would have none of that, and so I helped her get away.' He sighed. 'I only hope to God she's all right.'

'Don't you worry now.' Molly didn't want to let him

know how she, too, was worried. 'Nell will be ready when the bairn comes. She's young and strong, and she's nobody's fool.'

'I know that.' He made the sign of the cross. 'But, I mean ... look at poor Mrs Morgan, falling down the stairs like that, her baby gone and everything. It doesn't bear thinking about. Our Nell's bairn must be due soon, and she's on her own out there. Suppose an accident befalls her? I wish there was something I could do, but I've no idea where she is, and even if I did, she's that stubborn she wouldn't come back till she were ready.'

Molly was surprised. 'Would you really fetch her home, seeing as how your sister wanted rid of her bairn? Oh, I know she can't do much harm when it's here in flesh and blood, but Nell won't forget a thing like that.' A thought occurred to her. 'Have you any idea who fathered Nell's bairn?'

'None at all. She can be a stubborn little sod, can our Nell. All I know is she were made with child by somebody who won't come forward, and she wouldn't betray him no matter how many times I queried it. If you ask me, he must be a married feller.' Wringing his hands in the air, he groaned. 'God help the bugger if I ever lay hands on him, that's all I can say.'

Molly would have echoed the sentiment but just then she caught sight of Vincent Morgan. He was so close she could have reached out and touched him. It startled her; she and Don had been discussing a very private matter. For a moment she was unable to gather her wits enough to greet him.

Don, however, tipped his hat and muttered

condolences. 'A terrible thing, sir,' he stuttered. 'A terrible thing.' Embarrassed, he abruptly wished him and Molly good day and went on his way.

As he climbed into the carriage, Vincent noticed Molly regarding him curiously. He gave her a curt nod. Briefly he wondered who she was but he didn't pursue the thought. His mind was elsewhere – on Nell. She carried his child! He had forgotten all about her until reminded of her existence, and her condition, by the conversation he'd just overheard between that woman and Nell's father.

'Home is it, sir?' The carriage driver leaned his head down, awaiting instructions.

Vincent thought a while. 'No,' he answered. 'Take me to town, to my solicitor's office. As quick as you can.'

Chapter Eight

NELL HAD BEEN working at the baker's in Aylesbury for almost a month now, and every day was beginning to be more of a strain. 'Soon you won't be able to squeeze your backside behind this counter.' Kathy Johns was past her prime, a big, kind soul, with a heart of gold and a simple outlook on life. 'Another fortnight and I reckon you'll drop that bairn right where you stand.' She eyed Nell's huge belly with suspicion. 'No, not a fortnight,' she decided. 'I reckon it'll be ripe for dropping in less than a week. You've got a pink face, and that's always a sign the bairn's getting restless.'

Nell feared she could be right but denied it because she wasn't ready to lose her place here. 'I'll hold out till the day,' she promised, 'so don't you go worrying.' Knowing how Kath was counting on her, she was determined not to let her down.

'You're a hard little bugger.' The older woman looked at Nell and was reminded of the time she carried her own son. 'I never had a minute's bother when I carried our Lionel. I weren't sick or owt like that, but I pampered myself, if you know what I mean. I made the most of it, lying in bed till all hours and making out I were on my last legs every time I were asked to do any

297

work.' Winking heartily, she confessed, 'Once, I lay in bed a whole week while my husband waited on me hand and foot. Poor devil, he passed away when the lad were only two year old.'

'Oh, Kath, I am sorry.' Nell had noticed there was no man about but she hadn't liked to ask.

'Yeah, I'm sorry too,' Kath admitted. 'He were a good sort, and never had a day's illness in his life. I swear it were me as finished him off by being lazy and expecting him to carry me for nine months.' She gazed around at the pretty little shop with its bay windows and small-panelled bull's-eye panes. 'This was his pride and joy,' she said softly, 'but it's crippling work. You know yourself the long, hard hours our Lionel puts in. The pair of us have to work all the hours God sends to keep this place going.' She paused, letting the guilt wash over her as she often did when thinking of her late husband.

'Have you ever thought of selling?'

'Oh yes. Time and again, but I owe it to Lionel and his dad to keep it thriving. It's given us a comfortable life and I'd be a fool to give it up. I dare say the hard work will kill me in the end but it'll only be what I deserve.'

The shop bell rang and there followed a hectic few minutes while they served the rush of women who were on their way home from Aylesbury market. 'You astonish me,' Kath admitted, glancing at Nell who was shifting the loaves along the shelf.

Nell turned round. 'In what way?'

'Well, take a look at yourself. Big as a barge, only a week or two from birthing, and working like a navvy, up at the crack of dawn and never a complaint. You make me feel ashamed.'

'I love working here. You pay me well, and give us board and lodging. What have I got to complain about?'

'I don't know but if I were in your shoes, which I'm not, thank God, I'm sure I'd find *something* to complain about.'

Nell laughed. 'No you wouldn't. You say that but you work harder than any of us here, and I've never heard you moan.'

'You won't neither,' Kath replied hastily. 'I've done my moaning and it put my husband in his grave before his time. I'm serving my punishment and so I should.' She smiled, a broad, toothless grin. 'But you're right, Nell. This is a lovely little place and I've managed to save a tidy balance for my old age. I don't know what I've done to deserve it but not a day goes by when I don't thank my lucky stars. There's you and the lad, travelling the world on the back of a cart, not knowing from one night to the next where you'll lay down to sleep. You're about to drop your child, with no man to keep you, and still you can smile brighter than a summer's day.'

'What's the use of crying?' Nell wanted to know. 'It'll only make you feel worse. And anyway, I've got my health and strength, and once the baby's born I should be able to plan a proper life. You see, nobody wants you when you're big as a house, but I'm hoping it might be different when I can do a harder day's work. Me and Kit will handle it, don't you worry.' She looked at this big, kind woman and was grateful. 'You've been a godsend

to me these past weeks,' she said. 'I was at the end of my
tether when you took me and Kit in.' Her voice broke
as she recalled how hungry and cold they were, and
desperate for a friend.

Kath remembered too, and she smiled fondly.
'When you came into this shop with your sad blue eyes
and a belly like a ship, I didn't have the heart to turn
you away.'

'There were plenty who did though.' Nell had lost
count of the number of times she and Kit had been
chased from various establishments. It was a humiliation
she would never forget.

Filled with admiration, Kath told her, 'You're a
strong-spirited creature, Nell. I'm sure you'll pull
through, however many people turn you away.' She was
ashamed to admit it but she, too, was planning to turn
Nell away. 'God willing, I'll never have to face what
you've faced,' she said, 'because I don't reckon I'd have
the courage to go on.'

'You'd be surprised what strength you've got when
you need to find it.'

'I know my strength and it doesn't amount to a
thimbleful,' Kath admitted. 'I know it wouldn't run to
sleeping rough and living hand to mouth.'

'I know what you mean,' Nell answered from the
heart. 'It's not what I would have chosen either.'

'I gathered that.' For weeks now, ever since Nell had
appeared, rag-tagged and looking for work, she had
longed to quiz her about the awful circumstances that
saw her, a woman so advanced in pregnancy, on the
road with a lad who was obviously neither brother nor

son; he wasn't a brother because he was a Cockney and Nell was a northerner, and he wasn't her son because there were only seven or eight years between them. Moreover, they conversed as though they hadn't known each other all that long. It was a curious set of circumstances, and she was intrigued.

'You've never said why you were on the road,' she ventured cautiously, 'or why you weren't able to go home – that's if you have one. You've no man as far as I can see, and you never talk about your troubles.' She lowered her voice when a young woman came into the shop. 'Nell, remember this, if you ever feel like talking, I'm a good listener.'

Nell thanked her and then there was another peal of the bell over the shop door as a man and a woman walked in and she had to serve.

The minute the customers had gone, Kath resumed the conversation. 'I'm sorry, Nell,' she began, making Nell fear the worst. 'I've been trying not to say this because it's bound to make me sound heartless but,' she swallowed hard, 'there's no easy way to say it. I'll have to ask you to move on soon. It's not that I wouldn't like you to stay, or that you're not a good worker because you're the best I've had, and that's the truth.' She looked, and felt, guilty but went on anyway. 'It's just that I'm not young any more and I don't think I could stand the sight or sound of a baby in my house.' Stepping forward, she covered Nell's hand with her own. 'I'm not being hard, Nell. I wish I could let you have the baby in my house and then stay on afterwards, but I can't. Try to understand.'

Nell understood very well. The baby was her problem and she would never use anyone else, especially when they'd already given her time to breathe. 'I do understand,' she assured her. 'And anyway, I've already made plans. I meant to tell you tonight. Me and Kit will be moving on tomorrow, if that's all right.' In fact she had not made any plans but now was as good a time as any to get back on the road.

'You're a good lass.' Kath suspected Nell was lying. 'I know I'm forcing you out, yet here you are trying to make me feel better. Bless your heart, Nell,' she murmured. 'I'll miss you, I really will.'

Nell would be sorry to leave. She had worked and lived with Kath for the best part of a month and had grown to respect her. Now, putting on a brave face, she told her, 'I thought you wanted to help Lionel shut down the ovens for the weekend.' The shop closed at midday on Saturday, and there was only an hour to go.

'What if there's a rush?'

'I'll manage.'

Kath looked into that small pretty face, into those shining blue eyes, and she had to admire the woman Nell was. 'I know you will,' she said. 'When Monday comes and you're long gone, I expect I'll kick myself for letting you go.' She didn't want Nell to think she'd changed her mind though. 'I'm sorry.'

'Well, I'm not gone yet,' Nell announced with a quick smile. 'Your Lionel will be pulling his hair out, so go on, get out from under my feet.'

Kath half turned. 'You're sure now, Nell?' The last thing she wanted was a birthing right here in the shop.

The sight of blood and guts would frighten her customers away for weeks.

Nell brought all the cakes to the front of the cabinet. 'I'll be fine.' She seemed to read Kath's mind. 'I'm not about to drop the baby on the floor, if that's what you're worried about.'

Just then, Lionel poked his head round the bakery door. He was a good-looking young man of about twenty-two years, with thin brown hair and sorry eyes which were currently directed at Nell. 'If somebody doesn't come and help, I swear I'll leave the ovens dirty. I'm seeing Alice this afternoon, first time since we had a row, and I don't intend to be late.'

Kath swung round. 'I'm on my way,' she said, 'and don't you dare leave them ovens dirty, young man!' As she made to go out of the shop and into the bakery at the back, she caught sight of Kit. He was seated cross-legged, leaning against the gas lamp outside the shop. 'That lad of yours eats more than we sell,' she groaned, drawing Nell's attention to the boy.

Nell frowned. 'I asked him to deliver that loaf to old Mr Benson ages ago.' The loaf was wrapped up by his feet and there was a mangy old dog sniffing round it.

'You'd best get him away then before the dog runs off with it.' She had to chuckle. 'Look at him, though. I tell you, Nell, he must have hollow limbs 'cause I swear I don't know where he puts it all, I really don't.' She suddenly gasped. 'That bag of tarts wasn't for old Mr Benson too, was it?'

'Oh, my God, I'll kill the little devil!'

Completely oblivious of these two watching him, Kit

was contentedly stuffing his face with jam tarts which he took one at a time out of a brown paper bag beside him. His fingers, face and hair were smattered with raspberry jam and he even had a smear of it over his ear.

'I think it might be as well you're moving on,' Kath suggested light-heartedly. And before Nell could apologise again, she laughed out loud and made her way into the bakery. 'You'd think the lad would know where his mouth is, wouldn't you?' she asked with a chuckle, 'instead of stuffing his nostrils with the stuff.'

Nell called out, 'I'll pay for what he's eaten. Dock it out of my wages today.' This would not be the first time Kit's healthy appetite had cost her a pile of hard-earned pennies.

She sent Kit on his way with a fresh bag of tarts and a stern warning not to eat so much as a crumb.

Even so, she had to smile at him. 'What am I going to do with you, eh?' she mused. 'You'll have us in the workhouse before you're done.'

Before she finished for the day, there was one more delivery to make. It was only a few steps across the road to the cafe but it would give her the chance to get a breath of fresh air, and besides, if she sent Kit, he might eat the order, then she would be liable to Kath for yet more of her hard-earned money. She mentioned this to Kit when he returned from Mr Benson and he asked why he couldn't take the order. 'What? Sesame rolls?' he scoffed. 'Who'd want to eat *them*?'

The grimace on his face might have convinced her, but she wasn't taking any chances. 'You go and help in the bakery,' she ordered. 'I'll only be a minute.'

IN THE CAFE, the woman behind the counter eyed the stranger up and down. 'So, you've just made your way from Bedford, eh?' The man was tall and painfully thin, wearing a flat cap and long overcoat. He had good teeth and fine hands, and a ring on his finger that must have cost as much as a year's takings in the cafe.

Handing him his change, she was surprised when he returned a silver florin. He's after something, she thought. Information, I shouldn't wonder.

She was right.

'I've been all over,' he informed her. 'I travelled from up north a short time back. First stop was a place called Woburn. Do you know the convent there?'

She shook her head. 'Sorry. I don't know much outside Aylesbury. Some of us don't have time to wander.'

'So you haven't seen this?' Digging into his pocket he withdrew an old newspaper and began flicking the pages until he came to a certain article, which he pointed out to her. 'Here. Read that.'

Quickly, the woman perused the article. 'Oh, the murder in Ridgmont – Slater. Yes, I know about that,' she affirmed. 'Everybody knows how he killed his own brother and hid him in the cellar.' She shivered. 'Terrible business. Still, it were a good thing that young woman told the nuns or he might never have been discovered.'

'That's why I've been to Woburn,' he explained, 'to the Convent of Saint Mary Magdalen.'

Now she was interested. 'Why would you want to go there?'

'Some of the papers didn't make much of the young

woman,' he said, 'but this one gives a very detailed description. She's young, blue-eyed and fair-haired. She's also heavy with child. According to one woman I managed to speak to at the convent, a simple-minded creature by the name of Amy, this young woman in question was called Nell. There was a boy with her, a cheeky little Cockney lad, and they were travelling by horse and cart. I've followed them halfway across the country – been to Bedford, Ridgmont, Leighton Buzzard, and now Aylesbury. I have to catch up with her soon. I'm not as young as I was, and it's beginning to tell on me. Besides, it's costing me a fortune in transport – hiring carriages, train fares and the like.' He gave away more than he meant to when he confessed, 'Mind you, it's not my own money I'm spending. I'm on a job, you see. For a man who's wealthy and determined enough to get what he wants.'

'What's his interest in this young woman?'

'That's none of your business but if you can point me in the right direction, I'll make it worth your while. I'm sure she's here somewhere. According to the blacksmith in Leighton Buzzard, a woman and a boy did some work for him in return for shoeing her horse.' His eyes glittered. 'It was her, I know it,' he said. 'She asked where she might find other work and he sent her in this direction. So, where would a pregnant woman and a boy find work round here?'

The woman could see Nell through the window. She was halfway across the road. Any minute now she would be coming in through that door and he was bound to see how she fitted the description. 'I've no idea,' the woman replied craftily. 'You'll have to excuse me, I can't stand here talking. I've my own work to do.' With that she returned his newspaper and left him to make his way to a table.

Nell was surprised when the cafe owner came out to meet her. 'Oh, Mrs Potter, I was just bringing your sesame rolls.' She pointed to Kit. 'I'd have asked Kit only he ate a whole batch of jam tarts that should have been delivered to old Mr Benson. Not only that but he nearly let the dog eat the loaf. Kath wasn't too pleased, I can tell you.'

'Go back.' Mrs Potter placed her hand on Nell's arm and began to turn her away.

Nell didn't understand. 'It's all right,' she said. 'I'll walk back to the cafe with you. Happen I'll join you for a cup o' tea. I've been standing behind that counter all morning. The rest will do me good.'

She was astonished when Mrs Potter took the package from her hands. 'Listen to me, Nell!' she hissed, manoeuvring herself to block Nell's view of the cafe. 'Go back and don't turn round.'

'What's wrong?' Nell became anxious.

'There's a man in the cafe and he's asking after you.'

'Asking after me?' For one fleeting minute she wondered if it might be old John Butler come searching for her. 'Nobody knows where I am. Did he ask for me by name? What does he look like?' She would have peeped at the cafe but Mrs Potter was in the way.

'No, he didn't ask for you by name – well, not exactly. He asked after a woman travelling with a boy, a woman big with child. He mentioned the horse and cart too.' She glanced back and was shocked to see the man seated at the table near the window. If he was to look up now, he couldn't help but realise what she was up to. 'It's *you* he's after, Nell,' she insisted. 'And I don't like the look of him. He's a crafty looking bloke, got shifty eyes. He's up to no good, I can promise you that.'

Nell's heart turned somersaults. 'Why would anyone be after me?' It was obvious from Mrs Potter's description that it wasn't the old man.

'He wouldn't say but he's being paid to find you.' Tightening her grip on Nell, Mrs Potter turned her about and even walked a short way with her. 'He's a bad lot, Nell. If I were you, I'd make myself scarce.'

The man's suspicions were aroused. He was a master at asking questions and then letting others do his work. He had discreetly watched the woman hurry out of the cafe and rush to meet Nell. He saw Nell return to the shop and he saw the shutters come down.

'I'll be off then,' he said as Mrs Potter returned. 'I'm not paid to let the grass grow under my feet.'

Desperate to give Nell a chance to escape, Mrs Potter tried to delay him. 'I've been thinking, I might know the woman you're after.' She gave a sly wink. 'If I were to tell you what I know, how much is it worth to me?'

'You wouldn't play games with me, would you?'

'I've got no time for games, mister. I asked you what it would be worth if I sent you in her direction?'

He threw two half-crowns on the table.

'Not enough.'

He added another, with the warning that she shouldn't get too greedy because he had an idea he might know where to find the woman himself. 'I saw the way you rushed out of here just now,' he said. 'I'm not stupid.'

'Oh, I can see that.' She knew he'd guessed, and she had to think quickly. 'That's why you're talking with me now instead of going over there. The shop's closed but there are five people in the bakery at the back. You wouldn't want to burst in there and cause a fuss, would you? I mean, you wouldn't want the authorities sent for. There might be awkward questions.'

'Ah! So it *was* her!' He snatched his money up and hurried to the door. 'Why pay you when I'd worked that much out for myself?'

K ATH WAS ON her knees and up to her elbows in suds when the rapping came on the door. 'We're closed!'

He yelled through the letter box, 'It's a matter of urgency!'

'So is this bloody floor. Now clear off before I have you thrown off my step.'

This time when he rapped on the door, Kath thought he'd come right through the panels. 'What in heaven's name do you think you're doing?' She flung open the door with such fury that he fell in and almost floored her.

'I'm looking for the woman called Nell, the one that just came in here.'

'You must be mad. There's no one here of that name. There's me and my son, and that's all.' Swinging away she called out, 'Lionel! Come here quick!' Addressing the man, she said angrily, 'My son's a big, bad-tempered bloke. He'll soon have you on your way.'

Kath's colourful description did the trick. He was away across the road even before she'd finished speaking. 'I don't get paid enough to have my head kicked in,' he muttered, heading back to the cafe.

Mrs Potter looked out of the window. Kath winked at her, and she grinned back.

'What did I tell you?' she asked as the man hurried through the door. 'It isn't so easy, is it, eh? None of us likes parting with money but sometimes it's the easiest way.'

'How much?' Disgruntled, he sank into a chair close to the window, his eyes glued to the shop opposite. 'How much to lead me to her?'

Crossing the room, Mrs Potter sat beside him. 'More than three half-crowns, I can tell you that.'

'What will I get for my money?'

'You'll get her home address, that's what you'll get, with directions on how to get there.'

He had come so far. He was so close, he could taste it. 'How do I know you didn't warn her just now?'

'You don't. But I'm no fool either and you're not the only one who likes to make a shilling or two when the chance arises. If you want to get to Nell, you'd better deal with me because if you don't I *will* warn her, and she'll be away where you can't reach her.' She pressed her face close to his. 'So, what do you say? For a small consideration I give you the information you want and you do what you have to do. Only you leave me out of it. Once we've done our business, that's an end to it.'

'You're a grasping devil.'

'Then we're two of a kind, aren't we?'

'How much?'

'A guinea.'

'What? That's daylight robbery.'

'And you should know.'

'If you're lying, I'll be back.'

'A guinea, if you please.'

They did the deal and he left. 'Good shuts,' she muttered as he closed the door behind him. 'And good hunting, I don't think.'

'Nancy Potter, I never knew you were such a liar.' Her husband emerged from the back room, an ox of a man, with arms like pickaxes, a neck like a bull, and a nature as soft as butter.

'You heard what he said,' she warned. 'When he finds out Nell's long gone and that the address I've given him is a deserted house, he'll be back, looking for trouble.'

'He'll get it too,' her husband said, flexing his arms.

'Give over, Ernie,' she laughed. 'You wouldn't hurt a fly.'

'*He* doesn't know that though, does he?'

'No, you're right, he doesn't.' One look at Ernie and the feller would be off down the street like greased lightning. 'A guinea though,' she said, wide-eyed with wonder. 'What do you think to that?'

'I'll tell you what I think, Mrs Potter,' he said grandly.

'And what's that?'

'I think we might be able to have that holiday after all.'

'You might be right,' she agreed. 'What's more, it

JOSEPHINE COX

might be a good idea if we get packed and started right away.'

Half an hour later the shop was shut and the bags loaded on to the pony and trap. 'I hope he doesn't throw a brick through the shop window,' Mrs Potter said, glancing backwards.

'I don't think so,' Ernie replied. 'Not with next door's bulldog guarding the premises.'

'Cost us a shilling though.'

'A shilling well spent,' he declared with a grin. 'And we're still well in pocket.' Tapping her on the knee, he had the look of a man expecting a good time. 'I hope you're in the mood, Mrs Potter.' He couldn't stop grinning.

'What for?' When it came to frolicking, she was always two steps behind.

'For a bit of fun, if you know what I mean.'

'Course I am,' she replied cheekily as realisation caught up with her.

'You're a woman after my own heart, Mrs Potter.' He sent the bay mare into a trot with a touch of the crop. 'I feel like we're off on us honeymoon.'

'I hope you'll be gentle with me,' she entreated with a smile.

His answer was to gaze on her for a moment, his big floppy face filled with promise. It made her feel like a girl again.

They went away, counting the fruits of her good deed and giggling like two naughty children.

WITH A HELPING hand from Lionel, Nell climbed off the cart at the railway station. 'Are you sure you and your mam don't mind looking after the horse and cart for me?' she asked. 'I feel bad asking, especially as you've been so good to me and Kit.'

'It's no trouble. You've said we can use them until you get back, and that's good enough for me.' He glanced at the horse. 'Like I say, he'll be well looked after, so don't you go fretting. Besides, you're right not to travel on a cart in your condition.'

'And you'll keep my cradle safe?'

'It'll be there, safe and sound, for when you return.' He liked Nell. 'Where will you go?'

'North,' she answered thoughtfully. 'I'll go to Blackburn and when I get there, I'll decide what best to do.' Her heart sank. 'I left Blackburn because I was afraid. I knew Aunt Lilian would have made me get rid of the baby, and I dared not risk it. Now, though, I have to go back. But she can't be rid of the baby. It's too late for that, thank God. Besides, I'm older and wiser, and not so afraid.' Tears brimmed in her eyes. 'I did a cowardly thing and the shame grows with every day I'm away. Not once did I think of my father – what he really wanted or how he truly felt.' Her mind was made up. 'It's time to go home,' she decided. 'She can't take my baby from me now.' Her smile was curious. 'Maybe she never could.' She went to the front of the cart where she nuzzled the horse. 'You've been a good mate to me,' she told the kindly thing. 'Be good now, and it'll be no time at all before I'm back to take you home.'

Kit piped up, 'Where's home, Nell?' He was feeling

sorry for himself. While they'd been working at the baker's he'd never gone hungry. It was a new experience for him, and he liked it.

'Where the heart is,' she murmured. Nell, too, was sorry to be going but she had no choice. If Kath hadn't already asked her to go, she would have had to flee from the man Mrs Potter described as 'a bad lot'. Either way, it was time to move on. And, suddenly, the urge to go home was too strong to deny.

The idea of a stranger asking after her played on Nell's mind. Who was this man? And why was he looking for her? He was being paid, that's what Mrs Potter had said. So who was paying him to find her, and for what reason? It was very worrying.

Forcing all that to the back of her mind, Nell concentrated on more pressing matters. She had a train to catch, and plans to make. Time was catching up with her. The baby was due soon; she had a full wage packet in her purse, thank God, but only a vague idea of where she was headed. Once she got to Blackburn, what would she do?

Molly would never turn her away, she knew that, but was it fair to palm herself on that dear soul? And what about Bill? The thought of him seeing her big as a barge with another man's child made her heart stand still.

She could always go home, but why would she do that? All the hardship of these past months had been because of Lilian. Nell could just imagine what would happen if she turned up on the doorstep now. Lilian would either turn her away, after dousing her with a bucket full of pump water. Or she would drag her inside and steal the baby from her the minute it showed its face to the world.

It was a chilling thought and one which made Nell realise that, however desperate she might be, she could never, ever go back to that house.

'The train's coming, Nell!' Kit's excited voice shattered her thoughts.

There was a flurry of hugging, and now it was time to go.

The train was standing in the station, billowing steam down the platform. The rising grey vapour swallowed the disembarking passengers as they hurried away and, as it dissipated into floating, shifting clouds, it gave Lionel the appearance of a ghost. 'Look after yourself, Nell,' he called, waving them out of sight.

Nell wound down the window. 'Thank your mam again,' she cried. 'God willing, I'll be back before too long.'

'Don't worry!' he yelled above the din. 'Good luck!'

That was the last thing Nell heard before the train carried her and Kit away, and Lionel was only a speck in the distance.

'Cor, Nell!' It was Kit's first time on a train, and he was entranced. 'Listen. The wheels are singing to us.'

'So they are,' she said, 'so they are.' It was an exciting experience for her too. But she was bone-weary, and just now, when Lionel had helped her on board, she had had a niggling pain in the base of her back. It was there now, and it was getting stronger. Panic began to take hold of her. What if she went into labour on this train? What if she had the baby here, in front of all these people? It might die. She might die. And what about Kit? He was only a child, and all he had in the world was her. 'Calm yourself, Nell,' she chided. 'The baby won't come yet – please God!'

Kit dragged his attention from the outside world whizzing by. 'What did you say, Nell?'

'I was just saying, isn't it wonderful, Kit?' There was no reason to worry him. 'We're all dressed up in our Sunday best and travelling on a train.' She smiled through her fears. 'It's a real treat, Kit, and if all goes well it won't be the last.'

'Nell?'

'Yes, sweetheart?'

'When you've had your baby, will we really go back for the horse and cart, and the old man's cradle?'

Nell's face hardened with determination. 'Let anyone try and stop me!' Already she was fretting for the old horse. He had been with her since she was a little girl, and when she had needed him most he had been a loyal, faithful friend.

Similar thoughts were running through Kit's mind. 'I miss that scruffy old nag already.'

In an effort to raise a smile from him, Nell stared with horror. 'Oh, Kit! That's no way to talk about Kath!'

It did the trick, because he fell back in his seat and roared with laughter. 'I didn't mean *her*,' he protested, 'I meant the horse!'

Keeping up the pretence, Nell laughed with him, much to the indignation of other, more serious passengers, one of whom, a fat man in a pork-pie hat, complained to the attendant who in turn complained to Nell. 'Bleedin' misery!' Kit moaned, and was treated to a glare that might have curled his shoes. As it was, he had on a pair of sturdy boots, bought by Nell out of last week's wages.

Nell made herself as comfortable as she could, bearing in mind that her back was niggling, her stomach rested on her lap like a bag of spuds, and both her ankles were beginning to swell in her shoes. Nevertheless, she laid her head back, closed her eyes and imagined what she might do once they got to Blackburn town.

Try as she might, she couldn't think clearly. With every minute her back pain intensified, and her feet felt like rising dough in the oven. 'Hold on, Nell,' she muttered under her breath. 'You've come this far, you can't give in now.'

While Nell told herself one thing, her body told another. And all the while the fat man had his beady eye on her.

Nell dozed fitfully, then she shifted into a more comfortable position, and finally she got to her feet and hobbled up and down the aisle.

'What's wrong, Nell?' Kit was beginning to get worried.

Forcing a smile, Nell sat back in her seat. 'It's nothing,' she lied. 'Just a twinge or two, but Molly said that was only to be expected.' Oh, what she would give to have Molly here now!

'Is Molly the friend you told me about?' Round the camp fire, he had listened to many of Nell's stories and never forgot a single one.

'That's right,' Nell confirmed. 'You'll like her.'

'Will we stay with her, in Blackburn?'

'I don't think so. Molly has a family of her own and the house is very small.'

'If she's a proper friend, she'll squeeze us in. You would if you were her, wouldn't you, Nell?'

'Maybe.'

'Where will we stay then?'

'I'm working on it.' She kissed him on the forehead and he snuggled up to her, like he had done many times before. 'It's not for you to worry about, sweetheart,' she said, but he did worry, and Nell knew it.

Now it was Kit's turn to sleep. She held the boy close and stroked his hair and prayed they would be all right. 'Once we're in Blackburn, I'll know what to do,' she murmured. For one brief moment, she thought of Vincent Morgan. After all, this was his baby, and he was a compassionate man. But no! Her heart leaped with fear; if he knew she was having his child, he might well lay claim to it and that would never do; and anyway, Rosalyn may already have presented him with the child he craved.

T HEY WERE NEARING Liverpool. It was growing dark now. In the dark things seemed to intensify. Nell's pain intensified and she could no longer deny it. The baby wouldn't wait. Longer and deeper, the pains grew closer, until she could hardly bear it.

'Nell!' Kit's voice shook her. 'Are you all right, gel?'

She couldn't speak. Sweat was running down her

face and she was trembling violently. Reaching out, she took hold of Kit's hand, squeezing so hard it was all he could do not to cry out. Frantic, he looked up, straight into the fat man's beady eyes. Not a word was spoken but suddenly the fat man was calling out for the attendant. 'It's a disgrace!' Pointing to Nell, he physically pushed the attendant. 'Get her out of here!' he ordered. 'The woman's drunk!'

The attendant knew at once what the problem was, and it wasn't drink. His own wife had not long ago presented him with a son, and he recognised the pain Nell was in. There was little he could do except to say to her, in a surprisingly sympathetic voice, 'You'll not make it to Blackburn.' He recalled seeing her ticket. 'We'll be in Liverpool soon, love. You'll have to get off there, I'm afraid. The lad can get help. Don't worry, I'm sure he can find a way to get word to your husband.'

'She ain't got no 'usband.' When everyone gasped, Kit stretched an arm over Nell as if trying to protect her. 'So you can piss off an' mind yer own business!'

The attendant couldn't believe his ears. Nell looked such a refined young woman. He would never have thought her the sort to let herself get into this kind of trouble. 'Husband or not,' he was determined, 'you'll still have to get off at Liverpool.'

Nell understood and nodded her head in acknowledgement. She wanted him to move away, and the others to stop looking. The pains were bad enough, but these people were staring at her with open hostility and it was shaming her.

'Yer a cruel bastard!' Deriding the attendant, Kit only

echoed what Nell was thinking. 'Can't yer see she's hurting? Ain't yer got no 'eart?' He stared along the carriage. Besides the fat man, there were three other gents, and a gaggle of prim-faced women, all gawping. 'What you lot lookin' at?' he yelled. 'Bleedin' monkeys! Ain't yer never seen a woman have a baby before?' By now the tears were flowing down his face. He was angry and frightened. He loved Nell more than anything in the world.

The attendant caught him by the ear. 'Watch your mouth, son, and do as you're told. When we pull out of Liverpool station, you two won't be going with us. Understand?' All he got for his trouble was Kit's sharp teeth in his finger and another mouthful of abuse.

Enraged, he might have yanked the boy out of his seat but Nell's blue eyes pleaded. 'No.' That was all she said but he was humbled. 'I'm sorry, love,' he said quietly. 'There'll be somebody to help you in Liverpool, I'm sure.'

He walked away, wondering what his wife would say if she knew. No doubt she'd say he was all kinds of a coward, and she'd be right an' all.

From the back of the carriage he saw how the other passengers peered at Nell and the boy. 'The lad's right,' the attendant muttered. 'They *are* all bleedin' monkeys.'

A few minutes later he returned to Nell. Pressing a piece of paper into her palm, he whispered urgently, 'Go to this address. I'll keep the others back while the lad runs to the inn across from the station. You need a cab more than they do, missus.' Then he addressed Kit. 'There'll be a cab stood outside. You can't miss it, the horses are black as coal, big fellers. The owner's name is Alf. He'll be sitting in the inn aside the window. Fetch him out, tell him you want to go to this address and you need to be there in a hurry. Tell him Foster sent you. He's a good sort. He'll not let you down.'

He turned back to Nell. 'He'll take you to a place where they'll see you right,' he told her softly. 'They might not be the sort you'd normally visit, but they're kind-hearted and won't take a penny piece from you.'

'Thank you.' For the moment the pains had eased to a low, niggling ache, but instinct told her it was just the lull before the storm.

'I'm sorry,' he murmured sincerely before walking back through the gauntlet of scowling faces and the tutting and frowning, secretly hating every one.

By the time the train reached Liverpool, Nell was almost at the end of her tether. 'Come on now, missus.' Wanting to get her to the door of the carriage where she could alight before anyone else, the attendant helped her along the aisle. 'Remember now,' he told Kit, 'run straight to the inn and fetch the cabbie out. His name's Alf, and he'll be sitting aside the window.'

As the train juddered to a halt, Nell pushed Kit forward. 'Run, Kit,' she begged. 'Fast as you can.'

While the boy sped towards the inn, Nell stumbled her way to a bench where she sat crumpled in pain one minute and breathing easily the next. 'Hurry, Kit,' she kept muttering. 'Please hurry.' She glanced at the address on the paper given her by the attendant. It read:

'Miss Dawson's Home For Gentlewomen,
Guild House,
Albert Street.'

'What have I let myself in for?' Nell mused. 'Still,
beggars can't be choosers.' She laid a hand on her
stomach. 'Just you be patient,' she murmured. 'I thought
you wouldn't be ready for some time yet, but I was
wrong. Mind you, I never was any good at sums.'

Just then an elderly man strolled by. He glanced at
Nell and thought she might be ill; her face was flushed
and sweating, and she was bent in an uncomfortable
position, catching her breath, like you do when you're
in pain. 'All right, are you, love?'

'Right as can be,' she smiled, 'under the circumstances.' Now, when she leaned back, he could see she
was far gone with child. 'Thank you all the same.'

She was amazed when he sat beside her. 'Me and
my missus had twelve,' he confided. 'I suffered every
pain with her. It's always worse at night time. It were
the same pattern with every single one – we'd go to bed
of a night and come the morning we'd have another
mouth to feed.' He looked her up and down, curious
but not too bold. 'Why, you're nothing but a lass. Is
this your first?'

Feeling the pains coming on again, Nell tried hard
not to show it but he was an old hand. 'By the looks of
you it won't be too long before the child wants out,' he
said anxiously. 'I'll get a cab. Where do you live?'

Kit's voice reached them. 'Nell! Nell! It's all right.'
Red in the face and gasping for breath, he pointed to the

approaching cab. 'Look, Nell! I found him, right where the attendant said.'

There were enough helping hands to bundle Nell into the carriage. Once inside, with the door closed and Kit beside her, and the sound of the wheels rumbling against the cobbles, she gave a sigh of relief. 'Oh, Kit, I can't hold out much longer.' The pains were coming thick and fast, making her cry out. 'Tell him to hurry. Please, Kit, tell him to hurry!'

There was no need for Kit to tell the driver. He could see for himself. Nell was making the kind of breathless, terrifying noises women make when they're about to have a baby. 'Jesus! I'm glad I'm a man,' he muttered, slapping the reins against the two horses' rumps. 'Come on, you mangy devils, get a move on!' It was a good ten-minute drive to the perimeter of town.

Outside the house, he drew the cab to a halt and leaped down from his lofty seat. 'It's all right,' he told Nell. 'You're safe now. Lottie will look after you.' While he helped Nell down, he yelled at the boy, 'Bang on the door, lad! Get somebody out. Quick, damn your eyes!' Terrified that Nell might give birth there and then, he began to panic.

Kit didn't need telling twice. The noise he made banging on the door and yelling for somebody to come quick was enough to wake the dead.

'What the hell's going on out here?' The woman who had come to the door was young, with a painted, brassy face. She was wearing fussy, frilly clothes, with her blouse open to the breast and a long length of shapely leg showing. Her gaze fell on Nell and she realised at once. 'Bring her inside,' she said kindly. 'Alf, tell one of the girls to get things ready.' As they made their way up the stairs, she told Kit, 'And you, boy, find the kitchen and help yourself to what you fancy.'

'I ain't leaving my Nell!'

'Oh yes you are.' Flicking a thumb to Alf, she ordered, 'Get the brat out of the way. This is women's business.'

'Go on, Kit. I'll be fine.' Nell's soft voice had a calming effect on the boy. With his eyes following her all the way, he let himself be taken to the kitchen where the pantry was filled with every delight imaginable. But he couldn't eat. 'Not while Nell's up there,' he thought, 'with them strangers doing God knows what to her.'

'Come on, me beauty.' Lottie eased Nell on to the bed. 'Let's make you comfortable first,' she said, taking off Nell's shoes. 'Then we'll see how impatient this little bugger is, shall we?'

Lying on her back, Nell had a good view of the room. There were pink, frilly curtains above the bed, chairs dressed with drapes of gold, and a silk, ribboned table-cloth. The room was filled with a fragrance that stuck in the throat.

Two young women came in carrying bowls and towels; both wore low-cut gowns that left little to the imagination.

'Good God!' Nell exclaimed. 'I've been delivered to a whorehouse!'

'That's right,' Lottie laughed. 'This is Sue and Babs. And I'm Lottie.' She held out her hand in friendship. 'Pleased to meet you.'

Taking her hand, Nell shook it gladly. 'I'm Nell,' she said. 'And you're an angel.'

IT WAS PITCH black. He had waited all evening, and now, cold and miserable, he decided to enter the house. 'Bring her back,' that's what Morgan had said. 'Bring her back but be careful not to hurt her.' He laughed, a soft sinister sound that rippled through the air, disturbing the night creatures. 'I won't hurt her,' he muttered, moving stealthily forward. 'Unless she struggles, then it'll be lights out and no mistake. She can't struggle if she's unconscious, can she, eh?'

In a few minutes he was round the back of the house and in through the open kitchen window. 'Very careless,' he chuckled. 'Any rascal could get in here.'

Guided by the bedroom light, he cautiously made his way upstairs. 'She won't even know what's hit her,' he muttered. Softly, he pushed open the door and was riveted to the spot. The room was empty. There were curtains up at the windows but not a stick of furniture to be seen. The floor was stripped bare and cupboard doors ajar, as though someone had left in a hurry.

Incensed, he went from room to room. They were all empty. 'The bitch!' he cried, going downstairs at a run. 'That bitch at the cafe told her and now she's made a run for it!' He stood in the middle of the parlour, a match burning low in his fingers. 'It doesn't make sense though,' he mused. 'How could she have got all the furniture out of here without me knowing? I've watched this place like a hawk and I've seen nothing.'

The match burned out, but another light was beginning to dawn in his mind. 'That bloody woman at the cafe! This house was empty all along and she knew it.' He was hopping mad. 'Wait a minute! There's got to be

325

somebody here. Who lit the lamp in the bedroom?'

As he turned, he got the shock of his life. A ghostly figure was coming towards him, lamp in hand. In the halo of light it seemed unearthly. 'Jesus!' In his terror he actually screamed out loud, and still the figure came towards him.

The only way out was through the window and he lost no time. With one desperate leap he was through it and rolling about on the grass outside; dazed, he lay there for a minute. Suddenly the figure was bending over him. 'Who are you?' it said. 'What are you doing here?'

To his immense relief, he realised it was nothing more sinister than a grey-haired old woman who, judging by the way she cupped her hand to her ear, was deaf. That would explain why she hadn't heard him running through the house. She must have lit the lamp upstairs, then gone one way while he went another. 'Answer me,' she insisted. 'If you've come to see Mr Hayden, you're too late. He died last week and all his possessions were sold yesterday.' Her eyes widened. 'You're not the landlord, are you?' she asked hopefully.

'No, I'm not the landlord,' he said, scrambling to his feet. 'Get out of my way, you silly old fool!' He still hadn't quite got over the shock of it all.

The poor old thing couldn't hear him. 'I beg your pardon?' she said, blocking his way. 'Look, I know someone was supposed to be coming for the key.' She held it up for him to see, a big iron thing, threaded through a large hoop. 'I've got it here, see?' She tried thrusting it into his hand. 'I don't mind telling you I'll be glad to be rid of it. The house seems so spooky now it's empty. I've lived next door to the old fellow for many a year, looked after him when he was ill. He was all alone, you see. He had no family or friends, except for me, of course.'

'Was there a young woman called Nell?' He was clutching at straws.

'What's that you say?'

He raised his voice. 'A YOUNG WOMAN BY THE NAME OF NELL – SHE'S WITH CHILD – TRAVELLING WITH A BOY. WAS . . . SHE . . . HERE?'

The old woman laughed with relief. 'Oh no, dear. You've got the wrong place. She works at the baker's. Nice young thing, she lives with the family over the top of the shop.'

She was still chattering away as he went down the street at a run. 'I should have known,' he raged. 'I ought to teach that bitch a lesson but I've wasted enough time. I'll have to be content with taking the girl back and collecting my reward.'

But he was disappointed yet again. This time, there was no light and no one at home. 'If you're looking for Kath, you've just missed her.' The little girl ran towards him. 'She's gone to the inn with Lionel. My dad's gone too. I expect they'll all be drunk when they get back. They always are.' She would have skipped away but he called her back.

'Was Nell with them?'

She shook her head. 'Nell's gone.' Her bottom lip stuck out in a sulk. 'Kit's gone too. They've gone on the train. I wanted to go with them but Nell said I was too small. She promised to come back one day, and that she'd bring me a present.' Her smile returned. 'I like Nell. I like Kit too, but sometimes he pulls my hair. I don't like it when he pulls my hair.' Again the sulk.

'You said they'd gone on the train?' Stooping, he held her by the shoulders. '*Where* did they go?'

'Dunno. Me mam asked Kath, and Kath told her to mind her own business.' Something about him prompted her to ask, 'Are you a bad man? Me mam says all men can be bad.' That said, she was on her way, occasionally glancing back as if worried he might follow her.

'Damn and bugger it!' He'd been outwitted and he didn't like it. His pride was badly dented. 'Ganged up on me, the devils, that's what they did. Got her right out from under my nose and I fell for it like the bloody fool I am!'

It only took a minute for him to decide. Once the decision was made, it was easy. He climbed the gate at the back and crept round the house, making certain there were no signs of life. 'Setting fire is one thing, but murder is another. I've made enough mistakes for one night.'

The scullery window was open and the curtains flapping gently in the breeze. The match was struck and slipped in through the window, and in no time at all the curtains were alight. He waited a minute to be certain before making his getaway.

By the time he reached the end of the street to summon a hansom, the fire was well and truly ablaze. 'The nearest railway station,' he told the cabbie. 'And be quick.'

Behind him the blaze lapped up to the ceiling.

He was well on his way when the alarm was raised. They managed to save the horse but the fire was too far gone for them to save the baker's shop, or the living quarters above. 'Must have left an oven on,' one chap said.

'Aye, that was Lionel, I expect,' said another. 'That's what comes of thinking o' your sweetheart instead of keeping your mind on your work.'

They ferried buckets of water and even tried to beat out the flames with the clothes from their backs. When the firemen arrived they, too, did everything humanly possible. In the end, though, all they could do was watch from the roadside while Kath's livelihood and everything she owned was razed to the ground.

Chapter Nine

'IT'S A GIRL!' The cry echoed round the walls. After two days in labour, Nell had given birth to a beautiful baby girl. But she had paid the price.

Weakened by the prolonged and difficult ordeal, she lay exhausted, only her blue eyes seeming alive as they followed Lottie across the room. She was aware that her child had been born, and she'd heard them cry it was a girl, but now when she tried to raise her arms to take the child to her breast, they fell to her sides, lifeless, like lumps of wood. The whole of her body felt as if it had been run down by a coach and four. She couldn't move. She didn't even have the energy to open her mouth and speak.

Silently, the tears trickled down her haggard face; tears of joy and sadness.

Lottie understood. 'It's all right,' she said softly, placing the child into Nell's arms. 'You've been through hell, and it's only thanks to the strength inside you that you're here at all.'

Another voice intervened. 'You have to sleep now, dear,' it said. 'In the morning, you'll feel stronger.'

Raising her gaze to the face, Nell saw that it was an older woman, small and round, with kind eyes and a white mobcap over her grey hair. 'You've got a lovely little girl,' the woman murmured, 'and she's got the prettiest blue eyes, just like yourself.'

With every little movement seeming like torture, Nell turned her head to gaze on the face of her daughter. She could not see her eyes. She was sleeping now. So small and beautiful. A little miracle.

'Look, Nell, here's the boy come to see you.' The woman stood aside, allowing Kit to come forward.

'I've made the baby a cradle,' he whispered, his trembling voice betraying the fear he still felt for her. 'See, Nell?' Holding the tiny cradle aloft, he showed it to her. 'I whittled the ends down so they wouldn't be sharp.' His face was beaming with pride. 'Do you like it?'

The cradle was a work of art. Many things could be fashioned from wood and they might all look splendid, but when they were fashioned with love, as this was, they had a special significance. 'Why, it's beautiful!' The older woman clapped her chubby hands together. 'You've done her proud,' she told the boy.

Shaped round and deep, it was perfect, each thick, sturdy strand woven so tightly one into the other that they formed a smooth, safe cradle. 'I made it from a thorn bush,' he explained, his concerned gaze mingling with Nell's. 'It's for your baby, Nell, for your little girl.' Suddenly he was sobbing uncontrollably. 'Oh, Nell, I thought you were gonna die,' he cried. 'I 'eard 'em say how ill you were an' I didn't know what to do, so I ran off into the field and tried not to think about it.' His face was all crumpled with sorrow but, like Nell's, his tears were a mixture of sadness and joy.

His outburst touched Nell deep inside. Slowly, she moved her hand across the bed towards his. Their fingers entwined and for a long, wonderful moment they held each other.

'Get better, Nell,' he whispered. 'I ain't got nobody but you.'

When she nodded, her eyes moist with emotion, his breath caught in his throat. 'I'll polish it,' he promised. 'When you wake up tomorrer, you'll see. I'll have this cradle shining like nuthin' you've ever seen.' He was excited now, his fears slowly diminishing. Nell had strength in her grip. She wouldn't give in easily. But she had closed her eyes, the touch of a smile still on her lips. 'Nell! Wake up, Nell!' His fears were heightened again.

'No, leave her now.' Lottie edged him away. 'She's had a real bad time. She'll rest now. Don't you worry, she's made of strong stuff, is your Nell.'

'She'll be all right, won't she?' he pleaded. 'She won't die, will she? She can't die!'

Nell could still hear the voices but they were so far away. No, she wouldn't die, she vowed, not now anyway. There was something very special to live for, wasn't there? What was it? Her baby, yes, that was it. The woman in the mobcap had said she had a beautiful baby girl. Oh, how wonderful! She had a baby girl. She longed to hold her, to nuzzle her face close to her daughter's soft, new skin.

In her dreams she laughed with joy. Her mind wandered. It was summer, and she was walking across her beloved fields back home. Bill was with her, and the baby. Bill was holding the baby and oh, he did love her.

They looked so right together, and there was Kit, up a tree, swinging from a high branch like a little monkey. 'Come down from there,' she cried, afraid he might fall and hurt himself.

For a moment she was so afraid. But then she gazed on her family and her heart swelled with love. The sun shone on her face and the breeze lifted her hair, and all was well in her small world. Suddenly, Bill was holding her hand and they were making their way to that pretty cottage. She smiled at the memory. Near the cottage was the same river where she had very nearly met her end. Bill had saved her then. He had saved her since, and now at last they were together. Life was good. Someone up there had been kind. And for all of her life, she would remember how, but for the grace of God, it might have been so very different.

But oh, she was so weary just now. And why was Kit crying? Did he really think she would die? 'No, Kit,' she could hear herself call out, but it wasn't her. 'Bill!' Someone was calling Bill's name. Oh, where was he? 'Bill! Don't leave me . . . please don't leave me!'

Lottie dipped the muslin into the bowl of cold water and mopped Nell's brow. 'Who's this Bill she keeps crying out for?'

Kit had been allowed to stay a while longer. Standing quietly by, and overawed by all that was happening, he secretly willed Nell not to die. 'She told me about him once,' he revealed. 'He's Molly's son.'

'Who's Molly?'

'She's Nell's best friend in Blackburn.'

'This Bill. Is he the father of Nell's bairn?' It was

334

the little round woman in the mobcap.

Kit shook his head. 'I dunno about that. Nell never said.' All the time he was answering the questions, his gaze rested on Nell's face. 'All I know is, when she talked about him, her eyes sparkled, like stars in the sky.'

In her dreams, Nell smiled. Bill was here, she knew. 'Bill.' Now he was gone. Bill, where are you? No. It was all gone, and nothing seemed real. But she wasn't afraid now. Not any more.

Sleep overcame her. She drifted to another world; a calmer, gentler world where there was no pain. Only peace and rest and the promise of a brighter tomorrow.

For the next few hours, the women remained vigilant. 'I think the fever's passing.' The woman in the mobcap smoothed Nell's brow with a doused cloth. 'She's not out of the woods by a long chalk, but her breathing's easier.'

Pouring milk into a dish, Lottie touched Nell's lips with it. 'I'm never having children.' She kept her voice low, glancing to where Kit was curled up asleep on the settee. 'Look what this poor little cow's been through. It's worse than bloody torture.'

'It isn't the same for everybody.' The little woman's name was Rose. 'It's how you're built inside. Look at me.' She proudly displayed her rotund stomach. 'I've had six healthy childer and popped 'em all out easy, like corks from a bottle.' She chuckled softly. 'Still and all, I have to admit, this one's been through the mill.' Her sympathetic gaze went to Nell's sleeping face. 'To tell the truth, I didn't think she'd make it as far as she has.'

Lottie smiled. 'You're not the only one who thought that. She wasn't well enough to carry a bairn, if you ask me. I've been talking to the boy, and it seems they've lived a hard life up to this past month or so.'

'She's so young, and thin too. Now the bairn's here, you can see how undernourished she is. It seems to me that this past month or so that the boy mentioned wasn't enough to undo the longer damage of what went before.'

'She'll be all right now.'

'What makes you so sure?'

'Because I know a fighter when I see one, and this girl is a fighter through and through.'

'You're right. She's proved that already.' But she had seen things in her life that defied belief. Fate was a fickle thing and could turn the cards at any minute. 'Let's just hope she lives to tell the tale.'

———————

THE MAN CORNERED the attendant who so far had been uncooperative. 'Maybe this will help to loosen your tongue.' Pressing a handful of coins into his palm, he asked, 'The girl and the boy. Before you got it into your head that I was out to make trouble, you started telling me where I might find them.'

'That girl looked like she needed a friend.' The attendant hadn't forgotten how Nell had suffered right before his eyes.

'I *am* a friend.' Having followed Nell's trail from Aylesbury, and still smarting from being outwitted by her and the others, he didn't mean to lose her now.

'Hmm.' The attendant peeped at the money in his

hand and was convinced. 'I sent her to the whorehouse.'

The man was so shaken his mouth fell open. 'You did what?'

'Don't look so shocked. They might be loose and willing for a shilling, but they're kindly folk.' He grinned. 'You might be interested in the long-legged brunette,' he said, regarding the man's dark, miserable countenance. 'She never has a smile for anybody but she's magic between the sheets.'

'Get on with it, you fool, where can I find this place?'

'Hey! Just you watch your tongue.' He clicked the coins together in his fist. 'Your lousy money doesn't give you the right to belittle me.'

'Sorry.' He had to keep the attendant sweet. 'But it's important I find her. You see, she's from a good family and they're very worried about her.'

'And so they should be.'

'So?' Beneath his smile he felt like punching the attendant from one end of the train to the other. 'All I need is the address.'

Once he'd got it he was off and heading for the first hansom cab he saw, which was the very same that Nell had sat in; it was parked in its usual place, outside the inn. Its lazy owner was parked in *his* usual place, at the table beside the window.

A brazen, dark-haired girl was touting for a client. In fact, she had been touting for a client these past two hours or more. Her feet ached, her back was cold, and her stomach rumbled for a bite to eat.

Loitering beneath the gas lamp on the opposite side of Lostock Street, she was considering calling it a night.

'Nothing doing here,' she muttered, impatiently beginning to stroll back and forth. 'No men, no money, no sodding nothing!'

Sweeping the area with her eyes, she noticed the man. He was pacing the ground outside the inn, every now and then peering in the window as if debating whether to go inside. 'Wait on though.' She let her gaze wander from his head to his toes. 'He looks a likely lad.' She was impressed by the way he was dressed, respectable, and wearing a tie. 'Looks like he might be worth a bob or two,' she muttered, spitting on her finger and smoothing her eyebrows. 'He's a sour-looking bastard but there's nothing else doing, so I might as well give it a try.'

Sauntering over, she quickened her steps when it was obvious he was about to go inside the inn. 'It's no use looking for the cab driver,' she called out. 'He's in there all right but he's blind drunk.' Nodding towards the inn, she led his gaze to the man in the window. 'That's Alf, and if you ride with him in that state, you take your life in your hands.'

'Piss off, you baggage!'

'I can get you a reliable cabbie but it'll cost you a shilling.'

'I said piss off!'

Taking an immediate dislike to him, she began to walk away. 'Please yourself, you miserable bleeder, but you could search all night and still not find one. There's a big card game going on in town and all the cabbies have taken the night off.' She should know. If they'd been here, one or two might have paid for a quick fumble out of sight, like they usually did.

The man looked around. She was right, the place was deserted. 'Hey you!' He chased after her. 'Hang on a minute!'

She swung round, her painted lips parted in a smile. 'Thought you might change your mind.'

'Get me a cab and you'll get your shilling.' He walked towards her, hand outstretched and a silver shilling nestling in his palm. 'I'm in a desperate hurry. I need taking to a place on the outskirts of town.' He fished in his pocket for the address. Drawing out the slip of paper on which the attendant had written, he read in the light of the gas lamp, 'Lottie Dawson, Guild House. I'm told everybody knows it.'

When she screeched with laughter, he was visibly startled. 'What's so bloody funny?'

She thrust her arm through his. 'Pay for a room in a boarding house and I'll show you a better time than any of them scrags at Guild House.' She winked brazenly. 'As long as you keep your mouth shut to Lottie.'

'I haven't got time for all that,' he refused bluntly. 'I'm looking for a young woman by the name of Nell. She's big with child and, from what I've been told, she's travelling with a boy.'

The look of surprise in her eyes encouraged him. 'You've seen her, haven't you?' he growled, taking hold of her by the arms. 'Tell me and I'll be generous. Where is she? Can you take me to the place?'

'I might.'

'What's that supposed to mean?' He squeezed her so hard she winced.

'You're hurting me. Take your fingers out of my flesh or I'll be away.'

'I have to find her. Is she at this place?' He thrust the paper under her nose. 'It'll be worth your while to help me.'

A terrible thought struck her. 'Are you from the authorities?'

'Do I *look* as if I'm from the authorities?'

She appraised him carefully. 'Come to think of it, yes, you do.'

'Don't waste time. I've come a long way and I want the job done with.' There he went again! That was twice he'd let slip too much of what he was up to.

'What job?' She edged away. 'What do you want with her?'

He had to think quickly. 'The girl's only seventeen. She got herself in trouble with some man and now there's a child on the way. Since she ran away from home, her poor mother's been half out of her mind with worry.' He congratulated himself on his wonderful ability to warp the facts so they suited his purpose. 'I'm here to talk to the girl, that's all. If she won't come home, that's all right. I just want to do what I was paid for, and that is to try to persuade her, nothing more.'

'You're a liar.' She was amused by his attempt to deceive her.

'Can't fool you, eh?' He could see she was fishing for more money, and it made him smile. 'You're a crafty bugger. All right, how much to take me to her?'

'Double what you've offered.'

'I thought you were one of Lottie's girls?' There was

just the merest inkling of admiration for this attractive creature.

'I am.'

'But you'll go behind her back to help me, will you?'

'And to swell my own pocket.'

'So, it's dishonour among thieves, is it?'

'No. It's every man for himself.'

'I see.' Her philosophy matched his own. His admiration heightened.

Staring him in the eye with a boldness that made his loins tingle, she took the grin from his face. 'She might not be able to do much talking though.'

'There's no more money, so you needn't get cunning.'

'I'm not after more money. She just might not be in a position to talk to you, that's all I'm saying.'

Shaking her again, he demanded, 'You'd better explain.'

'She's in a bad way.'

'Go on.'

'When they brought her in, she was a mess, fighting with the bairn, if you know what I mean. Two days in labour and losing more blood than she could afford. The bairn's born now, and out of danger. But, if you ask me, its poor mam isn't long for this world.'

'So she's had the child, eh?' It meant nothing to him that Nell had suffered and might be dying. He was only interested in the possibility that this new development could work in his favour. 'If I can't take the mother home, I might as well take the child.'

'You'll have to take me as well. It'll cost you though.'

'What?' He was losing patience.

'If you mean to steal the child you'll need me too, because much as I hate the job, I've been chosen to wet-nurse the newborn because I've got a brat of my own. You can't travel with a newborn and not have a full titty when it cries.' She laughed. 'Unless you're different from other men.'

'If I take you, it'll only be until I get where I'm going. After that, you're on your way. Right?'

'Right.'

'You'll have to leave your own brat at home. I'm not travelling the country with a woman and two brats.'

'That's no hardship. Lottie can look after him. She's got a heart o' gold.' She winked, a sly grin lighting her features. 'Mind you, if she knew what we were up to, she'd boot me out on the street in a minute, with all my belongings and the brat as well.'

'I'm not interested in your problems. All I want is to be away from here with the girl's newborn, as soon as we can.'

'You're a heartless bastard.'

'Maybe. But if we have a deal, it's to be done tonight.' He gestured towards the inn, and the cab outside. 'Can the drunk keep his mouth shut?'

'Yes, if you make it worth his while.'

He wondered if he wasn't involving too many strangers, but he had little choice. He had to take a chance or risk going away empty-handed. 'So she's too ill to get out of her bed, is she?'

'On her last legs, I'd say. When that poor cow gets out of her bed, she'll likely be thrown straight into a wooden box.'

'Well now, that's very interesting.' He was grinning again, delighted with his success in tracking Nell down. Now it would be easier than he thought. Not only would he be going home soon, but he would be taking the child to Morgan, together with the news that the mother was in no position to trouble him. 'From what you say there's no desperate hurry for me to get there.'

'No hurry at all.'

Pinning her against the wall, he bent his head and looked her in the eye. 'Are you still wanting more money?'

'As much as you can spare.'

'You'll have to earn it.'

'That's what I'm here for, mister.'

'How much?'

She licked his face, her warm, moist tongue sending signals all over his body. 'Like I said, I want as much money as you can spare.'

'I haven't had a woman for so long, I've forgotten what it's like.' He pressed his head closer to hers. 'I'll pay you what you're worth, that's all I can promise.'

'Then you'd better empty your wallet,' she murmured, 'because I always give my money's worth.'

She put her hands down, undid his trouser buttons, lifted her skirt and there, right where they stood, she showed him she was as good as her word.

DRIPPING WITH SWEAT and feeling as weak as a child, Nell rolled over in the bed, her eyes piercing the darkness as she tried to make out the figures furtively moving about at the foot of her bed. 'Who's there?'

Exhausted by even the smallest effort, she lay back on the pillow. 'Kit, is that you?'

There was a series of shuffling sounds and whispering voices, and then a dreadful silence.

'Kit?' Determined now, she pulled herself up by the bedrail, taking a few deep breaths before calling out again, 'Lottie? Please, I can't see you.'

Something bad was happening. Someone was near her baby. '*Who's there?*' Summoning every ounce of strength within her, she made her legs move until her feet were touching the floor and she was sitting on the edge of the bed. Dropping her hand to the bedside cabinet, she found the matches and lit the candle.

'Who's there?' Steadying herself against the bed as she went, Nell shuffled towards the cradle, her progress agonisingly slow. 'Who are you?' In the shadows she thought she saw someone creeping across the room.

Her suspicions were confirmed when the door suddenly opened and then closed, and in the wake of that short, sharp click, there followed an eerie silence.

'Kit?' Nell was frantic. 'Lottie, is that you?' The room was going round and every bone in her body felt like sponge, but still she pressed on, her instincts telling her to get the baby. *Get the baby!*

After what seemed a lifetime, she felt the cradle beneath her fingers. In the half-light she stared down, not wanting to believe what her eyes told her.

Suddenly the door was open and a shaft of light lit the room. 'Nell! What in God's name are you doing out of bed?' Horrified, Lottie lurched forward, just in time to catch Nell as she fell, seemingly lifeless, into her arms.

As she lifted Nell's weightless body into her arms, Lottie's eyes were drawn to the floor. At first she couldn't make out what it was, but then she realised. The rug was crimson with Nell's blood. 'God Almighty!'

She would have screamed for help, but just then the little woman in the mobcap appeared at the door. 'What's wrong? Whatever is she doing out of bed?'

Lottie laid Nell gently between the sheets. 'Get a doctor, Rose,' she pleaded. 'As quick as you can. And pray to God we're not too late.'

AS HE HAD done many times since Nell was taken ill, Kit sat beneath the oak tree, his eyes closed and his mind on Nell. At night, when Lottie's house was quiet and the attic room where he slept was alive with all kinds of noises, as if the very walls of the old house were sighing and groaning, he would creep down to Nell's room and watch her sleeping. 'Don't die, Nell,' he would softly plead. 'Don't go and leave me now.'

He said it now to the night sky. 'They talk among theirselves, Nell,' he whispered, 'that strange little woman and the doctor. They say you might not have enough strength to pull through, and that plans will have to be made for the baby.' His voice caught in a sob. 'That ain't the truth, is it, Nell?' Pride filled his young heart, sounding in his voice as he said, 'They don't know you like I do. They ain't seen how strong you really are, and how you never let *nuthin'* get the better of you.'

He managed a smile as he remembered all the escapades he and Nell had been through. 'You can't let her die, Lord.' In all his life he had never prayed, but he prayed now, his young eyes turned to the skies and his heart bursting with anger. '*You* made her ill, and you can make her better. She ain't done nobody no wrong. She's kind and good like folk are supposed to be.' He punched the ground with his fist, his eyes closing in anguish. 'If you take her away, I'll never talk to you again, and I'll be as bad as I can be!' That was his promise and, right or wrong, he meant every word.

Lying there with his eyes closed and his mind on Nell, he didn't hear them at first, but then he was alerted by the sound of twigs cracking under approaching footsteps. 'Poachers!' It was the only explanation at this time of night.

Having lived all his young life under various threats of discovery, his first instinct was to hide. Cautiously, he stole round the tree and waited for the intruder to appear, his ears alert to every sound and his scrawny little neck stretched to see who the intruder might be.

When he was frightened, his stomach rumbled. To his consternation, it rumbled now. Fearful of being found, he moved back, deeper into the spinney, at the same time pressing both hands over his stomach in an effort to quieten it. He wished he dared sneak closer, to hear what they were saying, but his instinct told him to stay hidden for the moment.

'Keep your eyes peeled!' Clutching the precious little bundle under his arm, the man glanced back to the house; lights were going on at every window. 'They've rumbled us,' he whispered hoarsely. 'Shift yourself, woman!' With a sharp kick to her rear, he sent her a pace faster. 'If the brat starts crying, we've had it.'

'How much further?' She had broken the heels of her boots and the overhanging branches were tearing at her face and hair.

They were now so close to Kit he could have touched them as they passed.

'Keep going,' the man urged. 'A few more minutes and we'll be out of this.'

'It seems a longer way out than it was when we came in.' She had no sense of direction here. When she was working, she rarely ventured further than the front path. This was a wilderness, and she was out of her depth.

'We found our way in all right and we'll find our way out. Just keep going.'

'How much further?' She was beginning to panic. 'I don't like being in the woods. It frightens me.'

'You're worse than bloody useless.' He cursed when a branch sprang back and slapped him in the face. 'I must want my head tested taking you to Blackburn.' They were moving away now, out of Kit's hearing.

'You wouldn't go far without me, that's for sure. Babies are like men,' she teased. 'They can't go long without a taste of titty.'

'Slag!'

'I've never been to Blackburn.'

'So?'

'If there's any business doing, I might take a fancy to it and stay on.'

'And leave your kid here? Some mother you are!'

'Aw, he'll be all right. Lottie'll look after him.'

'I don't want you hanging about in Blackburn when the job's done.'

'I don't see how you can stop me.'

'There are ways and means.'

'You don't frighten me.' But she was frightened. He had already proved himself a bad 'un.

'You'll stay in Blackburn just as long as it takes to deliver this package.' He held the baby close to his breast, not because he had any special feelings for it but because he didn't want to hand over damaged goods, especially when Vincent Morgan was paying him a small fortune. 'Your job will be done as soon as mine is,' he reminded her. 'After that, you can take your arse back where it came from.'

Her thoughts had already moved on. 'You're a liar.'

'Who are you calling a liar?'

'You haven't told me the truth about why you came here in the first place. You don't really think I believed your story about taking her home because her mother was going out of her mind with worry?'

'I don't give a sod what you believe!'

'What are you up to?'

'I told you, I'm doing what I'm paid for. Stop asking questions and keep your eyes open for the road. I don't want that drunkard to think we're not coming and bugger off.'

'Who's paying you?'

'None of your business, you nosy cow!'

'He must be rich.' She squealed when her ankle twisted in a tangle of twigs. 'Damn it!'

'Shut up, woman! Have you no sense?'

348

She had a one-track mind. 'How rich is he, this man who's paying you?'

Before he could answer, they came on to the road and the hansom cab parked there. Alf the driver was pacing up and down the grass verge. When he saw them running out of the spinney, he threw up his hands with relief. 'Thank Christ for that. I was just about to clear off.'

He bundled them inside, curious when the man handed the woman a small bundle. 'What's that you've got there?' He would have looked closer but the man came between them, letting him know in a curt voice, 'If you want paying, get us out of here, and quick!' He slammed the door shut and the child gave out a small cry.

Alf didn't hear it, or chose to ignore it. He suspected there was something very funny going on here. The man could be right. They'd better get out of here fast or he might find himself involved in shady business that could put him behind bars, and what good would money be then?

Without further ado, he clambered on to his seat and took the cab down the road at speed. 'I should have stayed in the pub with my jar of ale,' he grumbled. 'I was safe enough there.'

Bemused, Kit watched them leave. 'That's a funny how-d'you-do,' he muttered. 'They're a strange couple an' no mistake.'

Settling down at the base of the tree again, he tried to recall that part of the conversation he'd heard, but he was so tired. 'I'd best make my way back soon,' he mused. 'I'll go and see Nell.' Thinking about Nell brought the tears to his eyes again. 'I'll sleep in the chair beside her till morning.'

He closed his eyes, only for a minute, while he got his thoughts together. But once his eyes were closed, he didn't have the energy to open them. For too many days he'd forced himself to stay awake and now he was exhausted. Soon he was hard asleep.

I T WAS MORNING when he woke. Shocked to see daylight breaking through the trees, he ran all the way back to the house.

Lottie and Rose were in the kitchen when he burst through the door. 'Good God above, I thought it were a robber crashing through the door!' Rose was so overcome by the sudden intrusion that she fell into the rocking chair and sat there staring at him, hand on breast and mouth wide open.

'We thought you were still in bed.' Ushering him in, Lottie softly closed the door. 'Have you been out all night?' His clothes were covered in dew and he was cold to the touch. In fact he was so cold he could only chatter his teeth and nod his head.

'Wherever have you been?'

Rose got out of the rocking chair and laid her arm on Kit's shoulders. 'Don't question the boy,' she told Lottie. 'There'll be time enough for that when he's had a hot drink inside him.'

Kit was so cold and hungry he didn't have the heart to refuse. 'What about Nell?' he asked as he was propelled to the table and eased into a chair. 'Is she better now? Will she be all right?'

While Lottie talked to him, Rose got him a bowl of steaming hot porridge. 'Get that down you,' she said, seating herself alongside him. 'When you've eaten it all up, you can go and see Nell.'

Lottie had been quizzing him and now she conveyed his answers to Rose. 'He's been asleep in the woods all night,' she said with a look of horror. 'It's a wonder he wasn't set on by poachers.'

Rose mentioned how a courting couple had been attacked in those very woods not long back.

'I saw a courting couple.' Kit had finished his porridge and was now on his feet, ready to be taken to his beloved Nell. 'They were arguing summat rotten. She called him a liar and he said she was a slag.' He rolled his eyes at their antics. 'It's a wonder they didn't end up fighting.'

'What did I tell you?' Rose declared. 'If the rogues don't attack us, they attack each other, and if you ask me, some of 'em should know better than to roam the woods when they should be home in their beds.'

Kit was growing impatient. 'I want to see Nell now.'

Lottie stood up and taking him by the hand said gently, 'There's something we have to tell you. Sit down a minute, there's a good boy.' She glanced at Rose and the look of sorrow between them was like a physical thing.

Sensing there was something dreadfully wrong, Kit cried out, 'It's Nell, ain't it?' His heart was breaking, his grubby little face contorted with pain. 'You've let her

351

die! I hate you! You've let Nell die!' His awful cries echoed through the house.

'No, Kit.' Lottie held him by the shoulders. 'Nell's asleep just now but we had the authorities here last night and Noreen had to go for the doctor.' She wondered how she was going to tell this boy what had happened here when his sad green eyes looked up at her as if she might perform some kind of bloody miracle. 'It might be best if you don't see Nell right now,' she suggested kindly. 'Let her sleep.'

'Somethin' bad happened last night, didn't it?' He knew all the signs. 'If Nell's all right, why did you have to send for the doctor?' Suspicious. Always suspicious. 'And what were the authorities doing here?' Into his mind came the cellar at Slater's house and the dead face staring up at him. 'Were they after me and Nell?' His voice shivered. He knew from experience that the authorities could sometimes blame you even if it wasn't your fault. 'We didn't 'ave nuthin' to do with what Slater did,' he said shakily. 'But me an' Nell knew they might blame us anyway so that's why we snuk off.'

Lottie was taken aback. 'Who the devil's Slater?'

'Isn't that why the authorities came last night?'

'The authorities came because I sent for them.'

He couldn't believe his ears. '*You* sent for 'em? Why?'

'Because somebody crept into this house while we were asleep.' Hesitating, she glanced at Rose, who nodded encouragement.

Returning her attention to the boy, Lottie continued, 'It was Nell who woke me. I sleep in the next room, and when I heard her out of her bed, I rushed in and she collapsed in my arms. She was bending over the cradle when I found her, and it wasn't until I got her into bed that I realised – someone had stolen her baby. Nell was in a sorry state and that's why I sent for the doctor. He gave her something to make her sleep. She's had a terrible shock, Kit. I really don't think we should disturb her.'

In a second he had broken away from Lottie and was racing out of the room. He didn't stop until he came to Nell's bedroom door where he paused, unable for a minute to go in. He leaned his head against the door, softly sobbing. 'Oh, Nell, I should 'ave been with you. They wouldn't have dared take your baby if I'd been watching.'

Lottie's hand touched his shoulder. 'Go in then,' she whispered. 'Try not to make a sound.'

Together they went in.

At first, when he saw Nell lying there, so white and still, he feared his worst nightmare had happened, but then he saw her heave a sigh and for one heavenly minute he was at peace. Then his gaze went to the cradle, that rough and beautiful thing he had made out of his love for Nell, and he was lost again.

At Nell's bedside, he held her hand tenderly. 'I'm sorry, Nell,' he murmured. 'I should 'ave been 'ere, an' I'm sorry.' Then he cried as only a child can cry.

Gently, Lottie took him downstairs to the kitchen where three of the girls had now gathered. 'Poor little sod,' Annabelle muttered. 'He don't know what to do next.' Annabelle was small with masses of hair and short, thin legs which she was showing to some degree as she sat down and crossed them one over the other.

The other two were Sue and Babs. Sue was as tall as Annabelle was short, and Babs was a good deal older than both but still attractive. 'Come on, girls,' she said, looking at Kit and feeling sorry. 'Let's go upstairs. We're in the way here.'

Without protest, the other two followed, each carrying the mugs of tea provided by Rose.

Kit was crying again, and for once he didn't care who saw him. 'Come on now, Kit.' Lottie was on her knees before him. 'Nell wouldn't want to see you like this. She told me you were her little man, and men don't cry if they can help it.'

With the back of his hand he wiped away the tears. 'Did Nell really say I was 'er little man?'

'She did. Ask Rose if you don't believe me.'

Rose confirmed it. 'Soon after you both came here, that's what she told us, and she was so proud of you. Lottie's right. Nell wouldn't want to see you crying.'

He pondered a while, then in a sombre voice asked, 'What did the doctor say?'

Lottie explained. 'Nell was already weak from loss of blood. In fact, I don't know how she got out of that bed and as far as the cradle, but she did, and it only goes to show how determined she can be. Losing the blood has made her weak, but it won't kill her – at least that's what the doctor reckons. He's left us with a list of dos and don'ts, and what kind of food she's to be given. I won't lie to you, though. Nell's had a dreadful shock. She knows the child is gone and even though she's asleep, it's bound to play on her mind.'

'What will happen?'

'Well, she can go two ways. She can either give up altogether, or the need to find her child and have it back will make her fight all that much harder.'

'Nell will fight.'

'From what I've seen of her so far, I'm sure you're right.' When Kit actually smiled, she ruffled his hair. 'So, no more crying, eh? You have to be strong for Nell's sake. We'll do everything we can, Kit, I promise you.'

'Why are you being so good to me an' Nell?'

'What else would you have me do? Turn you away?'

'Other people would.' In fact, other people *had.*

'I'm not other people, Kit. If it was me in need, would you and Nell help me?'

'Course we would. Nell would help anybody. She saved an old man when he'd been shot, and she took me on when I 'adn't got nobody.' His eyes shone with pride. 'Nell's got a heart o' gold.'

'There you are then. There's your answer.'

He felt ashamed. 'I'm sorry.'

Lottie pulled herself up by the chair. 'Oh! I must be getting old,' she said with a grin. 'My legs are locked.'

Rose laughed out loud, telling her she was only a slip of a thing. 'I'll make us a fresh brew,' she said. 'What about you, Kit? Do you want some tea?'

He looked at Lottie. 'Can I stay with Nell?'

'Better not. She has to be kept quiet for now.'

'I'm hungry.'

Rose laughed. 'That's a good sign. I'll have a plate of bacon and eggs in front of you before you can say no thank you.'

While the two women pottered about the kitchen, Kit began to think through the events. 'I'm sorry I cried,' he said again. 'You won't tell Nell, will you?'

Lottie brought two cups of tea to the table. Handing one to him, she sat down. 'It won't go beyond these four walls,' she assured him.

He polished off the breakfast Rose put in front of him and afterwards asked if there was anything he could do to help.

'You can gather a bucket full of kindling from the woods if you feel you have to be busy,' Rose told him. 'Or you can sweep the yard. If you don't fancy either of them, you're free to do as you please.'

'I'd rather sweep the yard. I don't want to go in the woods again.'

'You'll find the brush outside the kitchen door.'

Lottie gave him an encouraging wink, which prompted him to ask, 'Can I see Nell before I go out? I won't make a noise, honest to God.' When she seemed about to refuse, he pleaded, 'Please, Lottie. Just for a minute?'

With a sigh she conceded. 'All right, just for a minute. But you're not to make a sound. She mustn't be disturbed, do you understand me, Kit?'

He nodded. 'I'll be quiet as a mouse.'

After he'd gone from the room, Rose wasn't so sure. 'Don't you think you should have gone with him?'

Lottie didn't think so. 'Two of us would make more noise, and besides, he knows how important it is for Nell to rest. That boy would walk through fire to keep her safe.' She sighed, suddenly feeling sorry for herself. 'I've never had anybody care for me like that. In a way, I envy her.'

'*I* care for you,' Rose protested. 'You've been a good friend to me and there isn't much I wouldn't do for you.' She gave a little chuckle. 'Though I might draw the line at walking through fire.'

'I didn't mean you, Rose. I meant all the men who have ever used me and thrown me aside.' She waved it all away. 'Oh sod it! Who needs them? None of them are worth a second thought, and anyway I've done all right, haven't I, Rose? I've got my own house, and a bit put by for when I'm out to grass. How many other women can say that?'

'Not many. Certainly not that lovely young girl upstairs. She's wearing little more than rags; she has no money that I can see, and no prospects. She's fighting for her life, and now some bastard's snatched her baby. If you ask me, she's got more than her share of bad luck to contend with.' Coming to the table where Lottie was seated, Rose prodded her on the shoulder. 'So don't you say you envy that young woman upstairs. Shame on you! Even the boy is a burden to her though I don't suppose she'd admit that for a minute because she loves him as much as he loves her. Them two need each other and they look out for each other. That boy is all she's got, especially now.'

'You're right, and I ought to think before I speak.' Sipping her tea, Lottie thought about Nell, and wondered about her background. 'She's a pretty girl, isn't she, Rose?'

'She might be, but the illness has dragged her down.

She's so thin, it's pitiful to see.' Folding the dishcloth, she laid it on the sink. 'I'll soon have the fat back on her,' she mused. 'Beef broth and dumplings, that should do the trick.'

'Who'd want to snatch the newborn, d'you think?'

Rose had her own ideas about that. 'I know the policeman said there's been a spate of child-snatching in the area these past weeks, passing Gypsies, he said, but I'm not so sure.'

'What are you getting at, Rose?' Lottie stood up and moved closer to the little woman. 'You've got something on your mind, haven't you? Out with it.'

'Whoever took that child out of its cot must have known the layout of this house. It was too easy, Lottie. He came in, went upstairs, found the right bedroom, took the child from its cradle and made his getaway, and not one of us heard a sound. And another thing, how did he manage to miss that creaking step halfway up the staircase? If he'd trodden on that, the whole house would have been awake.'

Lottie stared at her. 'I never thought of that, Rose,' she admitted. 'But if it *was* someone who knew the house, who do you reckon it could be? And why?'

'Greed.' Rose had no doubt. 'Somewhere along the way there must be money involved. Rich folk are always willing to pay a handsome sum for a newborn.'

Upstairs, Kit sat quietly watching Nell. 'I'll be strong,' he whispered. 'I won't cry any more, and I won't sleep in the woods.'

His mind flashed back to the couple in the woods. He remembered hearing what he thought was a baby's cry. Suddenly he was on his feet, his mouth and eyes big with astonishment. 'In the woods, I heard a baby cry! I heard bits of what they were saying!' Jubilant, he was almost in tears. 'They've got Nell's baby – they've got her baby!'

Lottie and Rose were still discussing the possibility that the intruder could have been someone known to them when Kit burst in saying he knew where the baby was. They sat him down and quizzed him.

Words tumbling one over the other, startled and excited, Kit went over what he'd remembered. 'Them sweethearts in the woods. They were going to Blackburn. That's where Nell lived, and her best friend Molly Davidson. That woman in the woods, she knew you, Lottie. I heard her say your name.' He began to struggle. 'Let me go. I have to find Nell's baby.' He hadn't realised the importance of what he'd seen and heard, but now there was no holding him.

Leaping up, he would have gone there and then, but Lottie held him back. 'The woman who knew me, what was she like?' When he described her, Lottie knew straight away. 'The bitch! I never did trust that one.' Grabbing Kit, she said, 'I'm coming with you.' She ran upstairs and was down in record time, dressed for an outing and carrying a wad of money in her bag. 'Take care of the girl, Rose,' she said. 'Me and the boy have things to do. First stop is a visit to our drunken friend Alf. He's the one who brought Nell here and he might know something.'

She marched outside where, in a matter of minutes, she and Kit were heading out in her pony and trap.

'Blackburn is a good way off,' she said. 'Just remember the name of Nell's friend. Molly, did you say?'

'Molly Davidson.' As they rode away, he glanced back at the house. 'Get better, Nell,' he whispered. 'We're going to get your baby back.'

Chapter Ten

AFTER TRAVELLING FOR what seemed an age, Lottie and Kit were ready for a rest. 'This looks a likely place,' Lottie said, drawing into an inn yard. 'I expect you want to visit the Gents. I'll take myself off to the ladies' room while you see to the pony and trap.' Climbing down, she pointed to the main entrance. 'When you've done, you'd best get the order. I'll have a shandy and a muffin. You get what you like.'

With that she straightened her hat and went off at a smart pace towards the side entrance, where she assumed the ladies' cloakroom to be. 'Why they can't put them closer to the main building, I will never know!' She was for ever irritated by the preferential treatment men received over women.

It only took Kit a few minutes to visit the gents. Nobody paid him any attention until he came into the beer parlour, where all eyes turned and fixed themselves on this little man with a big stride. 'A shandy and a muffin, please,' he told the mop-headed fellow behind the bar. 'And I'll have some pork crackling and a jug of sarsaparilla.' He felt very grand. In all his life he had never even been inside one of these places, let alone walked up to the bar and placed an order.

'Oh, will you now?' Seeming friendly enough, the man smiled at him. 'I think you'd best show me the colour o' your money first.' He sneaked a glance at the other men in there, who quietly sniggered.

'I haven't got any.' Kit knew they were laughing at him and he was ready for war.

'Oh, I see. Well, if you've got no money, how do you expect to pay for your order?'

'He's not paying for it.' Lottie sailed in. 'I am.' She stared at the men who immediately looked away. 'My money's as good as anybody's,' she said loudly, 'but if you don't want it, we'll go elsewhere.'

'Touchy, aren't you?' The barman made no move to serve her.

Grabbing Kit's coat collar, Lottie swung him round. 'Come on,' she said. 'I haven't got time to waste here.'

'Woa!' The barman called her back. 'No offence meant. It's just that we're not used to women calling in.' He bade Lottie and Kit be seated, and in a surprisingly short time he had their order before them.

'They're all the same!' Lottie snorted as he walked away. 'Men and their cronies, all the bloody same!'

'We're not staying here long, are we?' Wolfing his food, Kit was impatient to be on his way.

'Eat slowly or you'll get colic.' Lottie tapped him hard on the back of the head. 'I'm not stopping for you to be sick so you'd best take your time and it'll stay down.'

'Did that drunken man know anything?'

'Turns out he drove that couple you saw. I did get that much out of him, for a price, you understand.'

Taking a huge bite of her muffin, she swilled it down with a swig of ale. 'According to him, the couple did have a baby and he took them to Blackburn, but he wouldn't say where he dropped them off.' She took another swig of her ale. 'I expect he's been sworn to secrecy and been paid a handsome sum into the bargain. Mind you, he'd probably have told me if I'd emptied my purse for him but then we'd have had no money ourselves, and anyway, I'm not a rich woman.' She groaned, blowing out her cheeks in frustration. 'Happen I should have stayed at home.'

Kit was mortified. 'Don't say that, Lottie. Once we find this friend of Nell's, she might know who the man is and where he lives.'

'You don't give up, do you?' Filled with admiration, she recalled what Rose had said: 'Don't you say you envy that young woman upstairs.' Rose was right as usual, and putting herself out like this was a small thing to do for someone less fortunate than herself. 'Come on, you,' she urged Kit. 'Finish up and let's be on our way. If we're to find this Molly Davidson and get Nell's baby back, every minute counts.'

It was already growing dark when they got to Blackburn. 'We'll ask our way to the high street,' Lottie decided. 'People congregate around high streets and somebody might know her name.'

She was right about there being plenty of people there, but she was wrong about any of them knowing Molly's name. 'Well, that's that,' she moaned, leaning against the trap and wondering where to go next. 'We don't know any more than we did when we started off.'

'What about the inns?' Kit pointed to where the sound of accordian music was coming from. 'We could ask there.'

'We might as well.' Securing the pony and trap where it was, she led the way to the inn. 'But if we don't have any luck here, it'll be a case of tramping about and asking whoever we come across. With a bit of luck we should strike lucky before it gets really dark. After paying that leech, Alf, I'm not sure my purse would stretch to a room for two.'

A few minutes later they emerged from the inn with disappointed faces. 'You'd think *somebody* would know her!' Lottie was beginning to lose hope. Rounding on Kit, she demanded, 'Are you sure you've got the name right?'

'Nell told me,' he insisted. 'She said Molly was her best friend. Molly Davidson, that's the name she said.'

'Well, I'm not wandering the streets half the night, not for you nor anybody else. I've done my time on that lark and all it got me was a chill in the bones. We'll search for a bit longer and ask anybody we come across. After that, we'll see. We'll see.' In the back of her mind she wondered whether Kit had got it all wrong. Tired and irritated, she was ready to make her way home.

LILIAN REECE WATCHED her brother from the doorway, the way he sat, hunched in his chair, head in hands, looking for all the world as if he could end his life and think nothing of it.

'Why don't you go to bed?'

He kept his head down as he answered, 'I'm not ready for me bed yet.'

'There's work to be done tomorrow.'

'There's *always* work to be done.'

'You haven't slept properly for weeks now.' She came and stood over him, like a hawk over a sparrow. 'It's *her*, isn't it?' Poison marbled her voice. 'That's the truth of it. You can't stop thinking about her!'

'She's my daughter.'

'And I'm your sister.'

'Go to bed, damn you.'

'She's not thinking about you, I'll be bound.'

'Why should she? I've let her down.'

'Oh? And what about me? What about the shame she's brought on us? What would people think if they knew what she'd done?'

'I don't give a bugger what people think.' Now he looked up, his eyes red-rimmed and his face white from lack of sleep. 'It's not *their* daughter who's roaming the streets God knows where. It's not *yours* either. Nell's *my* daughter, and I feel bad for letting her down when she needed me. But then you wouldn't understand that, would you?' he sneered. 'You've let people down all your life and it doesn't bother you one bit. I wonder what people you've hurt that I don't even know about.' He laughed, a harsh sound. 'No wonder you're a lonely old woman. You don't know what it's like to love someone other than yourself, and you never will.'

'You're wrong, Don. I've always loved you.' For one terrible minute she nearly told him about the things she had done in order to keep his love for herself. She nearly told him how she had ruined his life and crippled his sweetheart. She was sorely tempted to confess how she had consorted with others to hide that wretched girl Mary away in a convent yet keep the baby, Nell, as a measure of grudging compensation to him.

For a long time, when he had had no thoughts for Mary, Lilian had lived for his love and respect. Now it was he who craved love and respect, but not from her. It was Nell's love he wanted. Nell's respect he longed for. He had a lot to make up for where Nell was concerned, and it seemed nothing else mattered; not her, not the farm, not even himself. But at least he was unaware of the wicked wrongs his own sister had done to him and those he loved. It was best he stayed in ignorance, Lilian determined, trembling inwardly at how close she'd come to telling him everything. All these years the guilt had been hers. His only shame was in making the girl pregnant and believing with all his heart that he was responsible for her untimely death. Playing on his shame had been an easy thing. Making him believe that he was a coward and a sinner had placed him at her mercy. To bend her brother into the pitiful creature he had become was a satisfying and powerful thing.

'I haven't heard from her in a while.' It was as if Don was talking to himself. 'I don't know where Nell is, or whether she's had the baby. I don't know if she's well or in need, and I don't know what I should do.' He was still weak. Deep down he was still the coward she had made him. He looked up, pleading with her. 'What can I do? Tell me what to do.'

Hatred shone in Lilian's eyes. 'You do nothing,' she

screeched. 'Your daughter is a slut, and I don't care if she ends up in hell.'

He stared at her hard, cruel face, and for one awful, knowing moment, he was closer to her than at any other time in his life. Only a moment, and then he couldn't bear to look at her. 'I don't want you near me,' he said hoarsely. 'Sometimes I can't stand to look at you.' In seeing her, he saw himself. It was a sad and sorry sight.

Shocked, Lilian stared at him. The worm is turning, she thought, and her wicked heart leaped inside her. 'I'll leave you be,' she promised. 'But you must put her out of your mind. If the slut can't keep in touch with her own father, then she's not worth worrying about.'

His voice came to her in a growl. 'I make no promise but this. Leave me be, or I'll drop you where you stand.' With his eyes boring into her, he raised his two hands, curving them in a gesture of strangulation.

Lilian was mortally afraid. She saw something in him she had never seen before, and it made her wary. Quickly, she left the room, pausing at the door to gaze on him once more, her face a study in regret. Not regret for what she had done, though; not because she had lied, telling him his sweetheart was dead; not regret because she had robbed her own brother of the only chance he might ever have had at happiness, or because she had condemned Nell to a life of unbearable loneliness. None of these things touched her conscience. Lilian Reece had only one regret and it soared through her now. 'I should have killed the child at birth,' she muttered. 'If I'd done that she wouldn't be coming between us now.'

As she climbed the stairs, a shocking but delicious

idea came into her mind. Looking down into the hallway, her eyes were drawn to a tall, glass-fronted wooden
case. Inside, three shotguns were lined up like brown-
uniformed soldiers. 'It isn't too late,' she murmured with
the softest smile. 'If Nell was out of the way, I'd have
him all to myself again.'

I T WAS ONE of those bright, chilly mornings that made
everything sparkle. With Nell on his mind as always,
Bill was working in the big barn when he overheard an
argument.

'What the devil made you bring a woman of that
sort into my house?'

'I had no choice. Someone had to wet-nurse the
child, and she was on hand. Besides, she was helpful in
getting the job done.'

'She wasn't too pleased when I sent her on her way.
I hope for your sake she doesn't decide to open her
mouth.'

'She won't. You paid her too well.'

'I've also paid *you* well.'

'I earned it, didn't I? The child is with you, isn't she?
No doubt you'll satisfy people as to where it came from?'

'People are gullible. They'll believe what they're
told.'

There was a pause as they came to a halt right
outside the barn. 'What about the mother? Is there really
no hope for her?' Vincent Morgan had been told
how Nell was at death's door. It saddened him. So, too,
did the fact that the child he craved was not a son

after all. But he had the child, and that was some small consolation.

Detecting a note of regret in Morgan's voice, the man gave him a curious look. 'The girl wasn't expected to last the night but I can make inquiries if you like.' He had no qualms about going back. They had no reason to suspect him there. Besides, he would expect to be handsomely paid.

'No. I have the child. The mother is of no consequence.' Vincent Morgan was a self-centred man, looking out for himself and giving no quarter to those who would cross him. In that respect, nothing had changed.

Bill was intrigued. Remaining by the door, he was careful not to make his presence known. By this time the two men had moved out of earshot. 'What was that all about?' he wondered, and returned to his work with a sense of unrest. 'I expect the poor kid is a result of one of Morgan's sordid affairs with some poor woman who is now on her last legs. The bastard!' These last few weeks, his respect for Vincent Morgan had diminished by the day. Lately, it was diminishing by the minute.

The two men walked as far as the main gate. 'There's no more to be done. Just keep your mouth shut.'

'As you wish.' The man turned his collar up against the cutting breeze, saying cunningly, 'I just thought, if the girl does recover, she might come looking for the child.' He walked away, confident that he would be called back.

Sure enough, he hadn't gone two paces when Vincent called out, 'Wait a minute.' Vincent hesitated as he faced the horror of what he was about to do, but then he thought of Nell and knew he had no choice. 'Make sure she's in no fit state to follow the child.'

The man tipped his hat. 'Consider it done,' he said slyly. 'I'll be back for my fee.' Turning on his heel, he walked away.

Vincent strode off in the opposite direction, going towards the house. 'Forgive me, Nell,' he said. 'But if I know you, you'll move heaven and earth to get back your child.' Thinking of Nell, and the strong character she was, he knew he had done the right thing. 'I'll raise the girl well,' he whispered. 'You have my word, she'll want for nothing.'

As he turned to close the door, he glanced down the drive and was alarmed to see Bill emerging from the barn. How long had he been there? Could he have overheard anything?

There was only one way to find out. He followed Bill to the stables.

LATER, BILL RECALLED the incident. 'I tell you, Mam, it's the strangest thing. One minute he's talking with this scoundrel, and the next he's chasing after me, asking if I'd seen him and the fellow, and whether there was anything on my mind.'

'And was there?' Molly had been bustling about laying the tea. Now she stopped and looked him in the eye.

'I'm not sure. Could be.'

'Is he up to no good, d'you think?'

'Who knows?'

'Has he murdered somebody?' Not that interested, she resumed laying the knives and forks beside the plates.

'Don't be daft, Mam!'

'Does it mean you'll be out of a job, or that you can't have the cottage?'

'It was nothing to do with me or the cottage.'

'Well, there you are.' Flashing him a smile, Molly went into the kitchen. 'So long as it doesn't affect you, that's all as matters.' From the kitchen she poked her head round the door. 'You're not worried, are you, son?'

'No, I'm not worried. Just curious, that's all. Still, it's none of my business what he gets up to.' And that was how he left it. There was no use worrying about something that had nothing to do with either him or his mam.

Following Molly into the kitchen, he inquired, 'Have you heard from Nell?'

Molly shook her head, a frown creasing her face. 'Nell ain't written a word to me for some time now,' she said, looking at him with troubled eyes. 'I've been worried, son. It's not like her.'

'Don't worry,' he told her, though he was deeply concerned. 'She'll write soon, you see if she doesn't.'

Molly had often toyed with the idea of telling him how Nell was expecting a child but she had always held back. Now, though, she had an instinct that Nell might be in need of help. 'There's summat you should know,' she began.

'Oh, and what's that?'

It almost tripped off her tongue but once again she

stopped herself. 'Nothing,' she said, with a quick smile. 'It can wait.'

His dark eyes appraised her face. 'You're sure now?'

'Aye.' The moment of truth was gone. 'I'm sure.'

For some inexplicable reason, he couldn't rest. 'Never mind about a dinner for me,' he told Molly. 'I'm off out.' Slinging on his jacket, he went up the passage to the front door.

'Where are you going?' Molly called after him.

'Off to see Nell's dad. There's something I need to know.'

I T WAS DARK, and the houses all looked the same. 'Are you sure this is the right street?' Lottie took the pony and trap down the street at a leisurely pace, peering at the door numbers as she went. 'If this is another wild goose chase, I'm off home. I've had enough. Why couldn't that bloody man have given you the number?'

'There!' Kit pointed at Molly's house; the lamp was shining from the window. 'That's the one. The man in the shop said she had flowered curtains and a pot dog in the window, and look, it's just like he said.'

Even before the trap had stopped, he was off and knocking on Molly's door. 'Molly Davidson!' he yelled. 'Molly Davidson!'

Molly flung open the door. 'Jesus, Mary and Joseph! Is there a war on or what?' Red-faced and breathless after running down the passage, she gave him a piece of her tongue. 'You little bugger! What are you up to, eh?' For two pins she would have clipped his ear, but when he started gabbling with excitement about how 'We've come from Nell. Her baby's been stole, and we 'ave to find it,' she was shocked into silence.

Before Molly could get herself together, Lottie walked up. 'Can we come in?' she asked. 'We've come a long way, and we need your help.'

Molly found her voice. 'Is it right what he says?' She ushered the two of them inside. 'Have you come from Nell? What's the boy talking about? He said her baby's been stolen. Is that true?' Lottie's face told her the truth, and it was like a blow to the heart. 'Oh, dear God!' She clapped her hand to her mouth. 'Where is she? Why hasn't Nell come with you? Has anything happened to the lass?' Her voice broke. 'Tell me she's all right.'

It was Kit who answered, and in his innocence he only made matters worse. 'Nell won't die,' he declared. 'If she gets her baby back, I know she won't die.'

White as a sheet, Molly took hold of Lottie's shoulders and said in a small, frightened voice, 'I'll not take another step until you put my mind at rest.'

D ON REECE WAS just coming out of the house when Bill arrived. 'If I don't get out, she'll either drive me to an early grave or I'll swing for her,' he said as he hurried down the street with Bill beside him. 'Day and night, she never lets up. It's nice to see a friendly face,' he added, grinning at Bill with a humour he certainly didn't feel. 'What can I do for you?'

'I want to talk about Nell.'

Don came to a halt. 'Oh?' He was wary. Where Nell

was concerned, he was always wary, even with those he trusted. 'In that case, we'd better go back and talk inside.' He liked Bill Davidson. He was a fine young man, and it was a pity that he and Nell couldn't have found something in each other to draw them together. 'With a bit of luck we can hide ourselves away in the back room and she'll not bother us. Unless you'd rather we carried on to the inn and shared a jar of ale together?'

'Thanks, Don, but if it's all the same to you, it might be more private in the house. You know what it's like at the inn at this time of a night. We'll not be able to hear ourselves think.' What he had to say wasn't for everyone's ears.

Don gave him a sideways glance. 'Sounds serious.'

Bill's smile gave nothing away. 'Serious enough,' he answered, and Don wondered what could be so important as to bring this young man all the way across town on such a bitter, cold night.

HUNCHED AND PAINED, Molly sat in the chair as though she'd been felled by a blow. 'That poor lass. Some folk are meant to take the world on their shoulders, and it seems Nell is one of them.'

'She's certainly had her share of ill fortune.' Lottie had told Molly everything. 'But she's a fighter. Anyone can see that. Kit might well be right. If we can find where her bairn was taken, it might give her a reason to live.' She lowered her voice in case Kit returned. He was outside seeing to the pony. 'The doctor doesn't hold out much hope, and to tell you the truth, neither do I.'

The first person who came into Molly's mind was Bill. 'Bill will have to be told,' she said, adding confidently, 'He'll know what to do.'

'Bill?' Lottie recalled the name.

'That's my son.'

'Nell called out his name when she was feverish.'

'Aye, well, I'm not surprised.' Molly sat up in the chair, even managing a little smile. 'She loves him, you see.'

'I gathered that.' There was no man in her life, only leeches and rogues, but she made herself remember what Rose had said, and she didn't envy Nell, not one bit.

Fired now by the determination that Nell must come home, Molly took charge of the situation. 'Soon as ever the lad's finished, he can go and fetch our Bill.' She paused, thinking how one thing led to another. 'Funny thing though, our Bill went off to see Nell's father. Not five minutes afore you arrived.'

Outside, Kit waited while the horse gulped down the water from the bucket. 'Thirsty, were you, old feller?' He patted him on the neck. 'Hungry too, by the way you gobbled up them carrots. You shouldn't be hungry though, not after that wad of hay we got you when we stopped to rest.' He thought fondly of another friend left along the way. 'Me and Nell had a good horse but we had to leave him with Kath at the baker's. She'll look after him though, and when Nell's better, we'll go and fetch him back.'

His voice faded, tears clogging his eyes. 'I miss her,' he whispered. 'Nell's the only one who's ever cared about me. I wish she were my mother.' His mind turned to something that had been troubling him ever since he and Lottie had come to look for Nell's baby. 'I don't reckon Nell will want me around when she comes home. I expect I'll be on my own again.' Deep down, though, he couldn't believe it. 'Maybe she won't be rid of me,' he declared hopefully. 'Maybe she'll let me get work close by so we can see each other now and then.' The idea cheered him up, and he finished seeing to the pony with a whistle.

When he returned to the house, Molly was ready. 'I want you to go straight over to Nell's father,' she said. 'I've drawn you a sort of map so's you'll not get lost.' Spreading the paper on the table, she pointed out the landmarks. 'You turn left at the bottom of the street, then past the Red Lion Inn. Then you go this way, along Viaduct Street, right to the bottom, then cut across this field to the lane.' Kit listened carefully and nodded his understanding. 'Tell Bill about Nell,' Molly instructed. 'Tell him his mam'll have his things ready by the time you get back.' Then she sent Kit off at a run.

'Much as I'd like to run all the way to Liverpool and fetch Nell home,' she said to Lottie, 'there's nothing we can do till our Bill gets back, and he'll likely be a while. The men won't be in for at least another hour, so we're on us own for a time yet.' Molly had taken stock of her visitor, surmising she was a woman who might enjoy a tipple. 'You'll want summat to warm you through,' she suggested with a wink. 'What takes your fancy?'

'I could murder a drop o' gin.'

'A drop o' gin it is.' Waddling to the dresser, she

took out two glasses and a bottle of the clear stuff. 'Get that down ye.'

Handing one of the glasses to Lottie, she sat herself in the chair. 'Now then, let's get down to brass tacks. This woman who you think took Nell's young 'un. What does she look like? And the feller. He were paid, you say?'

Lottie sipped at her gin. 'According to Kit, the man mentioned being paid, yes. And he and the woman talked about coming to Blackburn.' Leaning forward in her chair, she said sourly, 'I've been good to that little slut. I'll wring her bloody neck when I lay hands on her. If she thinks she can come into my house of a night, creeping about as if she owns the place, stealing babies and running off, leaving her own brat for others to look after, well, I'm telling you, she's got a bloody shock coming!' Red-faced and angry, Lottie settled back in the chair and took another long sip of gin. 'That girl of yours is one reason why I want this newborn found, but the girl who took advantage of my good nature, that's another matter, and I'll not let it rest, you can depend on that.'

Molly had stopped listening. She was deep in her own thoughts, a light beginning to dawn in her mind. Of course! Why didn't she think of it before? 'There's only one man who has money to burn in these parts,' she said. 'One man who might have good reason for wanting Nell's young 'un – Vincent Morgan!' She almost leaped out of the chair. 'If it was Morgan who fathered Nell's bairn, it could be him who wants it back. You see, his own wife died. She were big with child and the two of them were lost in a tragic accident. The man has money and land, but no childer. If he is the father of Nell's bairn, it's likely he'd do anything to get his hands on it.'

'Lives near here, does he?' Lottie commented. The gin was making her sleepy. 'I'm getting too old for tearing about the countryside.'

'But I can't be certain. If I accuse a man like that and it turns out I'm wrong, I could be in a heap o' trouble. But then again, if I'm right, we could maybe get Nell's bairn back that much quicker.' She scratched her head in frustration. 'On the other hand, if he *is* the bairn's father, what are we to do? He's a powerful man, with money behind him and friends in high places. What can folk like us do against that?' Like as not they'd end up in prison. 'Oh, but it's Nell's child. We have to do what we can.'

It was the biggest dilemma Molly had ever faced in her life. 'If I tell Bill about me suspicions, he'll be round there and God knows what might happen.' She would have to think carefully about which way to turn; the wrong way, and they could lose everything.

'WHO SENT YOU?' Standing on the doorstep in the face of a keen wind and disturbed out of a cosy armchair by a grubby boy, Lilian was not in the best of moods.

Kit had faced worse in his life than the likes of Lilian Reece. 'Molly sent me,' he answered boldly. 'I'm to fetch Bill. It's a matter of life and death.' He felt very important delivering such a message.

'Whose life or death?'

'I ain't telling you.' He didn't like the look or the sound of this woman. 'It's Bill I've to tell, not you.'

'Who told you Bill was here?'

'Molly said he'd come to see Nell's dad.' He took out the map she'd drawn. 'Look, she made me this map. I follered it like she said, so I must be at the right place. Molly said Bill was here and that I was to fetch him right away, because of Nell.'

'Nell, eh?' Lilian's ears pricked up. 'What's Nell been up to now?'

'Is he 'ere?' When she didn't respond, he insisted, 'He 'as to come with me. Please, missus.'

Intrigued, she quietly observed him in the light from the hallway. 'You're not from round these parts, are you?' His Cockney accent was conspicuous.

Biting his lip and not sure whether to trust her, he stood there, freezing cold and visibly shivering, regarding her while she regarded him. He had a job to do, and this woman was hindering him. 'You must be Nell's Aunt Lilian. She said you were a bad 'un.'

'Nell has a fanciful imagination.' Her hatred for Nell multiplied.

'Is Bill 'ere, or isn't he?'

Cunning now, she played him along. 'He's out but you can come in and wait if you like.' She sensed there was something going on she should know about. 'I've got some fresh-baked cookies and a jar of sarsaparilla.' Pushing the door open wide, she gestured for him to enter.

Instead, Kit began yelling at the top of his voice.

'BILL DAVIDSON! NELL NEEDS YOU. MOLLY SAYS YOU'RE TO COME QUICK!'

Startled when Lilian was thrust aside and two men appeared before him, Kit's first instinct was to run. But then the younger man spoke. 'I'm Bill,' he said. 'What's all this about Nell?'

Kit looked from one man to the other. They both seemed troubled. 'Molly sent me to fetch Bill, and that old hag said he weren't here.' Lilian clutched at her throat as if she was choking.

'Well, I am here, son. So now you can tell me. What do you mean by saying Nell needs me? Where is she?' Desperate, he bent to look into the boy's face. 'Don't be afraid.' He was in no doubt that Lilian had already interrogated him.

Kit was having second thoughts. ''Ow do I know you're not with *her*?' He pointed a cold, shaking finger at Lilian. ''Ow do I know you're not all out to make trouble for Nell?'

Bill replied in a quiet, firm voice, 'I wouldn't hurt Nell for the world. Trust me. Tell me where she is.'

'And I'm Nell's father,' Don added. 'Say what you've come to say, boy. If Nell's in danger, we mustn't waste time.' He nodded towards Lilian. 'This is my sister Lilian, and if she's been frightening you, you mustn't worry. Nell's right, her aunt is a bad 'un, but she won't hurt you and she won't hurt Nell any more, I can promise that.'

Reassured, Kit launched into a full account of events. Gabbling so fast his words ran one into the other, he told how Nell's baby had been stolen and how they'd come all the way from Liverpool to find it. 'And Molly says you're to come home and fetch Nell back, because she's been at death's door.' He'd heard that phrase used at Lottie's house. It was so terrible a prospect it had stuck fast in his mind.

Bill was shocked. He hadn't even known about Nell being with child. But there was no time to waste. He glanced at Don who was grey at the news. 'Don't worry,' he said, 'I'll fetch her back.'

'Yes, you fetch her home.' Don's voice grated with pain. 'For pity's sake, fetch the lass home!' He glared at his sister. 'If God's good and Nell's safe, I swear she'll never be driven out from under this roof again.'

Pulling Kit after him, Bill ran down the street. 'If you can't keep up, I'll have to carry you,' he cried. And while he ran he prayed that Nell was safe and that they would not be too late. There had been a time when he loved Nell only as a sister. But now all that was changed. His love for Nell was all-consuming, and he recognised it for what it was. All the same, he dared not hope she might return his love. Just to have her safe was all he could ask for now.

A SHORT TIME later, with her heart in her mouth, Molly watched as Bill drove away, going up the street like a madman at the reins of the trap. Lottie sat on one side of him and Kit on the other, both of them hanging on for dear life.

Molly hadn't had the courage to reveal to Bill the things Nell had confided in her, or what she suspected about Vincent Morgan. 'For now, all we want is for the lass to come home and get well. When she's ready, we shall know it all, I'm sure.'

'Tell Nell I'm waiting for her,' she called after them. 'Tell her old Molly loves and misses her.'

Chapter Eleven

'ARE YOU SURE you're well enough, dearie?' Rose was leaning over Nell, reluctantly helping her on with her robe. 'I know you're on the mend but I don't know that you ought to get out of bed just yet.' She had met many people in her life and they were all different, but she had never come across anyone with Nell's stubbornness and grim determination.

Nell would not be dissuaded. 'If I lie in this bed much longer, I'll never get strong,' she answered, her blue eyes still scarred by the loss of her child. 'I need to use the bathroom and afterwards I'd like to sit by the window in the parlour.'

'But it's only four o' clock in the morning, and it's chilly in that room at the best of times.' She studied Nell's face, that small lovable face, with its soft, troubled eyes, and her heart went out to her. 'I don't know, love,' she said kindly. 'I'd never forgive myself if you were to catch pneumonia.'

'Just for a while,' Nell pleaded. 'Then I promise I'll rest.' She couldn't sleep; she desperately wanted to follow Kit and Lottie and find her baby. She felt so helpless, lying in bed, too weak even to get dressed without help.

'I'll light a fire,' Rose conceded, 'and make a hot drink. That should keep out the chill.' Linking her arm with Nell's, she helped her to her feet.

Grateful to lean on Rose until she got to the bathroom, Nell graciously refused her help from there. 'Thanks, Rose,' she said, drawing away. 'I'll be fine now. I can manage on my own.'

'You're sure now?'

Nell nodded and smiled and her whole face lit up, but not the eyes. The eyes were the mirror of what she felt inside, and what she felt was a terrible loss.

A few minutes later, she was making her own way downstairs. Rose insisted on going first. Nell followed carefully, negotiating each step with painstaking deliberation.

As they entered the parlour, the cold struck like a slap in the face. 'Brr!' Rose carried the lamp forward, pushing back the curtains. Outside, the snow glimmered in the shifting moonlight. 'It's beginning to clear,' she observed. 'I've a feeling we've seen the last of the snowfall.' Pointing to the big armchair by the fireside, she told Nell, 'Sit here, love, I'll have a fire going in no time.'

As Nell made her way across the room, Rose regarded her with concern. 'Are you sure you're all right? Do you feel very cold?'

As a rule, Nell didn't mind the cold, but she felt it now, right through to her bones. For just the briefest minute she wondered if she should have listened to Rose and stayed in bed where it was warm. And coming down the stairs just now had tired her out. Yet she knew that if she was to get back on her own two feet she had to get the better of it. 'You're right, Rose, it is cold. I wouldn't mind another coat, if you can lay your hands on one.' She tried hard to stem the shiver she felt creeping on, but she couldn't and when it came it was with a visible shudder.

'You sit in that chair and be still while I fetch a blanket,' Rose told her.

In a minute she was back and carefully wrapped the blanket round Nell. It wasn't long before the fire was blazing away and the kettle perched on the gas ring in the kitchen. 'How do you feel now?' Rose asked, putting more coals on to the fire. 'Warmer, are you?' Bent on her knees, she looked up to satisfy herself that Nell's face wasn't blue with cold.

'I'm all right, thank you, Rose.' But she wasn't. She might be warmer and she might feel more comfortable, even a little stronger, but until she had her child back in her arms, she was only half alive.

'Rose?'

'Yes, love?'

'Who could have taken my baby?' Nell asked forlornly. Just to say it was painful. It made it too real, too terrible.

Pausing in what she was doing, Rose couldn't bring herself to look Nell in the eye. 'I don't know,' she answered honestly. 'But whoever it was should rot in hell for their wickedness.'

'Do you think they'll bring her back?'

'All we can do is hope.'

'I wish Kit was here.' It was only now that she

realised just how much he really meant to her. 'Lottie too.'

'Don't fret. They'll be back soon, I'm sure.'

'Where did they go exactly, Rose?'

Not wanting to raise Nell's hopes, Rose had made no mention of how Kit and Lottie had followed a lead on the woman who had worked in this very house and was apparently somehow involved with the theft of Nell's baby. Besides, when all was said and done, the boy might have got it all wrong. Maybe he was in such a state about Nell being ill that he let his imagination run away with him.

'It's not for me to say,' Rose replied cagily. 'All I know is the two of them went off on what might turn out to be a wild goose chase, but we'll know soon now, I expect.'

Rose brought the tea and set it on the table. Suddenly she stiffened. 'Did you hear that?' She stared at Nell, her back rigid and her face coloured with fear. 'A sort of rumble, in this very room.'

Nell nodded, her gaze darting round the room. It sounded again and Rose turned. The chair in the far corner was shrouded in shadow, and there, out to the world, was a girl, dressed for night life. She was slumped in the chair with her long legs dangling and her shoes kicked on the floor. And she was snoring.

'Why, it's Tilly, the little baggage!' Marching across the room, Rose took her by the ear, yanking her into a sitting position. 'Get off to bed!' she said. 'If Lottie was here, she'd have something to say and no mistake.'

'Gerroff, Rose!' the girl yelped, shaking free. 'You're

bloody well hurting.' Grabbing her shoes and trying to put them on as she went, she hobbled out of the room, looking daggers at Rose and swearing like a trooper.

'In at all hours that one,' Rose groaned, and Nell couldn't help but smile.

They talked for a while, mostly about Nell's baby, and what the chances were of it ever being recovered. 'I'll find her,' Nell vowed. 'Even if I have to scour the four corners of the earth.'

Rose was in no doubt about that but it was not a pleasant prospect. 'Leave it to the authorities, love,' she chided gently. 'They know how to deal with these things, and anyway, who knows what Lottie and the boy might find out before they make their way back. You mustn't give up hope.'

Right now, Nell didn't know which way to turn but she would never give up hope. *Never*.

Soon she fell asleep. Rose gazed at her sleeping face for a long, poignant moment. 'I can't begin to know what you're going through,' she sighed. 'I've never had children and never wanted any, I'm not the mothering kind, but you, well, you were made to have children. Look how you've nurtured that cheeky little boy, and how he adores you.' The slightest hint of envy touched her heart. 'Sleep now.'

At the door, Rose turned, looking again at Nell and thinking how small and vulnerable she seemed in the big armchair. But there was nothing small about Nell, she decided. Right now she might be vulnerable, but judging by the way that young woman had rallied round, she wasn't about to be counted out just yet. 'Straight out of her sickbed,' Rose sighed. 'Wanting to run before she can walk.' Softly, she closed the door. 'Still, while she's sleeping, she's not hurting.'

But Rose was wrong. Even in her sleep, Nell was fighting the world.

Rose went to the kitchen where she spent a minute or two seated at the table, finishing off her cup of tea. Afterwards she busied herself with this and that. 'Too late to go back to bed now,' she muttered, stifling a yawn. 'I'm too wide awake for sleep.'

Nell was dreaming. It was a strange kind of dream. All the people she loved were there – Bill, Molly, her father, Kit and the baby, all there and yet, try as she might, she could not reach them. There was a wall between them, seemingly insurmountable. Suddenly she was tearing at the wall with her bare hands; her knuckles were bleeding but she didn't mind because the more she battled, the nearer she came to her loved ones. It was a desperate dream and it was the desperation that drove her on.

So intense was the dream, so real to her, that Nell was jolted awake. At first she couldn't imagine where she was, but then it dawned on her. 'Rose?' There was no answer. Rose had fallen asleep at the kitchen table.

Nell called again. When only silence greeted her, she got out of the chair and wandered to the window. 'Such a beautiful morning,' she murmured. How much more beautiful it would have been if only she had her child with her. 'Please, God,' she whispered, 'don't let her be lost to me for ever.' Sitting on the windowsill, she marvelled at the wonder of a morning. 'It's like the world is new all over again.' She watched the dawn creeping into the horizon and she felt humble.

Being here, in someone else's house, so alone in spite of there being others all around, Nell wondered if there was any point in going on. In that moment the futility of her life seemed to overwhelm her and she looked beneath the strength that had kept her going all this time, and what she saw made her ask, 'What have you got, Nell? What makes you keep going when there's nothing ahead?'

She thought of Molly and her words of comfort and advice from when she was a small child; wise, wonderful words which time and again had proved to be true. The Lord gives with one hand and takes with the other – she remembered that particularly. 'If that's true, he's taken more than he's given back.' She smiled at her own philosophy. 'If Molly could hear you now, she'd say, "Get a hold of yourself, Nell Reece! There are plenty o' folk in this world worse off than you, my girl!" '

The smile broke into a laugh, 'You're right, Molly,' she admitted. 'I've never felt sorry for myself before, and it's not the time to start now. Somehow, God willing, I'll get my baby back. I'll keep Bill's friendship, and yours. My father will grow stronger with the passing of time, and there's always Kit.' Her heart warmed. 'He's a cheeky little sod but I don't know what I'd do without him, and that's the truth.'

Leaning back on the windowsill, she closed her eyes and counted her blessings. Life was worthwhile after all. Right now it was as bad as it could be but she had to cling to the belief that things would come right in the end.

'O NLY ANOTHER MILE and we're there.' Lottie was aching all over. Bill had driven furiously all the way, though the snow had slowed their progress, and twice they had had to stop and rest the horse. 'I shan't be sorry to get inside,' Lottie complained, straightening her hat. 'I need a cup of Rose's tea, a bath and then bed, in that order.'

Bill gestured to the horse. 'Much as I want to get to Nell, I daren't push the sorry old thing too hard.'

'I know, and I'm not blaming anyone. It's just that I feel bad about not finding Nell's bairn. But I know the girl Kit saw and she'll be back, and when she is I'll be waiting for her, you can count on that!'

'So will I, and the man with her. But just now all I want is for Nell to be right. After that, I'll track that pair down and when I do, God help them!' His jaws clenched hard and there was a look of murder in his dark eyes.

'I'll have to remember not to make an enemy of you.' Slyly regarding him in the early morning light, Lottie thought Bill was every woman's dream. There was a goodness about him, a strength that made you feel safe. Even when he was hurtling through the lanes, he was always in control, instilling confidence, and with just one thought in his mind. Nell.

'How far now?' Approaching a fork in the road where two lanes met, Bill slowed the horse to a trot.

'Turn right,' Lottie said. 'The house is half a mile along here.'

Kit had been sleeping in the back of the trap. Now he sat up. 'We're nearly there! We're nearly there!' He couldn't contain his excitement. Then his mood quickly changed and his voice dropped to a murmur. 'I promised we'd find Nell's baby.' He was stricken with guilt. 'An' we 'aven't.'

'Don't you worry about it.' Bill turned to smile at him. 'Once we've got Nell home, there'll be time to deal with the other matter.' His voice stiffened. 'There'll be no stone big enough for those two to hide under.'

Kit was reassured. He liked Bill. When Bill and Nell were ready to leave, Kit didn't dare think about whether they would take him with them. All he could do was hope and pray.

When Bill pulled the horse up, Kit was the first to jump off. Normally he would have considered it his duty to attend to the horse and trap, but he couldn't wait to see Nell. Running to the front door, he banged on it with his fist. 'Rose? We're back! Open the door!'

Thankful to see Lottie and the boy safely home, Rose opened the door with a smile to greet them, but Kit didn't even notice; he flew past her, heading for the stairs. 'She's in the parlour,' Rose told him, and like a flash he changed direction and went full pelt towards the parlour door.

He didn't burst in though. He recalled how very ill Nell had been, and slowly, with his heart in his mouth, he inched the door open and peeped inside. Nell was on the windowsill, her face pressed to the pane and her eyes closed. There was a blanket round her shoulders and she was clutching a cushion; her face was rosy from the fire and just for a minute he wondered whether he should wake her.

Just as he was about to turn and ask Rose, Nell

opened her eyes and saw him there. 'Oh, Kit!' She held out her arms, and he ran to her. 'I've missed you,' she told him, hugging him close. 'Oh, Kit, I'm so glad you're back.'

For a moment she closed her eyes, holding the boy close, but then some deep instinct made her glance up, and when she saw who had entered the room, her heart turned over. 'Bill!' She couldn't believe her own eyes. A thrill ran through her. She felt her face blush warm beneath his gaze. This was the last thing she had expected. Bill, of all people. The man she adored. The man she had feared she would never see again. And here he was, standing only an arm's reach away.

Overcome with emotion, she felt the tears rising and pressed a hand over her mouth to stop them. As he came towards her, the tears broke into sobs and she was lost for words. Her whole being wanted to tell him how much she loved him; how much she had always loved him. But something stopped her. A touch of pride, the fear of humiliation, the idea that by revealing her love she would alter their relationship for the worse. For whatever reason, she was still afraid to tell him.

When he gathered her into his arms, with her head on his shoulder and her small, pale hand holding his, Bill felt his love for Nell spill over. But this was not the moment. Besides, how could he be sure of her love? How could he open his heart to her now? What gave him the right to think he could reveal his love and expect her to love him back? So many things he wanted to say, and he dared not. Instead, he held her close, his dark eyes gazing down on her lovely face, making Nell wonder for the first time whether he really did love her after all. 'I've come to take you home, Nell,' he said softly. 'Molly's waiting for you.'

Nell nodded her head. 'Thank God,' she murmured, smiling through her tears. Bill was here, and she was going home. If only her baby was going home with them, she thought, everything would be worthwhile.

Lottie sent Kit for a cab, and by the time it arrived, Nell was warmly wrapped against the cold, with her meagre belongings waiting at the door. Bill was holding her, now and then asking if she was all right, and smiling when she assured him that nothing would keep her from going home, now that he was here.

They heard the cab approaching up the lane and said their goodbyes. 'I won't forget your kindness,' Nell told the two women. They told her it had been an experience they wouldn't have missed for the world, that she was to get well and maybe one day pay them a visit.

Nell promised she would.

Troubled and afraid, Kit jumped out of the cab. 'Nell?' He tugged at her hand.

'What is it, sweetheart?'

'Are you taking me with you?' The tremor in his voice gave him away.

Nell hugged him to her. 'What do you think?' she said. 'How could I leave my little Cockney sparrer behind, eh?'

'I love you,' he whispered.

'I love you too,' she answered, wiping away his tears with the back of her hand. 'You and me, we're partners, aren't we?'

He nodded, still gazing up at her.

'Well then, can one partner carry another partner's bag?' She ruffled his hair, smiling when he answered with feigned indignation.

''E might. It all depends on what the tip might be.' His spirits were restored. ''Ow about a tanner?'

Mimicking his accent, Nell replied gruffly, ''Ow about a fick ear?'

'No need to get touchy, missus.' Skipping to the door he picked up her bag and carried it to the cab.

Bill had witnessed the little episode and was moved by the affection these two showed each other. 'The boy seems to be worth his weight in gold,' he said. 'A good friend.'

'One day I'll tell you about that scruffy little lad,' Nell murmured. 'Then you'll see how I might not have got through without him.'

'Then we both owe him a great deal.'

Nell felt his arm tighten about her. She heard the passion in his voice, and it gave her courage. Soon she would tell him. And if her feelings were not returned, at least she would know. Life could never be complete without him but she had Kit and, God willing, she would have her daughter.

'Blackburn,' Bill told the driver. 'Do you know the way?'

'I know it,' he answered, his calm manner belying the grinding fear inside him. He knew the way to Blackburn all right, because only a short time before he had taken a couple there, a devious couple who had come from this very house in the middle of the night, carrying what he suspected to be a child. The man had paid him well, asking if he knew how to keep his mouth shut, and of course he did. Especially when by opening it too wide he might just hang himself.

So Alf smiled and chatted, and when the company were on board, he took off at a steady gait, just like he'd been ordered. Not like last time when he was made to drive as though he was fleeing from the devil himself.

Lottie and Rose waved them off, with the other women hanging out of the upstairs bedrooms, half-naked and shouting good wishes.

'Interesting place,' Bill commented, and when Nell glanced at him, he was quietly smiling.

Much to her delight, Bill continued to hold her close, his body-warmth pulsating through her, and his long work-worn fingers wrapped round hers. Soon, she thought. When the time is right, I *will* tell him. She wondered how he really felt about her having borne another man's child. She wondered, also, what he might say when he learned who the father was.

'I WON'T HAVE her here!' Lilian screeched. 'If she takes one step over this threshold, I swear I'll kill her, and you with her if you go against me!'

'Give me the gun, Lilian.'

'Do you mean to have her back? And the bastard with her?'

'She's my daughter, and her child is my grandchild. Yes, I mean to have her back, and nothing you can do will make me change my mind.' He was defying her, and it felt good. But he was afraid, too. She had taken the shotgun from the cabinet and he couldn't get it from her. In the mood she was in, anything could happen. 'Give me the gun and we'll talk.'

Seated on a chair by the door, she kept the gun pointed at him, her eyes like two hard stones glittering in her face. 'I'm not moving from this door,' she hissed. 'I'm warning you, stay away.'

Haggard and weary, he stared into her wild eyes. 'Have you gone mad, woman?' She'd been on and on at him since Bill had left to fetch Nell, until finally things had come to a head and she'd grabbed a shotgun.

'It's her! She's the one who's taken you from me.' She glared back, her face contorted with terrible loathing. 'She deserves to be punished.'

A sound outside made her jerk her head round. It was then that he launched himself at her. There was a dull thud as she fell to the ground, then she was looking up and suddenly the air was split by the sound of the shotgun going off.

Silence descended and, as he stood looking down, he realised his sister had been shot. 'God Almighty! What have I done?'

Falling to his knees he cradled her in his arms, rocking her back and forth, his shirt soaking up her blood, and wailing like a child. 'I didn't mean to kill her,' he kept saying. 'I didn't mean to kill her.'

But maybe he did. Maybe, after all the years of being dominated by this spiteful, selfish woman, he had finally snapped. Maybe he had wanted her dead, and maybe she deserved it. But Lilian was his sister and, good or bad, she had always been there. She had loved him in her own way, and now he had killed her with his own two hands.

For a moment he looked up and shut his eyes, for he couldn't bring himself to look on her.

When he glanced down again, she was staring up at him, her eyes wide open and blood trickling from the corner of her mouth. She didn't say anything, but he knew she wanted to.

He suspected she had vile, dreadful things to say. And he couldn't bear it.

PART FOUR

January 1891
ALL THINGS
ARE EQUAL

Chapter Twelve

M OLLY WAS PACING back and forth, occasionally rushing to the front door and peering down the street, groaning when there was no sight of them. 'Aw, come on, son, come on.' Since five o'clock that morning she had been out of her bed, doing anything and everything to keep herself busy.

She cooked the breakfast and saw her men off to their work. She cleaned the windows and scrubbed the floor; shook the mats and white-stoned the front step; she gossiped with the neighbours and bemoaned the government; took down the curtains and dipped them in dolly blue.

Frustrated, she strolled to the shops and passed the time of day with the mild and impressionable Nancy Doggett who had only four months back buried her husband. 'This is Arnold,' she told Molly, proudly displaying the big ugly fellow at her arm. 'We're thinking of getting wed,' she whispered.

Astonished, Molly weighed the fellow up and down and thought Nancy was in for a terrible life. She told her so in front of him. 'You silly bugger,' she declared, hoping Nancy would have the common sense to listen. 'I'd 'ave thought you'd had enough o' men, especially when the last one gave you fourteen kids, never did a day's work, and beat the living daylights outta yer every Friday night.'

Nancy was speechless. Arnold threatened to give Molly a black eye.

'Yer can try!' Molly squared up to him. 'But I can tell yer, it won't be me as comes off worse!'

Nancy started crying and one of the customers in the shop took Molly to task; John Pearson was the local moneylender, a little squirrel of a man with a moustache and prim bowler hat. 'You shouldn't talk to her like that,' he reprimanded. 'The woman has a right to marry who she likes.'

'Nobody asked you to poke your nose in.' Molly was up in arms. 'I'm not surprised you're on his side, yer no better than Nancy's last husband yerself. Everybody down Addison Street knows you take a poker to yer poor missus – black and blue from her arse upwards she is. It's common knowledge how you threw the poor sod out in the middle of the night just because she wouldn't let yer have yer oats. And here she is, big as a ship with her ninth. Shame on yer!'

Leaving his shopping on the counter, Pearson scurried off down the street before she could reveal any more of his shameful secrets.

Molly's parting words to Nancy were kindly. 'If you've any sense at all, lass, you'll dump this bugger afore he leads yer the same merry dance as yer old man afore him.' With that she gave her an encouraging smile, scowled at the fellow beside her, and waddled off home with her bag of muffins.

She couldn't rest. She dished up the dinner and chatted to the men round the table. They asked about Bill and Nell, and what was happening, and she had to report that she'd heard nothing. She'd expected them to turn up in the afternoon but there had been no sight or sound of them. 'I hope to God she's all right.'

Getting out of her chair with her dinner untouched, Molly went to the window for the umpteenth time. 'Where are they, our Joe?' she asked, returning to clear the table. 'Don't yer think they should have been here by now?'

'Aw, sure they'll be here soon enough.' Joe stroked her hand as she collected his plate. 'Stop worrying now, will ye? If Nell's as poorly as the boy said, then they'll have to take it easy, sure they will.' He looked at Molly with a flicker of anger. 'It were a shock to all of us when we found out Nell had a bairn. You're a secretive bugger, our Molly.'

'I have to be, with a house full o' nosy men!'

Sam had a question. 'Why would anyone want to steal Nell's bairn?'

Tommy was quick to give his own opinion. 'I've heard how a newborn can fetch a tidy sum in the right quarters.'

Molly reprimanded him. 'That's a terrible thing to say, Tommy. Stealing a bairn is a wicked thing. Any bairn is worth more than a fortune to its own mammy.'

Tommy was hurt. 'I know it's wicked,' he protested. 'I only said I'd heard it, that's all.'

'Aye, well, there's some terrible things in the world, so there is.' Joe was in philosophical mood. 'Whoever did it should rot in hell, so they should.'

It was Sam who dropped the bombshell. 'Is Nell's bairn belonging to our Bill?'

Everyone stared at him but, unlike young Tommy, he didn't flinch. 'I just wondered, that's all. I mean, Nell hasn't got a boy friend as far as I know. Bill might be a good nine years older than Nell, but anybody can see he's besotted with her.'

Joe was shocked. 'Sure, he looks on Nell like a sister, the same as you lot do.' He glanced at Molly and something in her face told him he just might be wrong.

Except for Sam, the possibility had never occurred to any of them before, and it was a sobering thought that kept them silent, until suddenly there was a sound at the front door.

'It's them!' Molly ran along the passage, the men following.

Bill was helping Nell over the threshold. 'We're home, Mam,' he told her. 'I promised I'd bring her back and here she is, a bit worse for wear maybe, but we'll soon put that right.'

He had his arm round Nell's waist and the warm, wonderful way he looked at her told the watching men all they needed to know. They glanced at each other, sure now that Bill was head over heels in love with Nell and, by the way she was gazing up at him, she returned his love. 'Told you,' Sam whispered to Jack. And there was no denying it.

Beside herself with excitement, Molly surged forward. 'Oh, thank God,' she said, pressing Nell to her breast. 'Thank God, you're back safe and sound.'

Nell felt safe. She felt wanted and loved like never

before. 'It's so good to see you,' she told Molly, then she looked beyond to where the men were standing. 'It's good to see you *all*,' she murmured, and the tears shone brightly in her eyes.

One by one the men hugged her, before Bill protested, 'She needs her rest.'

'I'm all right,' Nell insisted, with Molly's fat little arm round her shoulders. 'I slept most of the way, and I'm not a bit tired.' Looking towards the door, she saw Kit standing there, a small, scruffy boy, pressed against the door jamb and seeming just a little bit lost.

Nell held out her hand. 'Come here, Kit.'

Nervously he edged forward.

'This is Kit,' she told them, taking hold of his hand and drawing him towards her. 'He's been a real friend to me.'

Joe stepped forward. 'Sure, any friend of Nell's is welcome in this house,' he said, and he promptly took charge of the boy. 'Come on, son, I expect you could eat a slice of meat pie, couldn't you, eh?'

Kit's face lit up. 'Gravy too?'

'Aye, gravy an' all if you want it.' And the two of them went into the parlour like old friends.

Nell followed, her heart more content but still sore. Her mind was with her baby. She recalled holding the infant, that tiny warm being that was no longer a bump on the front of her body but a real little person, breathing and seeing. She could feel her now, the way she had nestled close. Belonging. Then, with shocking suddenness, her daughter was gone. Nell couldn't get to grips with that.

Keeping hold of her, Molly went along the passage, chatting all the way. When she felt a deep sigh ripple through Nell, she knew what was on her mind. 'Don't you worry about your baby, my gal,' she chided. 'Our Bill won't rest till she's found.'

Bill remained at the door, his troubled gaze following Nell as she went. If it was the last thing he did, he would have the child back, and then he would dare to ask Nell if she might consider being his wife. Don had given his blessing the night before, just before Kit had come hammering on the door. 'But at the end of the day,' he had concluded, 'it's for Nell to say.'

As Nell walked away with Molly, there was another watching from the door. The very same man who, if he chose, could take them right to the door of the house where Nell's baby had been delivered. 'Will she be all right?' Alf asked Bill, who was counting out the fare. 'I mean, she's a nice girl. I don't expect she'll ever get over the loss of her bairn, will she?'

Bill was curious. 'What do you know about Nell's bairn?'

'Well, I just heard your mam talking, and then there were a few words I overheard in the cab.' He became flustered. 'It's nothing to do with me, though I were thinking what a terrible shame it was, a thing like that.' He was embarrassed, something he never was when he'd been drinking. Now, though, stone-cold sober, he could see the enormity of what he'd done. 'I've got young 'uns of my own,' he remarked quietly. 'There are times when you'd give the buggers away for a shilling but still you'd wring the neck of anyone who might snatch 'em away.'

Bill's suspicions were aroused. 'How did you know the bairn was snatched away? Nothing was said about that in the cab, and I don't believe it was mentioned just now.'

Alf cursed himself for being so loose-tongued. In that unsettling moment, with Bill's dark, questioning eyes on him, he could have murdered a jar of best ale. 'I must have heard it somewhere,' he stammered. Holding out his hand, he requested, 'Two shillings, if you please, guv, then I'll be on my way.'

Bill had the two shillings in his fist but deliberately withheld it. 'You know something, don't you?'

'Only the same as other folk.' His Adam's Apple bobbed up and down as he nervously swallowed. 'No more than that, guv, I swear.'

Bill persisted. 'You say you've got bairns?'

'Four.'

'How old?'

'The eldest is five, the youngest only a few weeks.' He stepped back a pace. 'Two shillings, guv. I'd best be off now.'

Now that he was certain the man knew more than he was letting on, Bill had no intention of letting him go. 'You *do* know something,' he accused, grabbing the fellow by the scruff of his neck. Aware that they might be overheard, Bill stepped out on to the pavement and closed the door behind him. 'You'd best tell me what you know,' he threatened, 'because you're going now-here till you do.'

'I don't know anything.'

'You'd rather I beat it out of you?'

'I don't know nothing!' Alf repeated.

Bill realised he had to take a gamble. If he used his fists, he still might not get the information he wanted. It was a known fact that under duress some men would clam up more, even die before they'd tell. But that would take courage and he didn't believe this fellow had any. On the other hand the fellow seemed to have a conscience, otherwise he wouldn't have been so concerned about Nell.

He tried another tack. 'Two shillings, you say?' Putting on a smile, he thrust the money into the man's palm. Digging into his pocket, he added another coin. 'And here's threepence for your trouble. Off with you now, back to your missus and the young 'uns.' He emphasised the last few words. 'I don't suppose Nell will ever see her bairn again but that's not your problem, is it, eh?' He leaned his face forward, almost touching the other man's nose with his own. Still smiling, but with a sinister tone to his voice, he declared, 'I'll tell you this though, it won't be long before I find out who's responsible, and when I do, well, God help 'em, that's all I can say.'

Slowly, Alf climbed into his cab. For a long, awkward minute he looked at Bill, before saying, 'If one of them responsible were to help you find that bairn, how would you reward him?'

Bill stepped towards the cab. 'Well now, let me see.' He scratched his chin and made the cabbie stew in his fear. 'If one of them responsible were to help me, I'd be that grateful I might even let him go in one piece . . . back to his missus and young 'uns.'

Now it was Alf's turn to take a gamble but, weighing up everything, he decided Bill was a man of his word. 'All right. I know where her bairn is,' he confessed. 'But I swear to God, I never took it.' He was gabbling now, his face covered in a film of sweat and his hands shaking at the reins. 'It were them two, him and her, they were the ones who took it.'

Suppressing his excitement, Bill answered coolly, 'I think you'd best tell me everything you know, don't you?' With that he climbed up and sat alongside the driver. 'Everything, mind. Every snippet. Every little detail. Then, if I'm satisfied, happen I'll let you be on your way.'

WHEN THE MEN left one after the other, Nell was worried she might be driving Molly's family out. 'Don't be so daft, lass,' Molly assured her. 'They're glad of an excuse to go courting. I don't suppose it'll be too long afore the lot of 'em are wed and off me hands. As for Joe, he's meeting a pal downtown, so we're left on us own for a time.'

Gratefully accepting the mug of hot cocoa, Nell said, 'Oh, Molly, you don't know how glad I am to be home.'

'Hey, lass. Many's the time I've stood at that window and wished you were back. And now you are, and we've a lot to catch up on.' Addressing Kit, who was seated cross-legged by the fire, she said, 'Buck up, me laddo. You can earn yerself a few pennies if you were to wash them dishes in the sink – after you've drunk your cocoa, o' course.'

'Cor!' He didn't need asking twice. In a flash he'd swallowed the cocoa and was off to the kitchen.

'It allus does the trick,' Molly chuckled. 'Offer 'em a few pennies an' there's nowt the little devils won't do.'

Nell's mind was elsewhere. 'Where's Bill?' She glanced anxiously at the door. 'He's been out there for ages.'

'Talking, like men do,' Molly answered. Now that she and Nell were on their own, she had a thing or two to ask. 'Have you told him how yer feel about him, lass?'

Nell shook her head.

'Are you going to?'

'I think so.' She would. It was just a question of when. 'Molly?'

'What is it, lass?'

'Why would anyone want to take my baby?'

Unusually for Molly, she had no answer. Taking hold of Nell's hand, she squeezed it hard. Then she put her arm round her and drew her towards her until Nell's head was resting on her shoulder. They were quiet for a time, each deep in their own train of thought, and each taking comfort from the other.

Molly suspected Vincent Morgan had taken the bairn, but until she was sure, it would be a dangerous thing to say to Nell. For now, it might be wiser to keep her own counsel.

Nell felt very strange, as though she had been cut off from everything and everyone, like a ship adrift, washed this way then that. Yet she knew she was with friends, and she knew her father was not too far away, but all that seemed not to matter in the light of what had happened. 'Do you really think Bill will find my bairn? The authorities don't seem to have had much luck so far, but then it's early days.'

'Aye, lass. And one man on his own can often do more than an army put together.'

'Sometimes I can't believe it's happened, and other times I think I'll go crazy.'

'Then it's just as well you know how to be strong.'

'I'll have to send Kit to let my dad know I'm here. I want to see him but I don't want to go there.'

'Good idea. I wouldn't want you to go there either. I want you to stay here.' She settled comfortably. 'Tell me all about yer adventures, lass,' she coaxed. 'It'll take your mind off things, if yer know what I mean.'

'Some other time, Mam,' Bill's voice cut in, startling the two women who hadn't heard him come in. 'I want a word with Nell, and it won't wait.'

Nell saw the hard look on his face and it made her afraid though she didn't know why. 'What's wrong?' Sitting up in the chair, she put her cup down on the hearth.

He stood over her, a handsome, towering frame of a man, his eyes brooding black as they bore down on her. 'I'll tell you what's wrong,' he said, clenching his fists at his sides. 'Vincent Morgan, *that's* what's wrong. Was he your lover, Nell? Was Vincent Morgan the father of your bairn?' He already knew. It was a bitter pill to swallow.

Nell's heart turned somersaults. She glanced at Molly's resigned face, then she lowered her gaze. It was enough to confirm his suspicions.

'Oh, Nell. Nell!' He dropped to his knees before her, his hands on hers and his eyes kinder as he asked, 'Was that why you went away? Was it, Nell?'

'He was never my lover. It was just the once, that's all. Just the once, and I wish to God it had never happened.'

'Are you saying you never loved him?'

'That's exactly what I'm saying, Bill.' She had waited for the right moment and here it was, and she would not let it go again. One glance at Molly's smiling face told her she wasn't alone.

'It's not Vincent Morgan I love,' she said firmly. 'It's *you*, Bill. It's *always* been you.' There! It was said and her heart sang for joy. If he turned her down or if she lost his friendship because of it, no one could say she had not spoken from the heart. And, for as long as she lived, she still had memories of the wonderful times she and Bill had enjoyed together. Those images would stay with her for a lifetime. Some folk never even had that much.

With awakening astonishment, Bill's expression began to change. First he stared at her in disbelief. Then he shook his head as though he was dreaming. He began to smile and then he was laughing out loud, laughing and swinging her round in his arms. 'Nell! Nell! And I love you, more than I can say.'

Nell was laughing and crying, and Molly too. 'See!' She put her arms round the two of them. 'Haven't I always said yer belong together?' she laughed. 'Haven't I seen the pair of yer grow like two peas in a pod?' She grabbed hold of Kit who had run in at the rumpus. 'See that?' she said, pointing to Nell and her man. 'Them two loved each other all the time and didn't even know it.'

One minute Nell was being swung round, and the next she was being kissed like she'd never been kissed before. Crushed in his arms she clung to him, his lips warming her mouth, and his arms holding her so tightly she could hardly breathe. 'Oh, Bill,' she murmured, drawing away and smiling into his dark, wonderful eyes. 'Is it really true?'

'Yes, Nell Reece, I love you. *I love you!*' He cupped her face in his hands and kissed her again. 'This night I'm the luckiest man on earth.' Gently now, he looked into her blue eyes and, in the softest voice, asked, 'Would you have me as the bairn's daddy? If I were to find your daughter, would you swear she was mine and no one else's?'

The blue eyes filled with tears. She dared not let herself believe it. 'You know where she is, don't you?' Tugging at his coat sleeve she begged, 'Don't torment me, Bill. Do you know where she is?'

'Answer me, Nell. Even if you were asked by the highest authorities, would you swear she was mine?'

'You know I would. There is no other man I would want for her daddy.'

He told her then. 'Vincent Morgan has her. The same cab driver who brought us here was paid to take two people and the bairn to the Morgan house. His wife died in what they called an accident, but I have my own ideas about that.'

Nell was shocked. 'Rosalyn is . . . dead?' That quiet soul who never did anyone any harm. What did Bill mean, he had his doubts it was an accident?

413

'He lost the child she was carrying and wanted yours. The cab driver heard it all. Morgan found out where you were and he had the child snatched. If we're to get her back, you must stick to your story, Nell. You *must* say she's mine and that we've been lovers for a long time. If you're prepared to do that, we can go and get her right now.'

Without hesitation, Nell replied, 'Let's get her, Bill. Oh, please, let's go and get her.' In the background she could hear Molly softly crying, but they were not tears of sorrow. They were tears of untold joy.

Nell was ready for anything. She was not afraid of Vincent Morgan, or of what might lie ahead. Besides, she had Bill at her side now.

THE LAST VISITOR Vincent Morgan expected was Nell. 'Good God, Nell! I was told you'd left the area.' A born liar, he knew how to pretend. 'There's no work here for you. I have all the staff I need.'

'I'm not here for work,' Nell replied stiffly. 'I'm here for my bairn.'

'Bairn?' He laughed in her face. 'What would your "bairn" be doing here?'

Bill intervened. 'Fetch the child, Morgan.'

'Who the hell do you think you're talking to?' One glance at Bill's face told him to expect trouble. 'What gives you the right to come here at this time of night?'

'The right of a father.'

'What are you talking about?'

'I thought I'd made myself clear enough.' Bill knew

414

the other man was playing for time to think. 'You've got my bairn in there,' he insisted. 'Mine and Nell's, and we've come to take her home.' He took a step forward, squaring up as he spoke. 'If you don't fetch her out *now*, I'll have no choice but to go in and get her myself.'

'Step one foot inside this house and I'll have you thrown out on your ear.' Shaken by the idea that Nell's baby might not be his after all, he was momentarily confused. 'What's more, the authorities might be interested to know how you've come here to threaten me.'

'Aye, and they might be interested to know how you paid to take what wasn't yours. Stealing a child is a serious offence, Morgan. A man in your position must know what punishment that carries.'

Whether it was fear or sheer desperation, Nell couldn't tell, but suddenly Vincent threw himself at Bill. The two of them fought like wild dogs. First Vincent was on top, then Bill had him pinned down hard. Vincent fought back and for a moment it seemed as though he might get the better of Bill. Then came the sound of hard knuckles crunching into Vincent's face; the blood spurted and he was blabbering like a baby.

Bill had him flat against the wall, holding him clear off the ground by his shirt. 'Happen you'll fetch the bairn now,' he growled. 'Two minutes, Morgan, then I'm in after you.'

Like a rabbit Vincent scurried inside. He didn't bring the child out. Instead he sent it out with one of the servants.

415

Bill took the baby and placed her in Nell's arms. He turned the blanket back to have a peep. 'She's lovely,' he said. 'Just like her mammy.'

Nell couldn't speak, she was so overcome. She had her daughter, and she had her man. The three of them walked away together, Nell carrying the baby and Bill with his arm round Nell. They made a fetching sight.

But not to the man who was looking from the bedroom window. What if Bill Davidson did call in the authorities and charge him with kidnap? There was no way of stopping him now. And the chances were he had a witness – somebody must have talked or how else had he tracked down the child so quickly?

He dared not take the risk. Calling one of the servants, he ordered, 'Pack my bags. I'm leaving for a long holiday.' So long he might never come back, he thought.

Molly was pale-faced and agitated when Nell got back. 'I sent Kit for your father like you wanted,' she explained. 'He's fetched bad news, lass. According to what he were told by a nearby farmer, there's been a terrible happening.' She made Nell sit down before going on gently, 'It seems your aunt's been shot and they've arrested your father.'

Numb with shock, Nell asked to go straight to the police station. Seeing how drained she was, Bill insisted on going with her.

While he went out in search of a hansom cab, Molly tried to comfort Nell. 'It never rains but it pours, lass,' she said, gazing at the infant and thinking how like Nell she was. 'It looks bad now, but the sunshine ain't far away, you'll see, and at least you've got your bairn safe in your arms.'

T HE SUNSHINE THAT Molly spoke of was a long time coming.

For two agonising months, while Nell's father was locked away, Lilian stuck to her story that her own brother had tried to kill her. It was only when she realised her time was near that she listened to Nell's heartfelt pleas and decided to tell the truth. Two days later, on 12 March, Don was released from prison.

That same evening, afraid and sure she would be called to answer for her terrible sins, Lilian sent for Nell and her father. 'I have something to tell you both,' she said. And the tale that followed was so barbaric, neither of them could take it in.

There, in that gloomy room, with only a candle to light the fear in her eyes, Lilian confessed how she had loved Don with a passion 'not befitting that of a sister'. She asked forgiveness for the terrible things she had done over the years, the worst being the way she had put a stop to Don marrying his girl when he made her with child. 'She was a sweet little thing,' she said, looking at Nell. 'Strong and fiery, like you in every way. That's why I could never stand you near me. It was like having her here all over again. I hated you like I hated her. I knew there would come a day when you might take his love away from me, just like she did.'

Don listened in silence. The spell in prison had made

him older, his face was thinner and his eyes were filled with pain. 'What did you do to her?' His voice was flat, accepting the inevitable but loathing her with every word she uttered.

'It wasn't just me,' Lilian muttered; every now and then she would pause, breathing with increasing difficulty. 'It was her parents too. They were devout, religious folk and when she got with child they knew she had to be punished. They disowned her and her fate was left to me. Neither of them lived long after that. I always thought it was the shock that killed them but it may have been their own consciences. I was stronger, you see. I never looked back . . . not until now.'

Nell saw the tears rolling down Lilian's face and she was shocked to the core. It seemed impossible that her aunt could cry. But the tears did not melt Nell's heart. She was thinking of what Lilian had said, and of the terrible things she had done to her father.

'We kept her safe until you were born,' Lilian told Nell, 'and then we took you from her. You were saved and she was condemned for her sins.'

Dark anger flooded Don's face. 'What did you do?' he demanded. 'For pity's sake, Lilian, what did you do to her?' He had never stopped loving that girl who was Nell's mother, not from that day to this.

'You always thought she'd died, and that's what I wanted you to believe,' Lilian revealed. 'The wretch you buried was a pauper. It worked well – a sly payment here and there, and people will do almost anything. You were too stricken with grief to ask questions. You blamed yourself and that suited my purpose. Under cover of dark, the girl was dispatched south, to a convent.'

His grief was overwhelming. 'What happened to her?'

Lilian's fear of him at that moment was greater than her fear of her maker, and though she wanted to clear her soul of all sin, she could not bring herself to answer.

It was too much for Don. What his sister had done went beyond his worst nightmare. 'We loved each other,' he said. 'We planned to wed, and you, *my own sister*, you ruined my life. I'll ask you again. What happened to her?' The words hissed through clenched teeth and there was murder in his heart.

Lilian looked at his face and knew she had lost him completely. 'The birthing was so difficult and bloody; the struggle damaged her spine and left her legs useless. I thought the good Lord in his wisdom had taken it on himself to punish her. But she survived, and that same night we delivered her to the convent.' She couldn't look on his face any longer. Fixing her gaze to the crucifix on the wall, she went on, 'Her parents gave a generous sum of money for her keep and I, too, gave a small amount. We weren't altogether wicked, you see. We wanted her out of our lives but we wanted her cared for.'

Nell was shaking her head, unable to comprehend the awful depths to which this woman had sunk. 'You monsters,' she uttered. 'You wicked, wicked monsters.'

Lilian had not yet purged herself of her sins. 'I believe she was already dying when we took her to the convent.' Shame enveloped her. 'Before casting her out, we held the girl down . . .' She swallowed and the sound seemed to fill that quiet room. 'Her father cut off her hair and stripped her naked. She was left on the steps of the convent with a note beside her. After that I don't know what happened to her, and I never wanted to know. With her own parents dead and gone, I thought it best to leave her to the mercy of others.'

'Which convent, Lilian?' Even the act of talking to her was nauseating.

She looked up at Don but didn't speak. Her voice cracked and then was silent.

All this time the nurse had remained with Bill at the back of the room, both of them deeply shaken by the story. Now, when it seemed it was all over, they stepped forward.

From somewhere deep inside, Lilian found the strength to lunge out and grab her brother by the hand. 'Forgive me,' she pleaded. 'I need you to forgive me.'

'Which convent?' He was hardened to her. There could be no forgiveness. Not now. Not ever.

Lilian glanced at Nell, as if pleading. 'I'm sorry.'

Nell gazed on that wizened face and she felt nothing. 'Which convent did you take my mother to?' she asked softly.

'Mary Magdalen . . .' Her voice was barely audible. 'I took her . . . to the Convent of Saint . . . Mary Magdalen.'

Don fell forward in his chair, his hands covering his face and his body racked with sobs. Silently, Bill came and took him away. Don never looked back.

Lilian and Nell remained.

'Why?' Nell whispered. 'Why?'

'Forgive . . . me.'

But Nell found that, like her father, she was too shocked, too hurt, to think of Lilian's soul. This woman had shown no mercy to her mother, and over the years she had shown none to her father or to herself.

Nell stood up and moved towards the door.

A small, pitiful voice called her back. 'Please . . . Nell?'

Nell could not leave without giving some comfort, deserved or not. Going back, she spoke softly. 'You found the courage to tell the truth about what happened,' she said, 'but it isn't for me or my father to forgive.' She even found the heart to touch her aunt's hand. 'It's for someone far greater than any of us. It's for Him to forgive, and if you're sorry enough, He won't refuse.'

T HAT VERY NIGHT, Bill took Nell and her father to the Convent of St Mary Magdalen, and on the way Nell told how she had been to that place before and had met a woman there who had stayed in her mind; a crippled woman with a brave heart, who got around on a contraption made for her by her friend, Amy. She had meant to come back one day and see them again. Old John Butler, too, if he hadn't gone travelling the world.

Mary was in the conservatory when she saw them arrive. 'Look, Amy,' she said. 'Isn't that the girl who was here with that Cockney boy?'

Amy was sewing but she looked up, stretching her neck to see. 'Well, I never!' she exclaimed. 'And who's that she's got with her now?'

Mary was not listening. She was watching the older

man striding along beside Nell, and she couldn't be sure but something touched a sleeping memory, and when she whispered his name it was like a cry from the depths of her soul. 'Don!' She sat, bewitched, waiting for him to look up and see her. 'It's Don!'

Now he was only feet away from where she was. Some pressing instinct made him look up. He saw her and his heart almost stopped. 'Dear God!' He almost fell in his tracks. 'Dear God! Oh, dear God above!' He could hardly speak for the emotion that tore through him. 'Nell . . . your mother is safe. She's safe, thank God.'

These two looked at each other and there were no words that could describe their feelings. Their vision might be blurred by the tears that tumbled down their faces but they knew. After all this time, they still knew.

When Don came into the conservatory, it was as though a whole lifetime slipped away. For Nell, too, it was an emotional moment. Here was the woman she had longed to come back and visit. Here was the same woman she had admired and liked right from the start. And now she was filled with joy to know that Mary was her own mother. 'I knew you two looked alike,' Amy said. 'I said to Mary, that girl looks just like you.' She recalled the birthmark on Nell's foot. She'd known all along that Nell and Mary belonged.

SOME MONTHS LATER, Don and Mary were wed. Mary had been dressed by Nell and Amy, and put into her new Bath chair, bought with the money her parents and Lilian had left for her care. Kit had the honour of pushing her chair up the aisle. Nell walked beside them, in a gown of blue, 'to match yer eyes', Molly said, and Bill smiled at her lovingly from the pews.

In that church, on that day, a certain, sorry soul was on Nell's mind. Lilian had confessed her terrible sin and now she must answer to her maker. And somehow, in spite of everything that tormented woman had done, Nell discovered it was not too hard to forgive her after all.

Later, when the festivities were still underway at Molly's house, Bill took Nell outside to see the night stars. The kitchen door was open and they could hear the laughter; they heard Don reminding Mary how the specialist she had seen was hopeful that she might be able to walk on her own two legs after a course of treatment, and how she'd be able to get about the house left to them by Lilian.

They heard Kath – who had arrived driving an old cart with Clarence between the shafts – describe how a developer had bought her burned-out baker's shop for a small fortune. And there was John Butler who hadn't gone round the world after all. Instead he said he was 'looking for a woman with brass'. Kath winked at him, and he fancied his chances.

Lottie and Rose looked fine and dandy.

Kit was in his best bib and playing with the baby in the cradle he had made for her and Molly and Joe were in their element.

Amy was going to live with Mary and her feller, just as Mary had always promised.

All in all, it turned out grand; even the kidnapper

got his come-uppance with a spell in jail, though the woman's sentence was suspended on account of her having a child to care for. Rumour had it that she had truly learned her lesson, and was now looking for respectable work. Lottie had laughed at the idea. 'She's a hot-arse,' she said. 'I'll give her a month before she's bedding the master.'

Outside, Nell nestled into Bill's arms. 'Your mam wants us to have a dozen children,' she laughed.

Bill kissed her soundly. 'And what do you want?'

Nell's blue eyes sparkled with love. 'I want you, and Kit, and our daughter,' she answered, 'and as many more as the good Lord sees fit to send. After all, there are two cradles to fill now Kath has brought John Butler's.'

'We'll see,' he answered. 'First, though, we have to make plans to get wed.'

In between the kissing and the cuddling, that's just what they did.

'I wonder what's on the cards for us?' Bill mused, looking up at the stars.

'Oh, wonderful things.' Smiling at him, Nell took a leaf out of Molly's book. 'You'll see,' she whispered. 'You'll see.'

In fact, what turned out to be on the cards was the cottage Bill had been working on. Vincent Morgan had put the place up for sale, and it went for a song in his absence.

They named their daughter Molly. Kit grew to be a prosperous businessman, with a chain of draper's shops. And they had two other sons, John and Edward, who set up a marine yard and made ships to sail round the world.

Nell and her mother grew closer over the years.

The cradle of thorns made by Kit, the most treasured of Nell's possessions, was handed down through the family for many generations to come.

Headline hopes you have enjoyed reading CRADLE OF THORNS and invites you to sample the beginning of Josephine Cox's compelling new saga, MISS YOU FOREVER, out now in Headline hardback...

Chapter One

‘G o on, you old bag. Get back to the slums where
you belong!’

The taunts rang in Kathleen’s ears. Tripping and
stumbling over the cobbles, she hurried away, wincing
beneath the onslaught of abuse and objects that followed
her.

‘You’d better run, old woman.’ The jeers were
merciless. ‘If you’re not out of sight in two minutes, we’ll
set the dogs on you.’ As if to endorse the threat, the two
bull mastiffs growled threateningly, straining at their
leashes, mouths dripping saliva at the thought of sinking
their fangs into her soft, ancient flesh.

‘What you got in that bag, then, eh?’

‘Huh! Crown jewels I shouldn’t wonder, by the way
she’s clutching it.’

The dogs went crazy to be loosed. ‘They fancy that
scraggy mongrel of hers for dinner,’ someone yelled,
and they fell about laughing.

As she fled, Kathleen prayed the thugs would not
carry out their threat. She know the danger, for they
were no different from many others who had made fun
of her along the way.

The old woman had lost count of the times when

she's been jeered at, spat at, laughed at, or chased away at the wrong end of a pitchfork. People were wary of newcomers, especially 'newcomers' with no fixed abode or means of earning a living. Generally, they tended to pour scorn and contempt on such as Kathleen. Being made unwelcome was something she had learned to live with. There were times when she met with kindness and compassion, but these occasions were few and far between.

Too old and too tired to run any more, she yearned to put down roots, but with each passing year the prospect grew more unlikely.

In her lonely treks Kathleen Peterson had travelled the length and breadth of Britain. She had tramped across the green fields of the Emerald Isle and climbed the hills of Scotland. She had stayed in the Welsh valleys, travelled every nook and cranny of England, but her heart always brought her back to her native Blackburn.

Yet Kathleen had neither home nor family, no one who would miss her if she never returned. Her life was in the diaries she so jealously guarded, and in the mangy old dog she had found snuggling up to her when she awoke in an alley one cold February morning.

He was a dolly mixture of black and brown, with a long, meandering splash of white down his nose, and a speckle of grey around his whiskers. He had one black ear that had been broken in a fight and hung sadly over his head like an eye-patch, while the other ear remained upright and finely turned to every sound. He reminded Kathleen of an old man she had known as a child; he, too, had had a black eye-patch and grey speckled whiskers that twitched when he talked. His name was Mr Potts. 'What else can I call you?' she had asked the dog, and so he was given the old man's name.

The two of them became fast friends. They made a comical sight as they walked the streets, Kathleen in her dark shawl and boots, with a threadbare, tapestry bag over her arm and her long grey hair in thick plaits that reached down to her waist, and the odd Mr Potts, head cocked to one side as he peered from under one ear, his body so close to her heels as they went that he might have been attached.

Having been on the road since first light, Kathleen had arrived in Liverpool. She had fourpence in her purse, earned from sweeping an undertaker's yard in Sheffield. She was hungry and cold, and, having consulted with the wise old Mr Potts, had decided that Liverpool was as good a place as any to stay a while. 'The market should be opening soon,' she explained. 'With a bit of luck we might go away with a bag of sweet potatoes.' She hadn't tasted a sweet potato in ages and her mouth watered at the prospect.

'Are you still 'ere, old woman? I thought we told you to piss off!' The four thugs who had taunted her earlier had followed her to the docks. 'What'ya got in yer bag, eh?'

Kathleen didn't have to look round. She recognised the voice. 'Come on, Mr Potts,' she urged. 'Let's be off, before they come after us.'

In spite of her scruffy, neglected appearance, the old woman spoke in a soft, genteel tone that might have shocked the rough crowd who saw her only as an object of derision. Like many others who had never taken the trouble to know her, they would have been astonished to learn that Kathleen Peterson, the unkempt and aged vagabond who tramped the roads and carried all her worldly possessions in a grubby tapestry bag, was once a fine, respected lady.

K athleen took a detour which brought them into a back alley. One of the yards was open. Its tall, wooden gate was split from top to bottom and hung from its hinges as though it might have been ripped off by some marauding drunk. From the house could be heard raised and angry voices.

'As long as they don't come out for a bucket of coal, we should be safe enough,' Kathleen decided, with a wry little smile. 'Be quiet and no one will be any the wiser,' she said, wagging a finger at the mongrel. She noticed the coal-hole door was ajar. Cautiously, she went inside; it was dark and cold, but not as cold as the street outside. 'Seems cosy enough,' she remarked. 'I'm sure no one would mind if we made ourselves comfortable for a while. And we can finish off the last of that pie, before it goes sour on us.'

Finding an old sack lying on the ground, she took it out and shook it, sending the black dust flying through the air. Then she laid it in a clean corner of the coal cellar and sat herself down, with the dog at her feet as always. As the cold struck through her thin shirt, she shivered. 'It's a hard life, Mr Potts,' she sighed.

Waiting for any little titbit she might have for him,

Mr Potts sat on his bony haunches, eyes bright and ear cocked, intently listening to every word the old woman uttered.

'It's not like it used to be, is it?' the old woman pondered softly. 'There was a time when you could walk the streets and be safe, when you could pass the time of day and not be afraid somebody might snatch your bag or run you through when your back was turned.' She chuckled. 'It doesn't matter to you though. All you're concerned about is having a full belly and a warm place to lay your head, and nobody can blame you for that, can they, eh?'

Her kind brown eyes misted over, her voice falling to a whisper. 'As for me, what does it matter? Who is there left to care about a silly old fool like me?' She gave a sad little grunt. 'Nobody, that's who.' Smiling into the dog's eyes, she cradled his hairy face between her two hands. 'You might be a funny looking thing, and you might have very little to say for yourself, but you've been a friend to me, and I'm grateful for that.'

Impatient now, the mongrel began to whimper, scratching at her with his paw.

She rummaged in her bag. 'Let's see what old Kathleen's got for you.' Laughing, she confessed shamefully, 'I weren't the only one watching the butcher throw his leftovers away. I'll have you know I fought off a hungry cat for this particular juicy bit, though in the end I couldn't see the cat starve and gave him a piece. So, you see, your dinner isn't as big as it might have been. Mind you eat it slowly,' she cautioned, taking out a muslin cloth and opening it to reveal a half-eaten meat pie. 'It might be all we get between now and tomorrow morning.'

In the house the row continued. 'Somebody's certainly got a temper,' she commented. 'Hope they leave us be.' Undaunted by the raging voices, she slid down and crossed her harms over her precious tapestry bag. 'I'll just close my eyes for a minute.'

This was always a sign she was settling to sleep. The dog knew it, and normally when she closed her eyes he would curl down beside her. But not this time. This time he remained wary, one ear cocked and a low, hostile growl issuing from his throat.

The old woman didn't hear it, for she was already asleep, warmed by the cider, and dreaming dreams of long ago.

While she slept, the four thugs crept up on her.

'The old hag's asleep,' the ringleader hissed.

'With no interfering docker to save her this time,' chuckled another. 'Let's get a look inside that precious bag of 'ers.'

MORE THAN RICHES

Josephine Cox

'You'll never let it go, will you?'

Taken aback by the hatred in her eyes, he wanted to tear out her heart. 'I'll let it go when you stop wanting him!' he hissed. Then he covered his head with his hands and cried like a child.

When Rosie's parents were involved in a train accident, her mother was killed and her father was left crippled, unable to earn a living and relying on Rosie to keep the wolf from the door.

With her mother gone and her sweetheart Adam away in the army, Rosie is lonely. She eagerly awaits the letters from him, but they never come. As she grows more disillusioned, Adam's best friend Doug goes out of his way to be charming and attentive. Alone and confused, Rosie blossoms under his evil influence. Soon she is carrying Doug's baby and her father has thrown her out of the house. Realising she has no choice, she agrees to marry Doug.

As if she isn't in enough trouble, Rosie's whole world falls apart when a warm and wonderful letter arrives from Adam . . . telling her he's on his way home.

'Driven and passionate, she stirs a pot spiced with incest, wife-beating . . . and murder'
The Sunday Times

FICTION / SAGA 0 7472 4657 2

A LITTLE BADNESS

FROM THE BESTSELLING AUTHOR OF
MORE THAN RICHES

Josephine Cox

Rita Blackthorn's heart was barren and hard. In all of her life she had never truly loved. But she had hated. She hated now, so deeply she could almost taste it. Beneath the loving gaze of her daughter's soft green eyes, her heart swelled with dark and dangerous emotions.

Young Cathy Blackthorn has never experienced any loving response from her mother; it is her beloved aunt Margaret, with a heart as big and warm as the summer sky, who has been more of a mother than her own could ever be. And when Cathy's father Frank Blackthorn brings home a London street urchin and announces this will be the son he and Rita have never had, Cathy despairs of ever winning her parents' love. But Cathy is a generous soul, and tries to give the young lad a chance to prove himself – one way or the other – but, unlike her best friend, David Leyton, something about him makes her more than uneasy . . .

'Driven and passionate, she stirs a pot spiced with incest, wife-beating . . . and murder'
The Sunday Times

FICTION / SAGA 0 7472 4831 1

A selection of bestsellers from Headline

LAND OF YOUR POSSESSION	Wendy Robertson	£5.99 ☐
DANGEROUS LADY	Martina Cole	£5.99 ☐
SEASONS OF HER LIFE	Fern Michaels	£5.99 ☐
GINGERBREAD AND GUILT	Peta Tayler	£5.99 ☐
HER HUNGRY HEART	Roberta Latow	£5.99 ☐
GOING TOO FAR	Catherine Alliott	£5.99 ☐
HANNAH OF HOPE STREET	Dee Williams	£4.99 ☐
THE WILLOW GIRLS	Pamela Evans	£5.99 ☐
A LITTLE BADNESS	Josephine Cox	£5.99 ☐
FOR MY DAUGHTERS	Barbara Delinsky	£4.99 ☐
SPLASH	Val Corbett, Joyce Hopkirk, Eve Pollard	£5.99 ☐
THEA'S PARROT	Marcia Willett	£5.99 ☐
QUEENIE	Harry Cole	£5.99 ☐
FARRANS OF FELLMONGER STREET	Harry Bowling	£5.99 ☐

All Headline books are available at your local bookshop or newsagent, or can be ordered direct from the publisher. Just tick the titles you want and fill in the form below. Prices and availability subject to change without notice.

Headline Book Publishing, Cash Sales Department, Bookpoint, 39 Milton Park, Abingdon, OXON, OX14 4TD, UK. If you have a credit card you may order by telephone – 01235 400400.

Please enclose a cheque or postal order made payable to Bookpoint Ltd to the value of the cover price and allow the following for postage and packing:

UK & BFPO: £1.00 for the first book, 50p for the second book and 30p for each additional book ordered up to a maximum charge of £3.00.
OVERSEAS & EIRE: £2.00 for the first book, £1.00 for the second book and 50p for each additional book.

Name ....

Address ....

....

....

If you would prefer to pay by credit card, please complete:
Please debit my Visa/Access/Diner's Card/American Express (delete as applicable) card no:

Signature .... Expiry Date ....